SWEENEY BOO

EAT,
AND LOVE YOURSELF™

BOOM!
BOX™

Designer
Marie Krupina

Associate Editor
Sophie Philips-Roberts

Editor
Shannon Watters

BOOM! BOX™

EAT, AND LOVE YOURSELF, April 2020. Published by BOOM! Box, a division of Boom Entertainment, Inc. Eat & Love Yourself is ™ & © 2020 Cécilia Dupuy. All rights reserved. BOOM! Box™ and the BOOM! Box logo are trademarks of Boom Entertainment, Inc., registered in various countries and categories. All characters, events, and institutions depicted herein are fictional. Any similarity between any of the names, characters, persons, events, and/or institutions in this publication to actual names, characters, and persons, whether living or dead, events, and/or institutions is unintended and purely coincidental. BOOM! Box does not read or accept unsolicited submissions of ideas, stories, or artwork.

BOOM! Studios, 5670 Wilshire Boulevard, Suite 400, Los Angeles, CA 90036-5679. Printed in China. First Printing.

ISBN: 978-1-68415-506-4, eISBN: 978-1-64144-664-8

DEDICATED TO EVERYONE WHO
STRUGGLES TO LOVE THEMSELVES.
YOU ARE BEAUTIFUL.
—S.B.

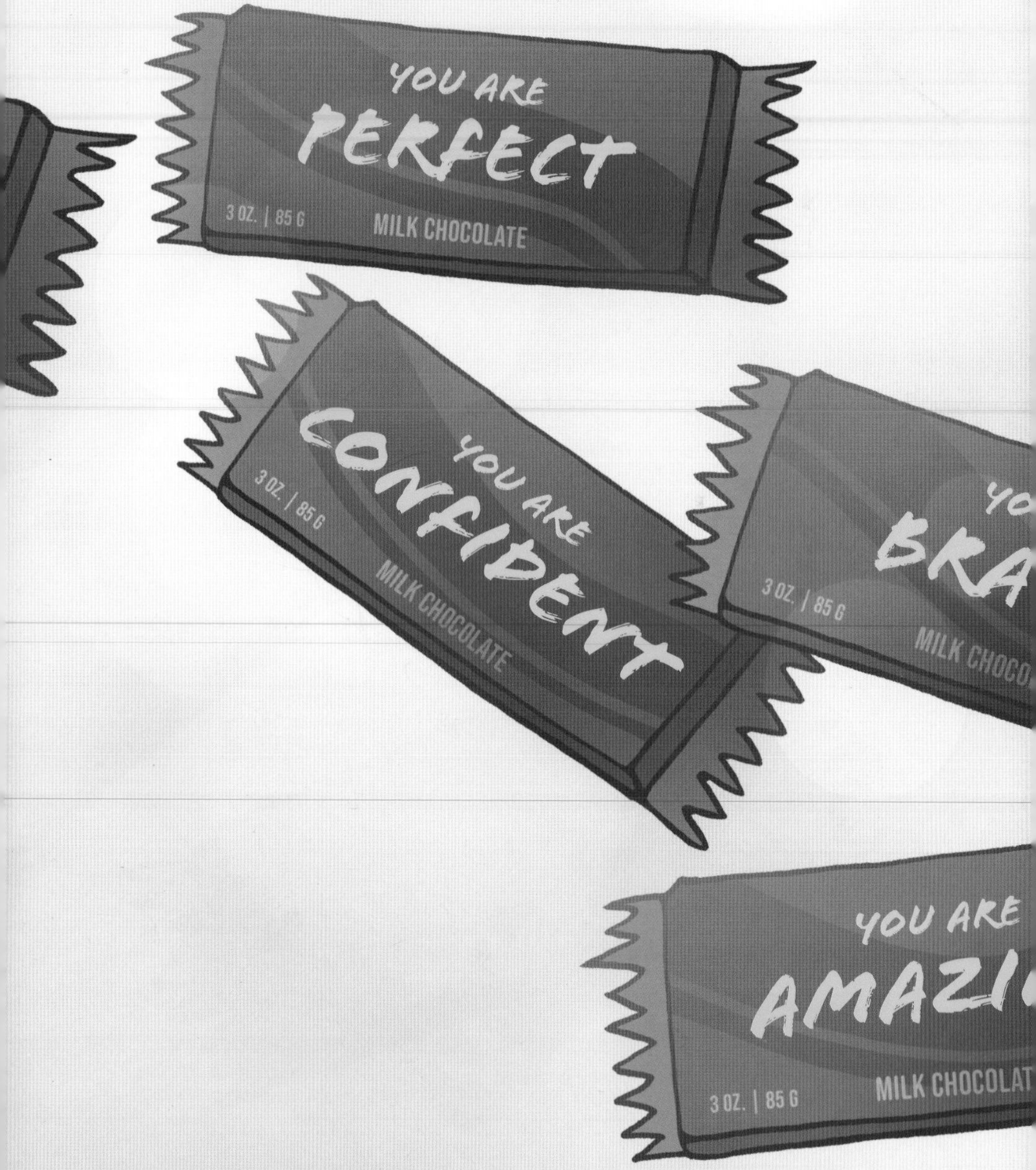
YOU ARE
PERFECT
3 OZ. | 85 G
MILK CHOCOLATE
YOU ARE
CONFIDENT
3 OZ. | 85 G
MILK CHOCOLATE
3 OZ. | 85 G
YOU ARE
3 OZ. | 85 G

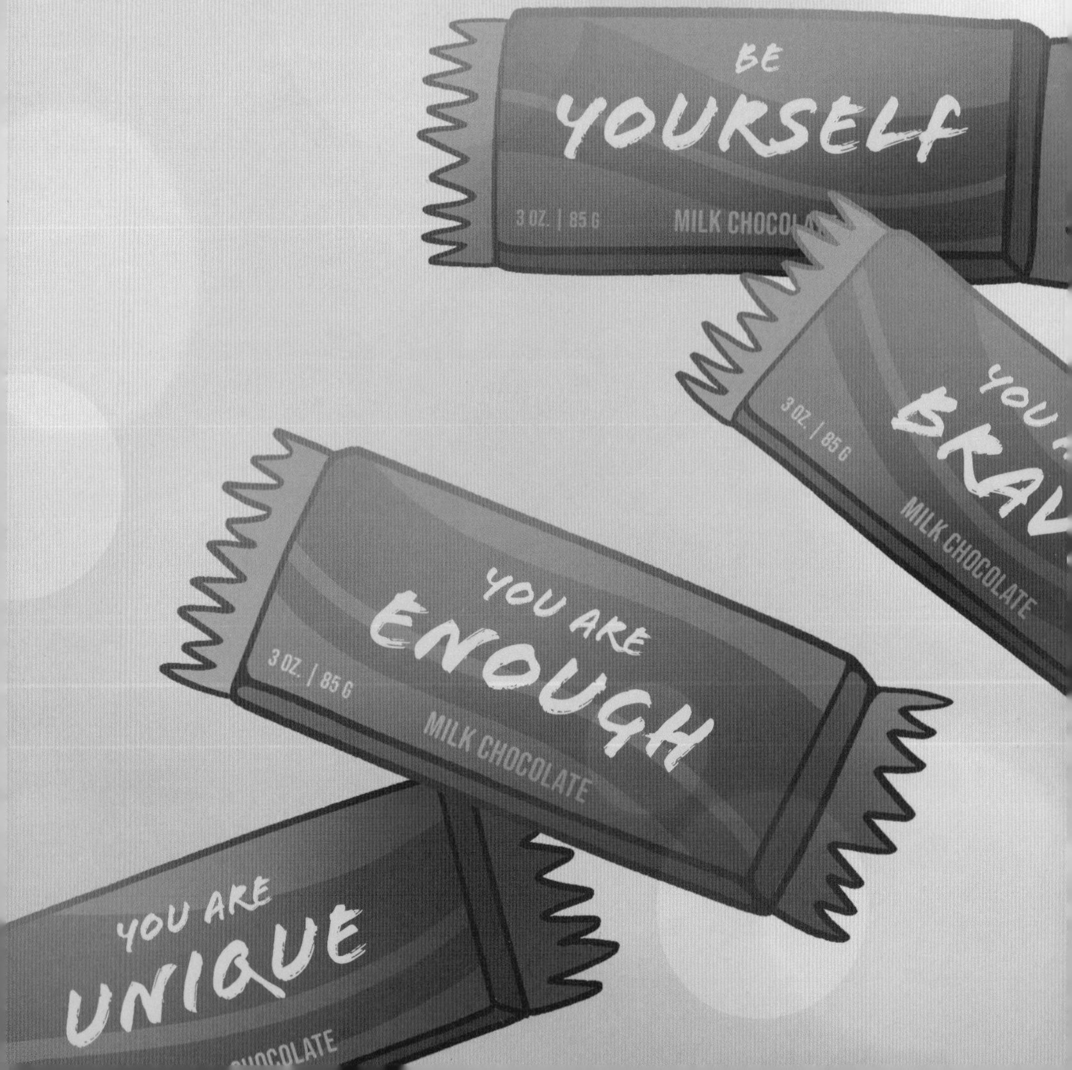
BE
YOURSELF
3 OZ. | 85 G
3 OZ. | 85 G
MILK CHOCOLATE
YOU ARE
ENOUGH
3 OZ. | 85 G
MILK CHOCOLATE
YOU ARE
UNIQUE

BE KIND TO
YOURSELF

Story and Art by
SWEENEY BOO

Colored by
JOANA LAFUENTE

Lettered by
DAVID HOPKINS

Script Translated by
EDWARD GAUVIN

3 OZ. | 85 G

MILK CHOCOLATE

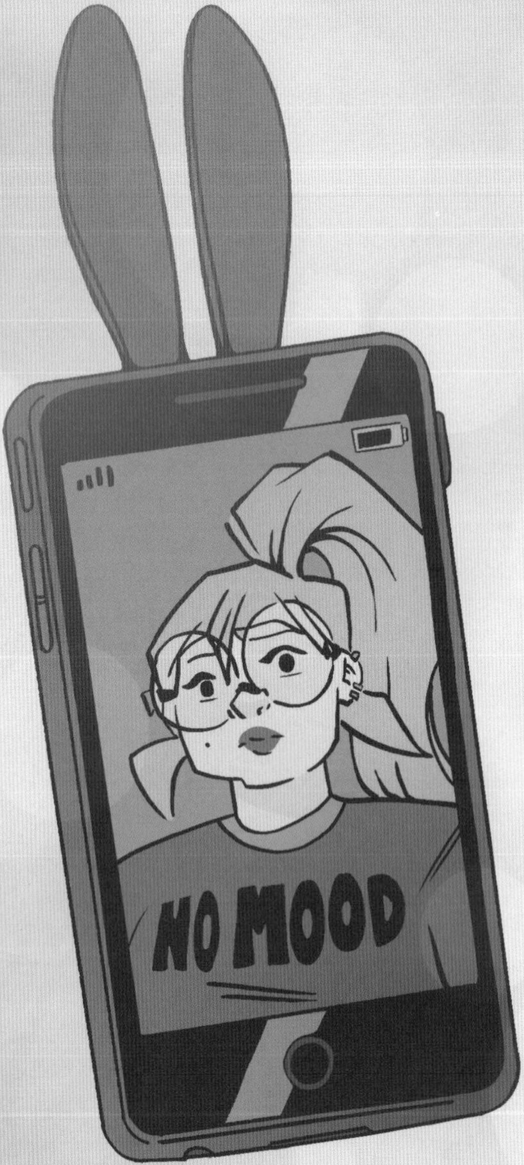

NO MOOD

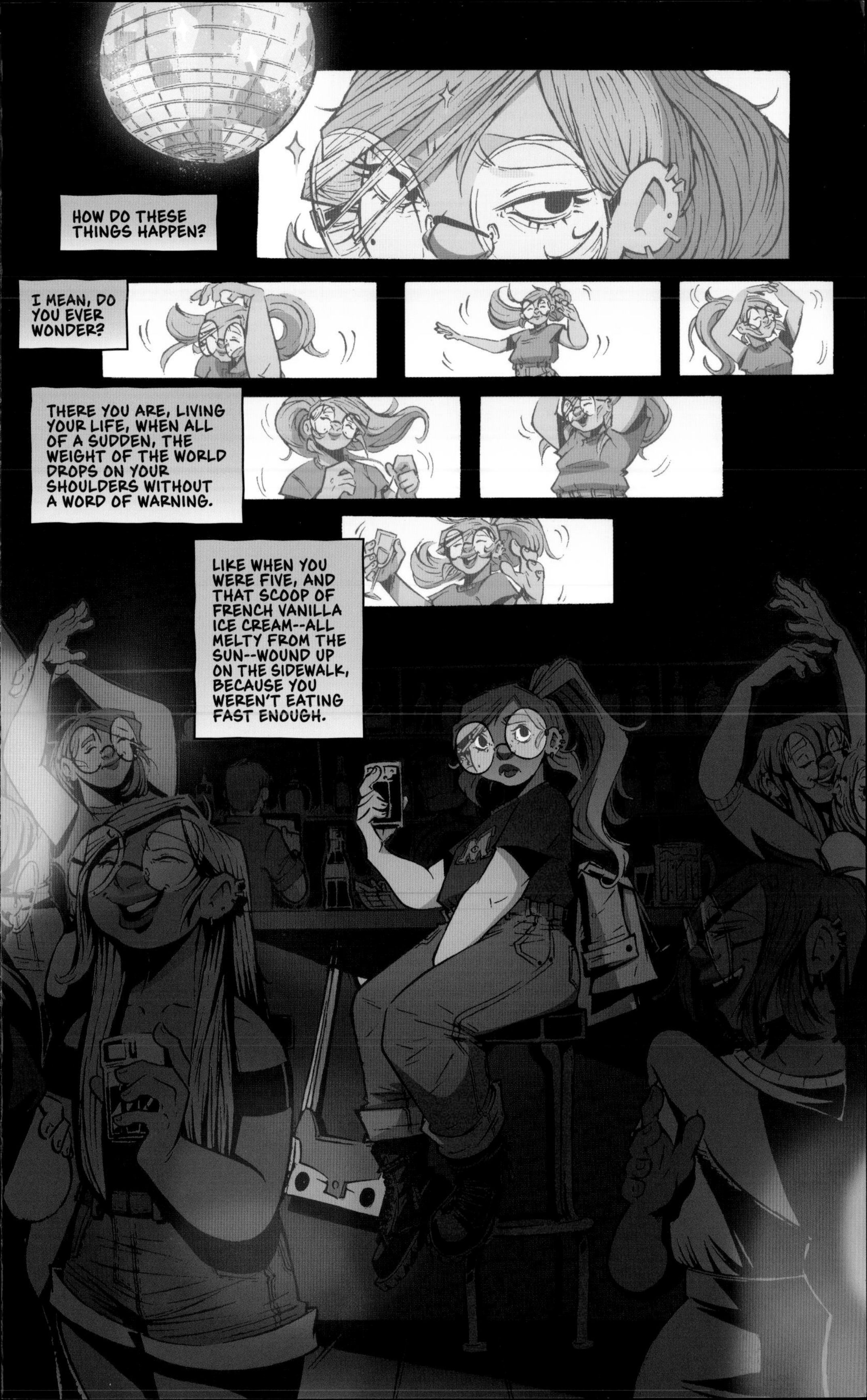
HOW DO THESE THINGS HAPPEN?
I MEAN, DO YOU EVER WONDER?
THERE YOU ARE, LIVING YOUR LIFE, WHEN ALL OF A SUDDEN, THE WEIGHT OF THE WORLD DROPS ON YOUR SHOULDERS WITHOUT A WORD OF WARNING.
LIKE WHEN YOU WERE FIVE, AND THAT SCOOP OF FRENCH VANILLA ICE CREAM--ALL MELTY FROM THE SUN--WOUND UP ON THE SIDEWALK, BECAUSE YOU WEREN'T EATING FAST ENOUGH.

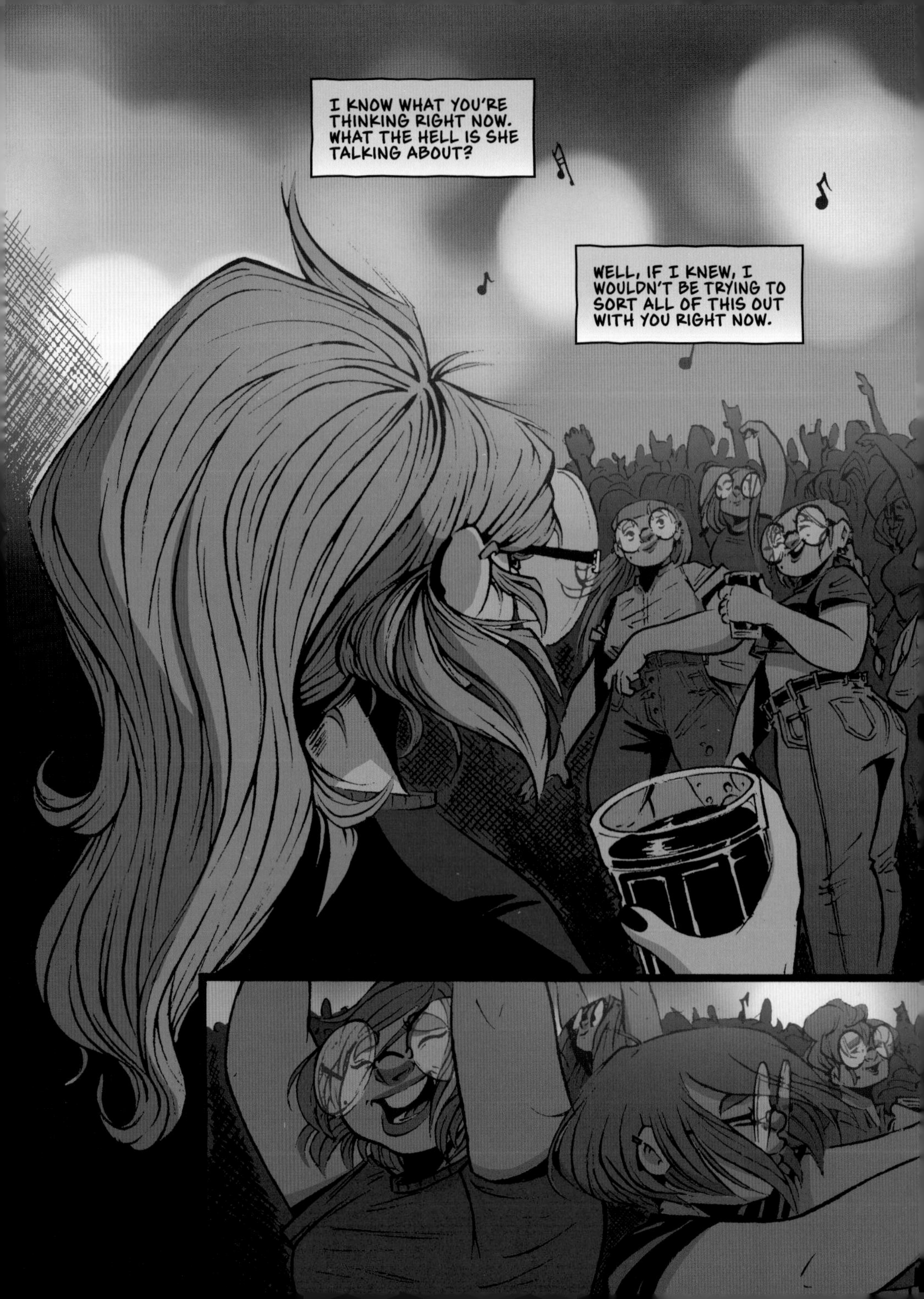
I KNOW WHAT YOU'RE THINKING RIGHT NOW. WHAT THE HELL IS SHE TALKING ABOUT?
WELL, IF I KNEW, I WOULDN'T BE TRYING TO SORT ALL OF THIS OUT WITH YOU RIGHT NOW.

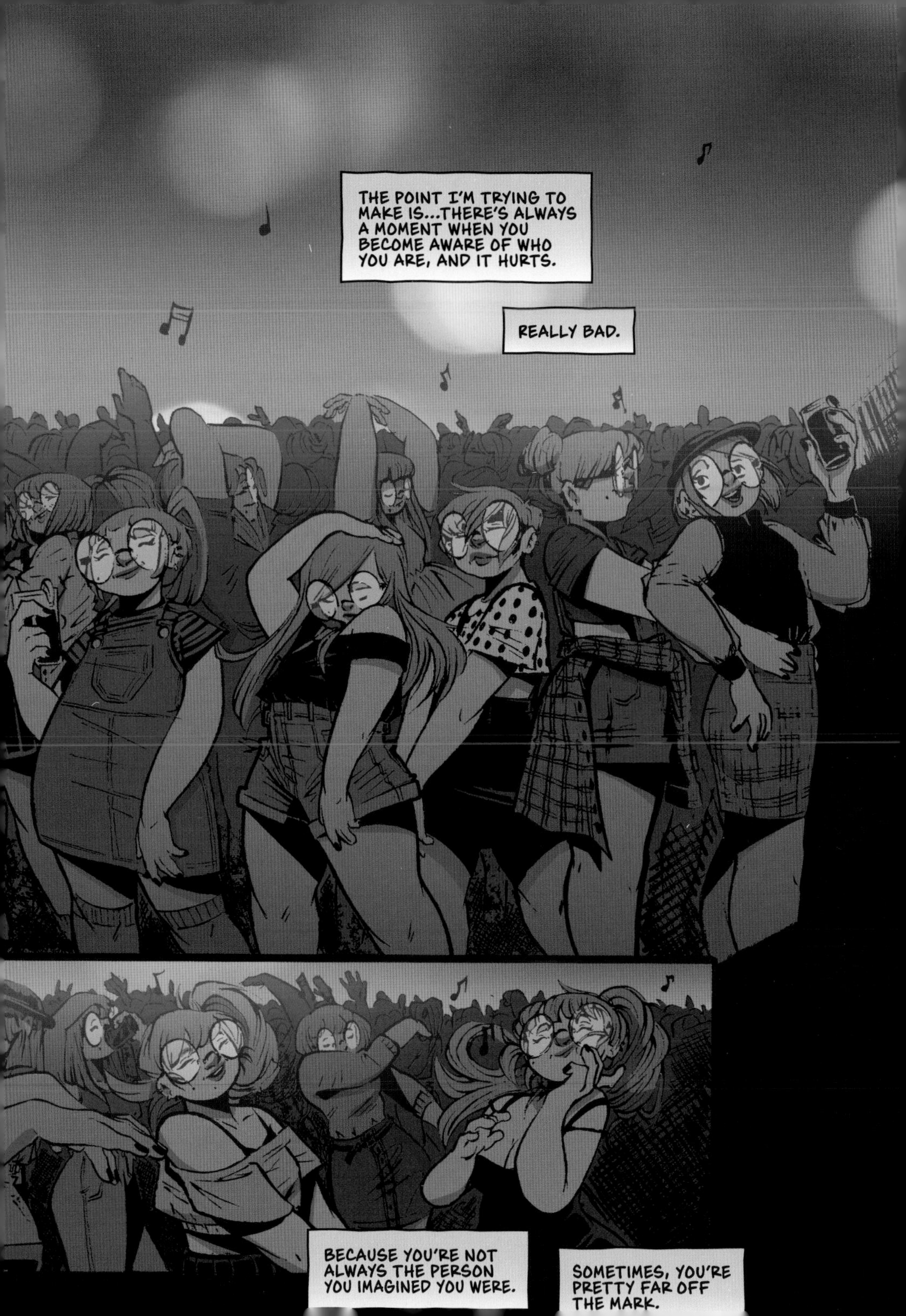
THE POINT I'M TRYING TO MAKE IS...THERE'S ALWAYS A MOMENT WHEN YOU BECOME AWARE OF WHO YOU ARE, AND IT HURTS.
REALLY BAD.
BECAUSE YOU'RE NOT ALWAYS THE PERSON YOU IMAGINED YOU WERE.
SOMETIMES, YOU'RE PRETTY FAR OFF THE MARK.

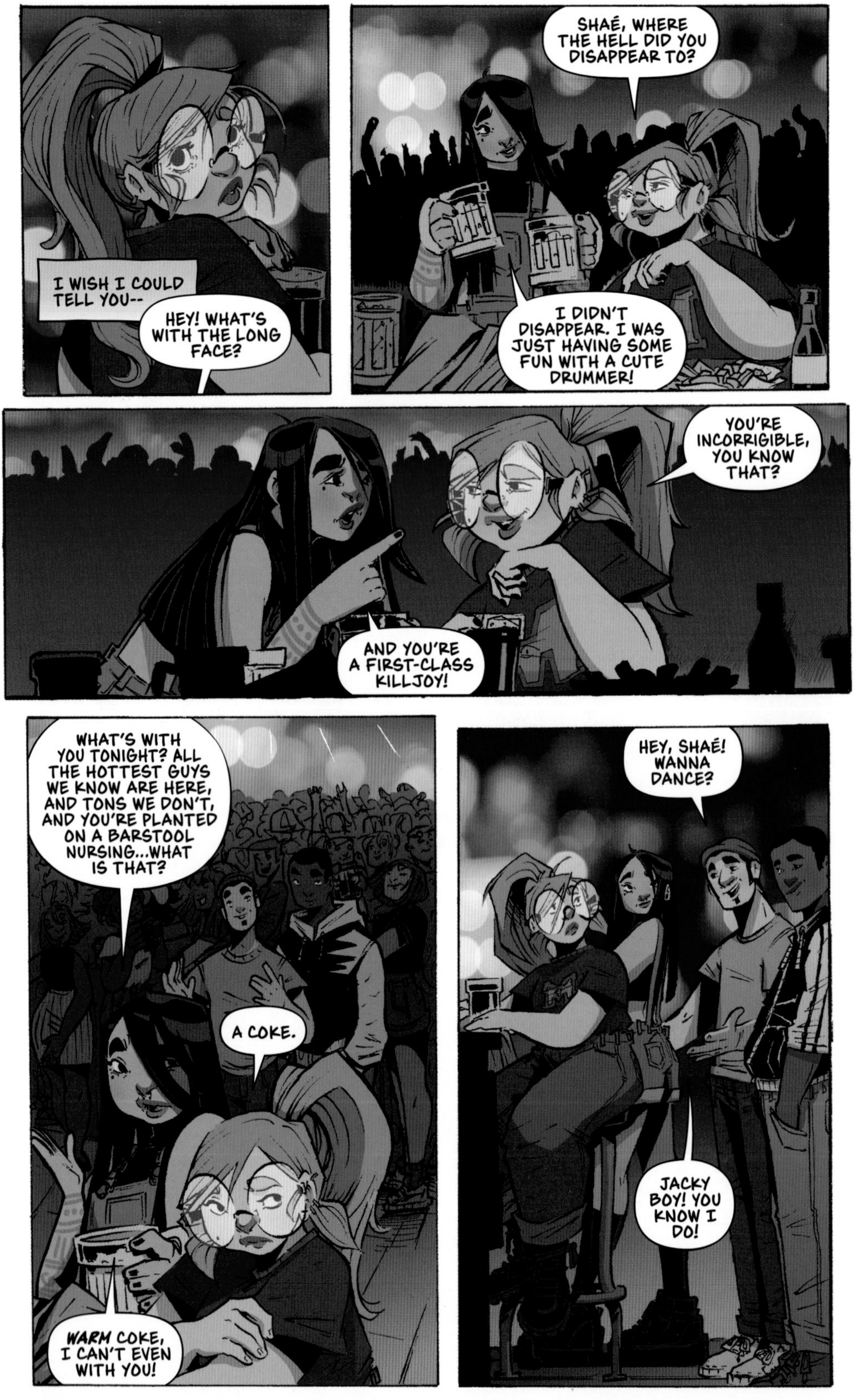
I WISH I COULD TELL YOU--
HEY! WHAT'S WITH THE LONG FACE?
SHAÉ, WHERE THE HELL DID YOU DISAPPEAR TO?
I DIDN'T DISAPPEAR. I WAS JUST HAVING SOME FUN WITH A CUTE DRUMMER!
YOU'RE INCORRIGIBLE, YOU KNOW THAT?
AND YOU'RE A FIRST-CLASS KILLJOY!
WHAT'S WITH YOU TONIGHT? ALL THE HOTTEST GUYS WE KNOW ARE HERE, AND TONS WE DON'T, AND YOU'RE PLANTED ON A BARSTOOL NURSING...WHAT IS THAT?
A COKE.
WARM COKE, I CAN'T EVEN WITH YOU!
HEY, SHAÉ! WANNA DANCE?
JACKY BOY! YOU KNOW I DO!

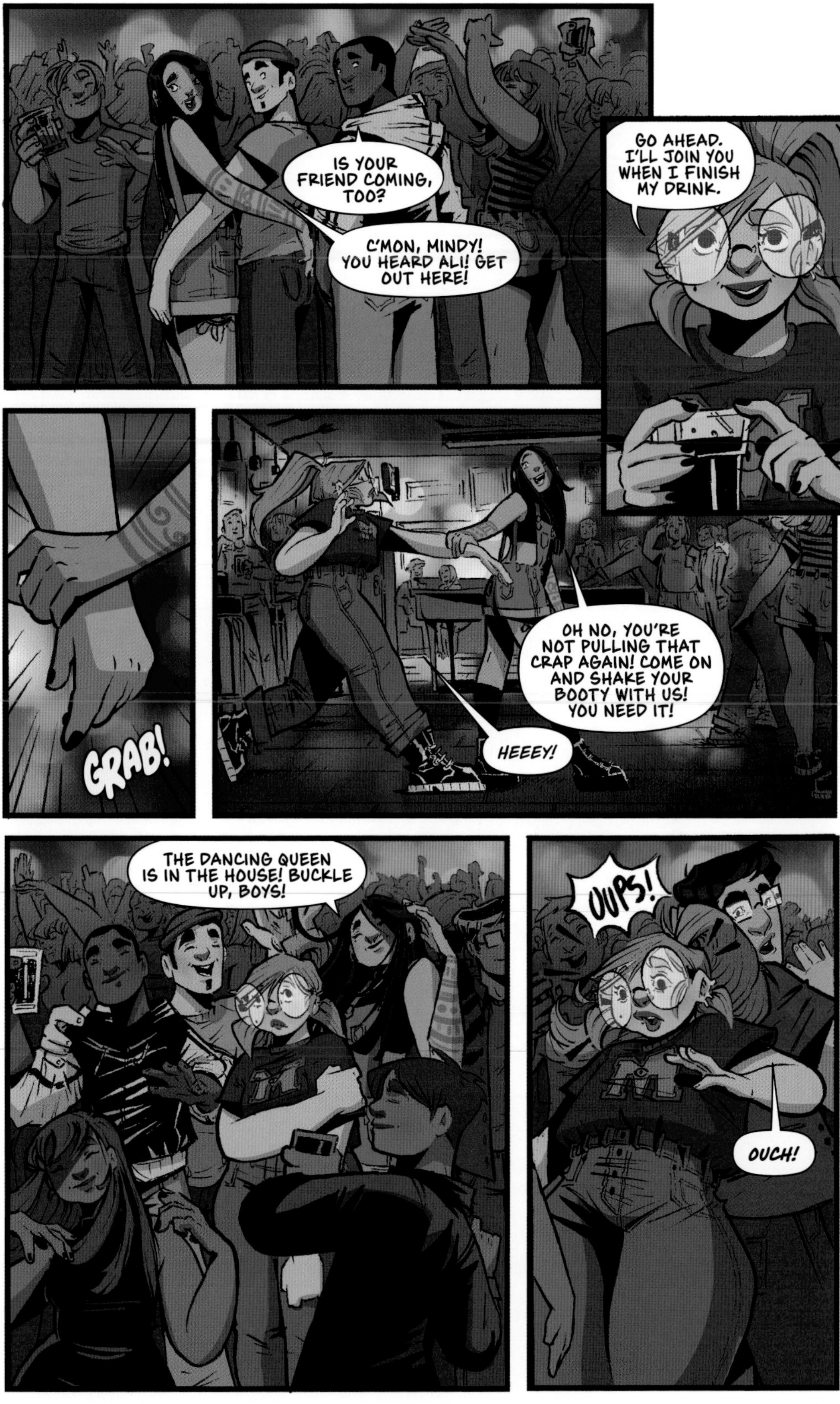
IS YOUR FRIEND COMING, TOO?
C'MON, MINDY! YOU HEARD ALI! GET OUT HERE!
GO AHEAD. I'LL JOIN YOU WHEN I FINISH MY DRINK.
GRAB!
OH NO, YOU'RE NOT PULLING THAT CRAP AGAIN! COME ON AND SHAKE YOUR BOOTY WITH US! YOU NEED IT!
HEEEY!
THE DANCING QUEEN IS IN THE HOUSE! BUCKLE UP, BOYS!
OUPS!
OUCH!

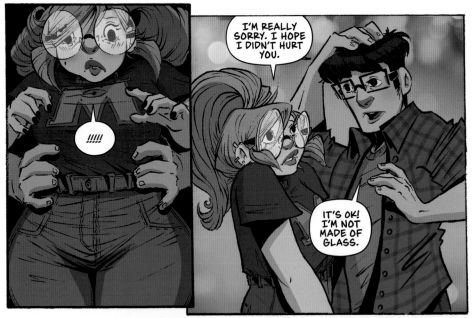

!!!!!

I'M REALLY SORRY. I HOPE I DIDN'T HURT YOU.

IT'S OK! I'M NOT MADE OF GLASS.

PARDON MY FRIEND, PRETTY BOY, BUT SHE'S SPOKEN FOR TONIGHT! YOU CAN TRY YOUR LUCK TOMORROW... THAT IS, IF SHE GIVES YOU HER NUMBER.

SHAÉ...

COME ON! GO!

MY NAME'S MINDYYYYYY...

I'M TOM! MY NUMBER'S 555...26.

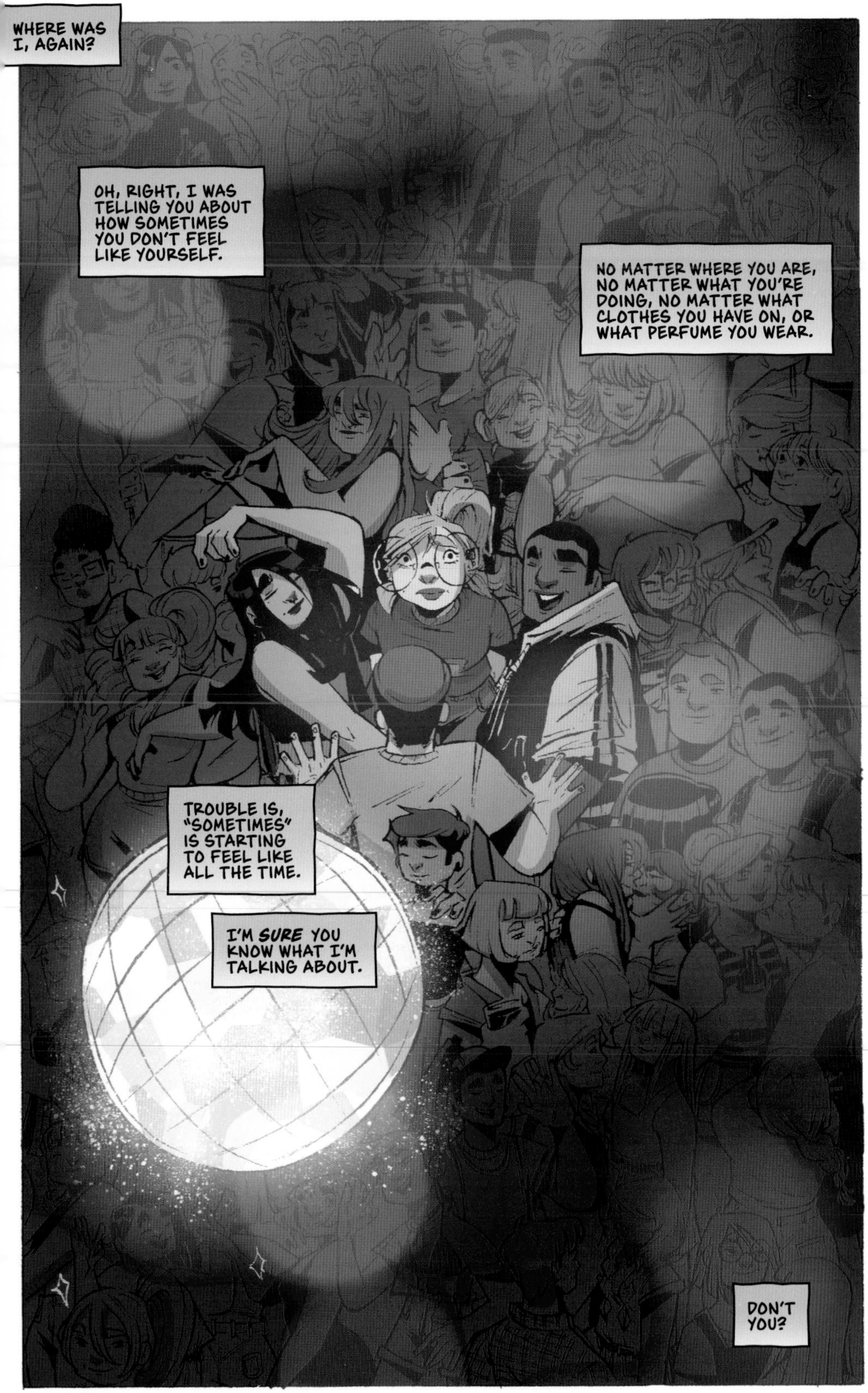
WHERE WAS I, AGAIN?
OH, RIGHT, I WAS TELLING YOU ABOUT HOW SOMETIMES YOU DON'T FEEL LIKE YOURSELF.
NO MATTER WHERE YOU ARE, NO MATTER WHAT YOU'RE DOING, NO MATTER WHAT CLOTHES YOU HAVE ON, OR WHAT PERFUME YOU WEAR.
TROUBLE IS, "SOMETIMES" IS STARTING TO FEEL LIKE ALL THE TIME.
I'M *SURE* YOU KNOW WHAT I'M TALKING ABOUT.
DON'T YOU?

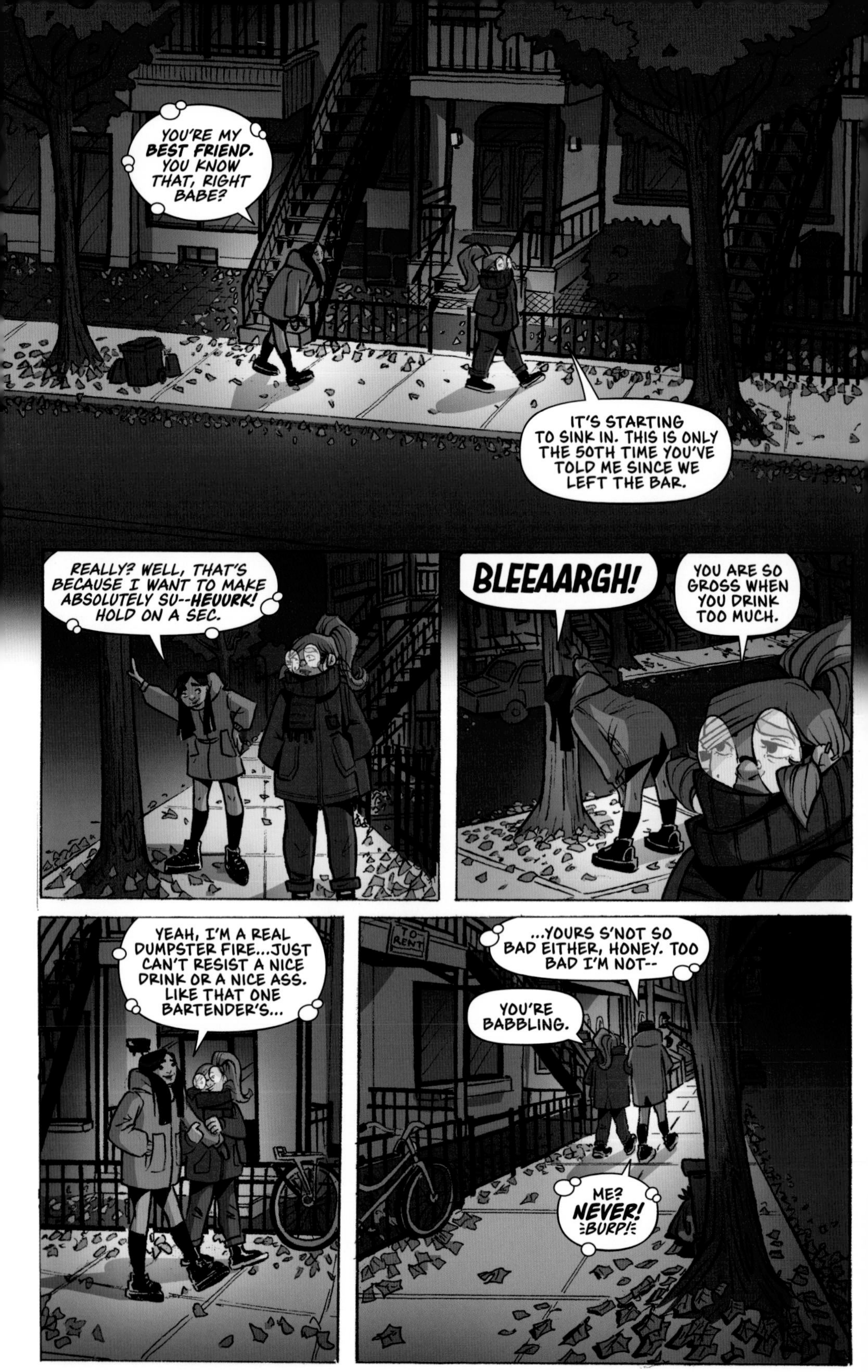
YOU'RE MY BEST FRIEND. YOU KNOW THAT, RIGHT BABE?
IT'S STARTING TO SINK IN. THIS IS ONLY THE 50TH TIME YOU'VE TOLD ME SINCE WE LEFT THE BAR.
REALLY? WELL, THAT'S BECAUSE I WANT TO MAKE ABSOLUTELY SU--HEUURK! HOLD ON A SEC.
BLEEAARGH!
YOU ARE SO GROSS WHEN YOU DRINK TOO MUCH.
YEAH, I'M A REAL DUMPSTER FIRE...JUST CAN'T RESIST A NICE DRINK OR A NICE ASS. LIKE THAT ONE BARTENDER'S...
TO RENT
...YOURS S'NOT SO BAD EITHER, HONEY. TOO BAD I'M NOT--
YOU'RE BABBLING.
ME? NEVER! BURP!

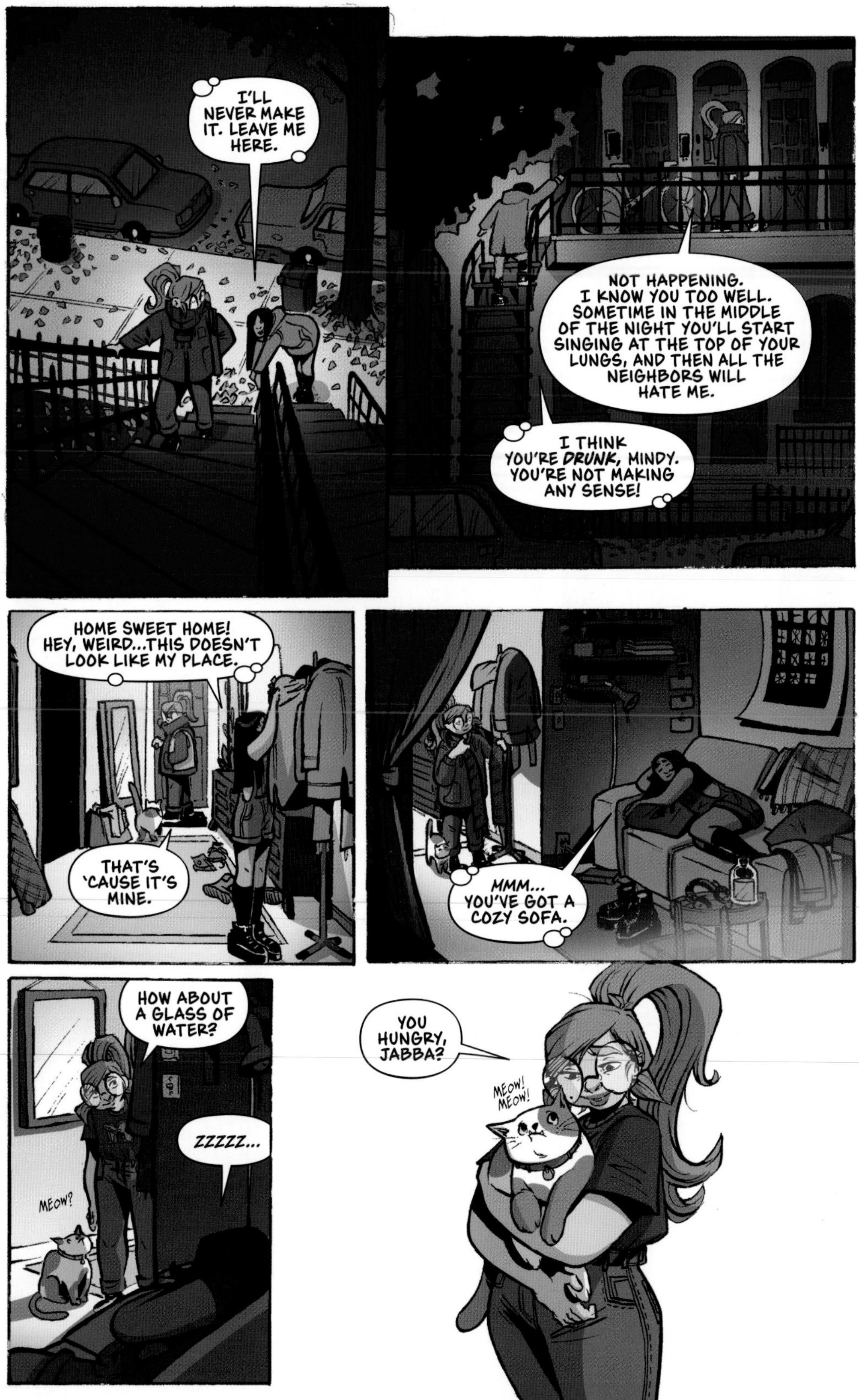
I'LL NEVER MAKE IT. LEAVE ME HERE.
NOT HAPPENING. I KNOW YOU TOO WELL. SOMETIME IN THE MIDDLE OF THE NIGHT YOU'LL START SINGING AT THE TOP OF YOUR LUNGS, AND THEN ALL THE NEIGHBORS WILL HATE ME.
I THINK YOU'RE DRUNK, MINDY. YOU'RE NOT MAKING ANY SENSE!
HOME SWEET HOME! HEY, WEIRD...THIS DOESN'T LOOK LIKE MY PLACE.
THAT'S 'CAUSE IT'S MINE.
MMM... YOU'VE GOT A COZY SOFA.
HOW ABOUT A GLASS OF WATER?
ZZZZZ...
MEOW?
YOU HUNGRY, JABBA?
MEOW! MEOW!

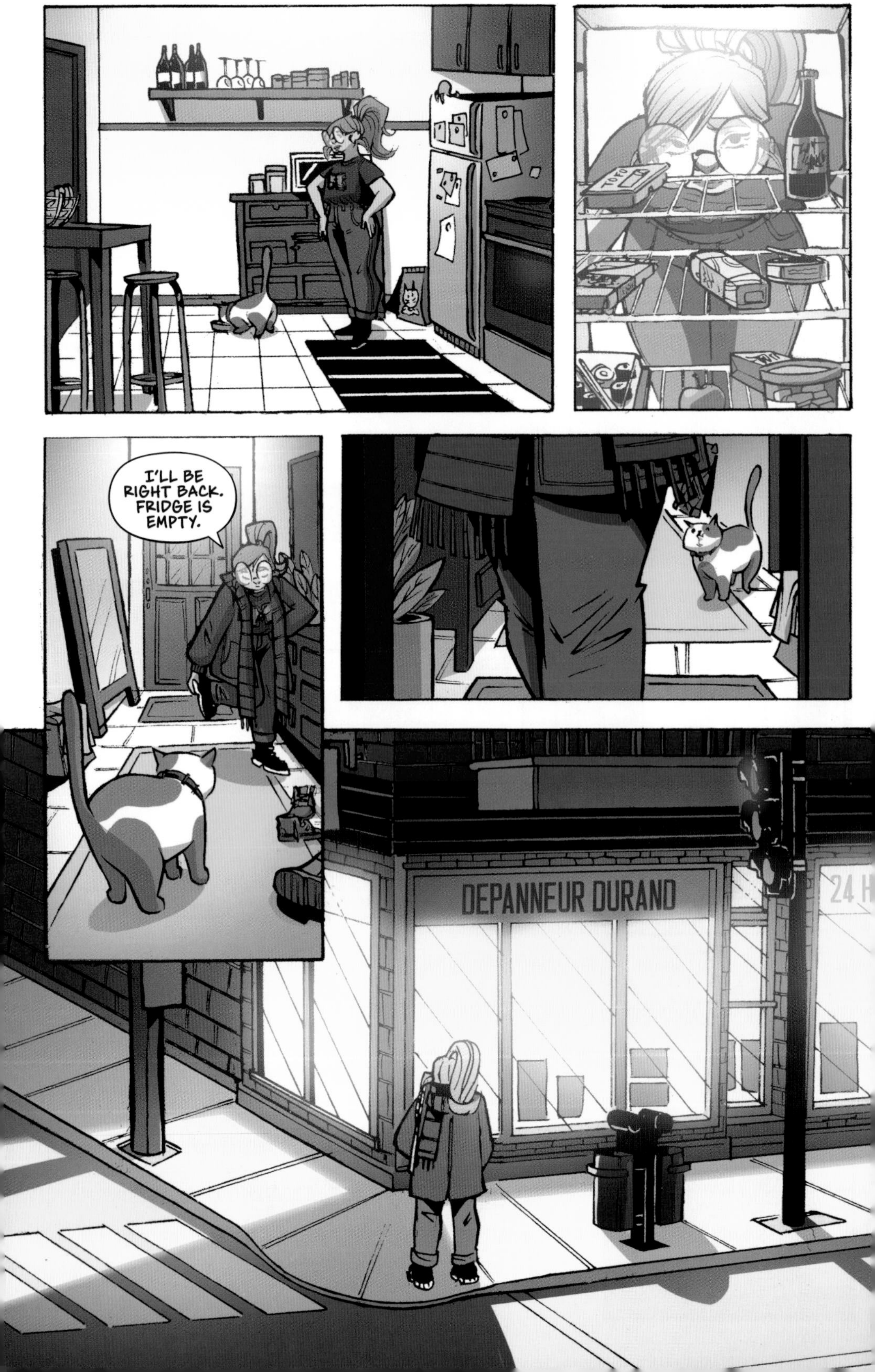
I'LL BE RIGHT BACK. FRIDGE IS EMPTY.
DEPANNEUR DURAND
24 H

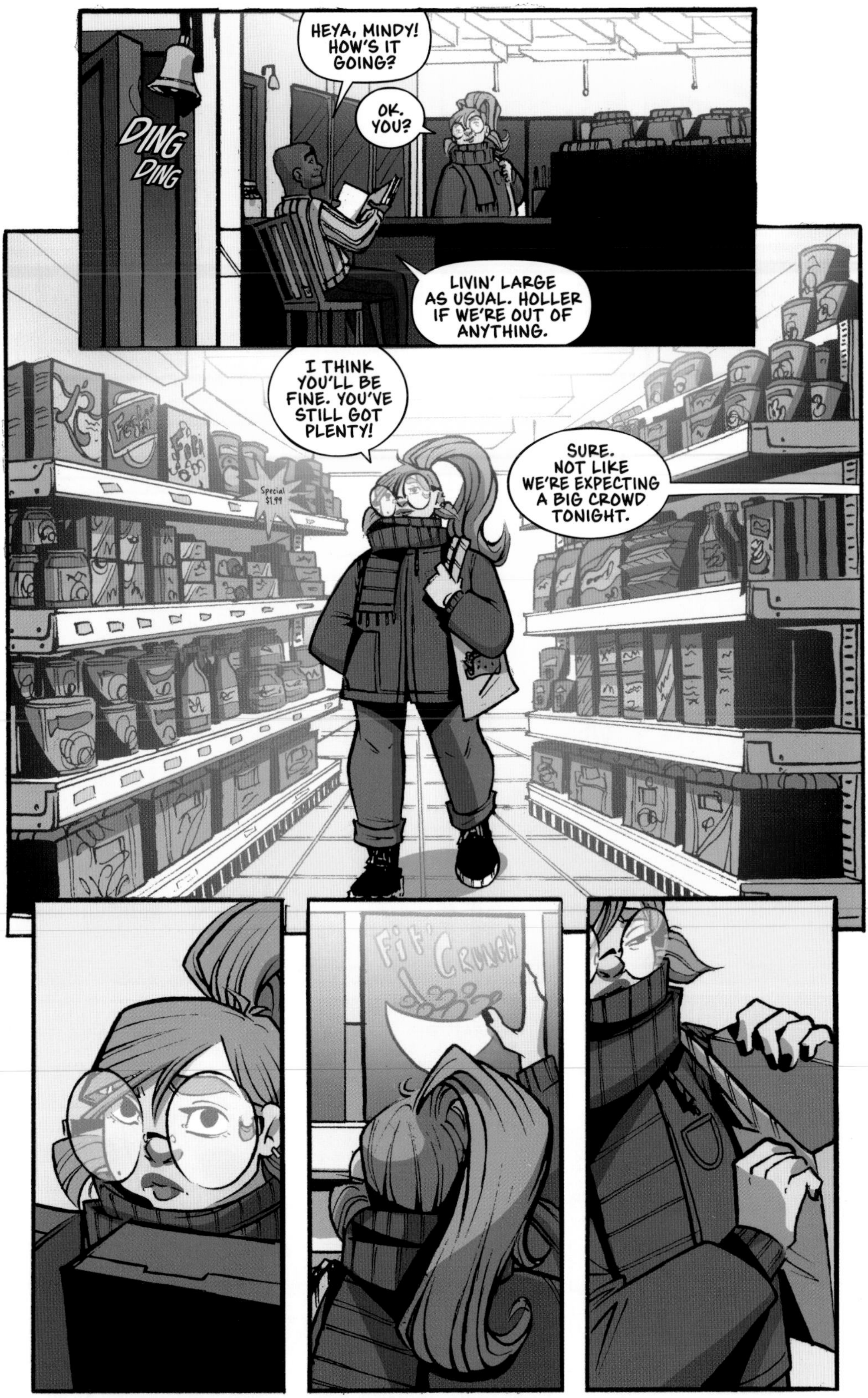
HEYA, MINDY! HOW'S IT GOING?
DING DING
OK. YOU?
LIVIN' LARGE AS USUAL. HOLLER IF WE'RE OUT OF ANYTHING.
I THINK YOU'LL BE FINE. YOU'VE STILL GOT PLENTY!
SURE. NOT LIKE WE'RE EXPECTING A BIG CROWD TONIGHT.
Special $1.99
FIT' CRUNCH

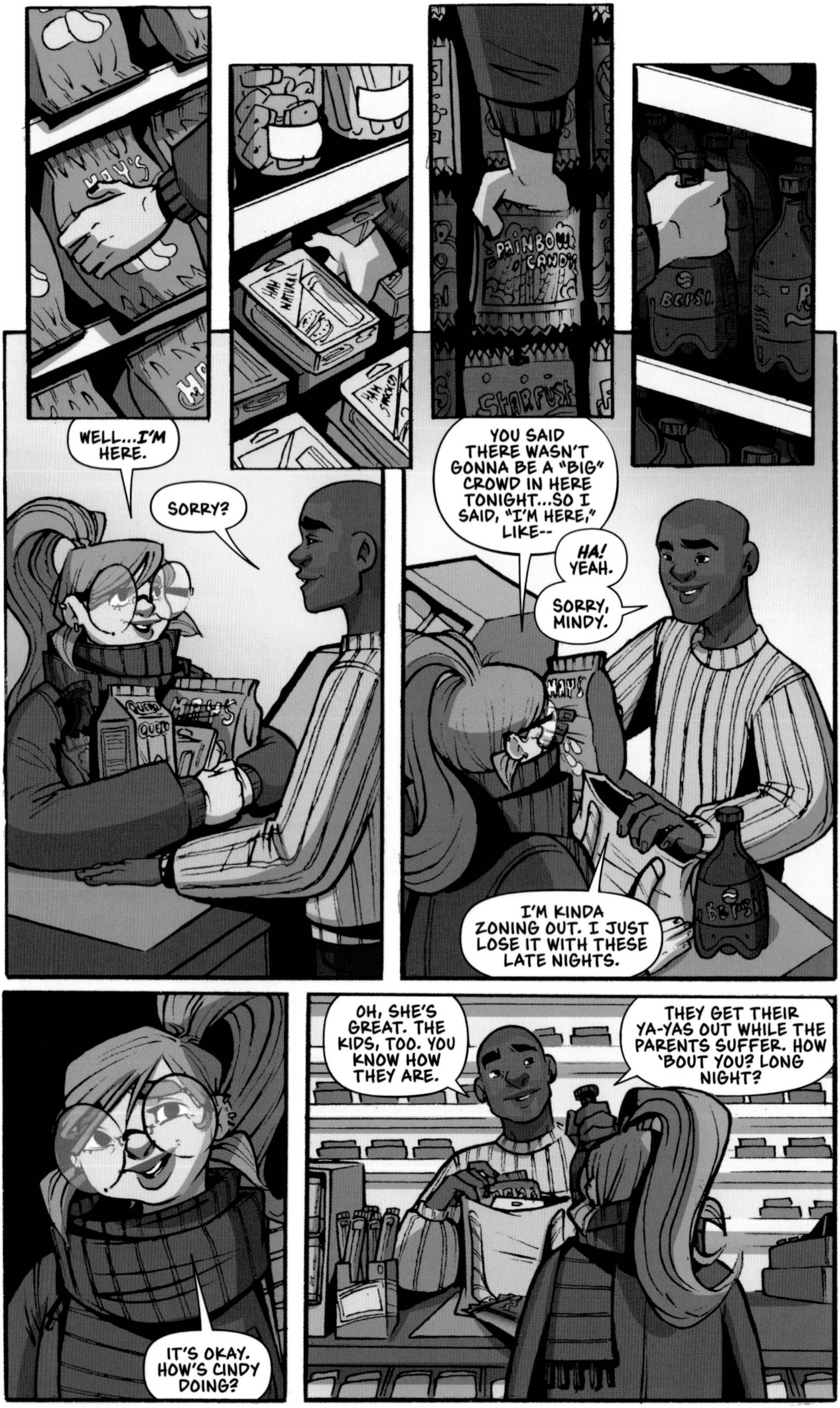
WELL...I'M HERE.
SORRY?
YOU SAID THERE WASN'T GONNA BE A "BIG" CROWD IN HERE TONIGHT...SO I SAID, "I'M HERE," LIKE--
HA! YEAH.
SORRY, MINDY.
I'M KINDA ZONING OUT. I JUST LOSE IT WITH THESE LATE NIGHTS.
IT'S OKAY. HOW'S CINDY DOING?
OH, SHE'S GREAT. THE KIDS, TOO. YOU KNOW HOW THEY ARE.
THEY GET THEIR YA-YAS OUT WHILE THE PARENTS SUFFER. HOW 'BOUT YOU? LONG NIGHT?

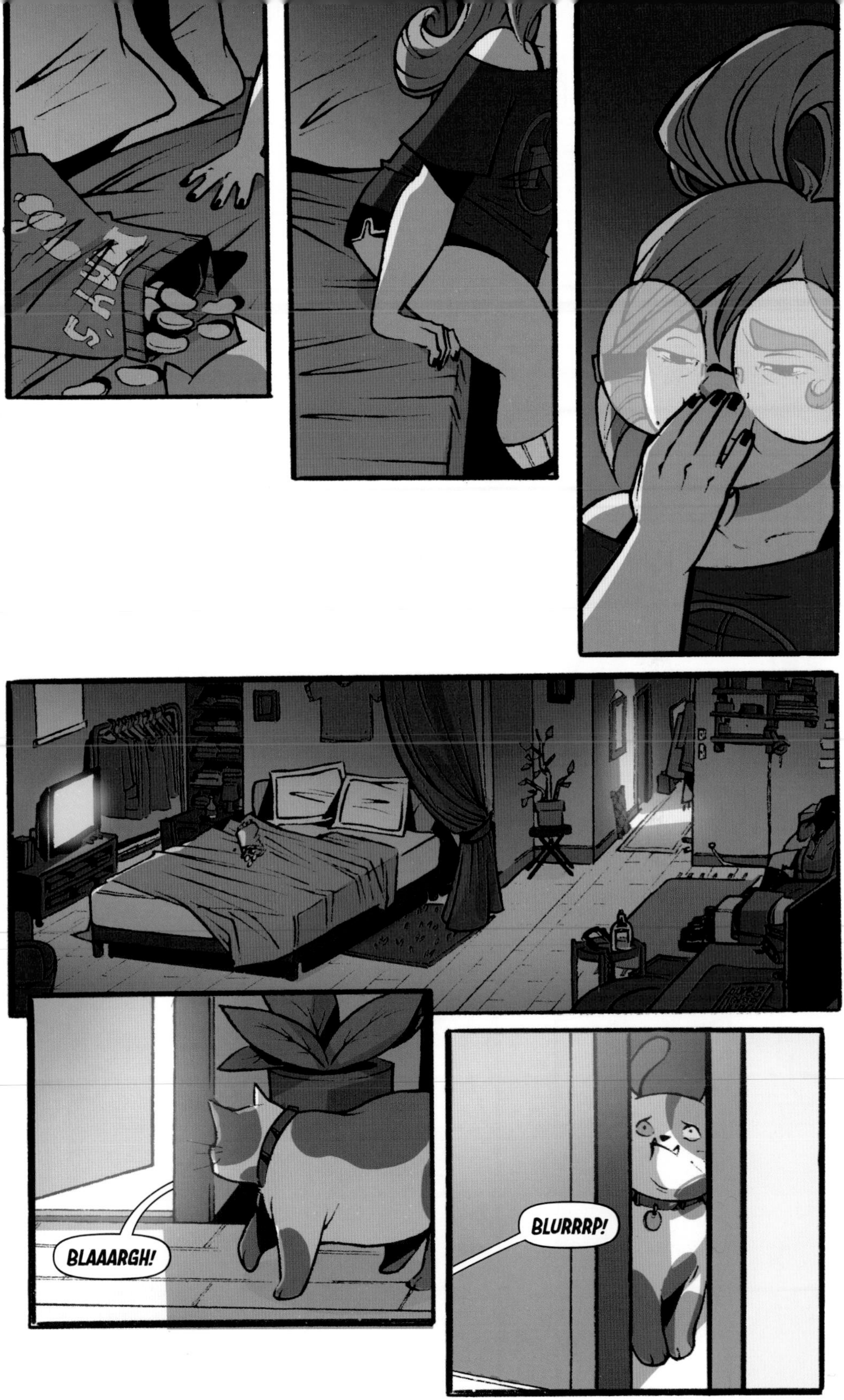
BLAAARGH!
BLURRRP!

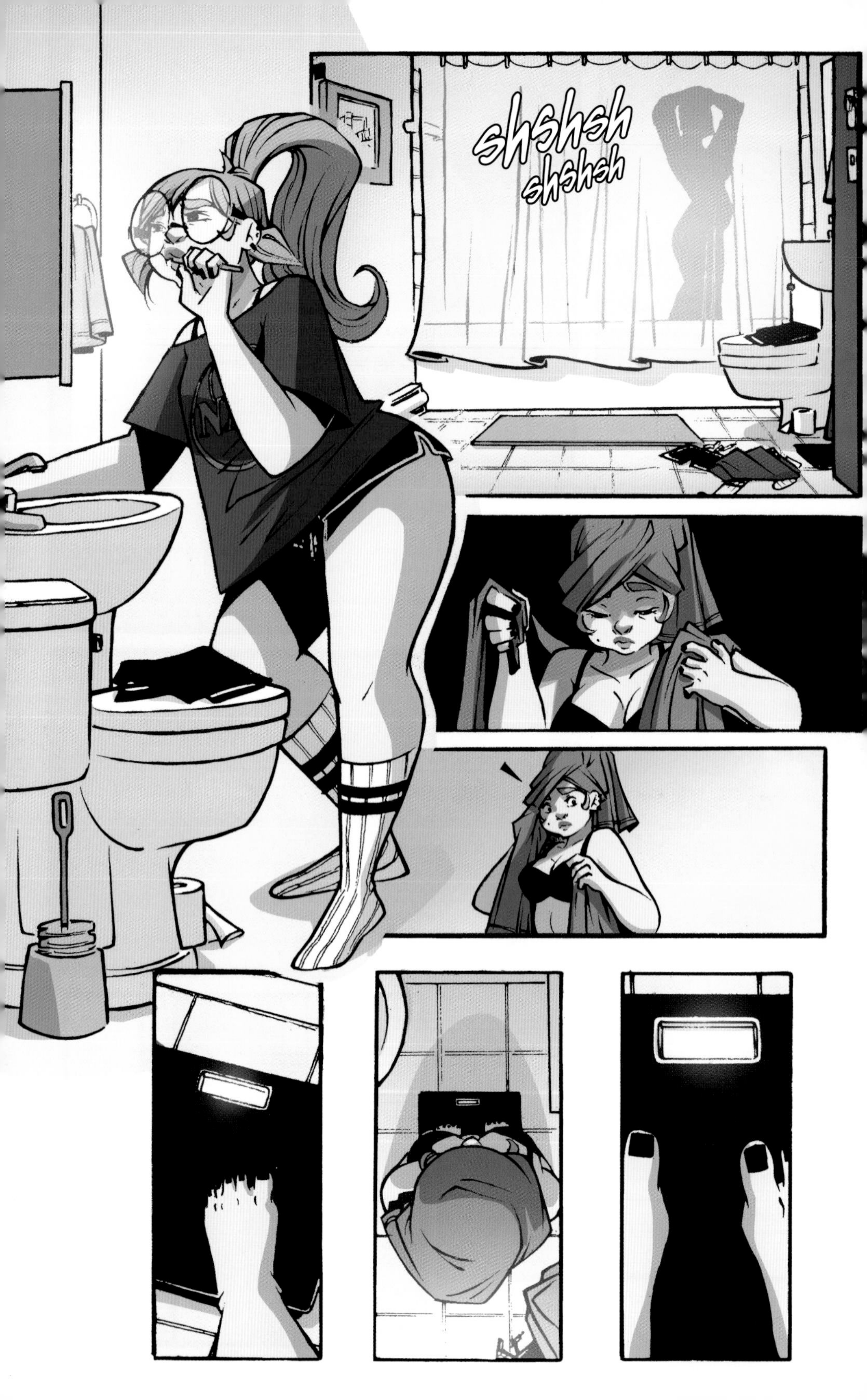
shshsh
shshsh

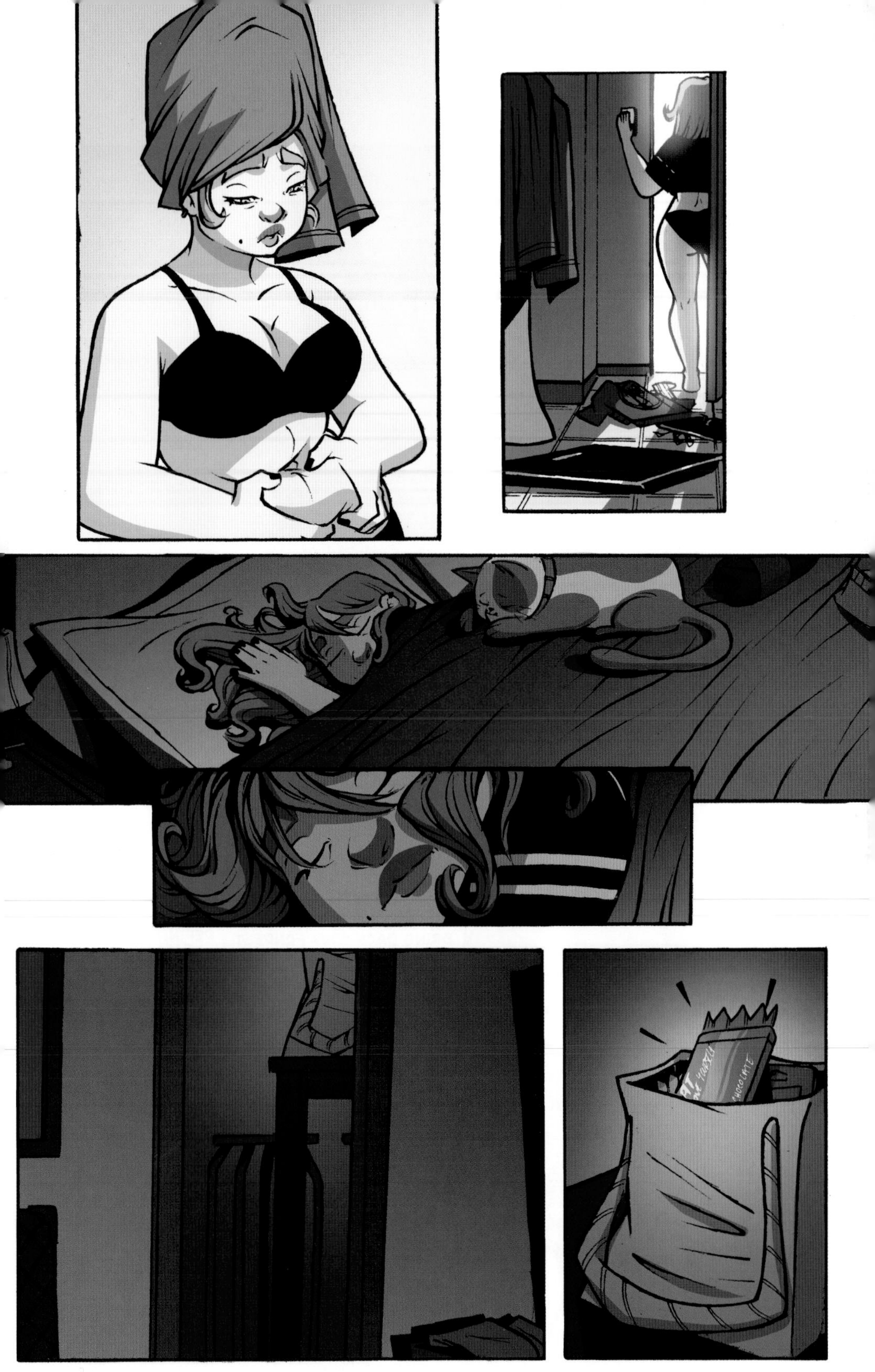
YOURSELF
CHOCOLATE

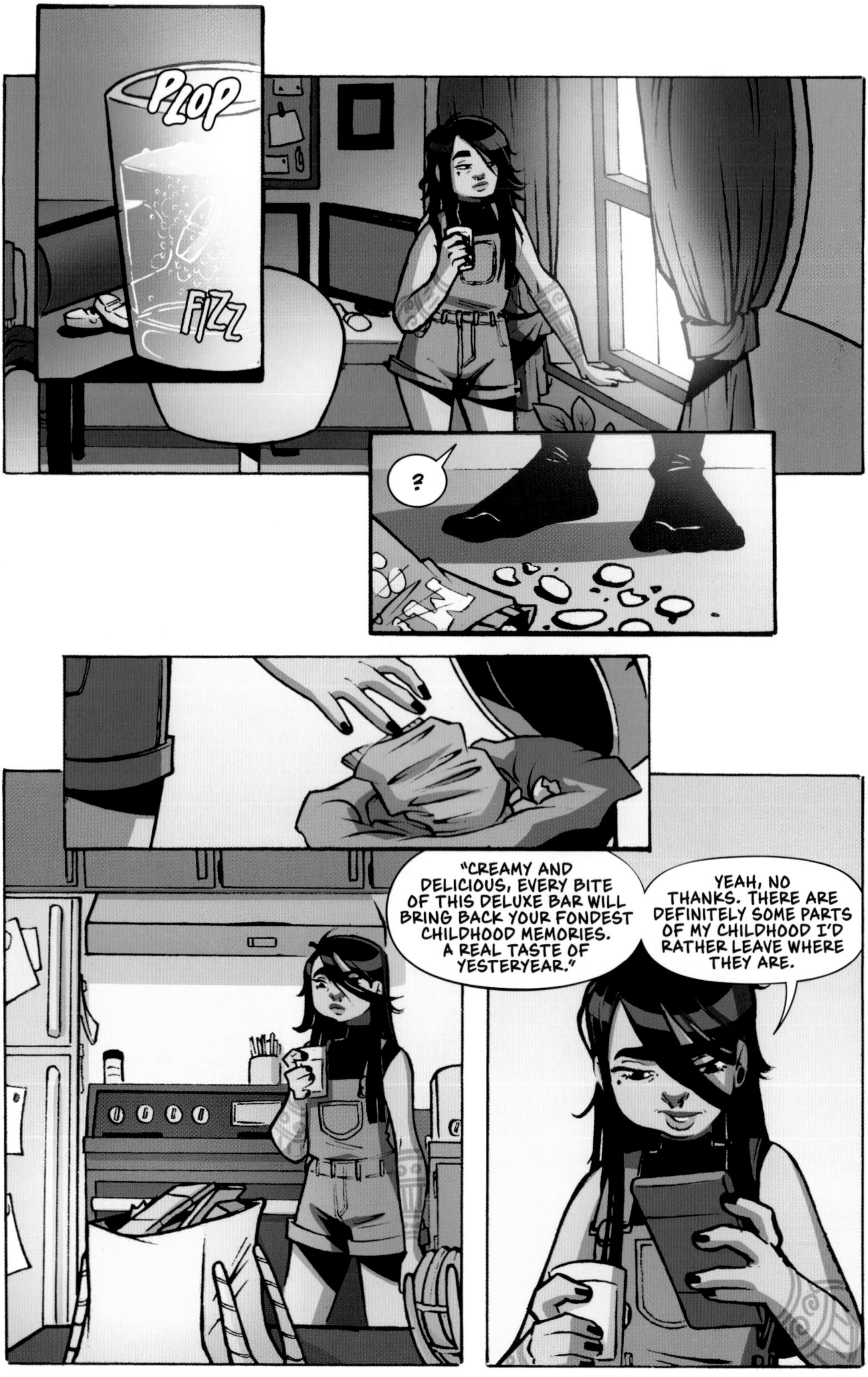
PLOP
FIZZ
?
"CREAMY AND DELICIOUS, EVERY BITE OF THIS DELUXE BAR WILL BRING BACK YOUR FONDEST CHILDHOOD MEMORIES. A REAL TASTE OF YESTERYEAR."
YEAH, NO THANKS. THERE ARE DEFINITELY SOME PARTS OF MY CHILDHOOD I'D RATHER LEAVE WHERE THEY ARE.

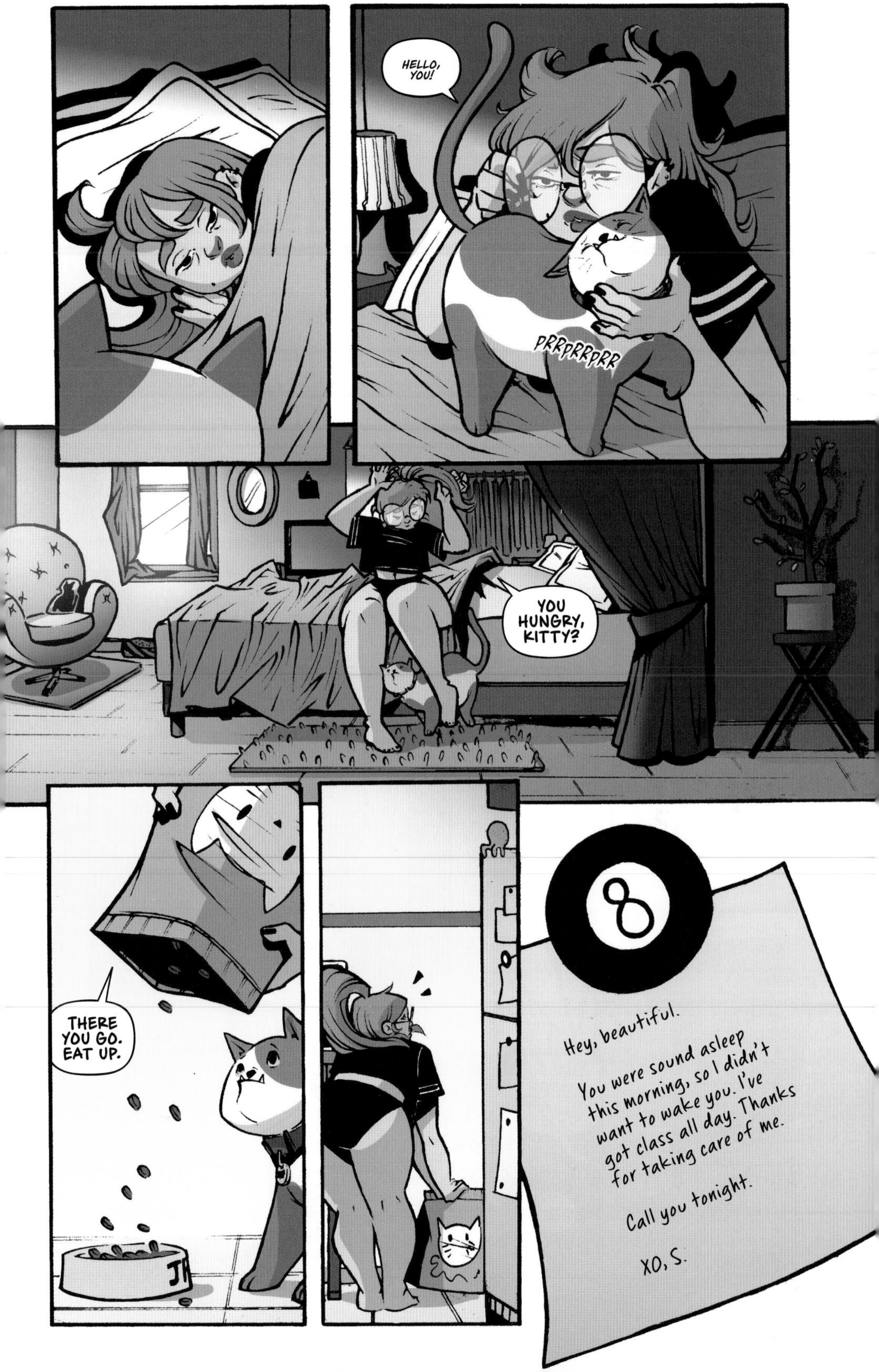
HELLO, YOU!
PRRPRRPRR
YOU HUNGRY, KITTY?
THERE YOU GO. EAT UP.
8
Hey, beautiful.
You were sound asleep this morning, so I didn't want to wake you. I've got class all day. Thanks for taking care of me.
Call you tonight.
XO, S.

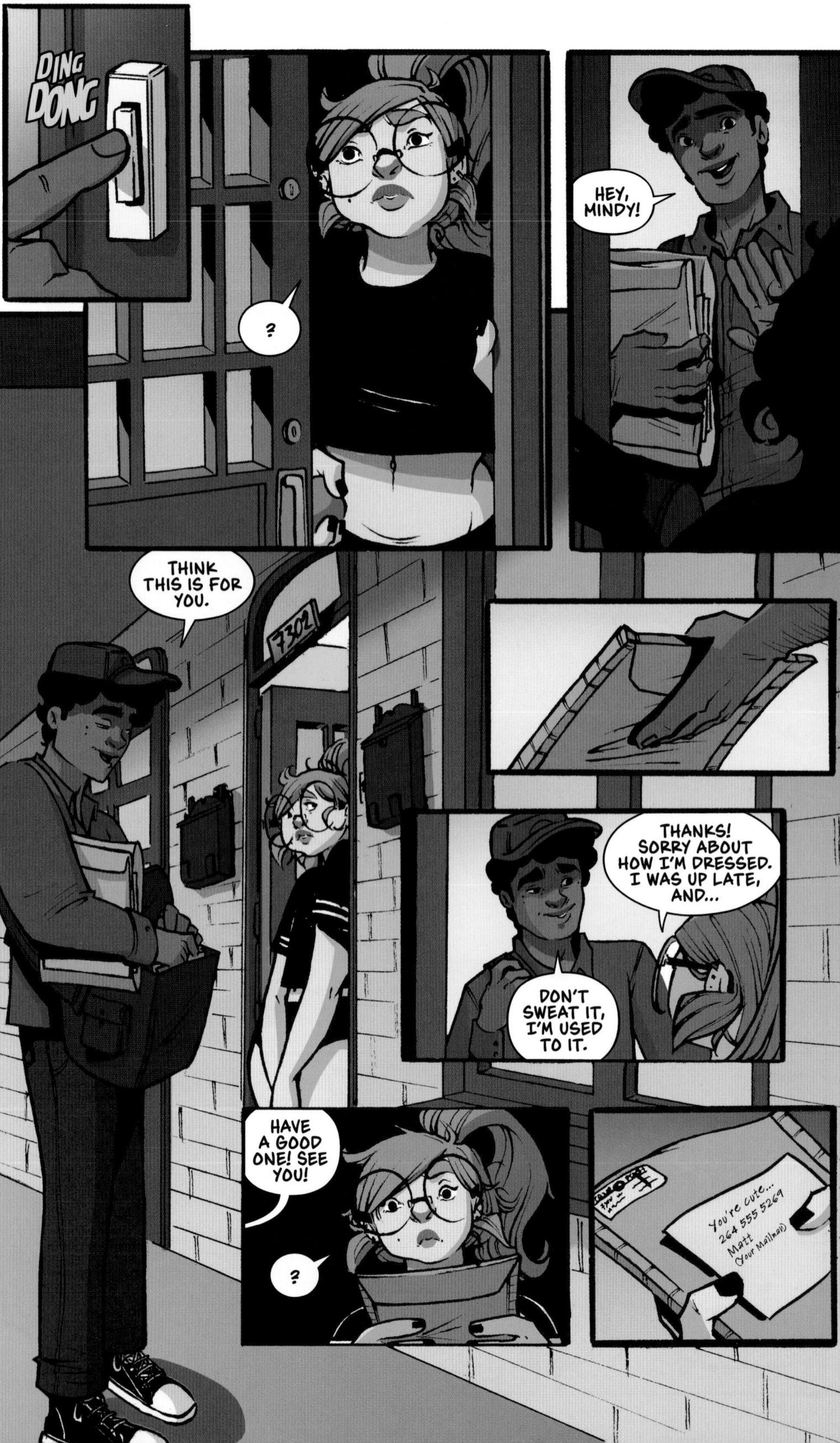
DING DONG
?
HEY, MINDY!
THINK THIS IS FOR YOU.
7302
THANKS! SORRY ABOUT HOW I'M DRESSED. I WAS UP LATE, AND...
DON'T SWEAT IT, I'M USED TO IT.
HAVE A GOOD ONE! SEE YOU!
?
You're cute...
264 555 5269
Matt
(Your Mailman)

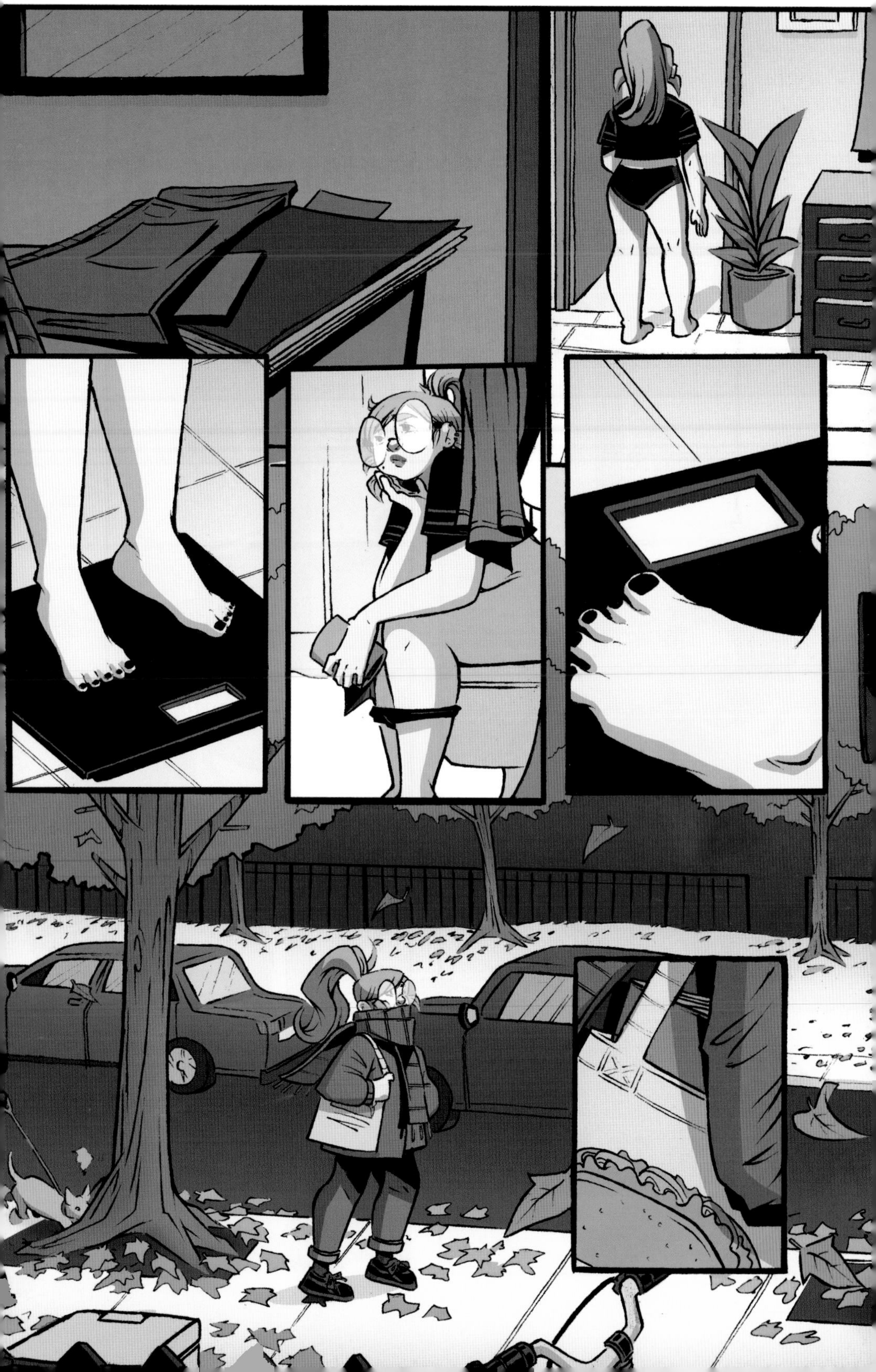

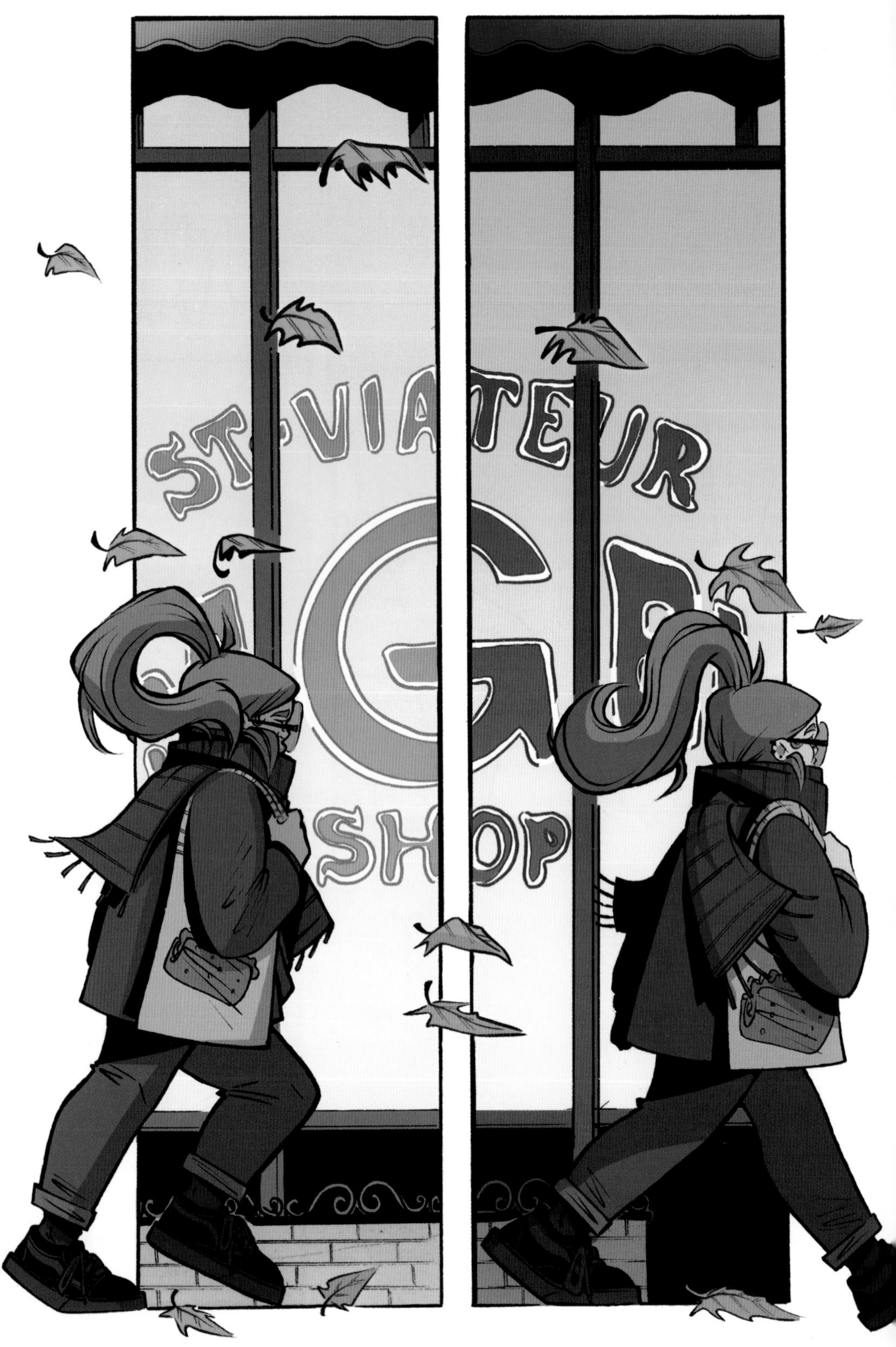
ST-VIATEUR
SHOP

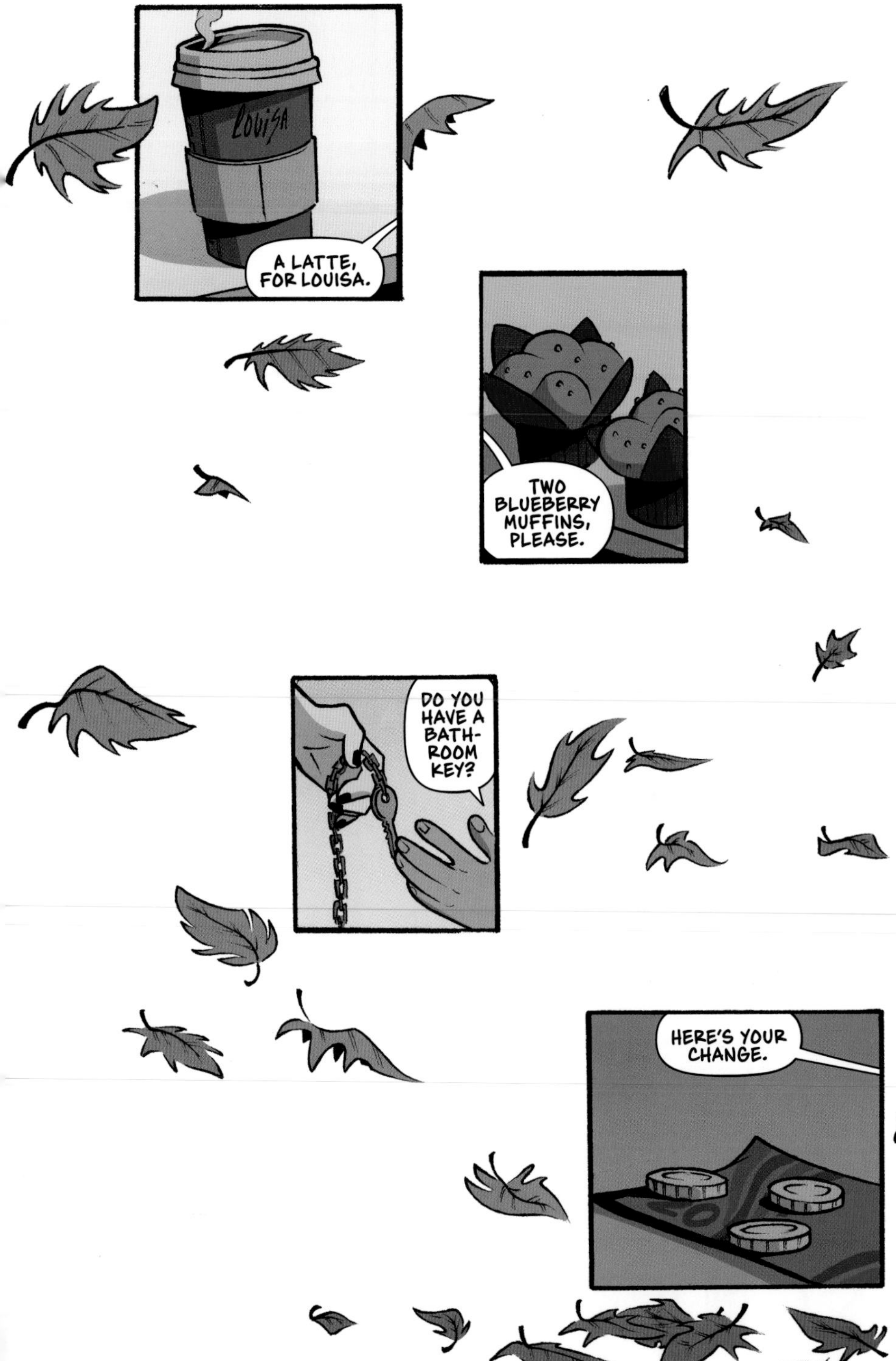
LOUISA
A LATTE, FOR LOUISA.
TWO BLUEBERRY MUFFINS, PLEASE.
DO YOU HAVE A BATH-ROOM KEY?
HERE'S YOUR CHANGE.

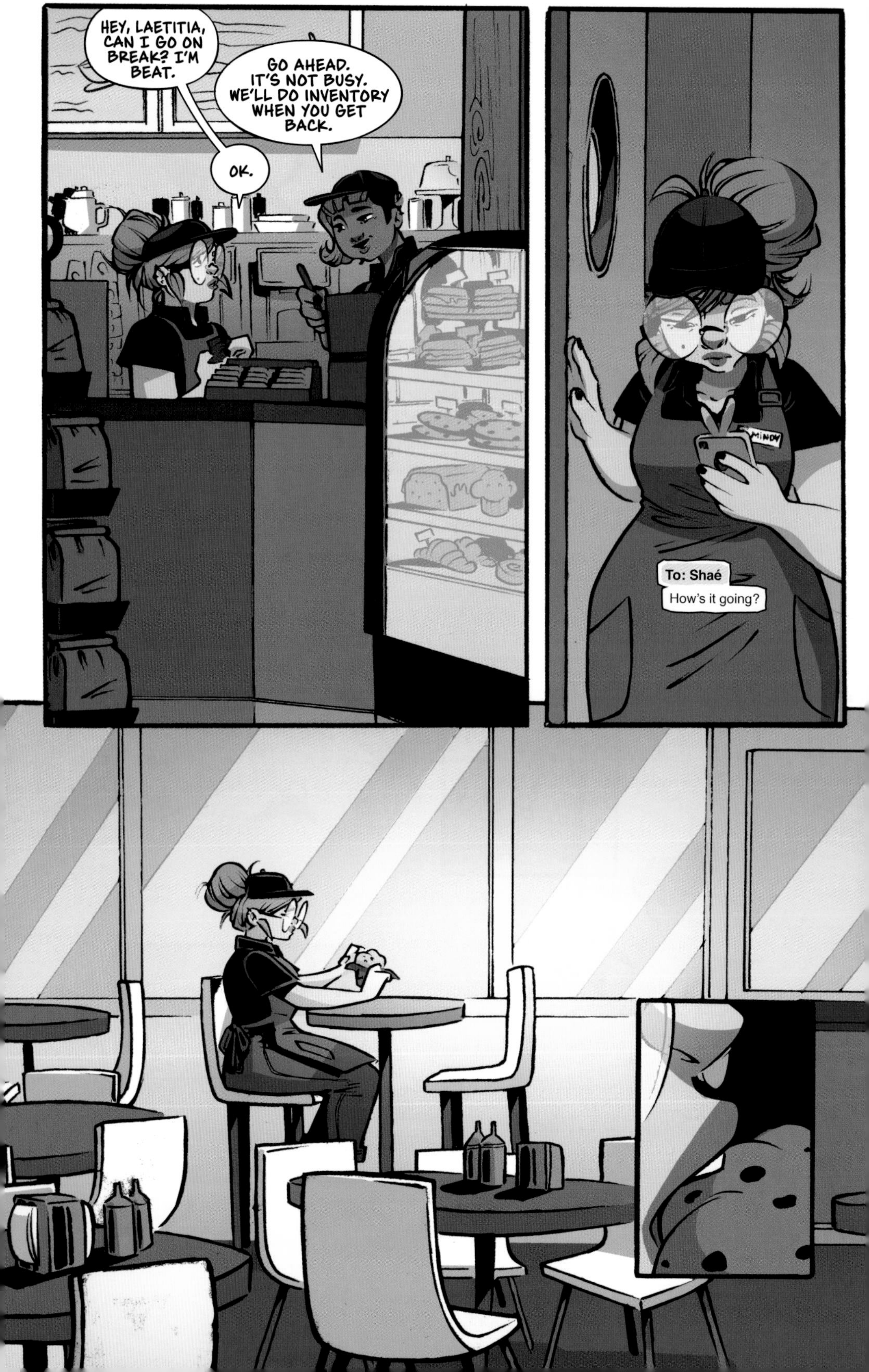
HEY, LAETITIA, CAN I GO ON BREAK? I'M BEAT.
GO AHEAD. IT'S NOT BUSY. WE'LL DO INVENTORY WHEN YOU GET BACK.
OK.
MINDY
To: Shaé
How's it going?

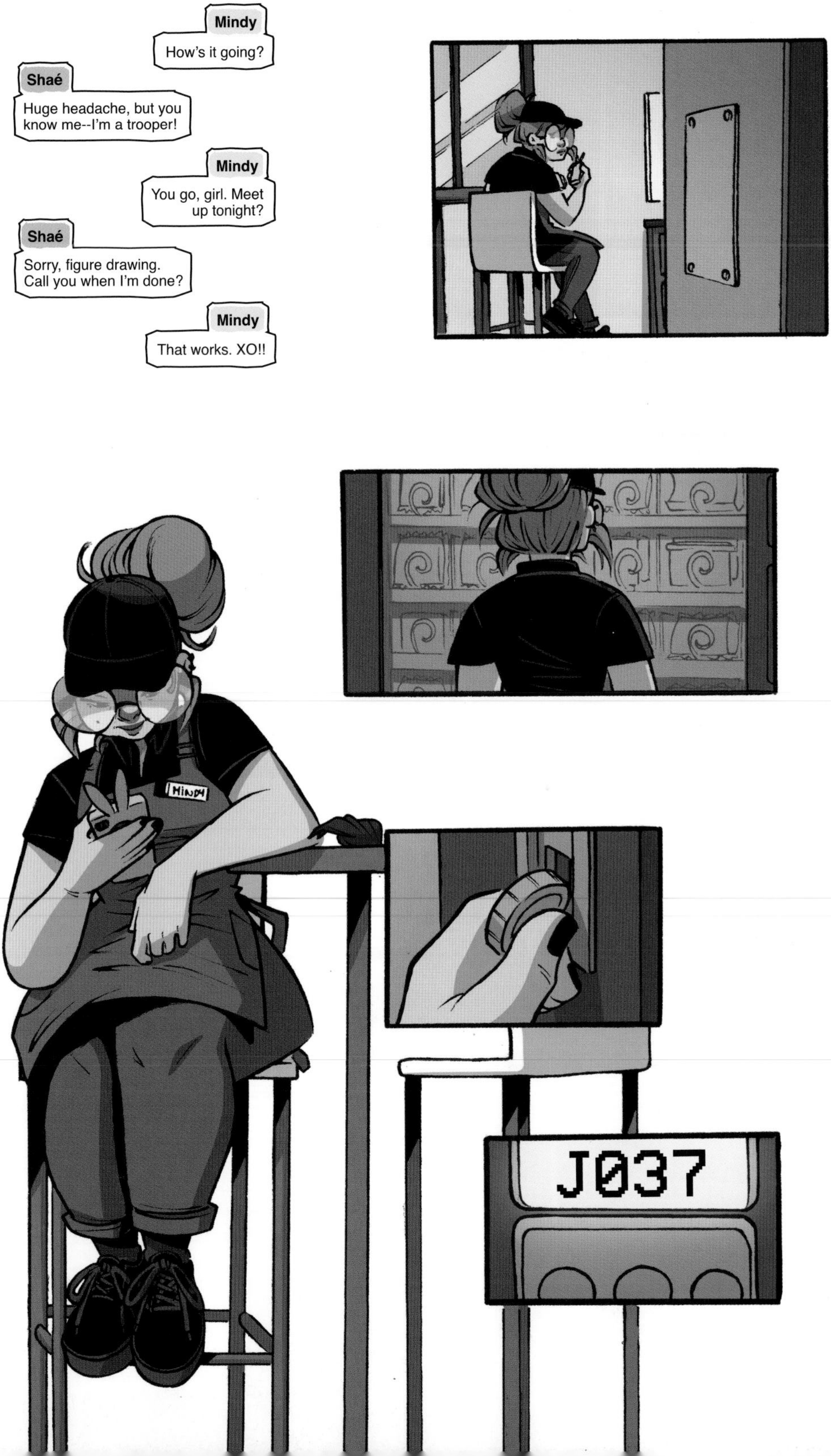
Mindy
How's it going?
Shaé
Huge headache, but you know me--I'm a trooper!
Mindy
You go, girl. Meet up tonight?
Shaé
Sorry, figure drawing. Call you when I'm done?
Mindy
That works. XO!!
MINDY
J037

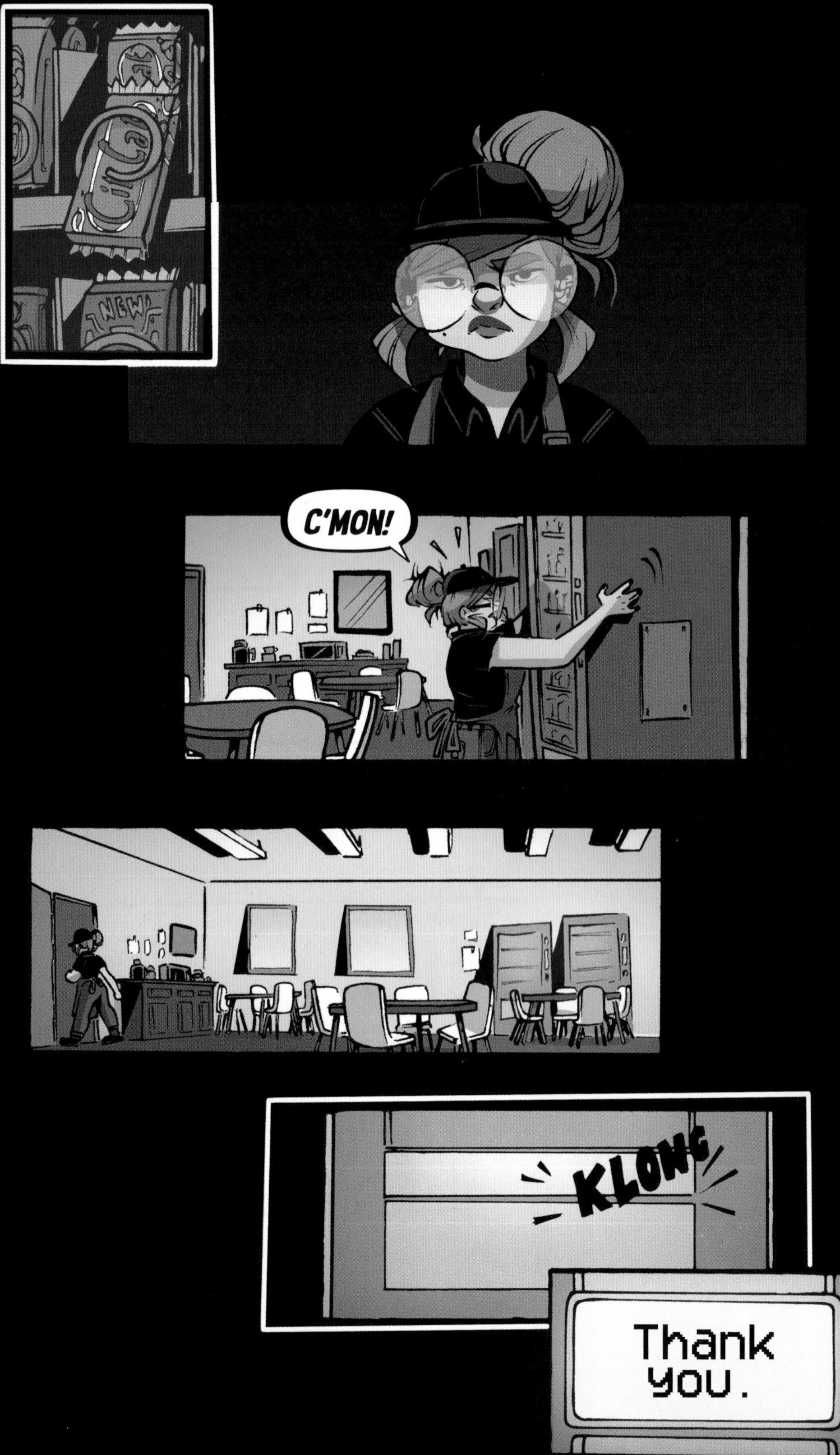
C'MON!
KLONG
Thank you.

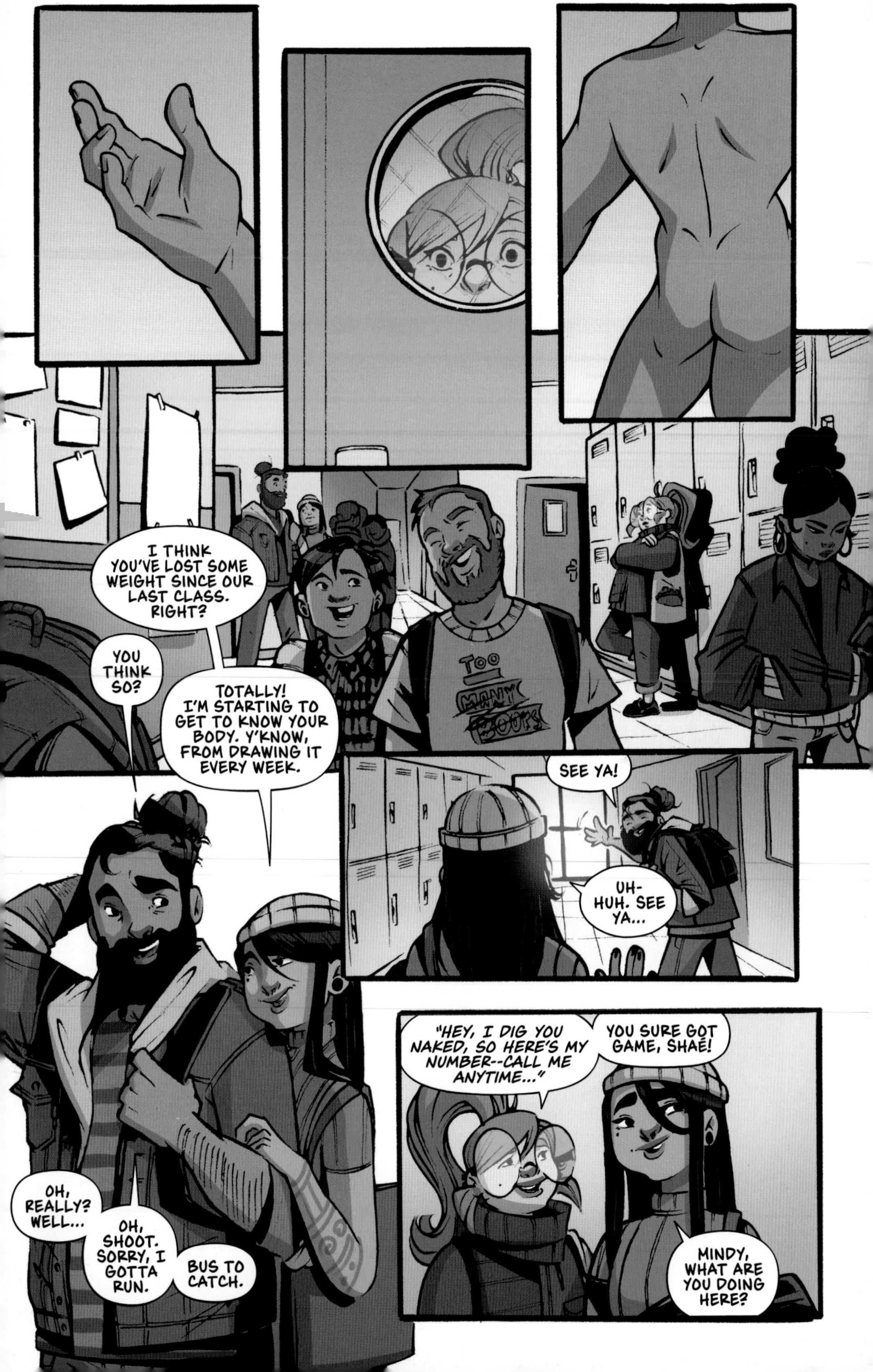
I THINK YOU'VE LOST SOME WEIGHT SINCE OUR LAST CLASS. RIGHT?
YOU THINK SO?
TOTALLY! I'M STARTING TO GET TO KNOW YOUR BODY. Y'KNOW, FROM DRAWING IT EVERY WEEK.
TOO MANY BOOTS
OH, REALLY? WELL...
OH, SHOOT. SORRY, I GOTTA RUN.
BUS TO CATCH.
SEE YA!
UH-HUH. SEE YA...
"HEY, I DIG YOU NAKED, SO HERE'S MY NUMBER--CALL ME ANYTIME..."
YOU SURE GOT GAME, SHAE!
MINDY, WHAT ARE YOU DOING HERE?

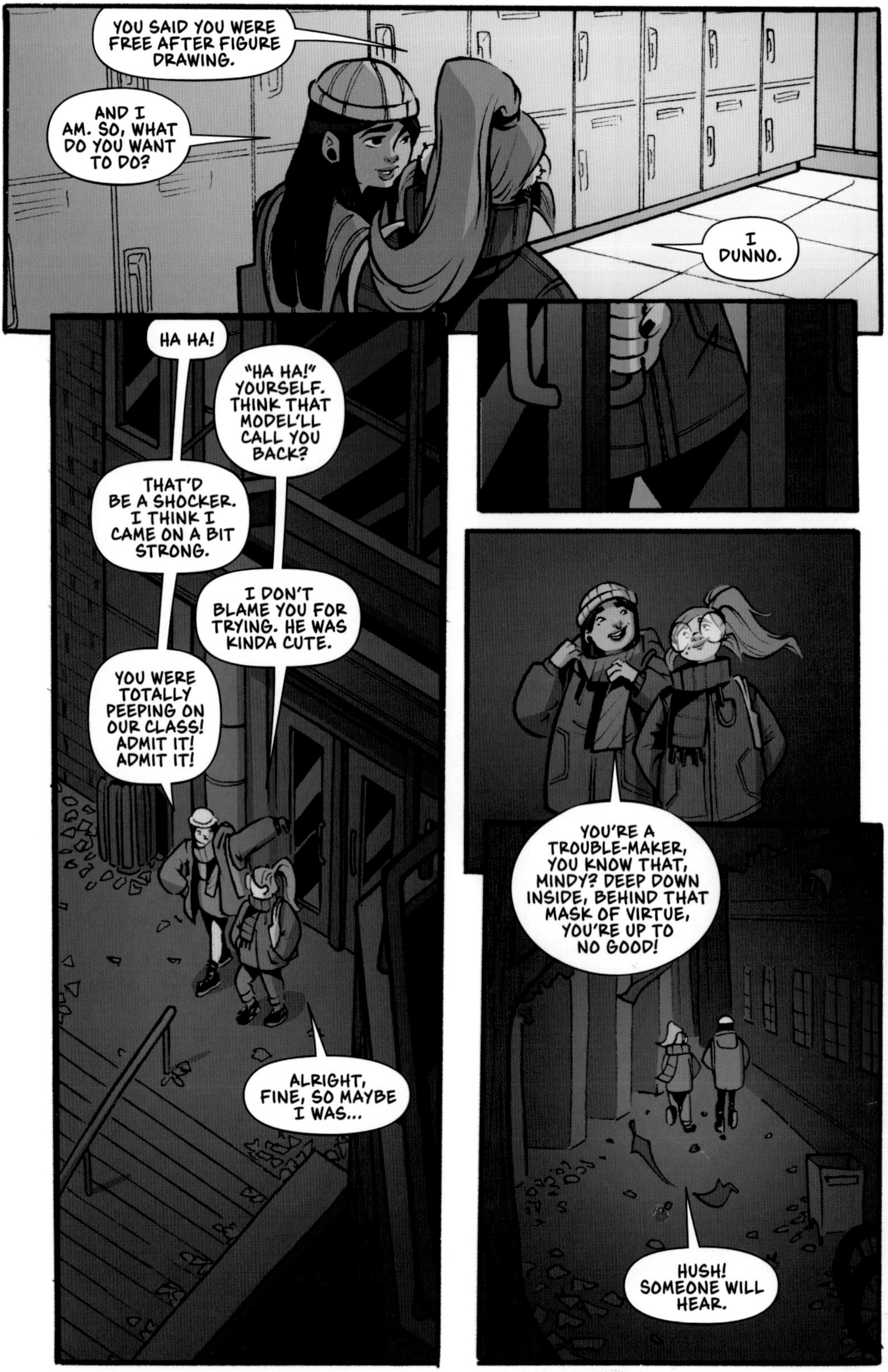
YOU SAID YOU WERE FREE AFTER FIGURE DRAWING.
AND I AM. SO, WHAT DO YOU WANT TO DO?
I DUNNO.
HA HA!
"HA HA!" YOURSELF. THINK THAT MODEL'LL CALL YOU BACK?
THAT'D BE A SHOCKER. I THINK I CAME ON A BIT STRONG.
I DON'T BLAME YOU FOR TRYING. HE WAS KINDA CUTE.
YOU WERE TOTALLY PEEPING ON OUR CLASS! ADMIT IT! ADMIT IT!
ALRIGHT, FINE, SO MAYBE I WAS...
YOU'RE A TROUBLE-MAKER, YOU KNOW THAT, MINDY? DEEP DOWN INSIDE, BEHIND THAT MASK OF VIRTUE, YOU'RE UP TO NO GOOD!
HUSH! SOMEONE WILL HEAR.

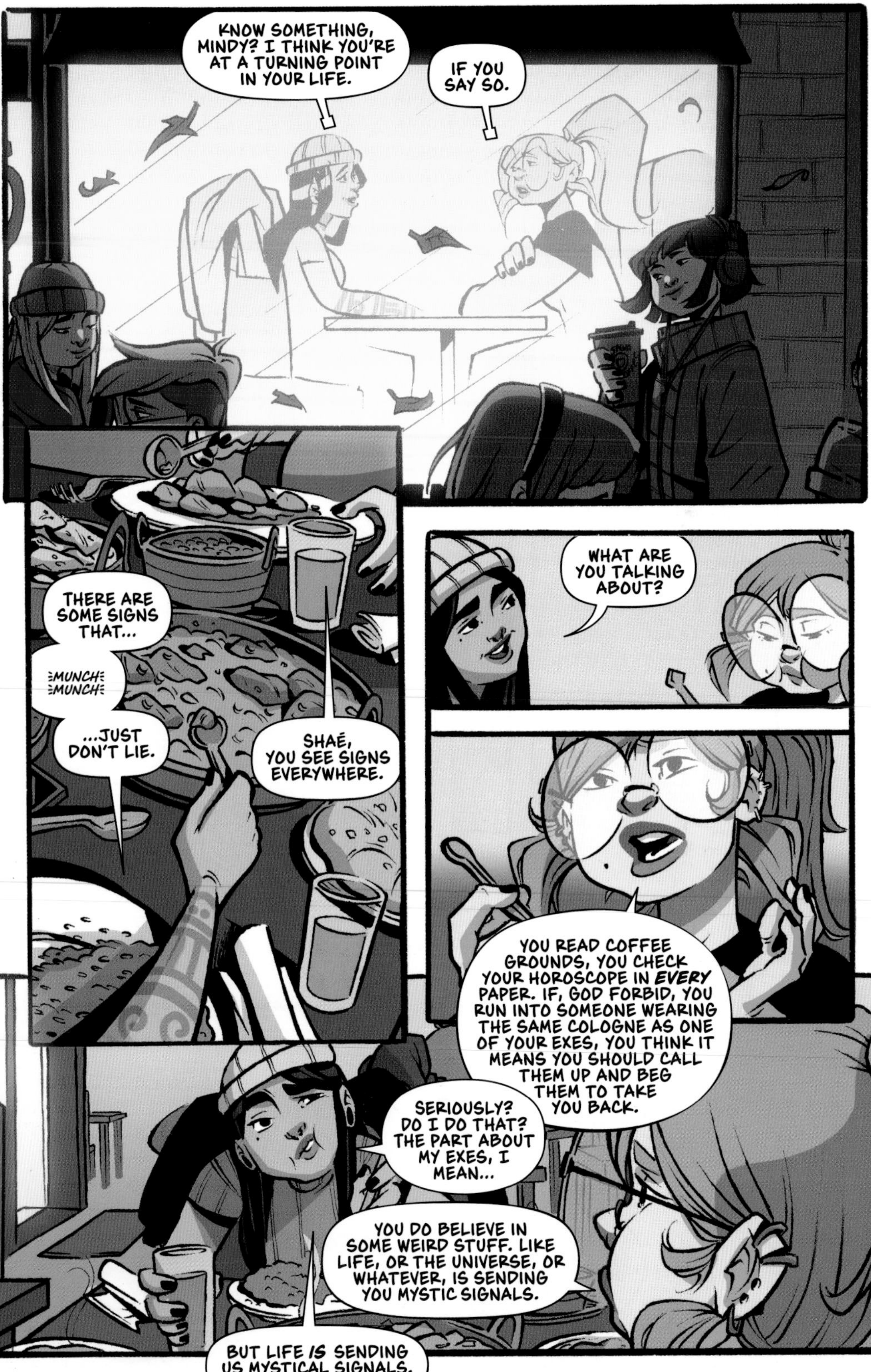
KNOW SOMETHING, MINDY? I THINK YOU'RE AT A TURNING POINT IN YOUR LIFE.
IF YOU SAY SO.
THERE ARE SOME SIGNS THAT...
MUNCH MUNCH
...JUST DON'T LIE.
SHAÉ, YOU SEE SIGNS EVERYWHERE.
WHAT ARE YOU TALKING ABOUT?
YOU READ COFFEE GROUNDS, YOU CHECK YOUR HOROSCOPE IN EVERY PAPER. IF, GOD FORBID, YOU RUN INTO SOMEONE WEARING THE SAME COLOGNE AS ONE OF YOUR EXES, YOU THINK IT MEANS YOU SHOULD CALL THEM UP AND BEG THEM TO TAKE YOU BACK.
SERIOUSLY? DO I DO THAT? THE PART ABOUT MY EXES, I MEAN...
YOU DO BELIEVE IN SOME WEIRD STUFF. LIKE LIFE, OR THE UNIVERSE, OR WHATEVER, IS SENDING YOU MYSTIC SIGNALS.
BUT LIFE IS SENDING US MYSTICAL SIGNALS. ALL THE TIME!

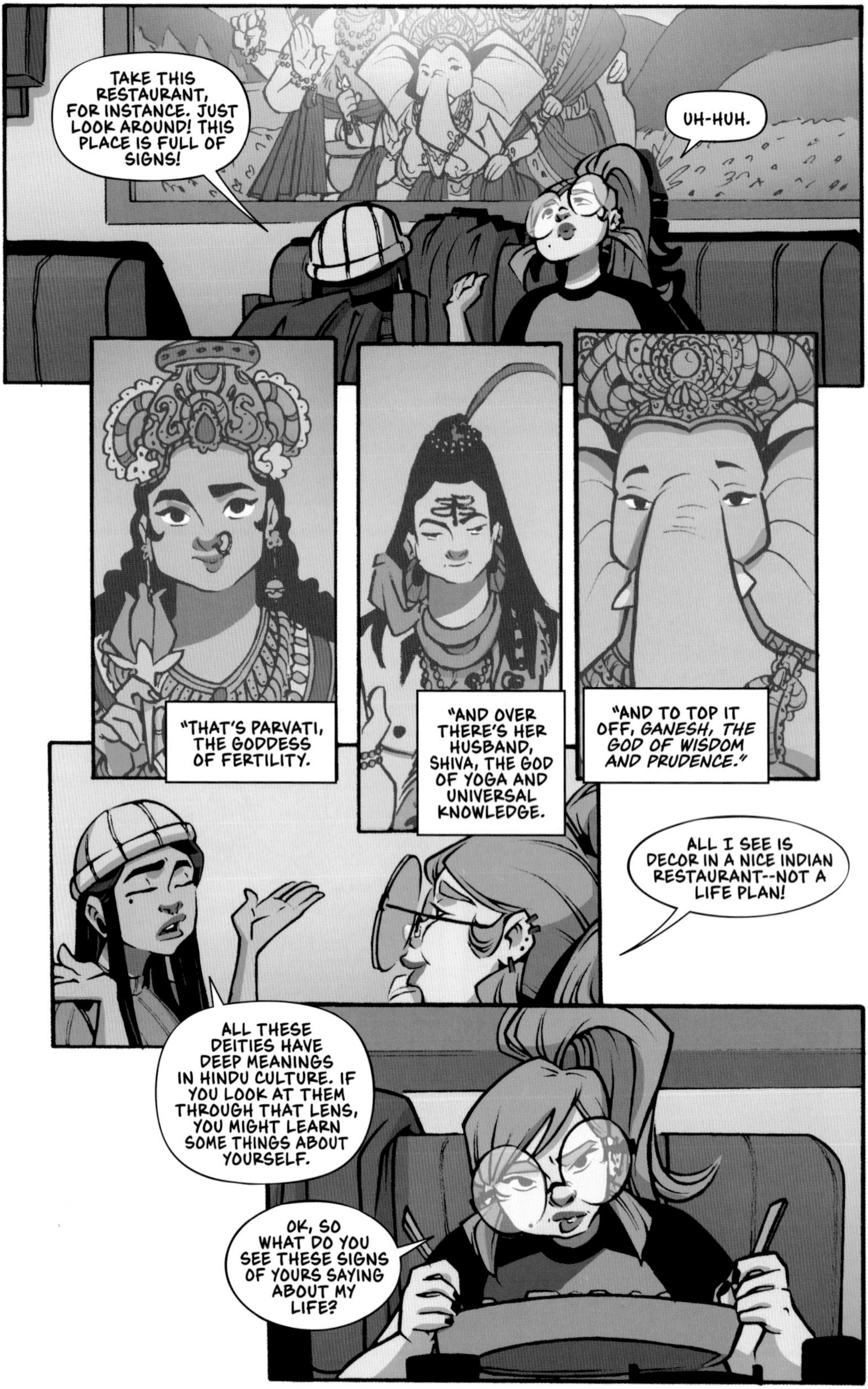
TAKE THIS RESTAURANT, FOR INSTANCE. JUST LOOK AROUND! THIS PLACE IS FULL OF SIGNS!
UH-HUH.
"THAT'S PARVATI, THE GODDESS OF FERTILITY.
"AND OVER THERE'S HER HUSBAND, SHIVA, THE GOD OF YOGA AND UNIVERSAL KNOWLEDGE.
"AND TO TOP IT OFF, GANESH, THE GOD OF WISDOM AND PRUDENCE."
ALL I SEE IS DECOR IN A NICE INDIAN RESTAURANT--NOT A LIFE PLAN!
ALL THESE DEITIES HAVE DEEP MEANINGS IN HINDU CULTURE. IF YOU LOOK AT THEM THROUGH THAT LENS, YOU MIGHT LEARN SOME THINGS ABOUT YOURSELF.
OK, SO WHAT DO YOU SEE THESE SIGNS OF YOURS SAYING ABOUT MY LIFE?

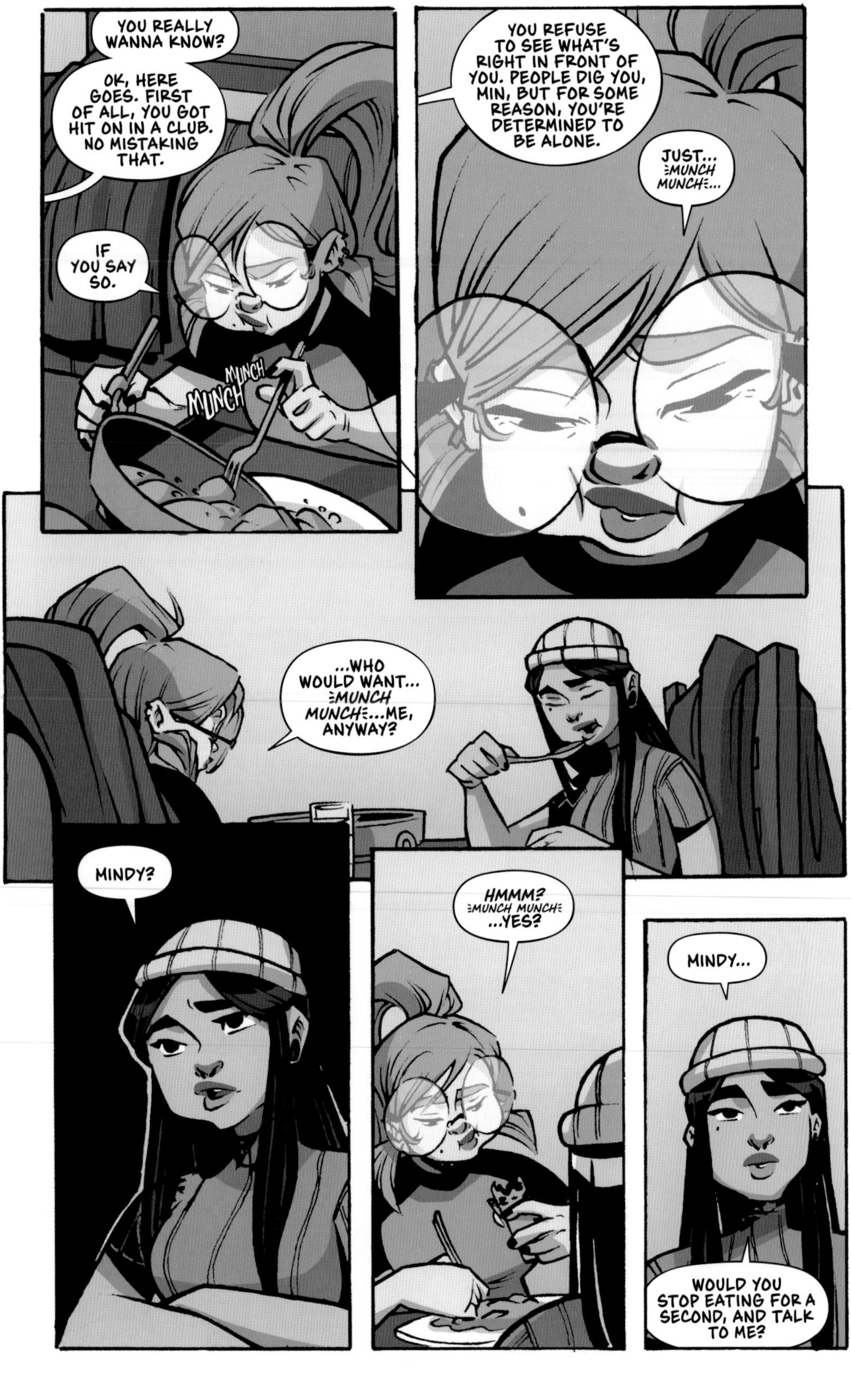
YOU REALLY WANNA KNOW?
OK, HERE GOES. FIRST OF ALL, YOU GOT HIT ON IN A CLUB. NO MISTAKING THAT.
IF YOU SAY SO.
MUNCH MUNCH
YOU REFUSE TO SEE WHAT'S RIGHT IN FRONT OF YOU. PEOPLE DIG YOU, MIN, BUT FOR SOME REASON, YOU'RE DETERMINED TO BE ALONE.
JUST... MUNCH MUNCH...
...WHO WOULD WANT... MUNCH MUNCH...ME, ANYWAY?
MINDY?
HMMM? MUNCH MUNCH ...YES?
MINDY...
WOULD YOU STOP EATING FOR A SECOND, AND TALK TO ME?

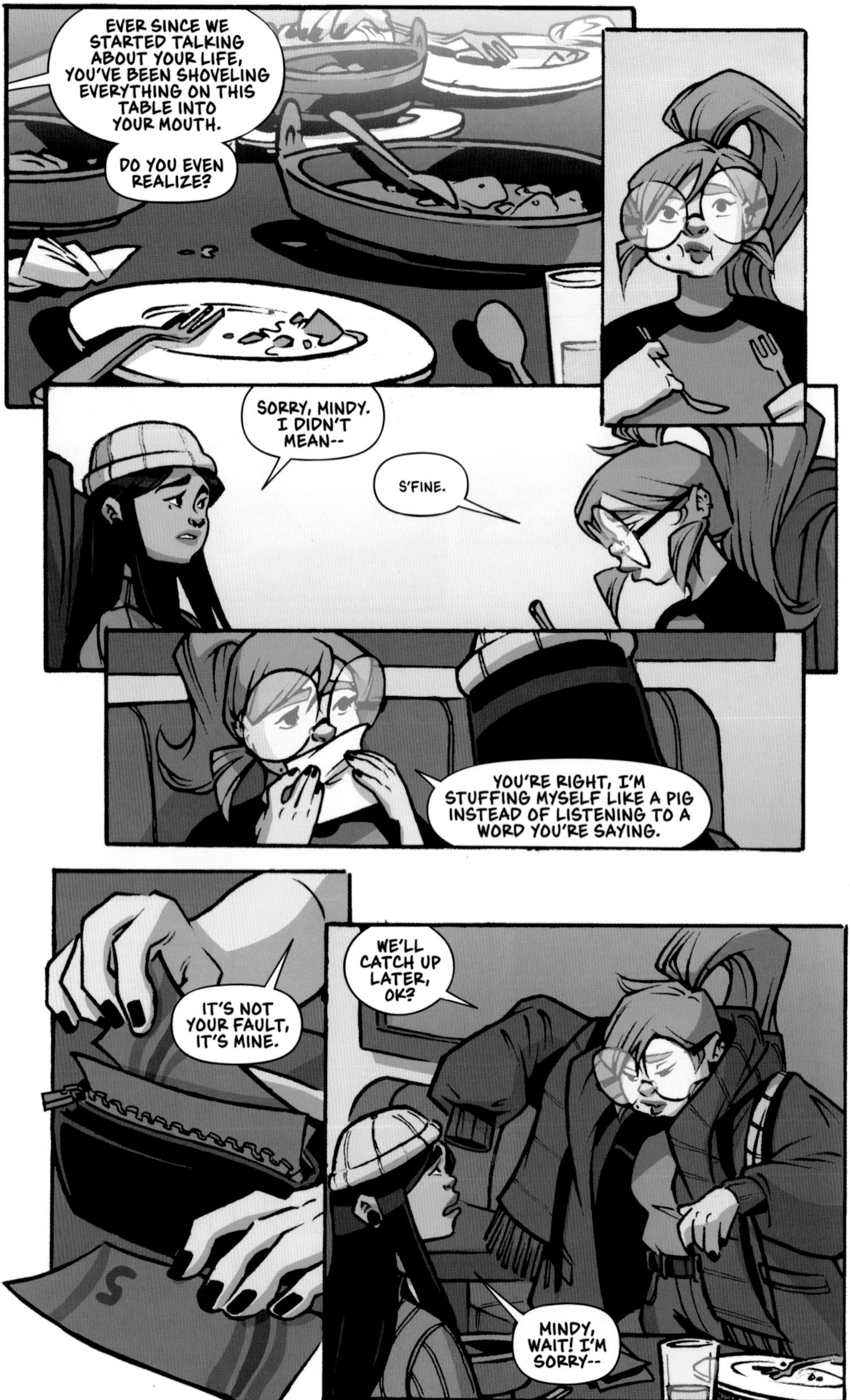
EVER SINCE WE STARTED TALKING ABOUT YOUR LIFE, YOU'VE BEEN SHOVELING EVERYTHING ON THIS TABLE INTO YOUR MOUTH.
DO YOU EVEN REALIZE?
SORRY, MINDY. I DIDN'T MEAN--
S'FINE.
YOU'RE RIGHT, I'M STUFFING MYSELF LIKE A PIG INSTEAD OF LISTENING TO A WORD YOU'RE SAYING.
IT'S NOT YOUR FAULT, IT'S MINE.
WE'LL CATCH UP LATER, OK?
MINDY, WAIT! I'M SORRY--

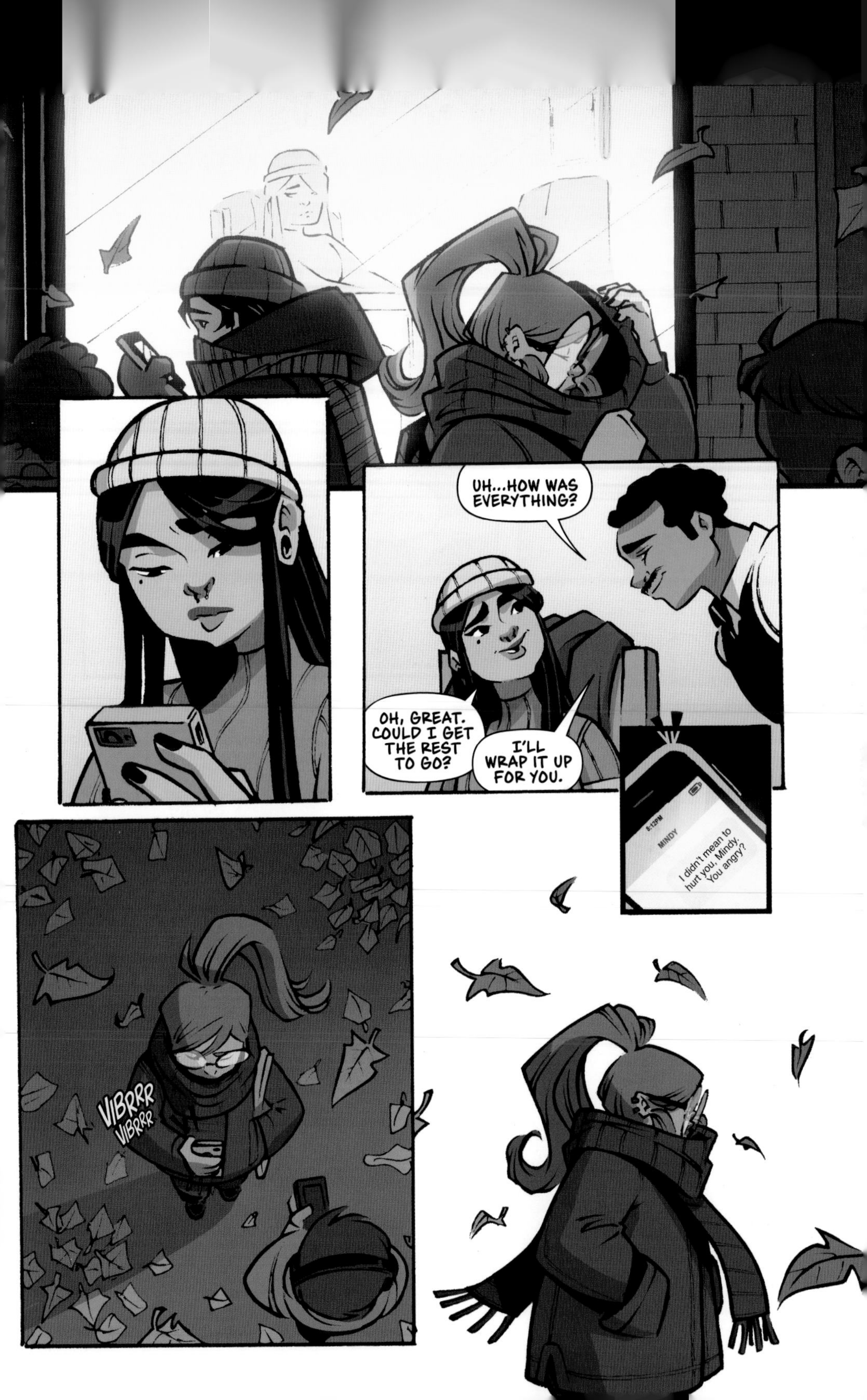
UH...HOW WAS EVERYTHING?
OH, GREAT. COULD I GET THE REST TO GO?
I'LL WRAP IT UP FOR YOU.
8:12PM
MINDY
I didn't mean to hurt you, Mindy. You angry?
VIBRRR VIBRRR

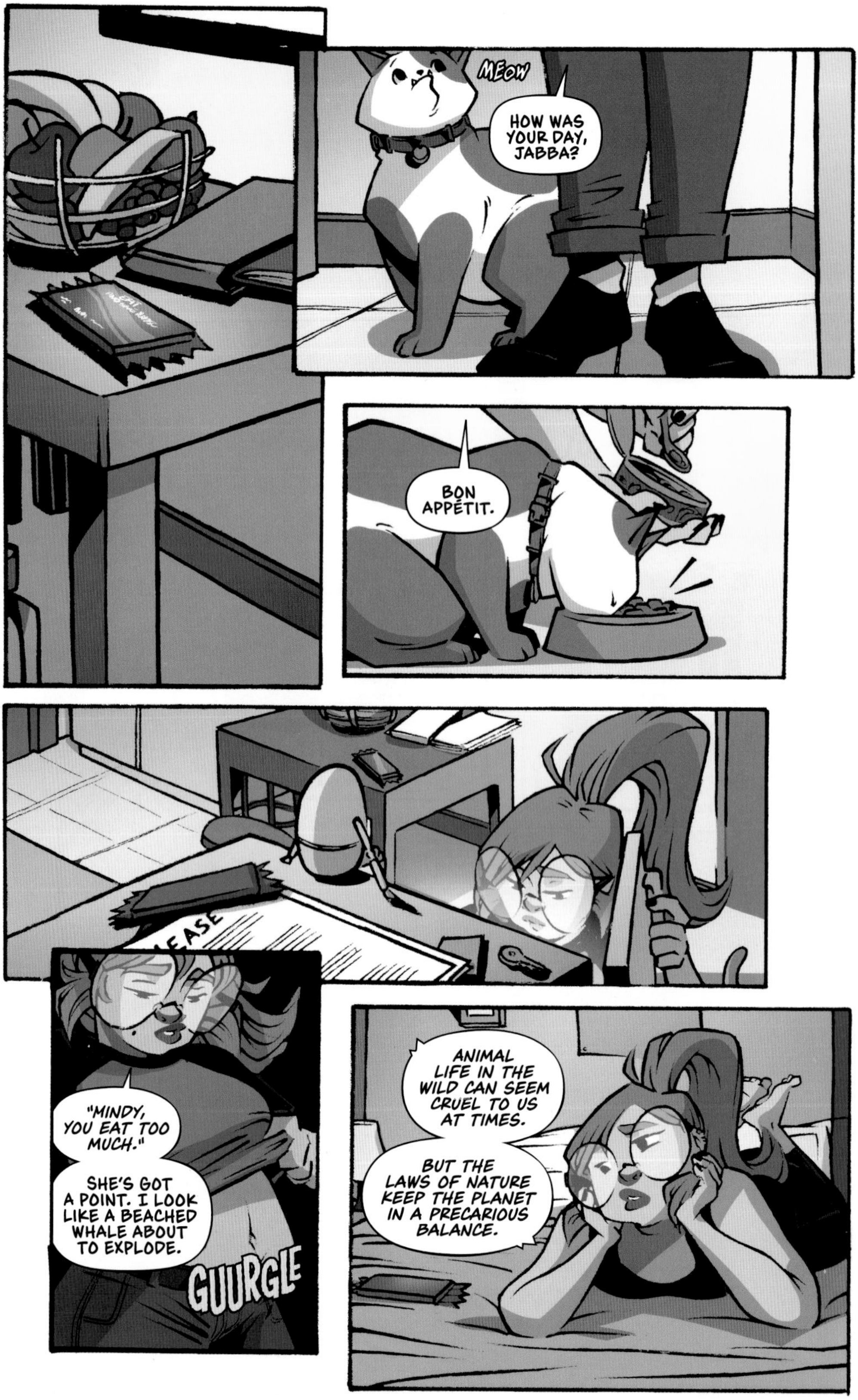
MEOW
HOW WAS YOUR DAY, JABBA?
BON APPÉTIT.
"MINDY, YOU EAT TOO MUCH."
SHE'S GOT A POINT. I LOOK LIKE A BEACHED WHALE ABOUT TO EXPLODE.
GUURGLE
ANIMAL LIFE IN THE WILD CAN SEEM CRUEL TO US AT TIMES.
BUT THE LAWS OF NATURE KEEP THE PLANET IN A PRECARIOUS BALANCE.

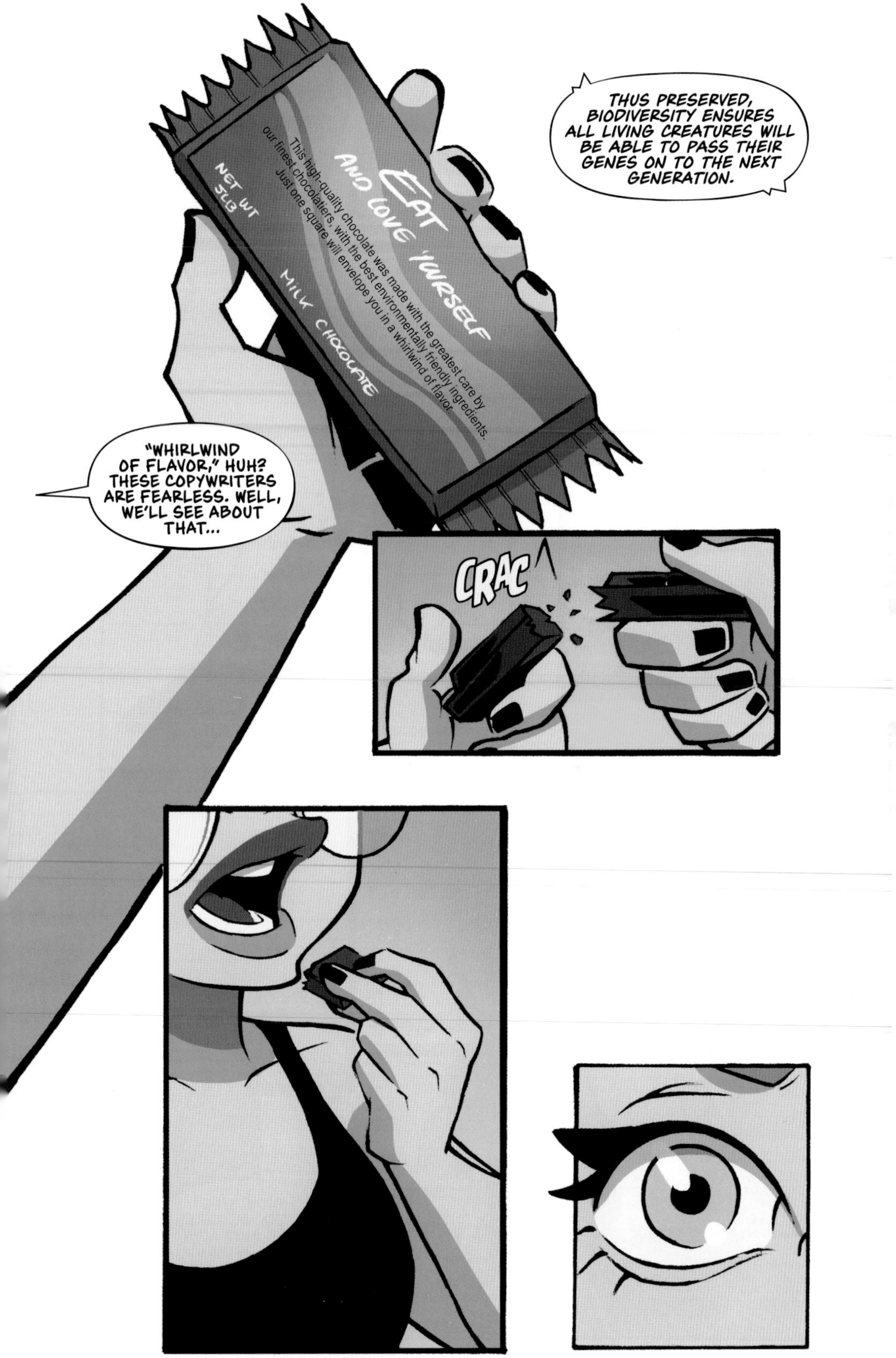
THUS PRESERVED, BIODIVERSITY ENSURES ALL LIVING CREATURES WILL BE ABLE TO PASS THEIR GENES ON TO THE NEXT GENERATION.
EAT AND LOVE YOURSELF
This high-quality chocolate was made with the greatest care by our finest chocolatiers, with the best environmentally friendly ingredients. Just one square will envelope you in a whirlwind of flavor.
NET WT
MILK CHOCOLATE
"WHIRLWIND OF FLAVOR," HUH? THESE COPYWRITERS ARE FEARLESS. WELL, WE'LL SEE ABOUT THAT...
CRAC

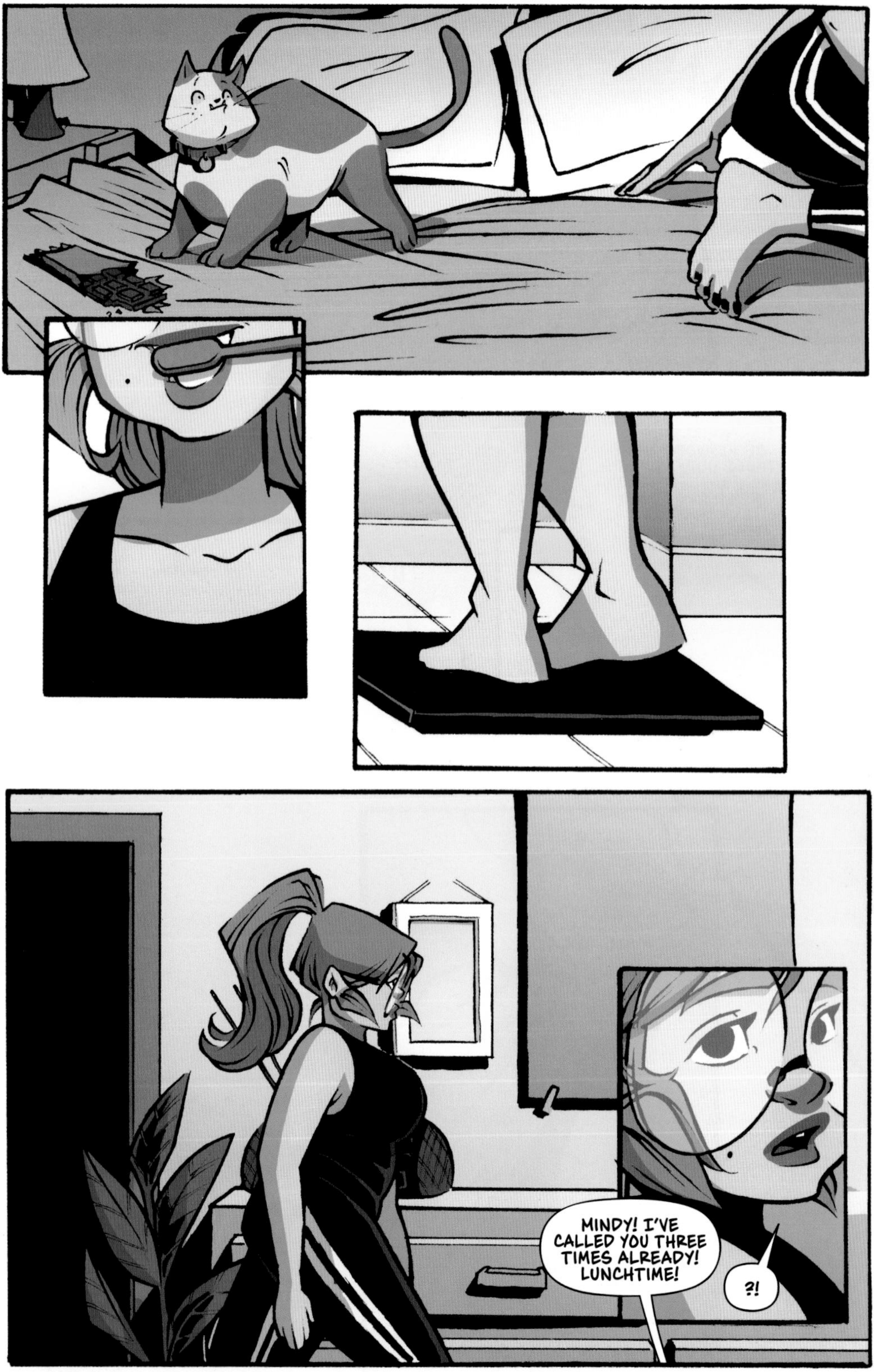
MINDY! I'VE CALLED YOU THREE TIMES ALREADY! LUNCHTIME!
?!

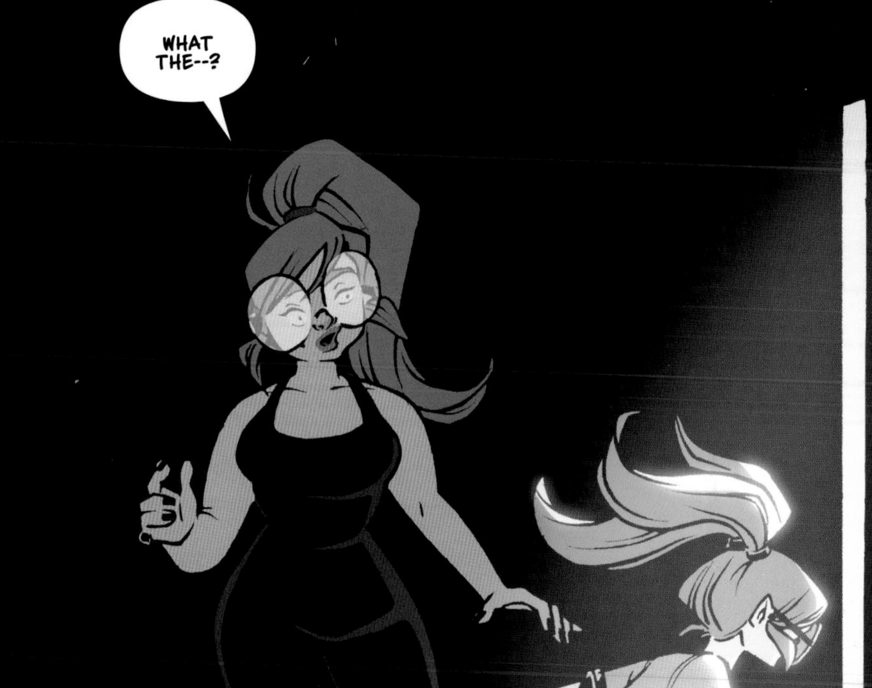
WHAT THE--?

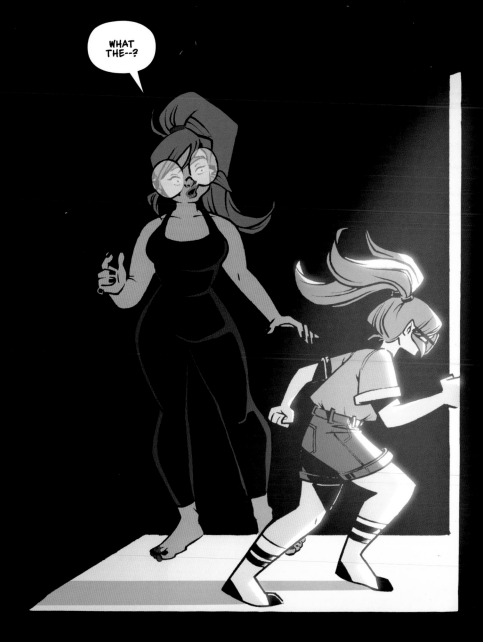

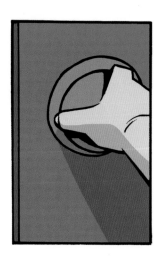

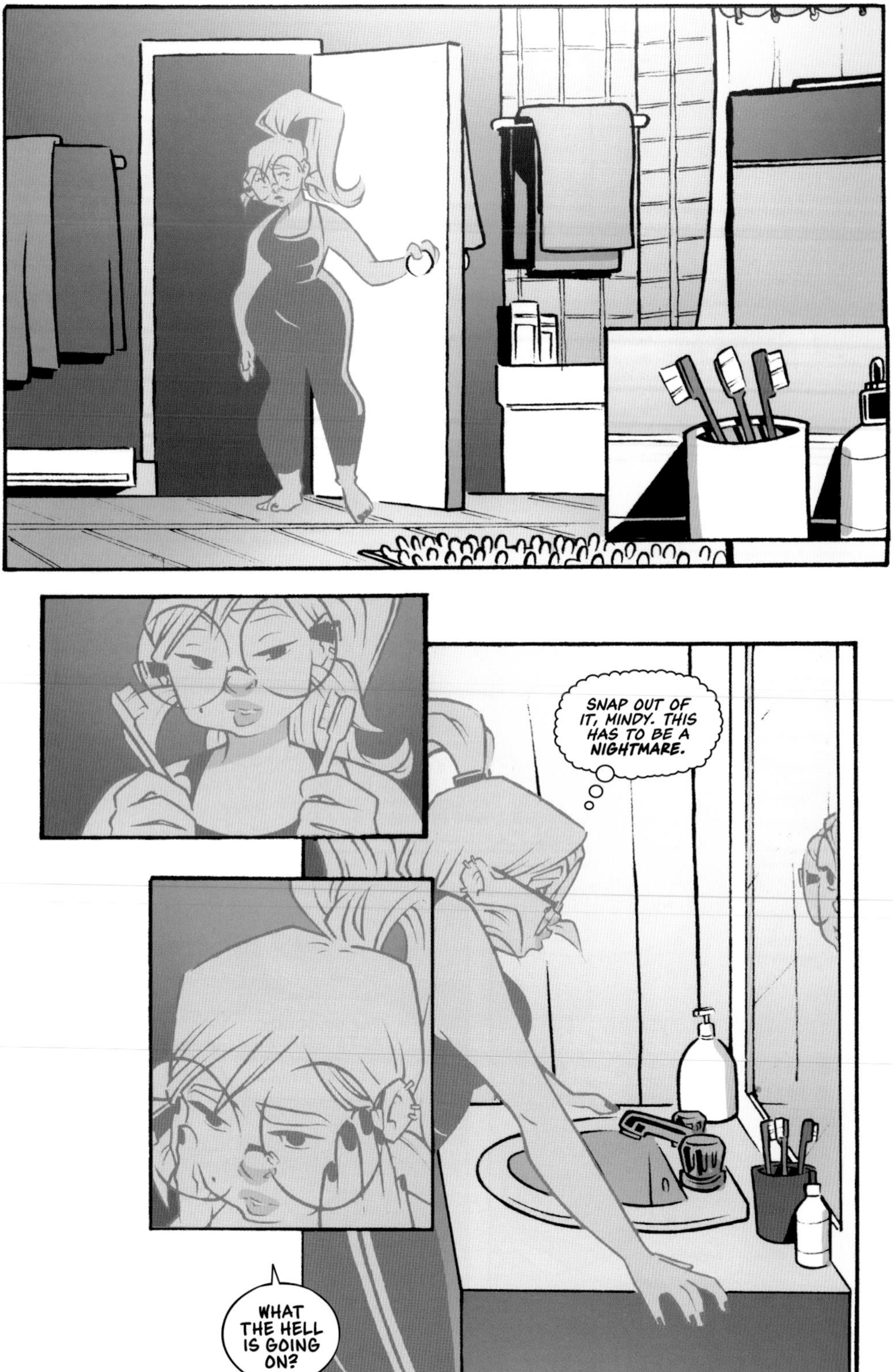
SNAP OUT OF IT, MINDY. THIS HAS TO BE A NIGHTMARE.
WHAT THE HELL IS GOING ON?

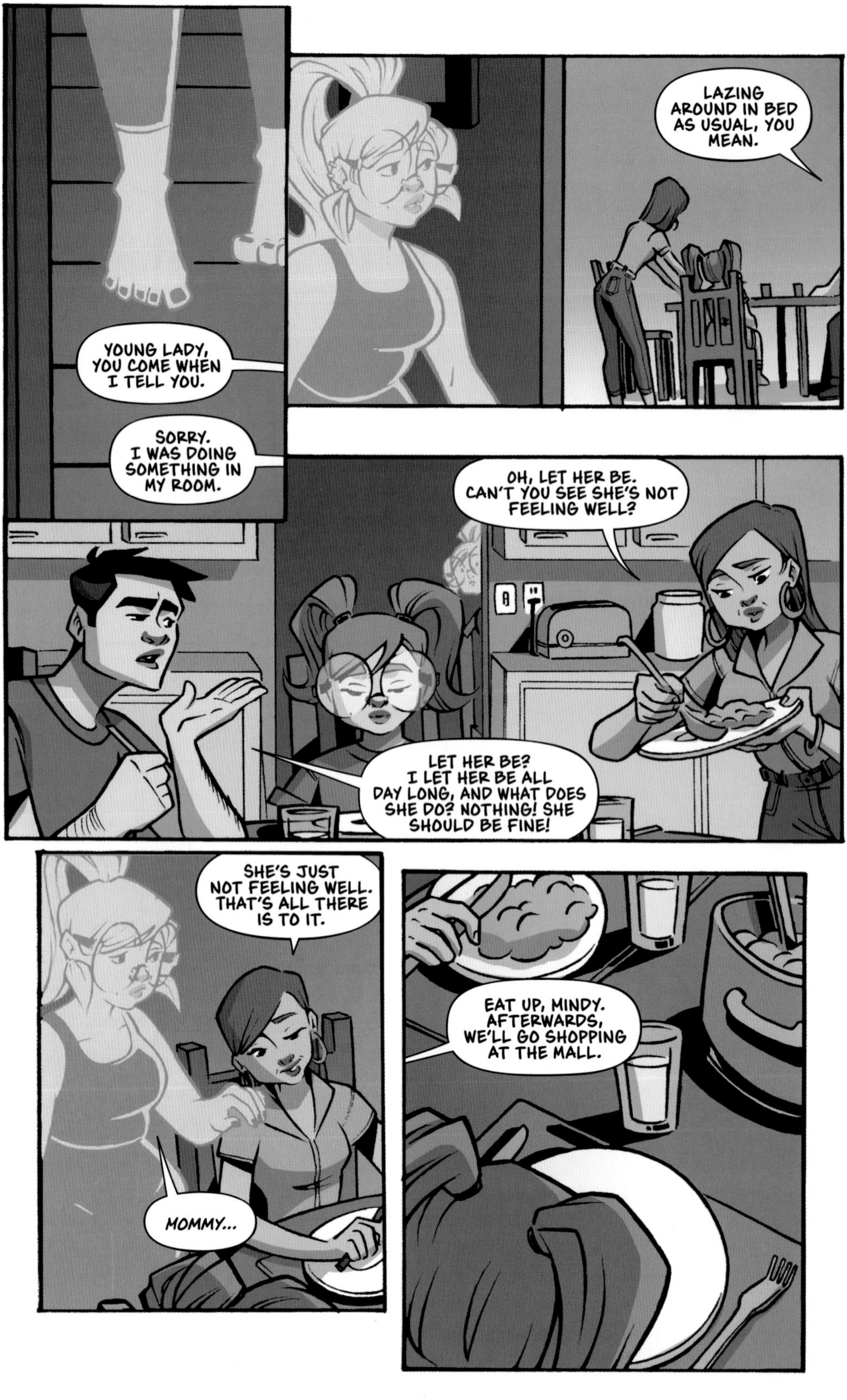
YOUNG LADY, YOU COME WHEN I TELL YOU.
SORRY. I WAS DOING SOMETHING IN MY ROOM.
LAZING AROUND IN BED AS USUAL, YOU MEAN.
OH, LET HER BE. CAN'T YOU SEE SHE'S NOT FEELING WELL?
LET HER BE? I LET HER BE ALL DAY LONG, AND WHAT DOES SHE DO? NOTHING! SHE SHOULD BE FINE!
SHE'S JUST NOT FEELING WELL. THAT'S ALL THERE IS TO IT.
MOMMY...
EAT UP, MINDY. AFTERWARDS, WE'LL GO SHOPPING AT THE MALL.

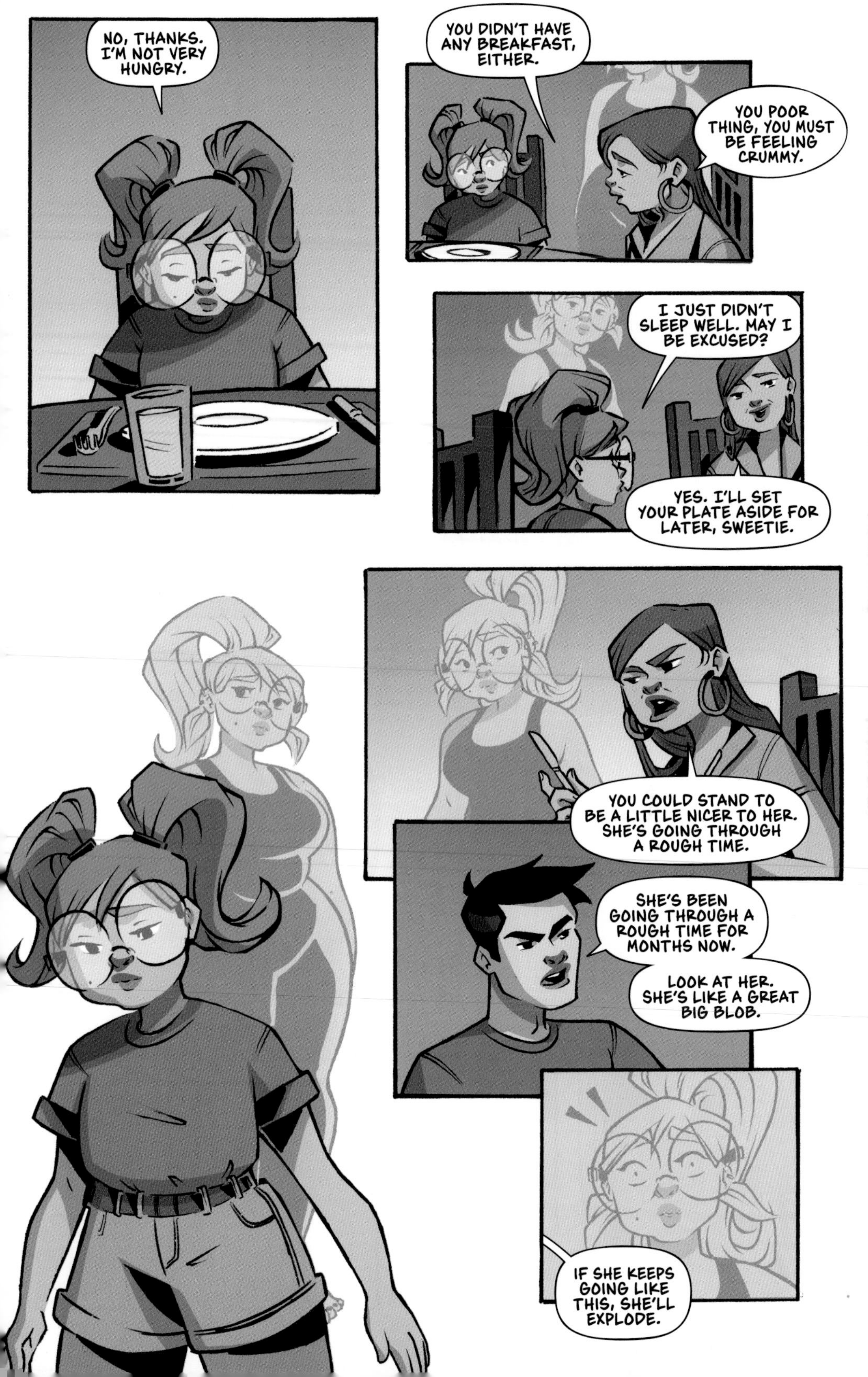
NO, THANKS. I'M NOT VERY HUNGRY.
YOU DIDN'T HAVE ANY BREAKFAST, EITHER.
YOU POOR THING, YOU MUST BE FEELING CRUMMY.
I JUST DIDN'T SLEEP WELL. MAY I BE EXCUSED?
YES. I'LL SET YOUR PLATE ASIDE FOR LATER, SWEETIE.
YOU COULD STAND TO BE A LITTLE NICER TO HER. SHE'S GOING THROUGH A ROUGH TIME.
SHE'S BEEN GOING THROUGH A ROUGH TIME FOR MONTHS NOW.
LOOK AT HER. SHE'S LIKE A GREAT BIG BLOB.
IF SHE KEEPS GOING LIKE THIS, SHE'LL EXPLODE.

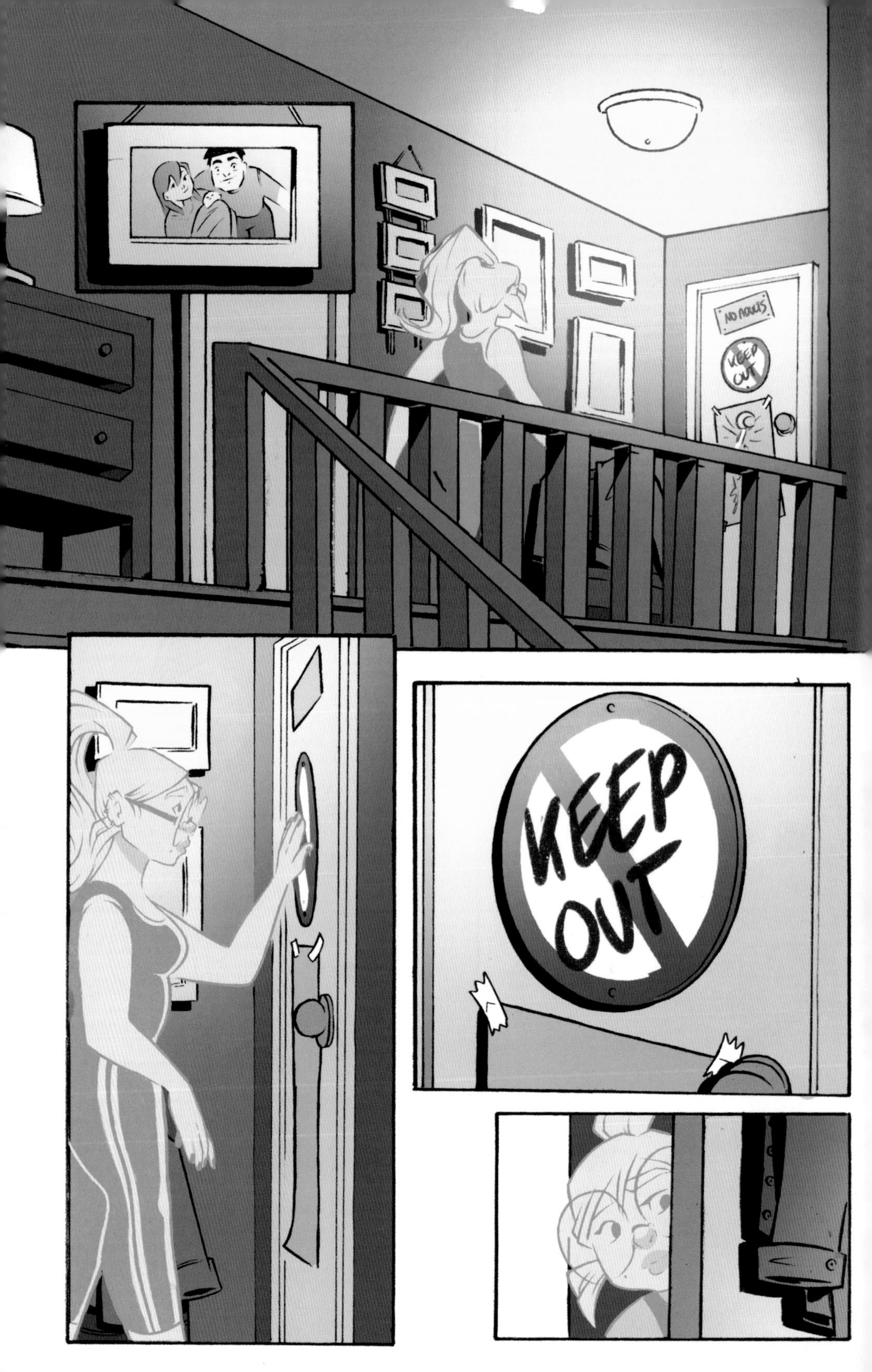
NO ADULTS
KEEP OUT
KEEP OUT

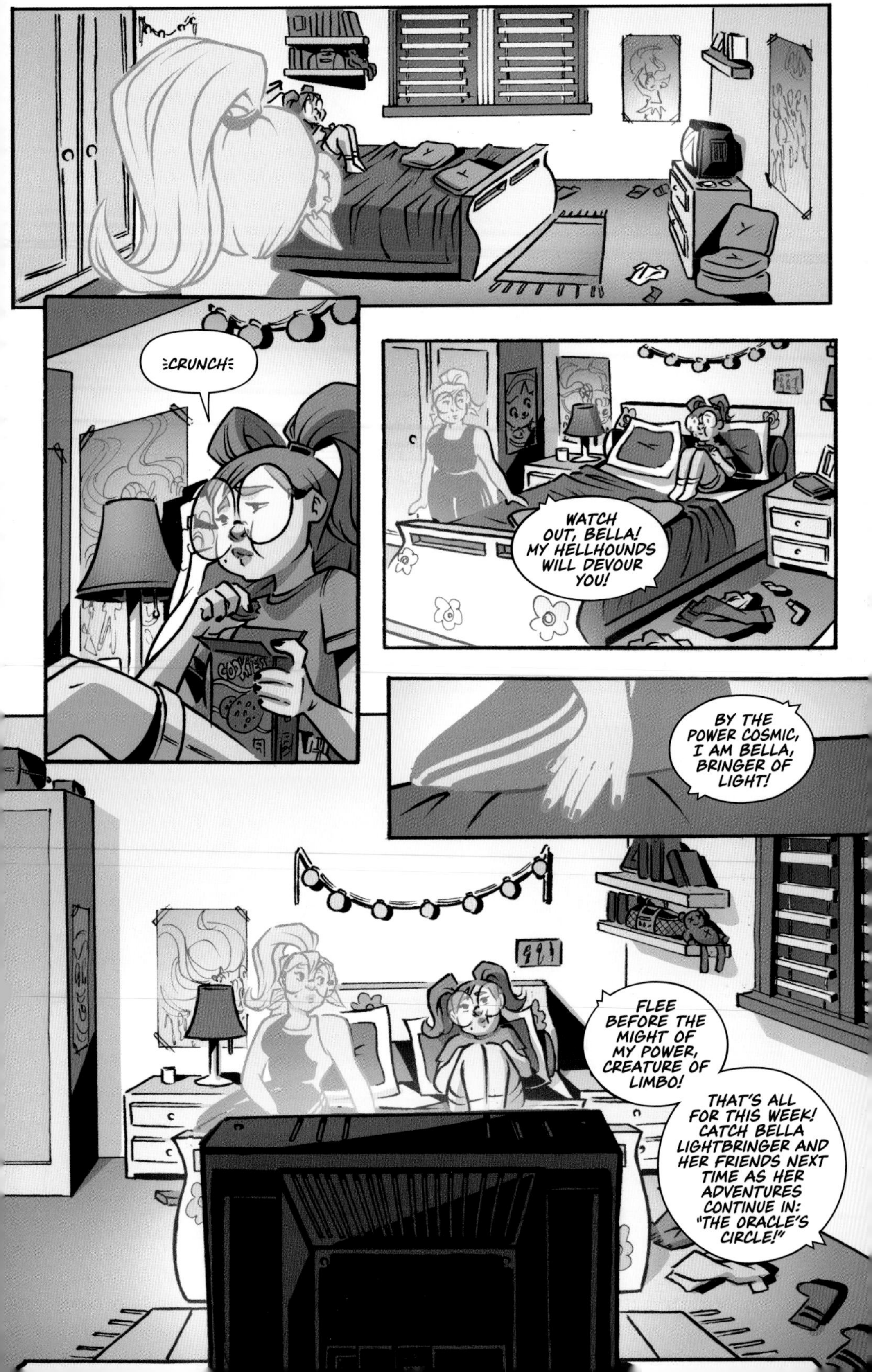

CRUNCH
WATCH OUT, BELLA! MY HELLHOUNDS WILL DEVOUR YOU!
BY THE POWER COSMIC, I AM BELLA, BRINGER OF LIGHT!
FLEE BEFORE THE MIGHT OF MY POWER, CREATURE OF LIMBO!
THAT'S ALL FOR THIS WEEK! CATCH BELLA LIGHTBRINGER AND HER FRIENDS NEXT TIME AS HER ADVENTURES CONTINUE IN: "THE ORACLE'S CIRCLE!"

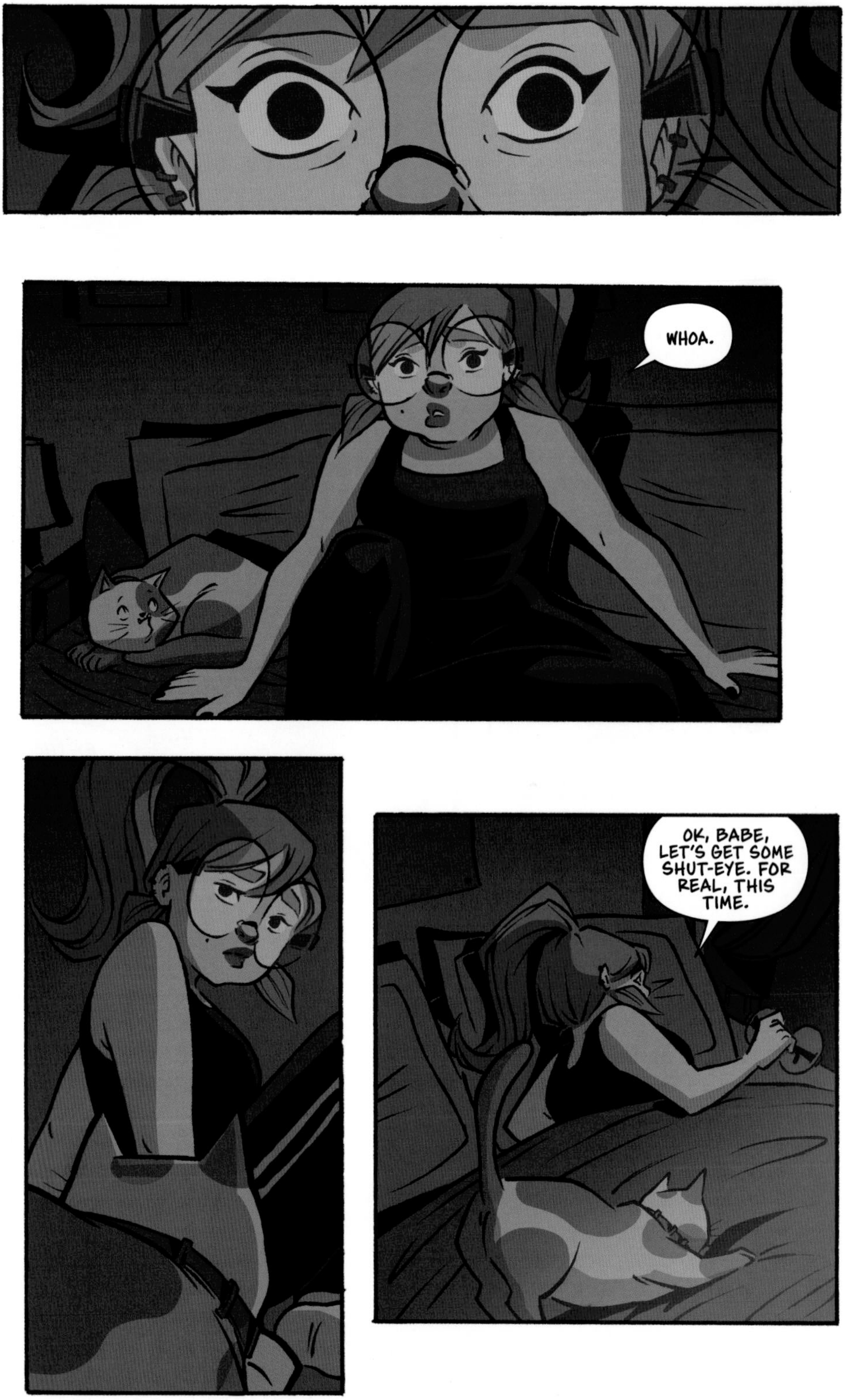
WHOA.
OK, BABE, LET'S GET SOME SHUT-EYE. FOR REAL, THIS TIME.

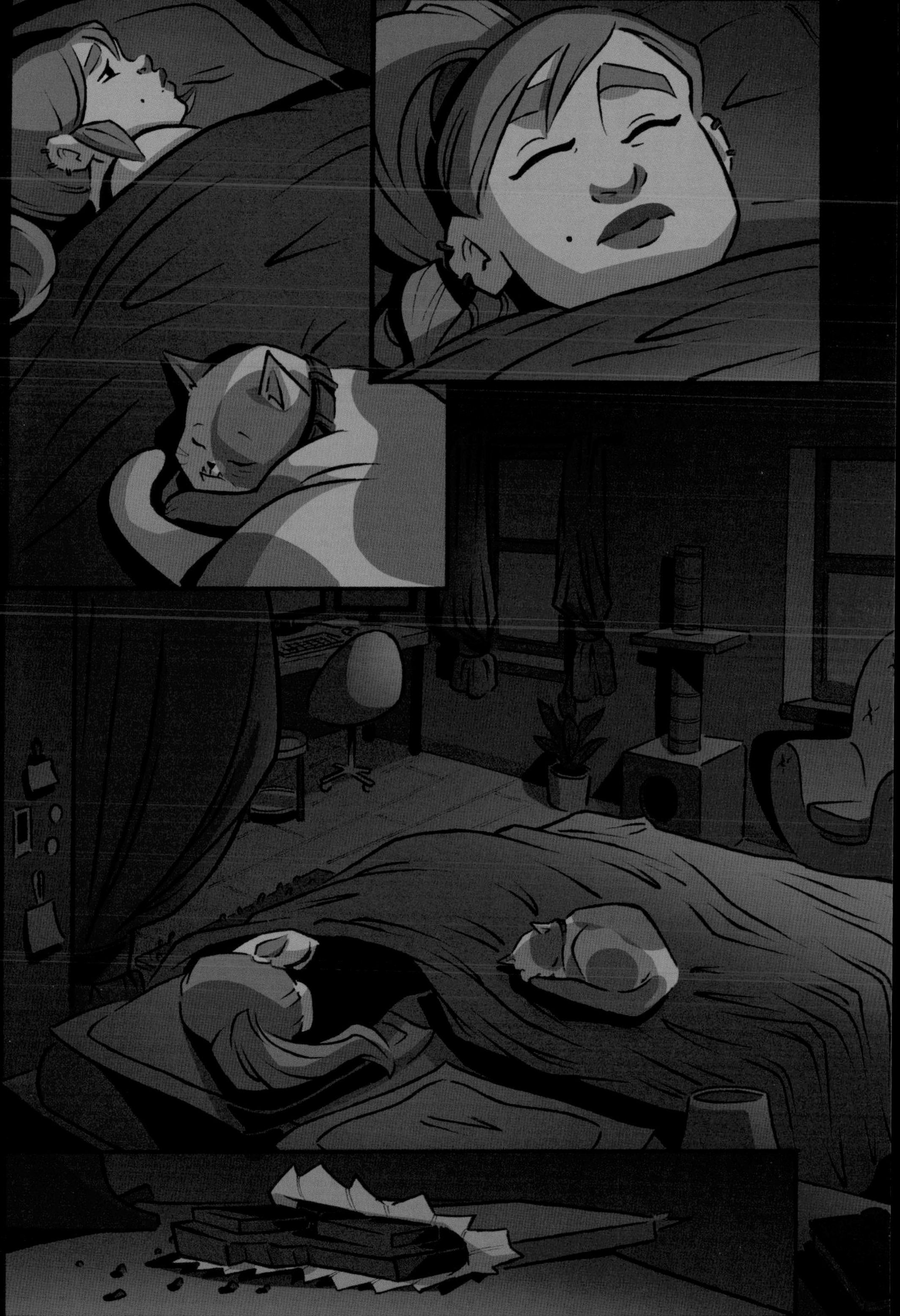

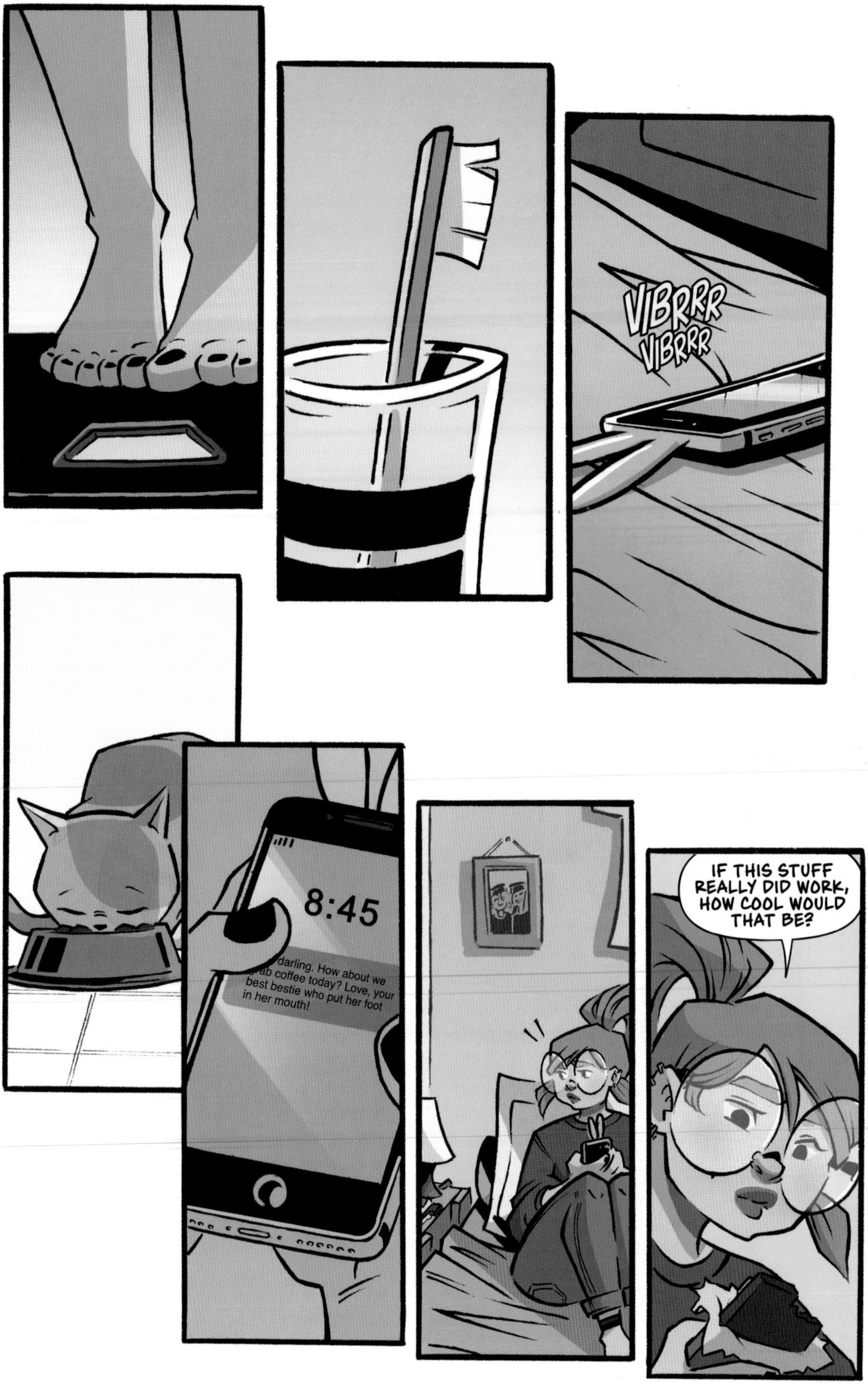
VIBRRR VIBRRR
8:45
darling. How about we
ab coffee today? Love, your
best bestie who put her foot
in her mouth!
IF THIS STUFF REALLY DID WORK, HOW COOL WOULD THAT BE?

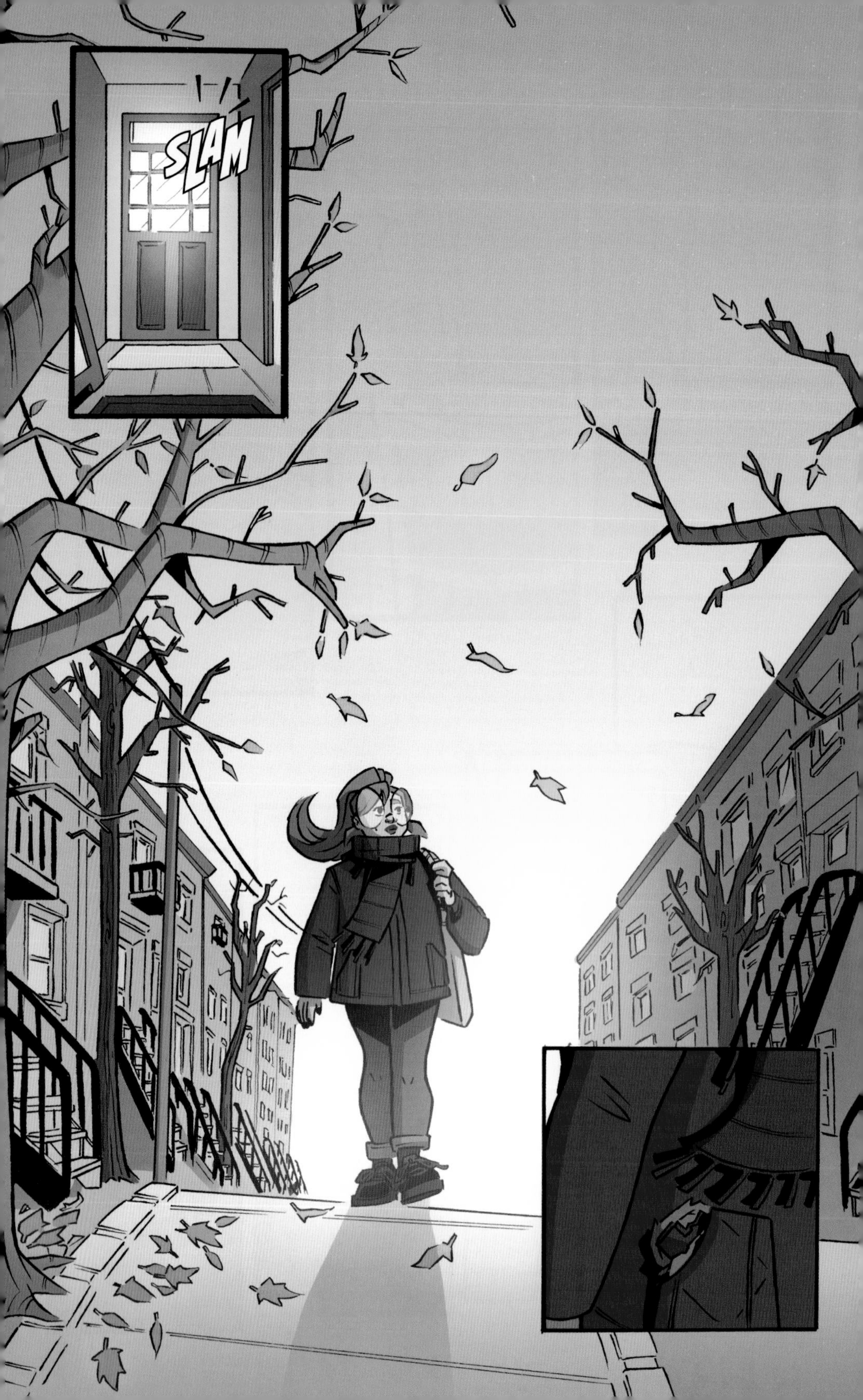
SLAM

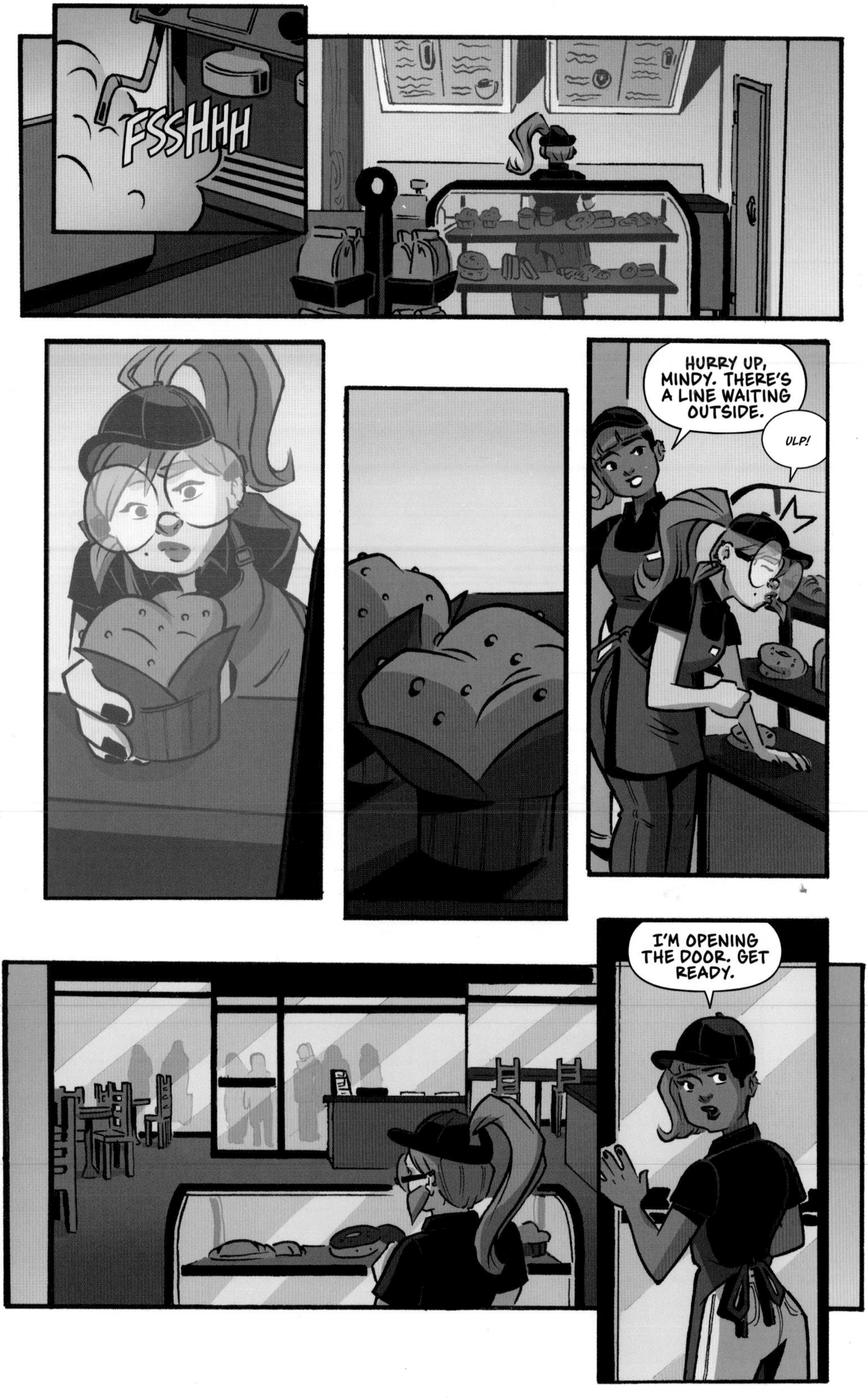
FSSHHH
HURRY UP, MINDY. THERE'S A LINE WAITING OUTSIDE.
ULP!
I'M OPENING THE DOOR. GET READY.

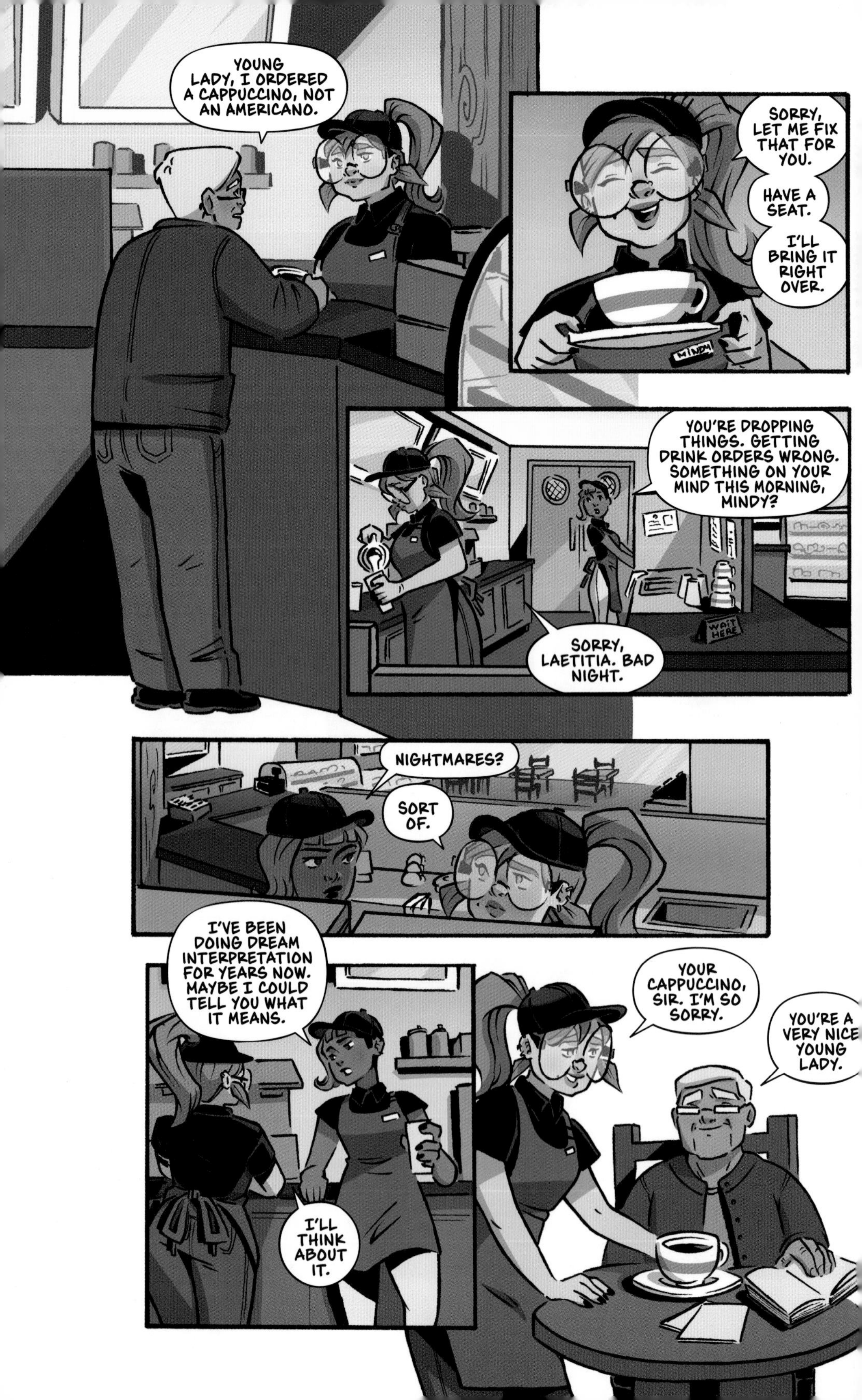
YOUNG LADY, I ORDERED A CAPPUCCINO, NOT AN AMERICANO.
SORRY, LET ME FIX THAT FOR YOU.
HAVE A SEAT.
I'LL BRING IT RIGHT OVER.
MINDY
YOU'RE DROPPING THINGS. GETTING DRINK ORDERS WRONG. SOMETHING ON YOUR MIND THIS MORNING, MINDY?
SORRY, LAETITIA. BAD NIGHT.
WAIT HERE
NIGHTMARES?
SORT OF.
I'VE BEEN DOING DREAM INTERPRETATION FOR YEARS NOW. MAYBE I COULD TELL YOU WHAT IT MEANS.
I'LL THINK ABOUT IT.
YOUR CAPPUCCINO, SIR. I'M SO SORRY.
YOU'RE A VERY NICE YOUNG LADY.

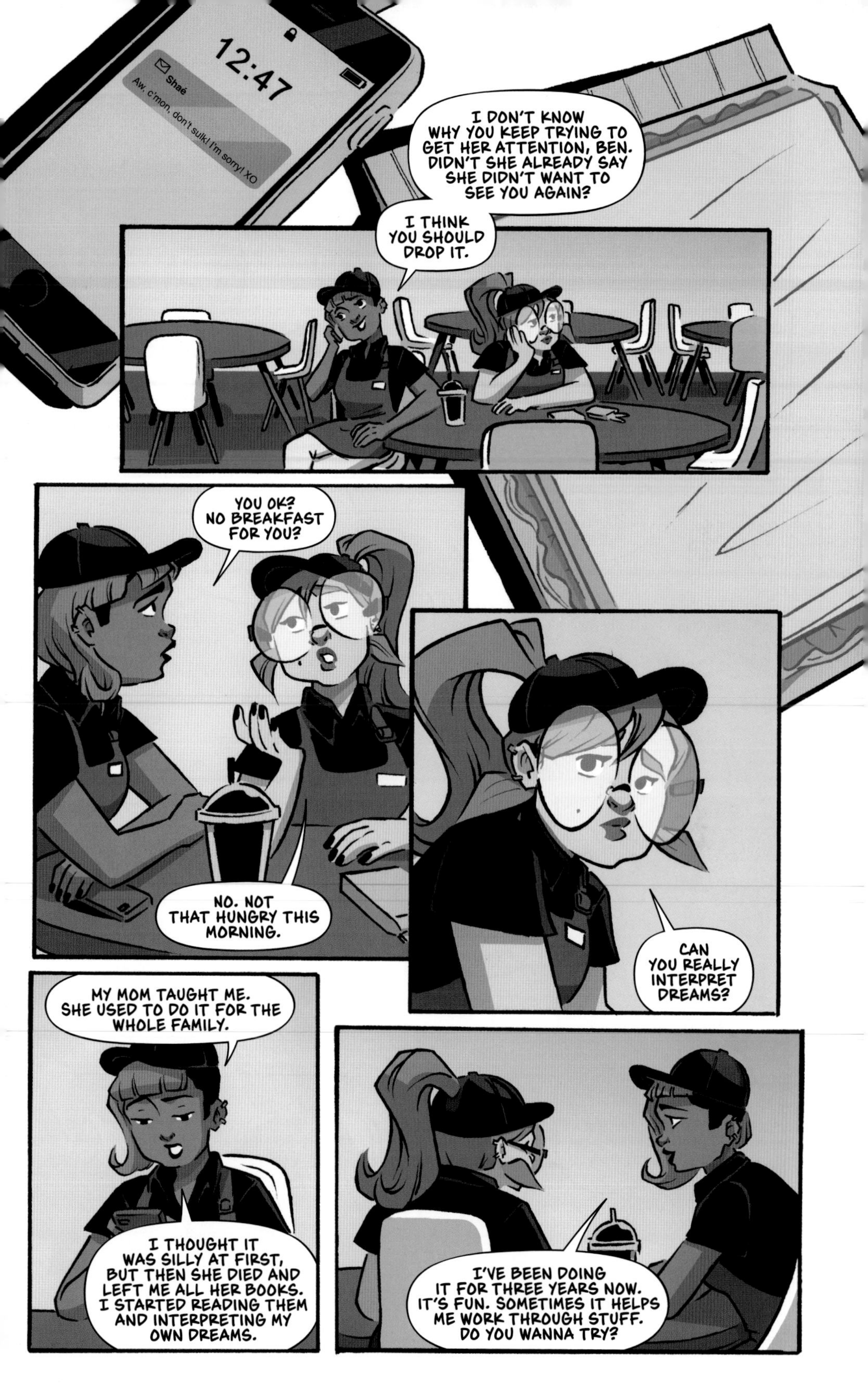
12:47
Shaé
Aw, c'mon, don't sulk! I'm sorry! XO
I DON'T KNOW WHY YOU KEEP TRYING TO GET HER ATTENTION, BEN. DIDN'T SHE ALREADY SAY SHE DIDN'T WANT TO SEE YOU AGAIN?
I THINK YOU SHOULD DROP IT.
YOU OK? NO BREAKFAST FOR YOU?
NO. NOT THAT HUNGRY THIS MORNING.
CAN YOU REALLY INTERPRET DREAMS?
MY MOM TAUGHT ME. SHE USED TO DO IT FOR THE WHOLE FAMILY.
I THOUGHT IT WAS SILLY AT FIRST, BUT THEN SHE DIED AND LEFT ME ALL HER BOOKS. I STARTED READING THEM AND INTERPRETING MY OWN DREAMS.
I'VE BEEN DOING IT FOR THREE YEARS NOW. IT'S FUN. SOMETIMES IT HELPS ME WORK THROUGH STUFF. DO YOU WANNA TRY?

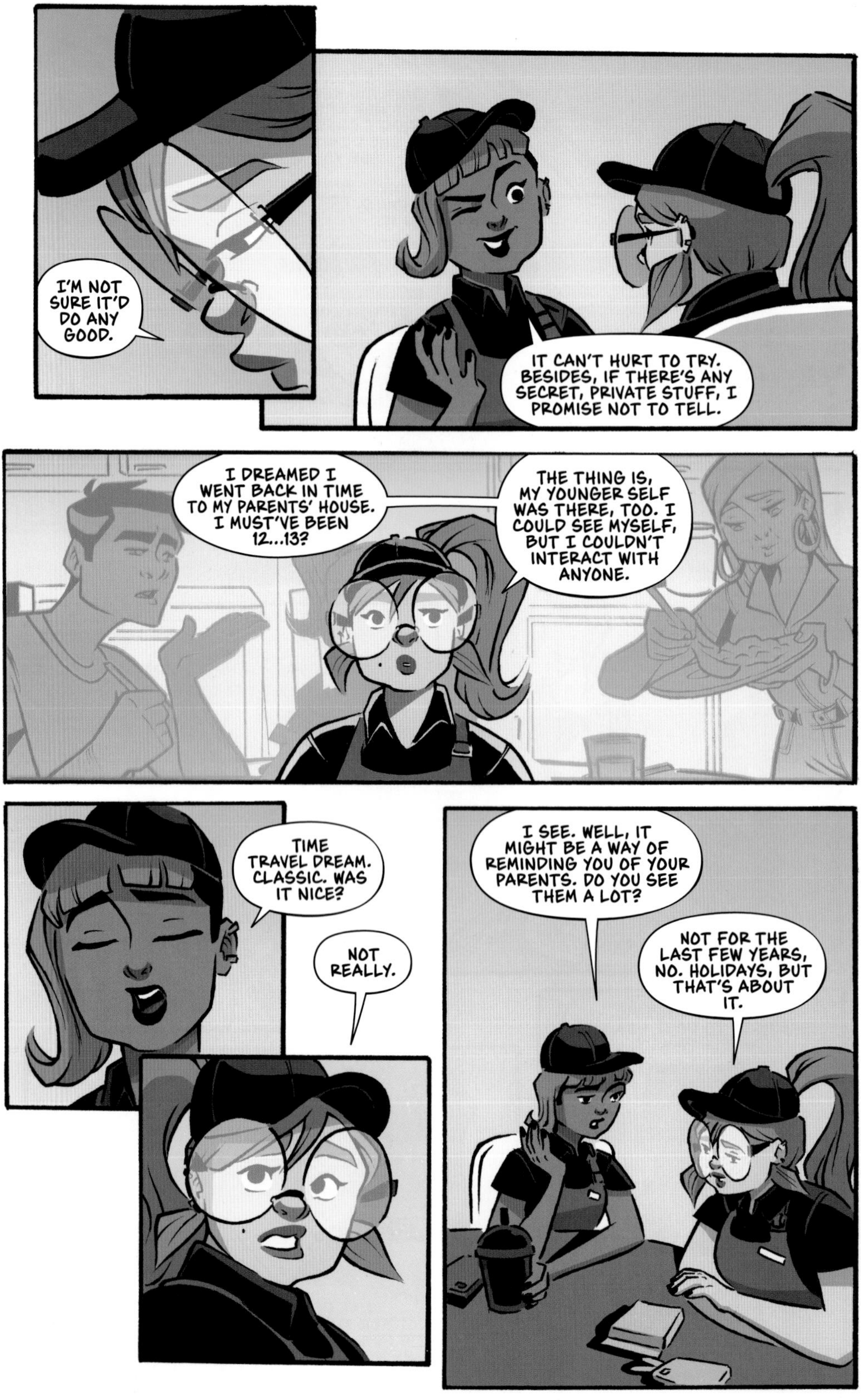
I'M NOT SURE IT'D DO ANY GOOD.
IT CAN'T HURT TO TRY. BESIDES, IF THERE'S ANY SECRET, PRIVATE STUFF, I PROMISE NOT TO TELL.
I DREAMED I WENT BACK IN TIME TO MY PARENTS' HOUSE. I MUST'VE BEEN 12...13?
THE THING IS, MY YOUNGER SELF WAS THERE, TOO. I COULD SEE MYSELF, BUT I COULDN'T INTERACT WITH ANYONE.
TIME TRAVEL DREAM. CLASSIC. WAS IT NICE?
NOT REALLY.
I SEE. WELL, IT MIGHT BE A WAY OF REMINDING YOU OF YOUR PARENTS. DO YOU SEE THEM A LOT?
NOT FOR THE LAST FEW YEARS, NO. HOLIDAYS, BUT THAT'S ABOUT IT.

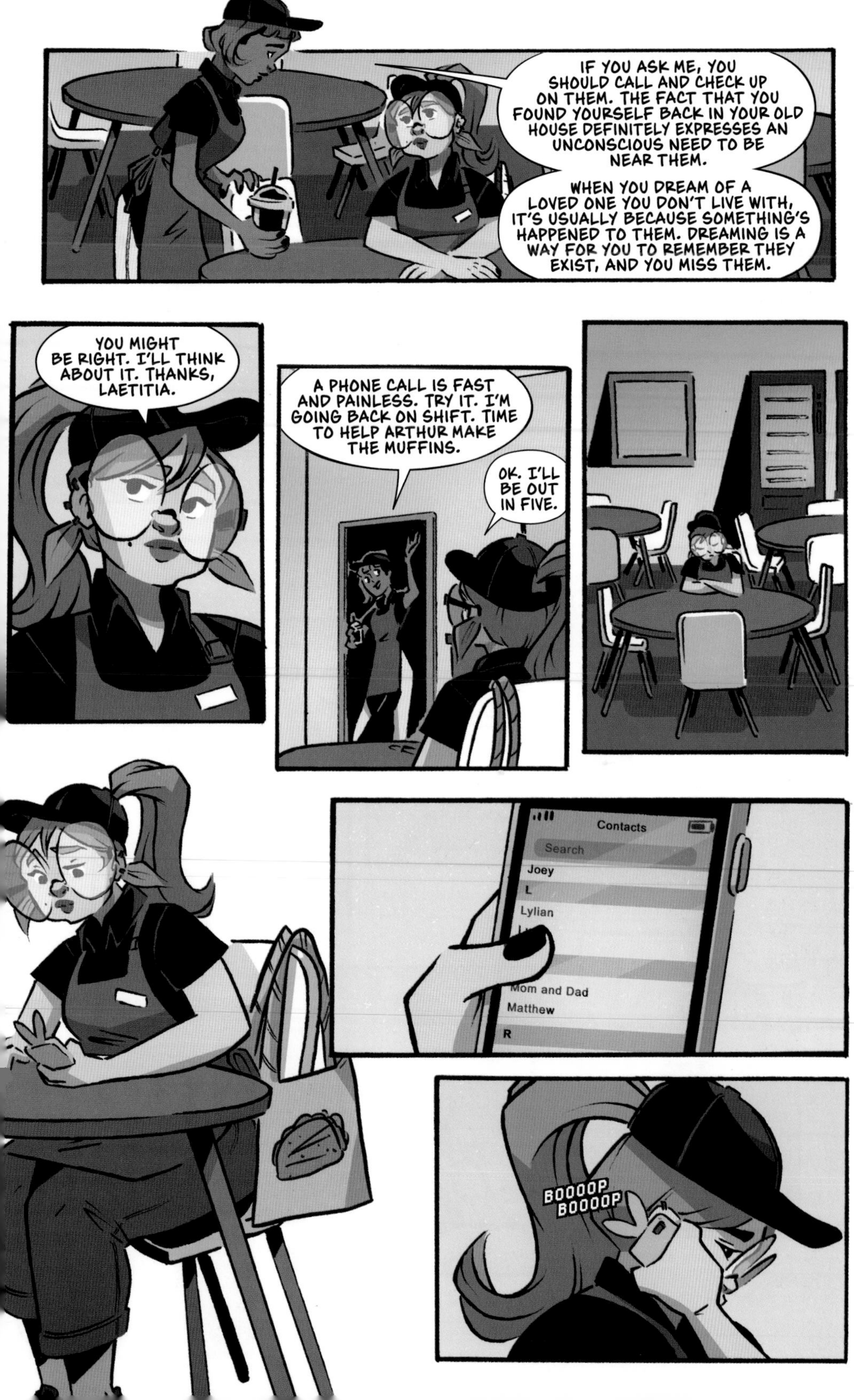
IF YOU ASK ME, YOU SHOULD CALL AND CHECK UP ON THEM. THE FACT THAT YOU FOUND YOURSELF BACK IN YOUR OLD HOUSE DEFINITELY EXPRESSES AN UNCONSCIOUS NEED TO BE NEAR THEM.
WHEN YOU DREAM OF A LOVED ONE YOU DON'T LIVE WITH, IT'S USUALLY BECAUSE SOMETHING'S HAPPENED TO THEM. DREAMING IS A WAY FOR YOU TO REMEMBER THEY EXIST, AND YOU MISS THEM.
YOU MIGHT BE RIGHT. I'LL THINK ABOUT IT. THANKS, LAETITIA.
A PHONE CALL IS FAST AND PAINLESS. TRY IT. I'M GOING BACK ON SHIFT. TIME TO HELP ARTHUR MAKE THE MUFFINS.
OK. I'LL BE OUT IN FIVE.
Contacts
Search
Joey
L
Lylian
Mom and Dad
Matthew
R
BOOOOP BOOOOP

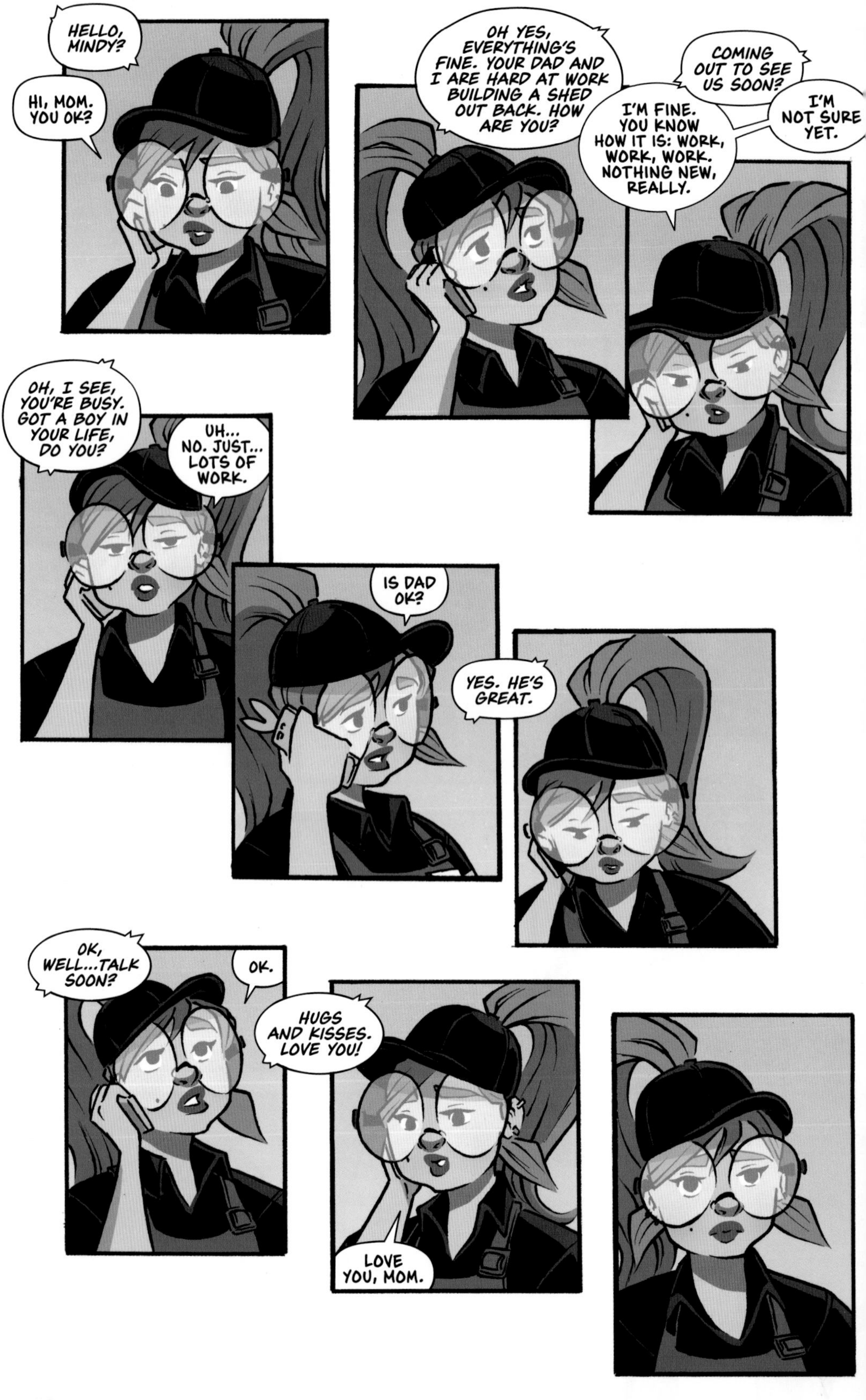
HELLO, MINDY?
HI, MOM. YOU OK?
OH YES, EVERYTHING'S FINE. YOUR DAD AND I ARE HARD AT WORK BUILDING A SHED OUT BACK. HOW ARE YOU?
I'M FINE. YOU KNOW HOW IT IS: WORK, WORK, WORK. NOTHING NEW, REALLY.
COMING OUT TO SEE US SOON?
I'M NOT SURE YET.
OH, I SEE, YOU'RE BUSY. GOT A BOY IN YOUR LIFE, DO YOU?
UH... NO. JUST... LOTS OF WORK.
IS DAD OK?
YES. HE'S GREAT.
OK, WELL...TALK SOON?
OK.
HUGS AND KISSES. LOVE YOU!
LOVE YOU, MOM.

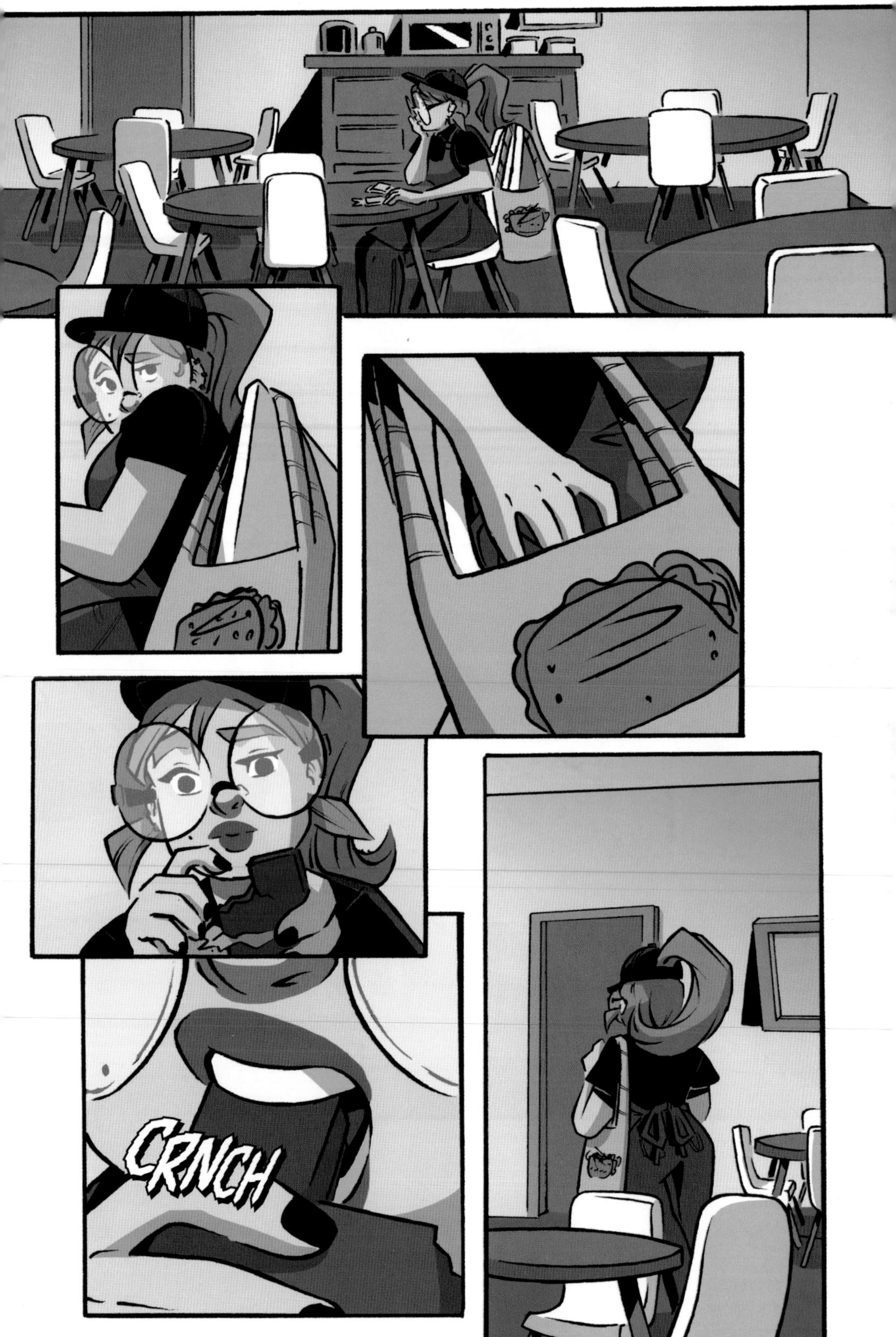
CRNCH

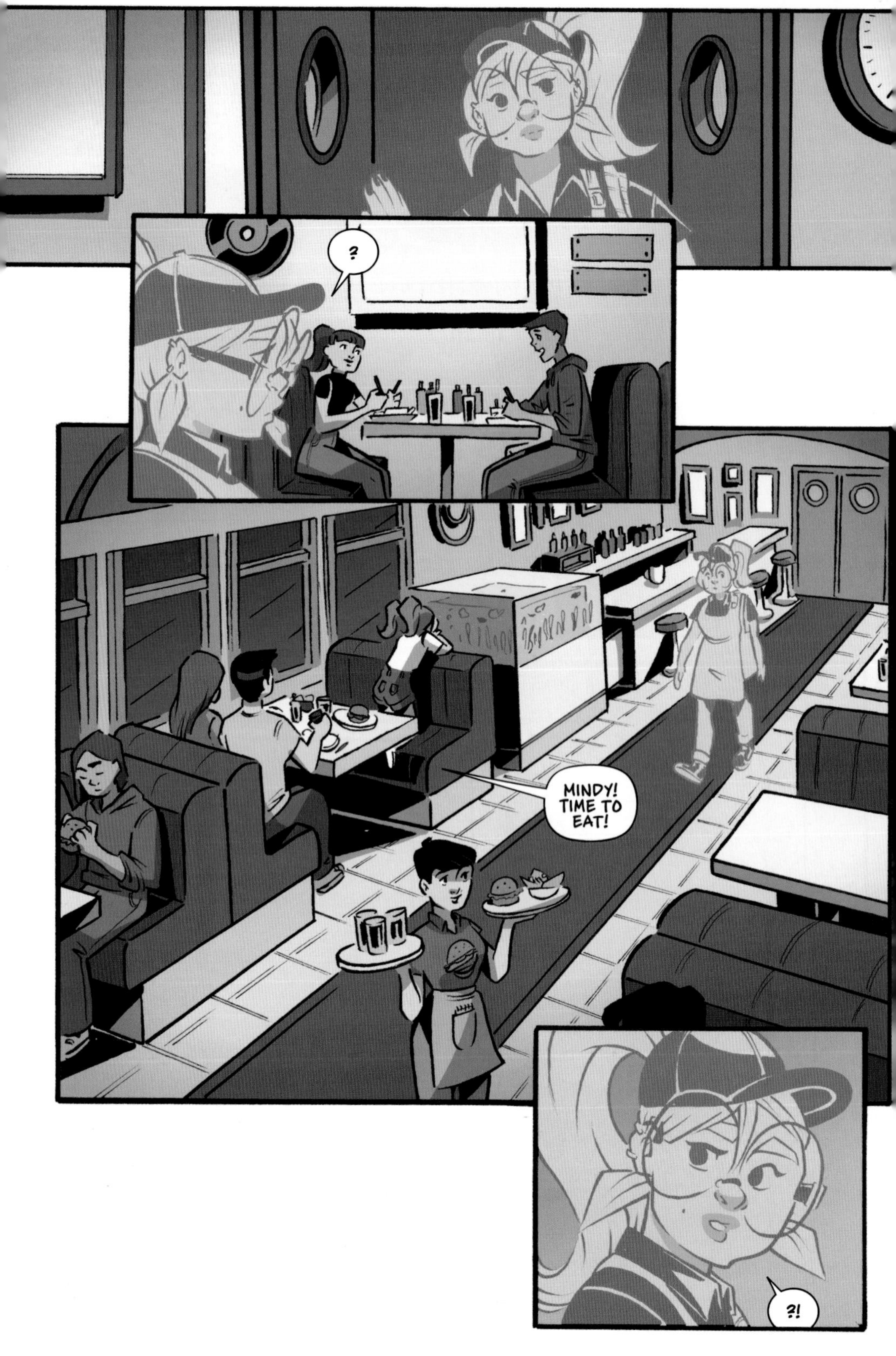
?
MINDY! TIME TO EAT!
?!

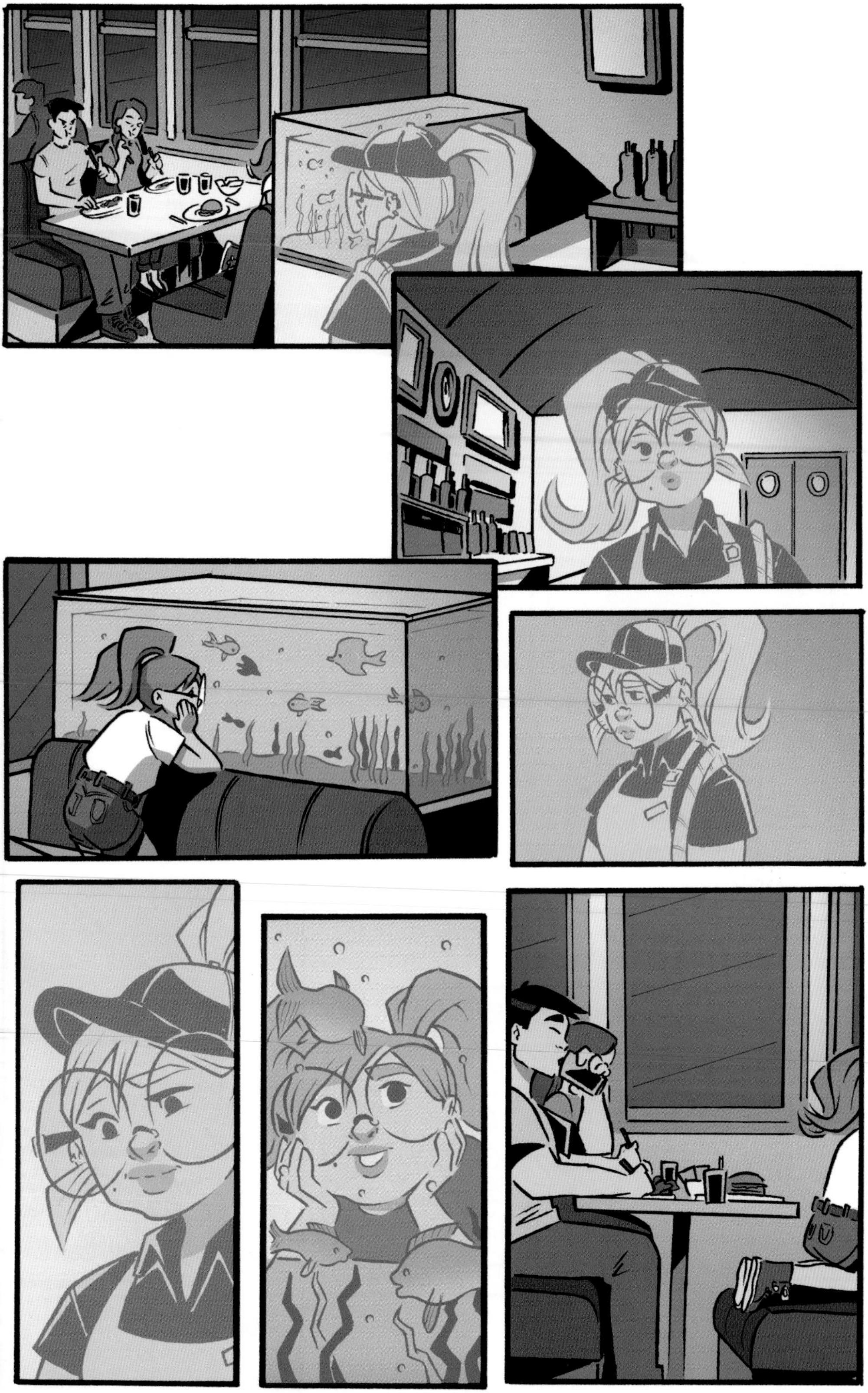

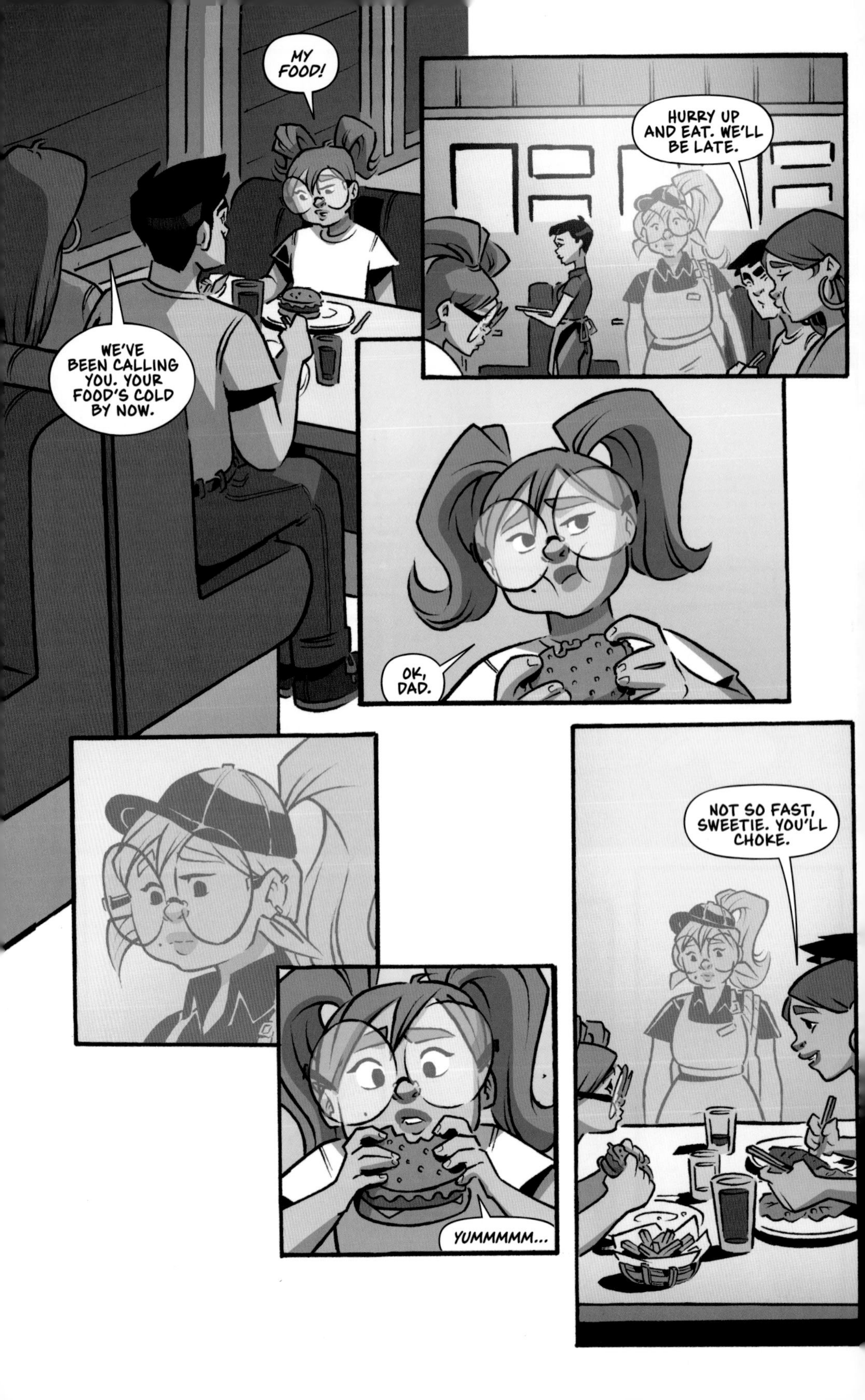
MY FOOD!
WE'VE BEEN CALLING YOU. YOUR FOOD'S COLD BY NOW.
HURRY UP AND EAT. WE'LL BE LATE.
OK, DAD.
YUMMMMM...
NOT SO FAST, SWEETIE. YOU'LL CHOKE.

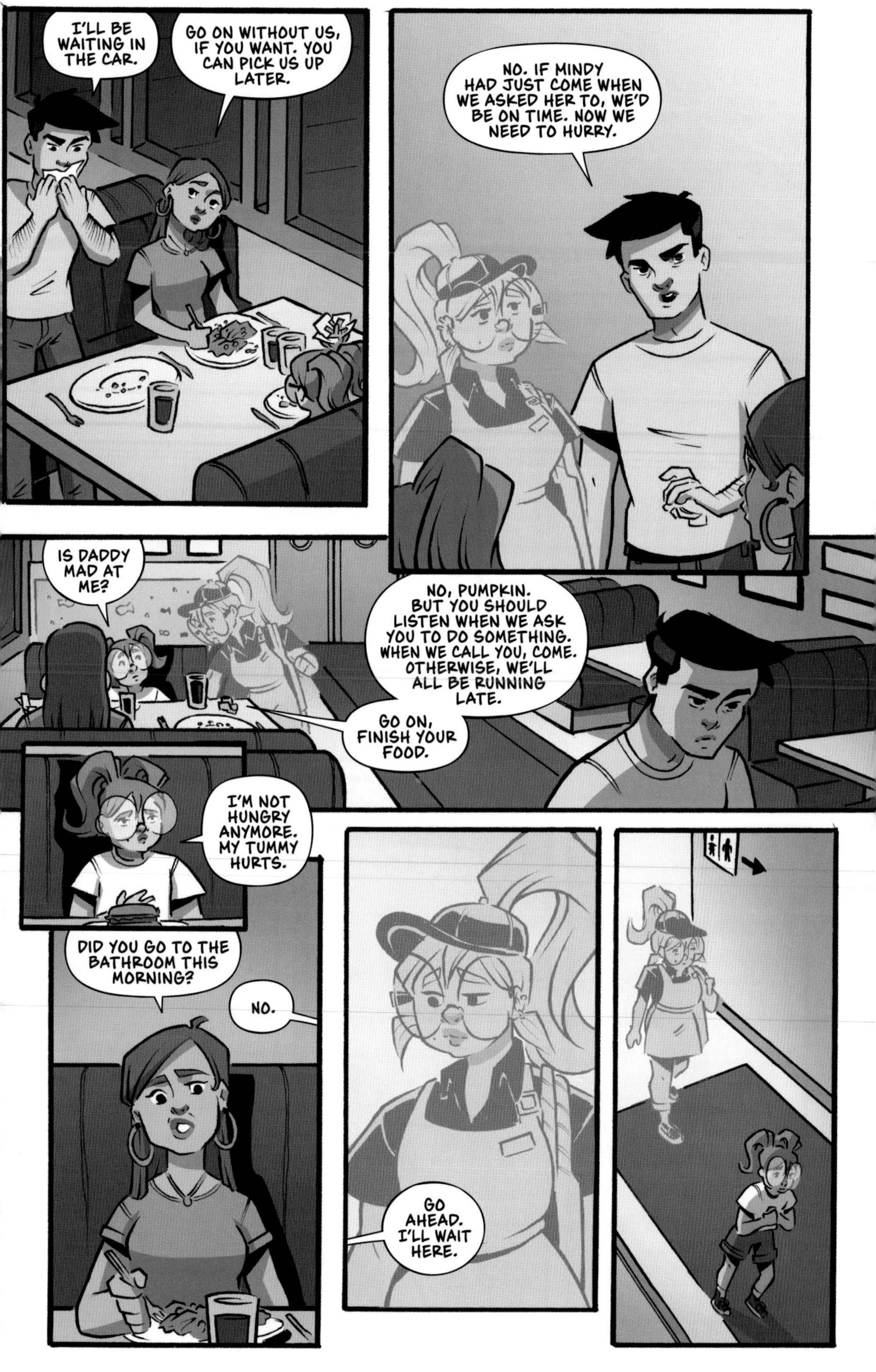
I'LL BE WAITING IN THE CAR.
GO ON WITHOUT US, IF YOU WANT. YOU CAN PICK US UP LATER.
NO. IF MINDY HAD JUST COME WHEN WE ASKED HER TO, WE'D BE ON TIME. NOW WE NEED TO HURRY.
IS DADDY MAD AT ME?
NO, PUMPKIN. BUT YOU SHOULD LISTEN WHEN WE ASK YOU TO DO SOMETHING. WHEN WE CALL YOU, COME. OTHERWISE, WE'LL ALL BE RUNNING LATE.
GO ON, FINISH YOUR FOOD.
I'M NOT HUNGRY ANYMORE. MY TUMMY HURTS.
DID YOU GO TO THE BATHROOM THIS MORNING?
NO.
GO AHEAD. I'LL WAIT HERE.

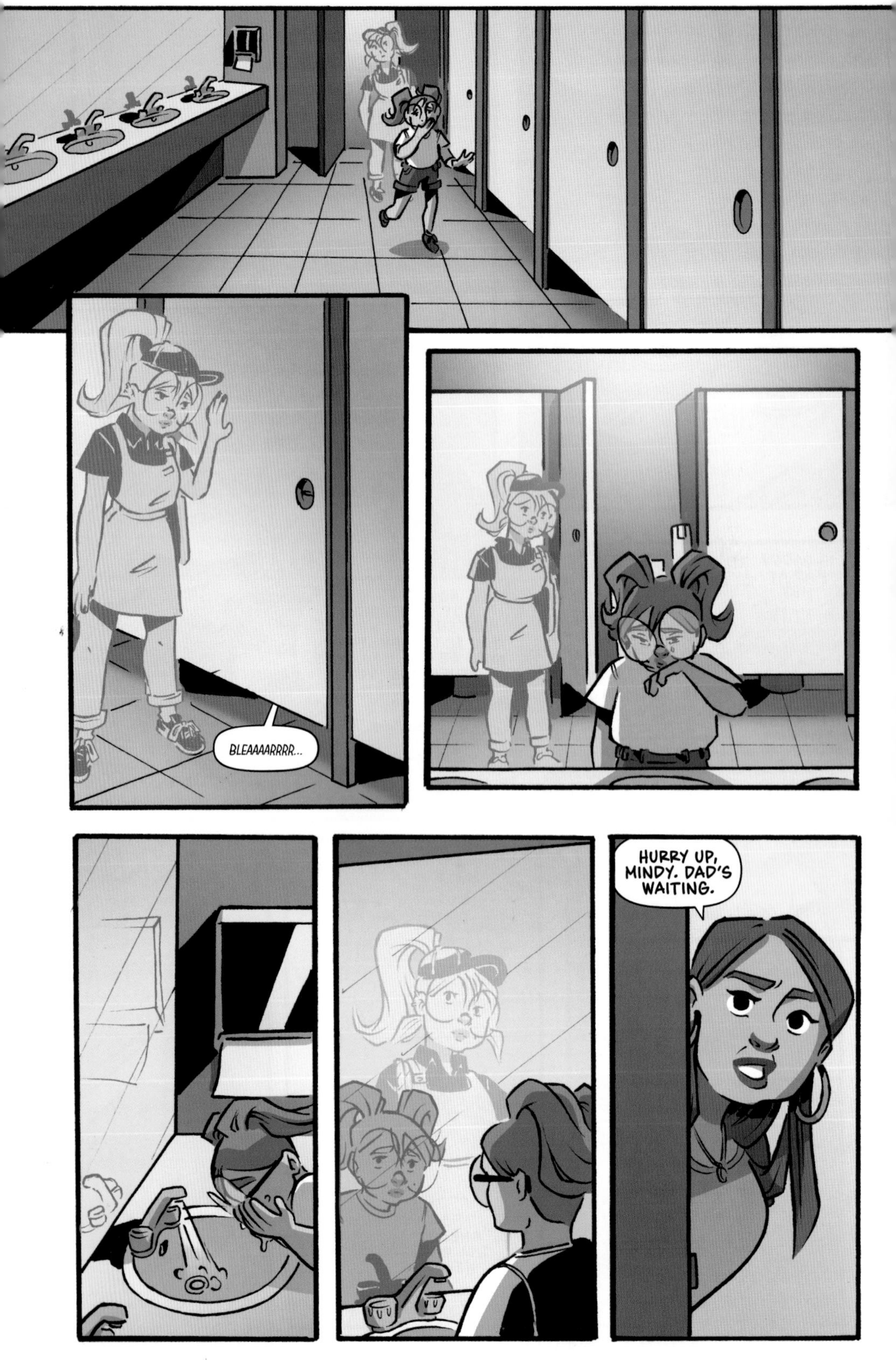
BLEAAAARRRR...
HURRY UP, MINDY. DAD'S WAITING.

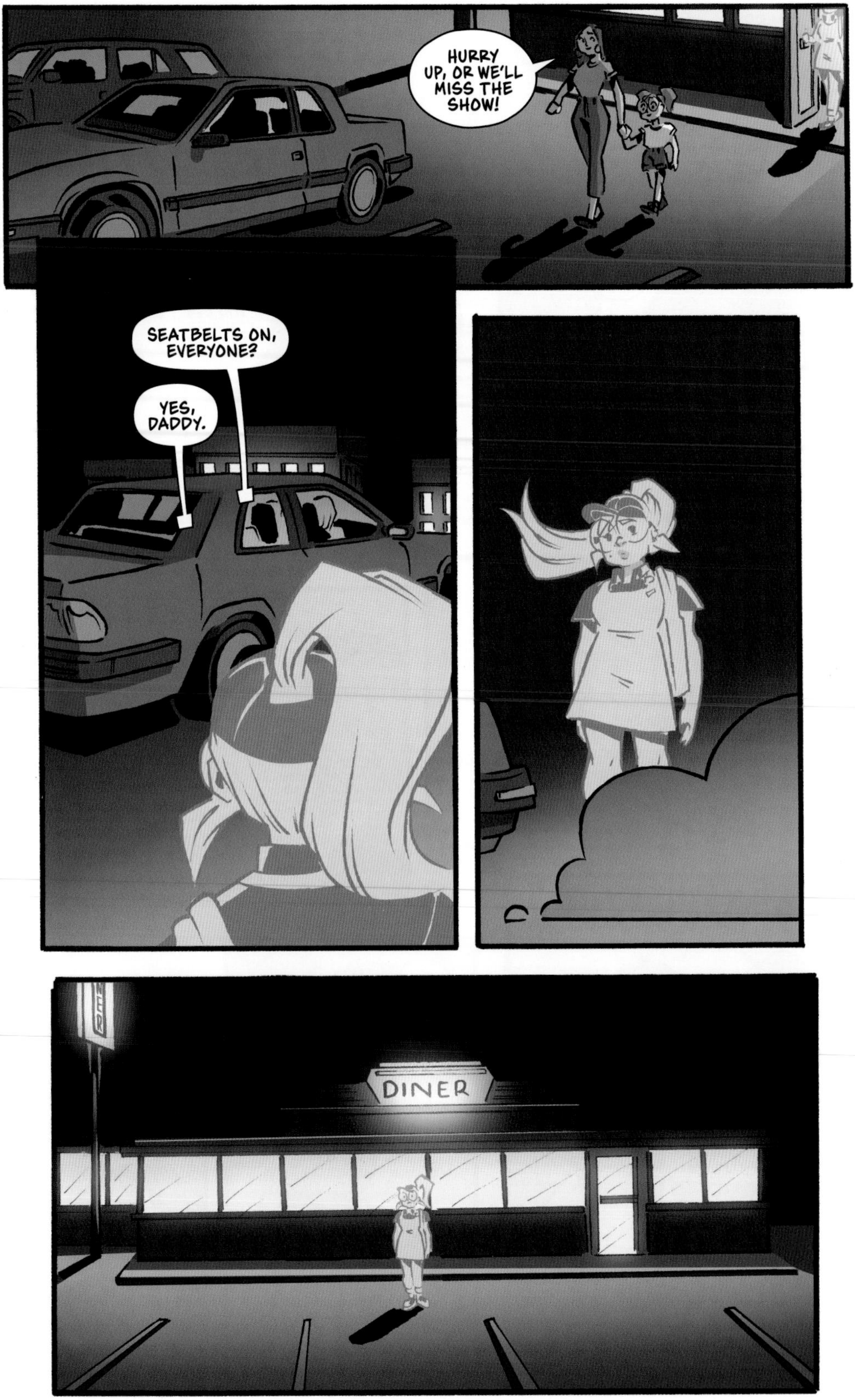
HURRY UP, OR WE'LL MISS THE SHOW!
SEATBELTS ON, EVERYONE?
YES, DADDY.
DINER

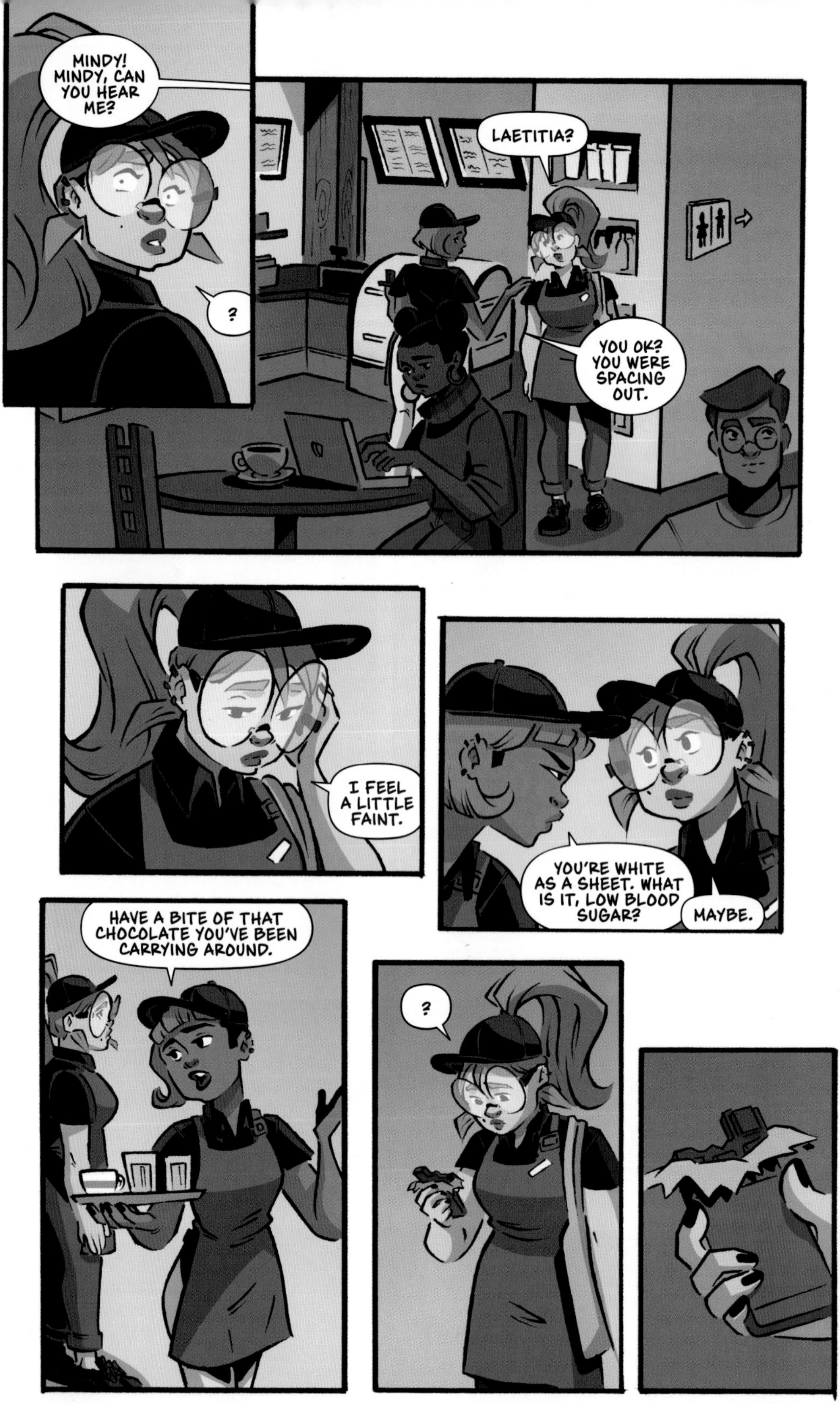
MINDY! MINDY, CAN YOU HEAR ME?
?
LAETITIA?
YOU OK? YOU WERE SPACING OUT.
I FEEL A LITTLE FAINT.
YOU'RE WHITE AS A SHEET. WHAT IS IT, LOW BLOOD SUGAR?
MAYBE.
HAVE A BITE OF THAT CHOCOLATE YOU'VE BEEN CARRYING AROUND.
?

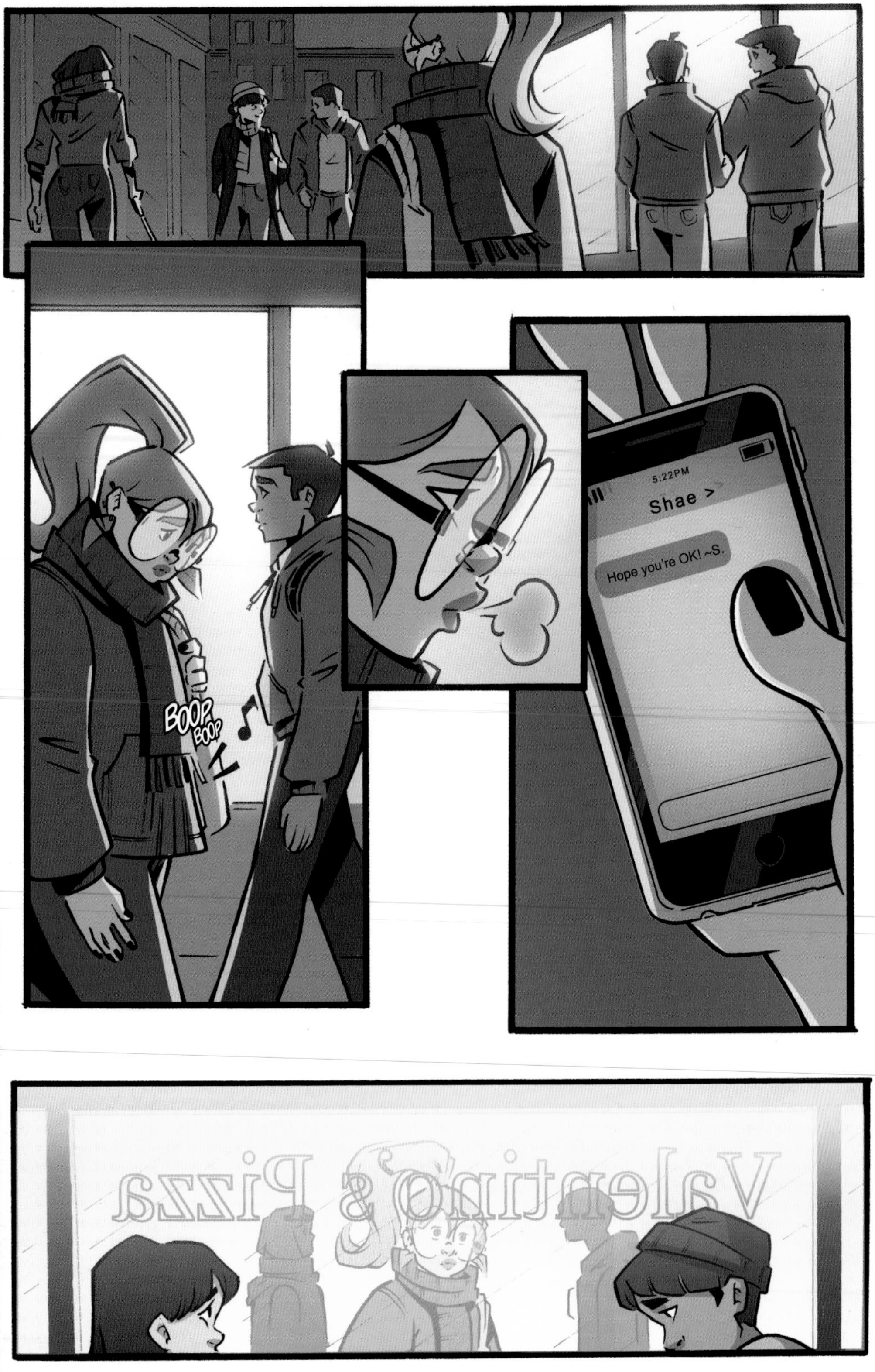
BOOP BOOP
5:22PM
Shae >
Hope you're OK! ~S.
Valentino's Pizza

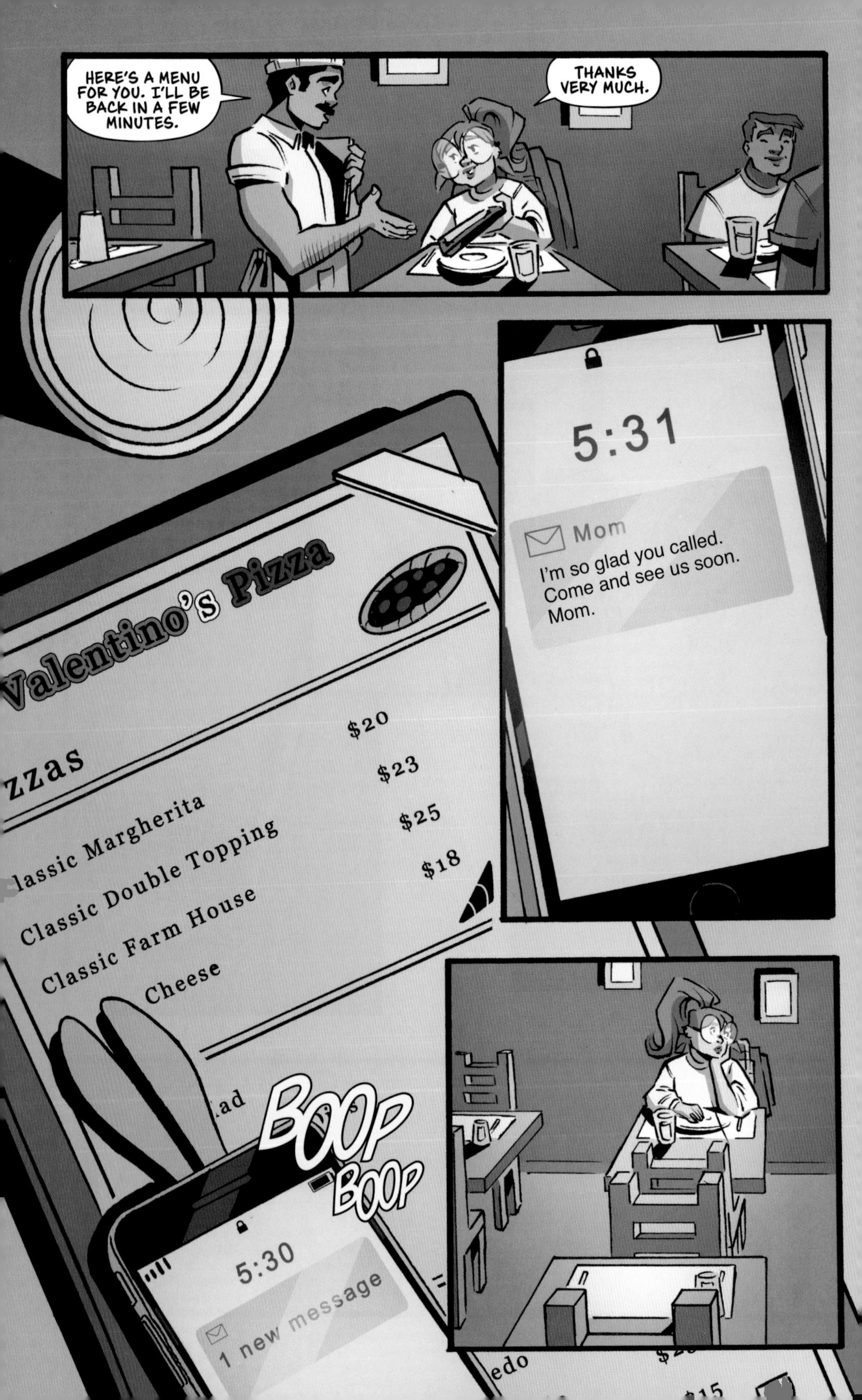
HERE'S A MENU FOR YOU. I'LL BE BACK IN A FEW MINUTES.
THANKS VERY MUCH.
5:31
Mom
I'm so glad you called. Come and see us soon. Mom.
Valentino's Pizza
zzas
lassic Margherita $20
Classic Double Topping $23
Classic Farm House $25
Cheese $18
BOOP
BOOP
5:30
1 new message

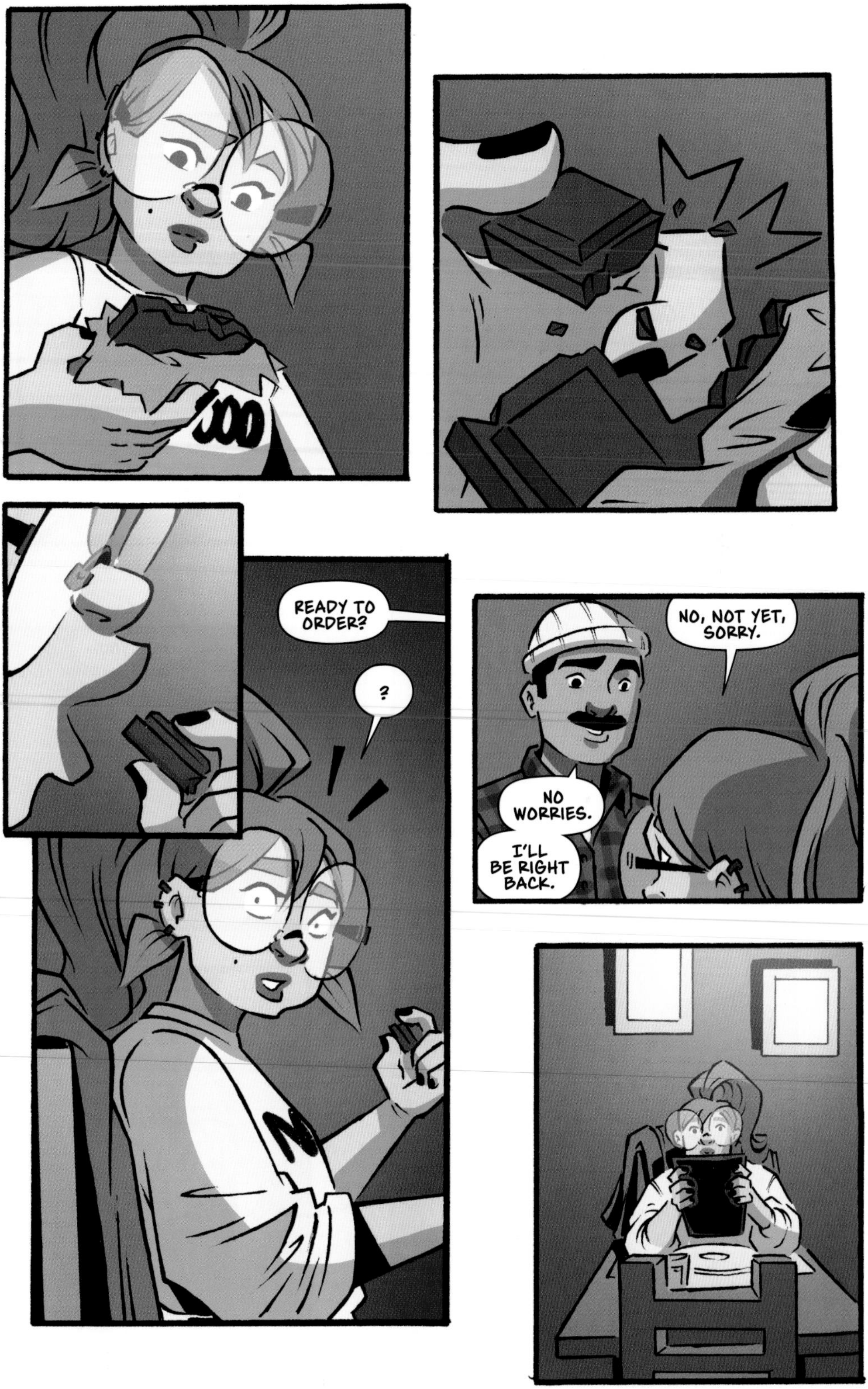
READY TO ORDER?
?
NO, NOT YET, SORRY.
NO WORRIES.
I'LL BE RIGHT BACK.

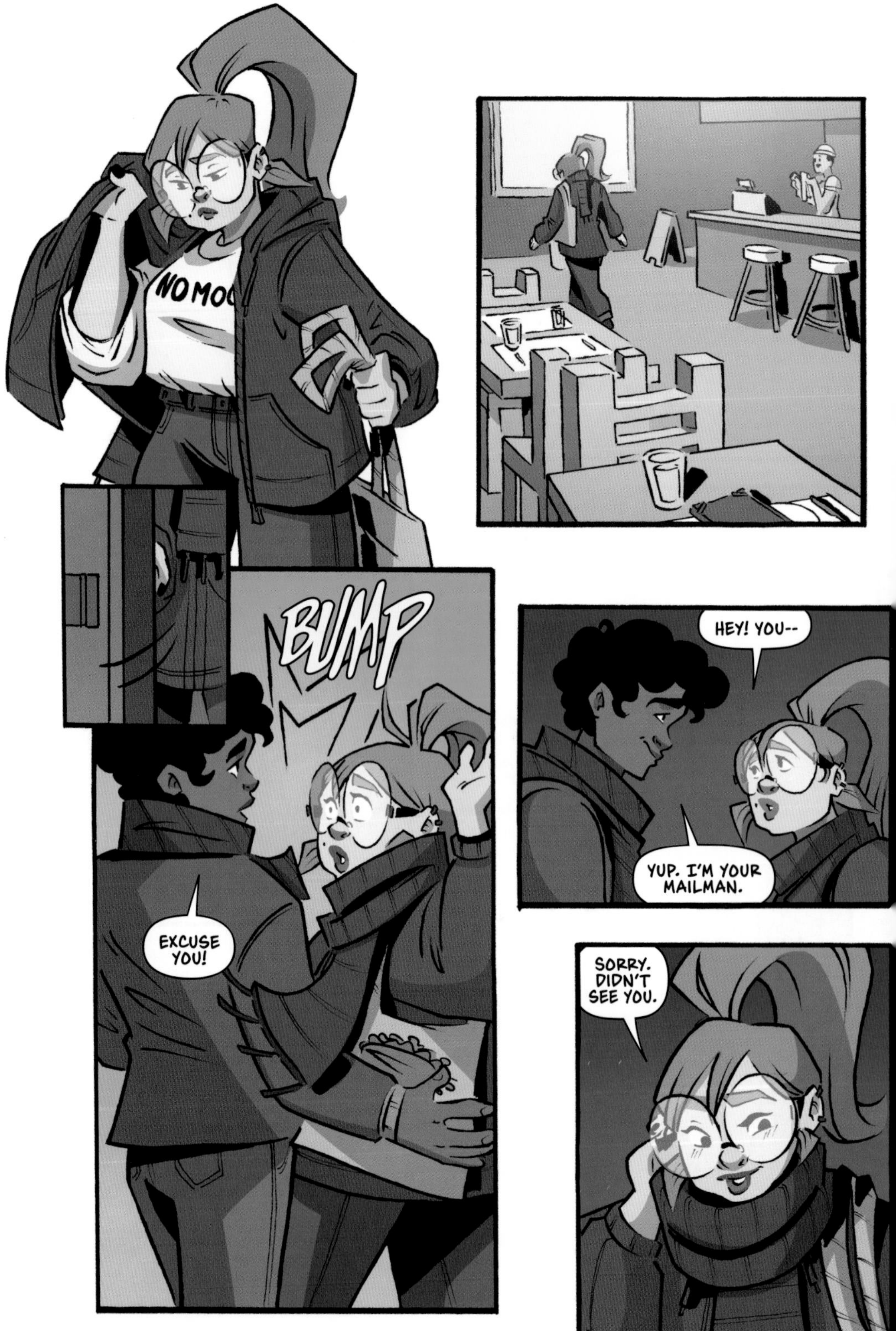
NO MOO
BUMP
EXCUSE YOU!
HEY! YOU--
YUP. I'M YOUR MAILMAN.
SORRY. DIDN'T SEE YOU.

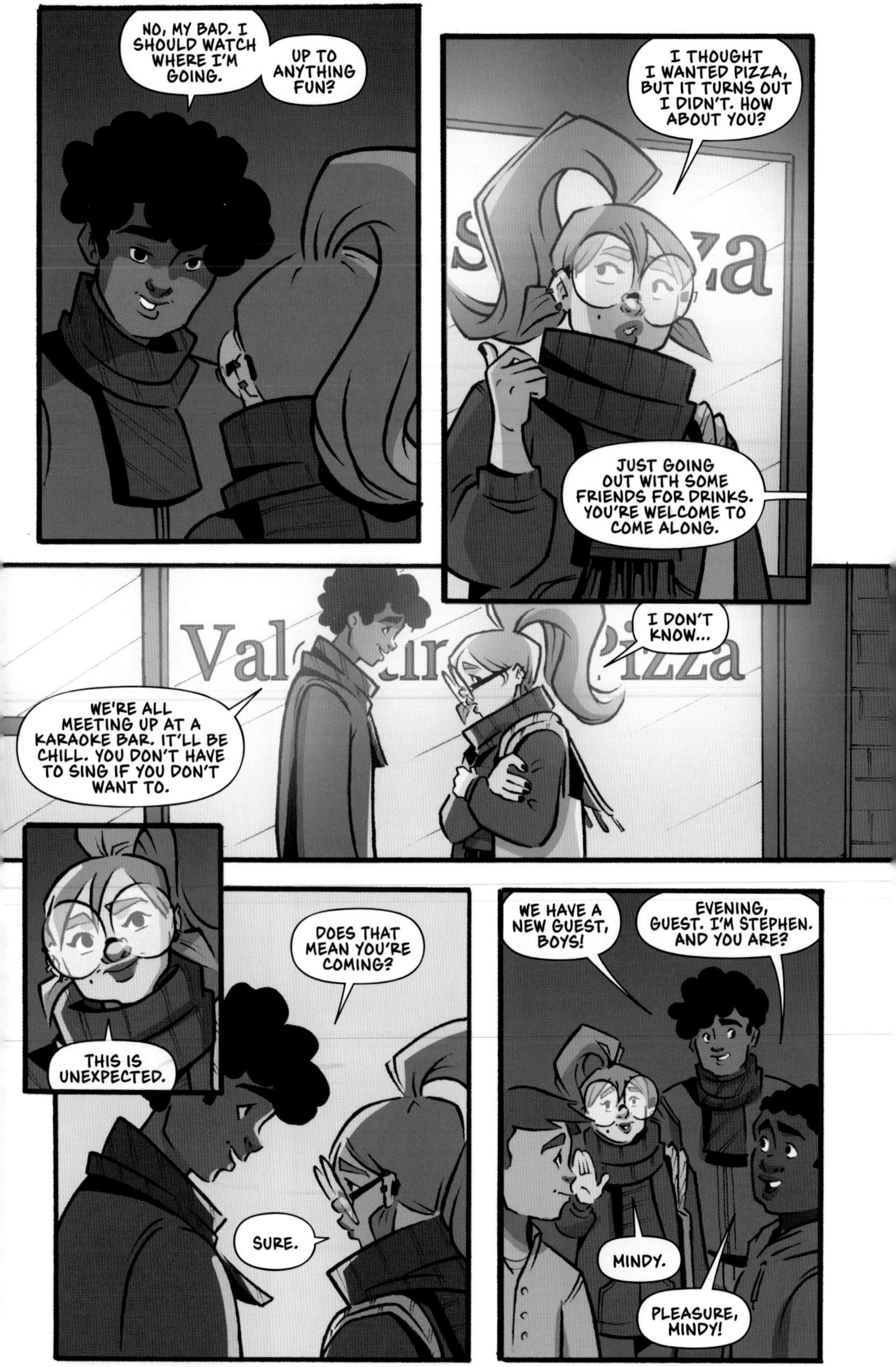
NO, MY BAD. I SHOULD WATCH WHERE I'M GOING.
UP TO ANYTHING FUN?
I THOUGHT I WANTED PIZZA, BUT IT TURNS OUT I DIDN'T. HOW ABOUT YOU?
JUST GOING OUT WITH SOME FRIENDS FOR DRINKS. YOU'RE WELCOME TO COME ALONG.
I DON'T KNOW...
WE'RE ALL MEETING UP AT A KARAOKE BAR. IT'LL BE CHILL. YOU DON'T HAVE TO SING IF YOU DON'T WANT TO.
THIS IS UNEXPECTED.
DOES THAT MEAN YOU'RE COMING?
SURE.
WE HAVE A NEW GUEST, BOYS!
EVENING, GUEST. I'M STEPHEN. AND YOU ARE?
MINDY.
PLEASURE, MINDY!

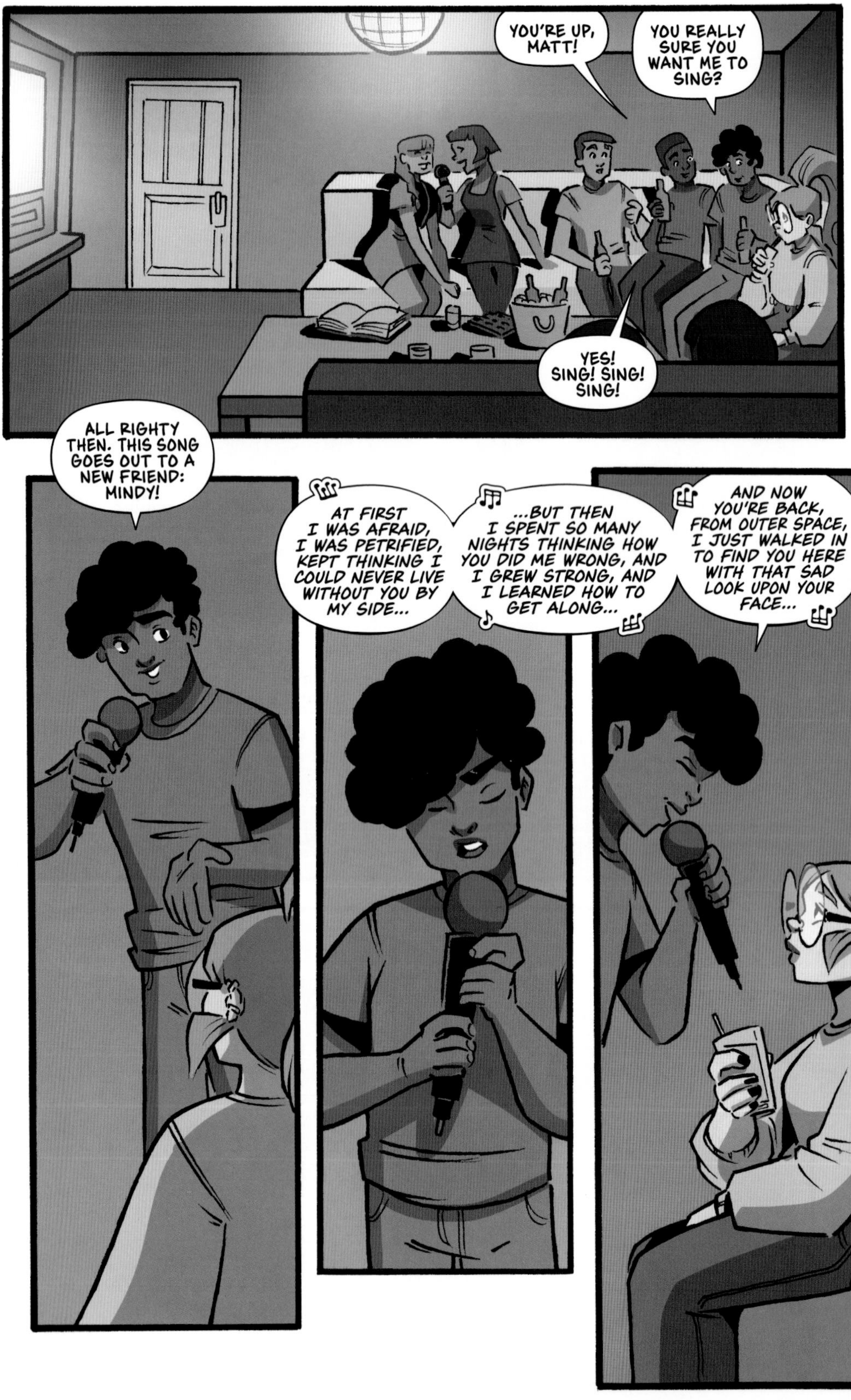
YOU'RE UP, MATT!
YOU REALLY SURE YOU WANT ME TO SING?
YES! SING! SING! SING!
ALL RIGHTY THEN. THIS SONG GOES OUT TO A NEW FRIEND: MINDY!
AT FIRST I WAS AFRAID, I WAS PETRIFIED, KEPT THINKING I COULD NEVER LIVE WITHOUT YOU BY MY SIDE...
...BUT THEN I SPENT SO MANY NIGHTS THINKING HOW YOU DID ME WRONG, AND I GREW STRONG, AND I LEARNED HOW TO GET ALONG...
AND NOW YOU'RE BACK, FROM OUTER SPACE, I JUST WALKED IN TO FIND YOU HERE WITH THAT SAD LOOK UPON YOUR FACE...

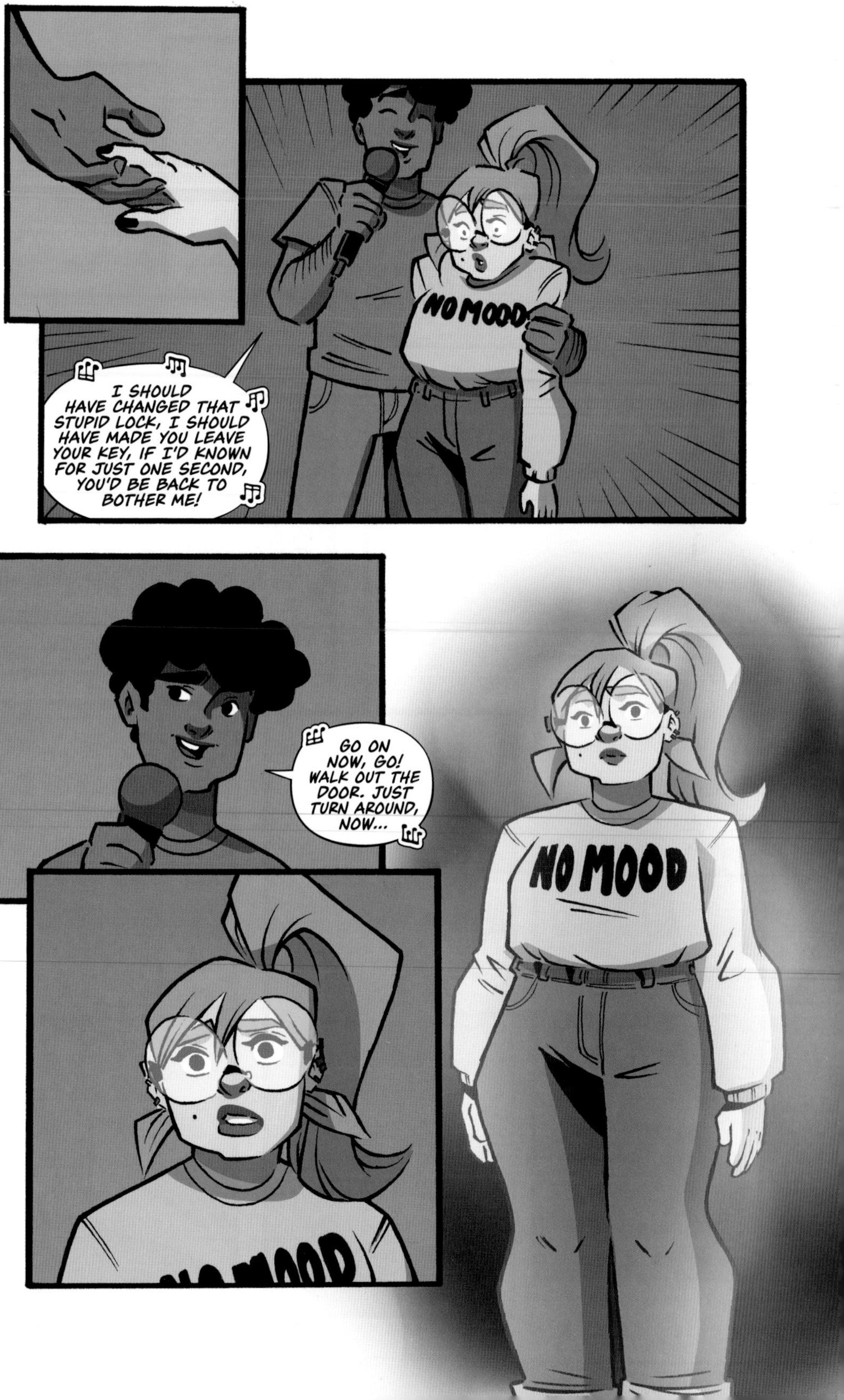
I SHOULD HAVE CHANGED THAT STUPID LOCK, I SHOULD HAVE MADE YOU LEAVE YOUR KEY, IF I'D KNOWN FOR JUST ONE SECOND, YOU'D BE BACK TO BOTHER ME!
NO MOOD
GO ON NOW, GO! WALK OUT THE DOOR. JUST TURN AROUND, NOW...
NO MOOD

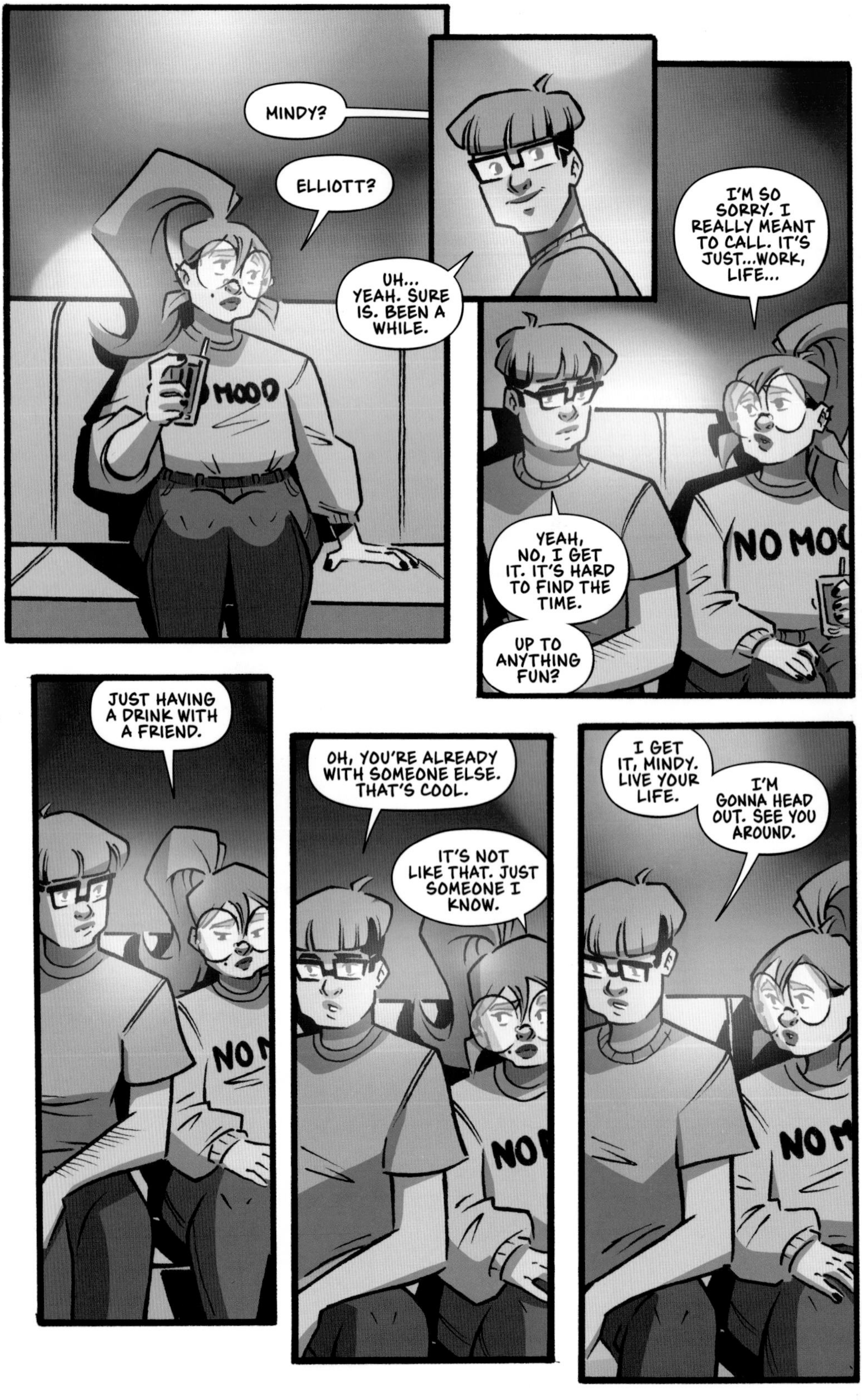
MINDY?
ELLIOTT?
UH... YEAH. SURE IS. BEEN A WHILE.
I'M SO SORRY. I REALLY MEANT TO CALL. IT'S JUST...WORK, LIFE...
YEAH, NO, I GET IT. IT'S HARD TO FIND THE TIME.
UP TO ANYTHING FUN?
NO MOOD
JUST HAVING A DRINK WITH A FRIEND.
OH, YOU'RE ALREADY WITH SOMEONE ELSE. THAT'S COOL.
IT'S NOT LIKE THAT. JUST SOMEONE I KNOW.
I GET IT, MINDY. LIVE YOUR LIFE.
I'M GONNA HEAD OUT. SEE YOU AROUND.

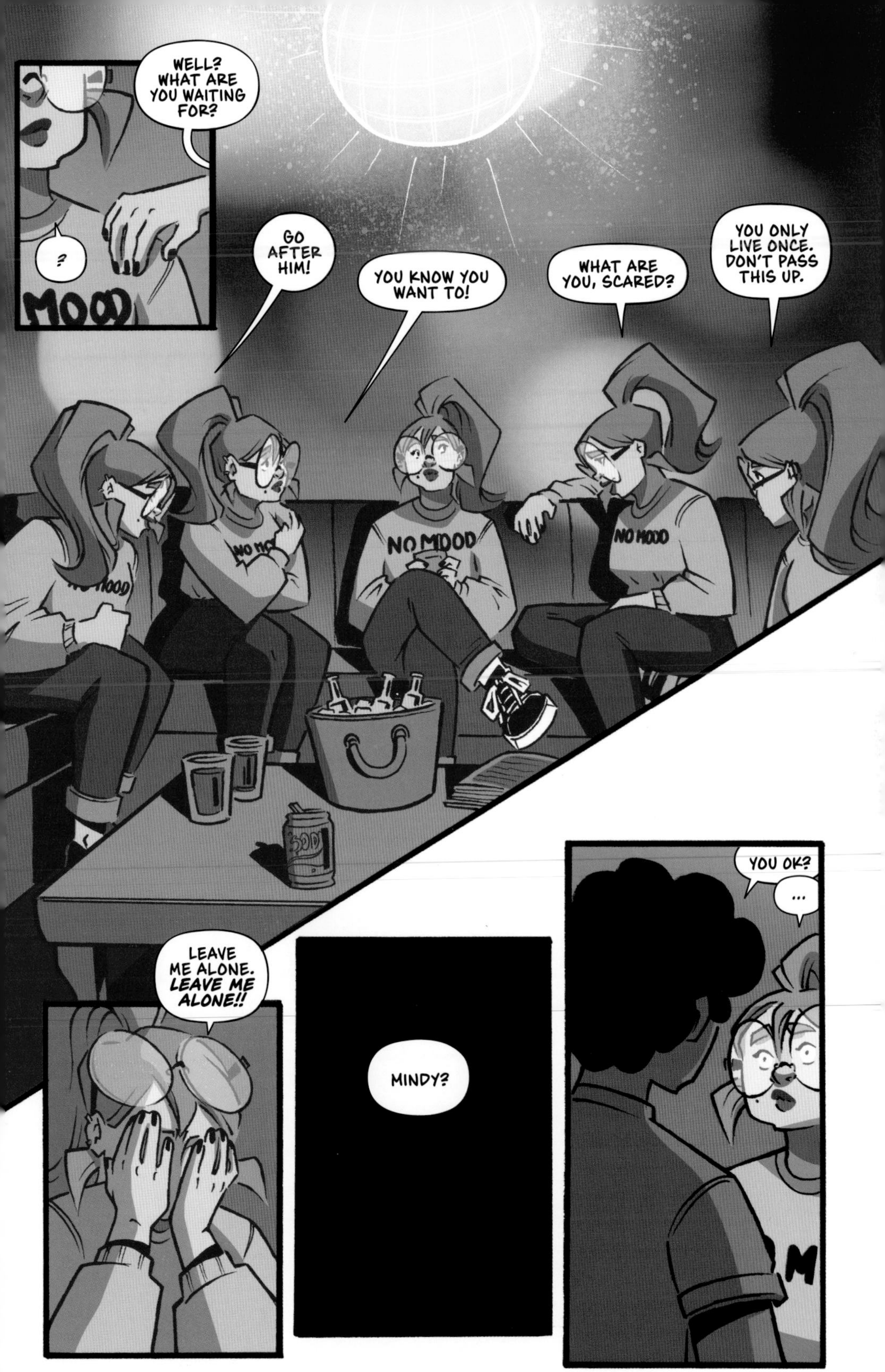
WELL? WHAT ARE YOU WAITING FOR?
?
MOOD
GO AFTER HIM!
YOU KNOW YOU WANT TO!
WHAT ARE YOU, SCARED?
YOU ONLY LIVE ONCE. DON'T PASS THIS UP.
NO MOOD
NO MOOD
NO MOOD
YOU OK?
...
LEAVE ME ALONE. LEAVE ME ALONE!!
MINDY?

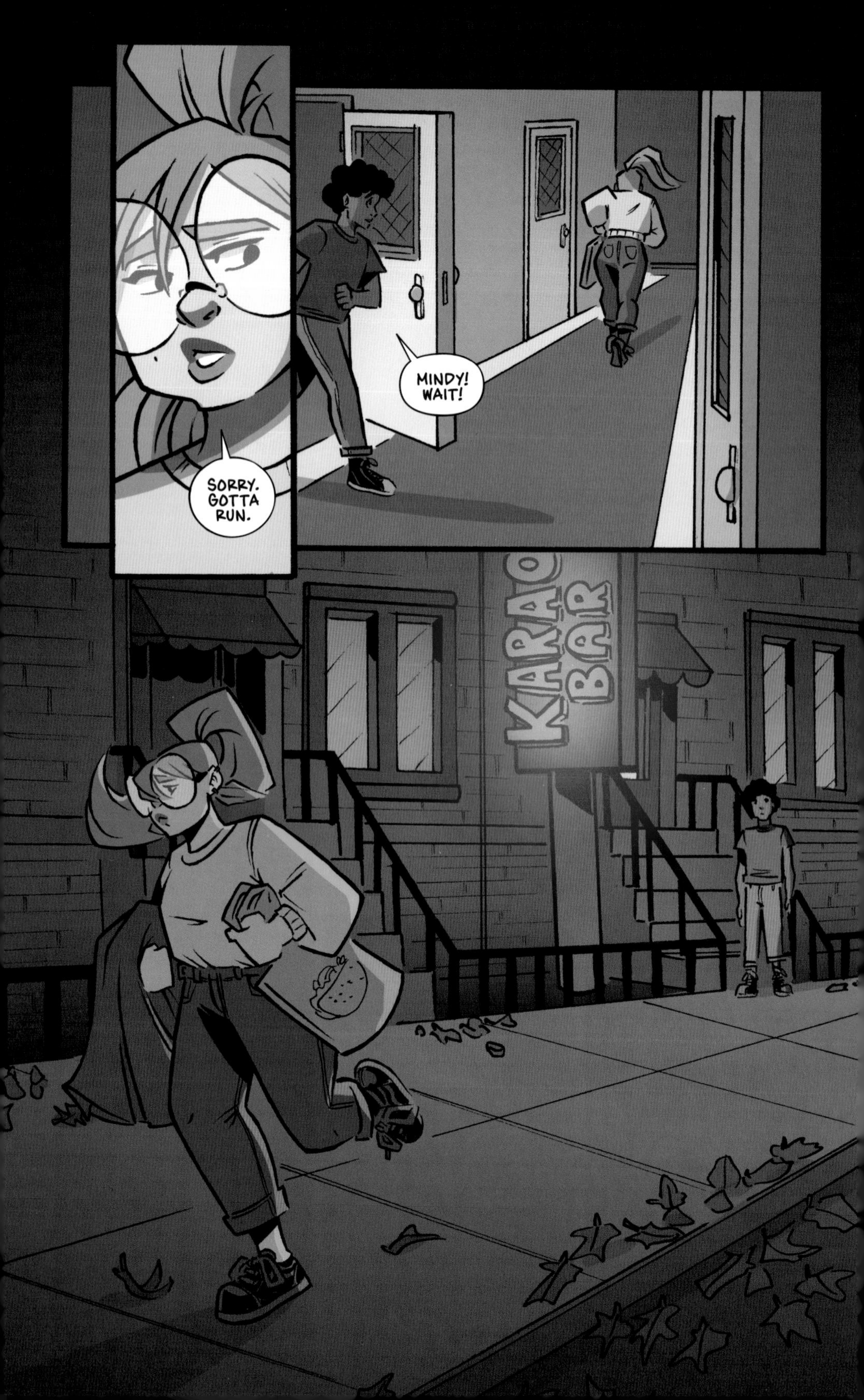
SORRY. GOTTA RUN.
MINDY! WAIT!
KARAO
BAR

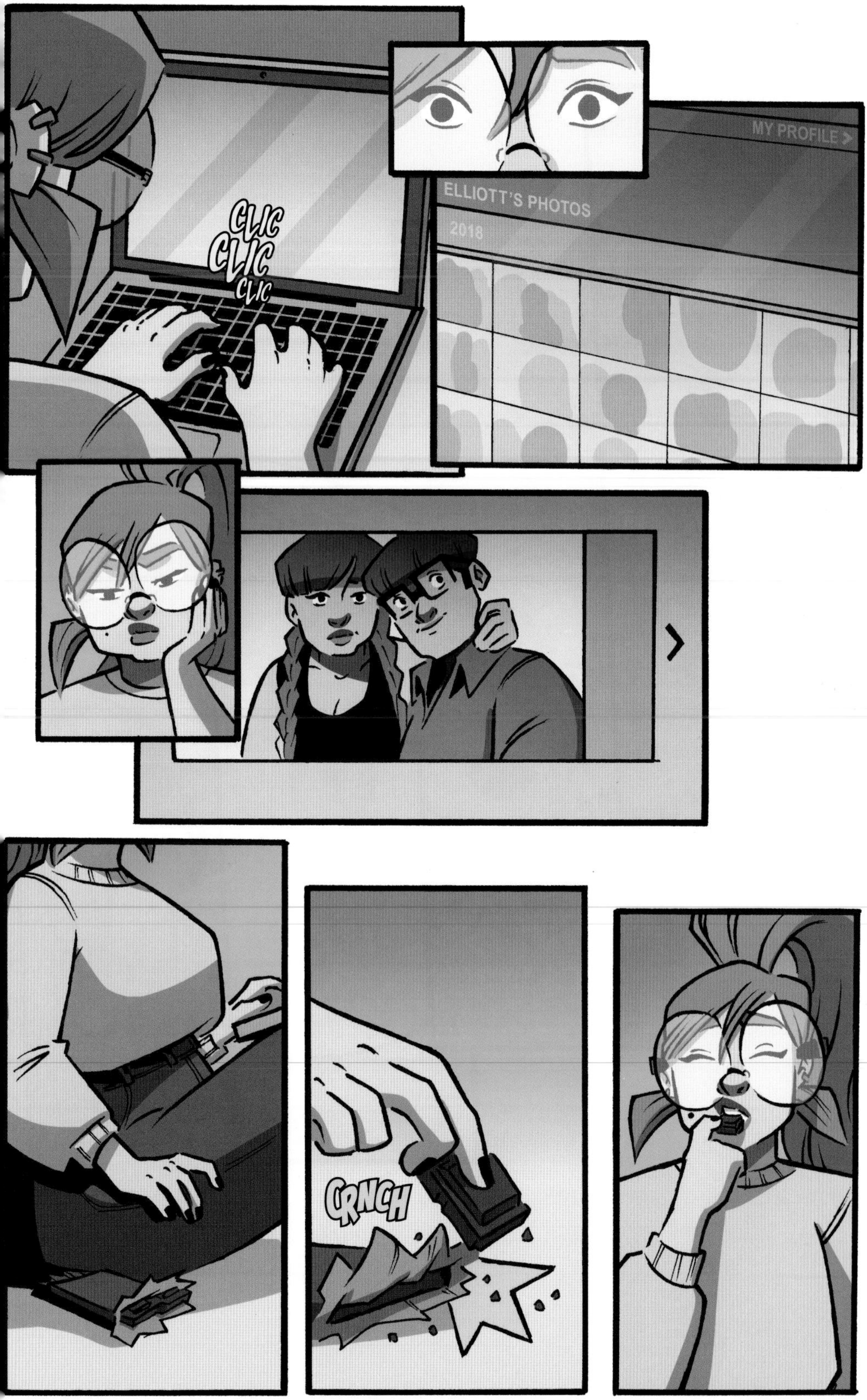
CLIC
CLIC
CLIC
MY PROFILE
ELLIOTT'S PHOTOS
2018
CRNCH

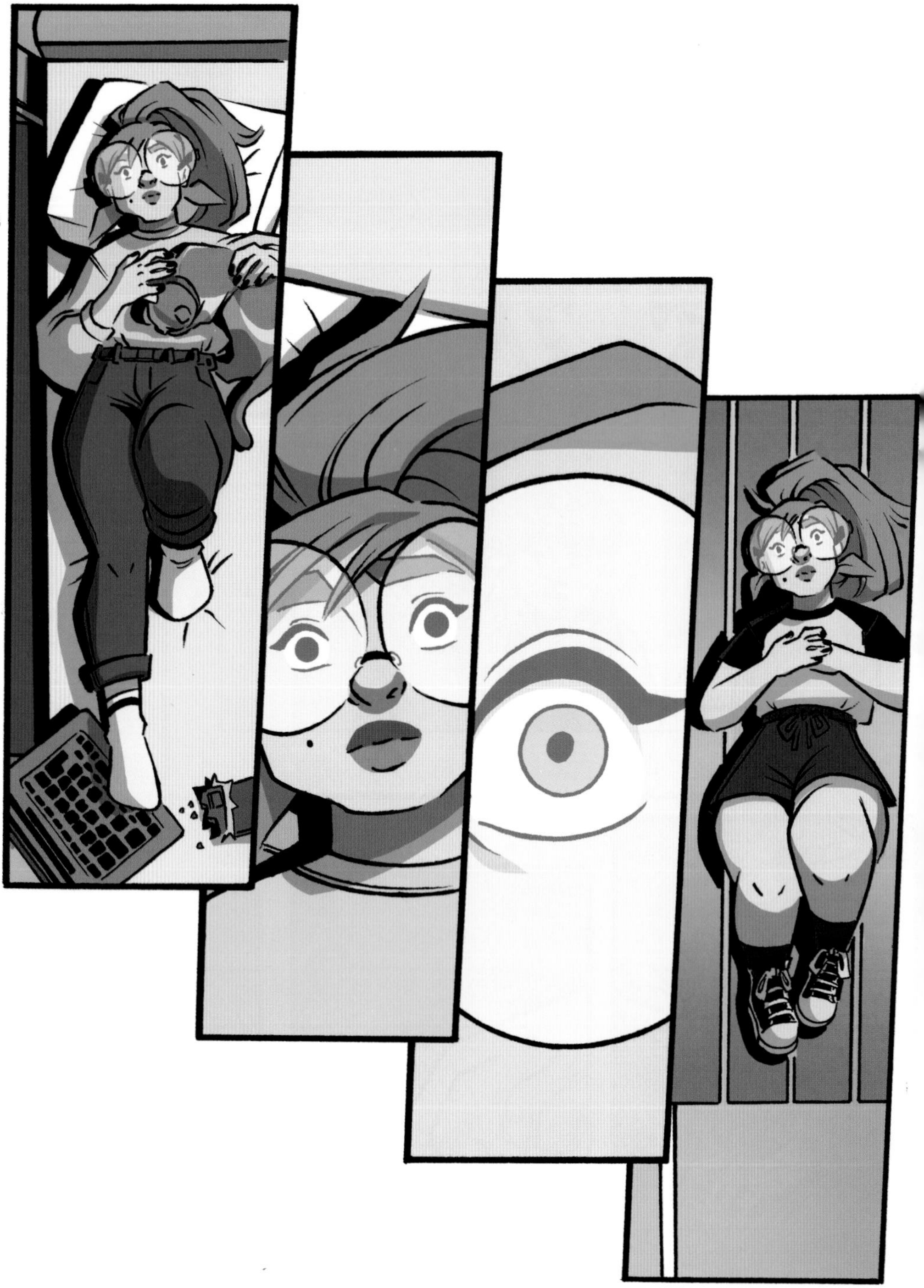

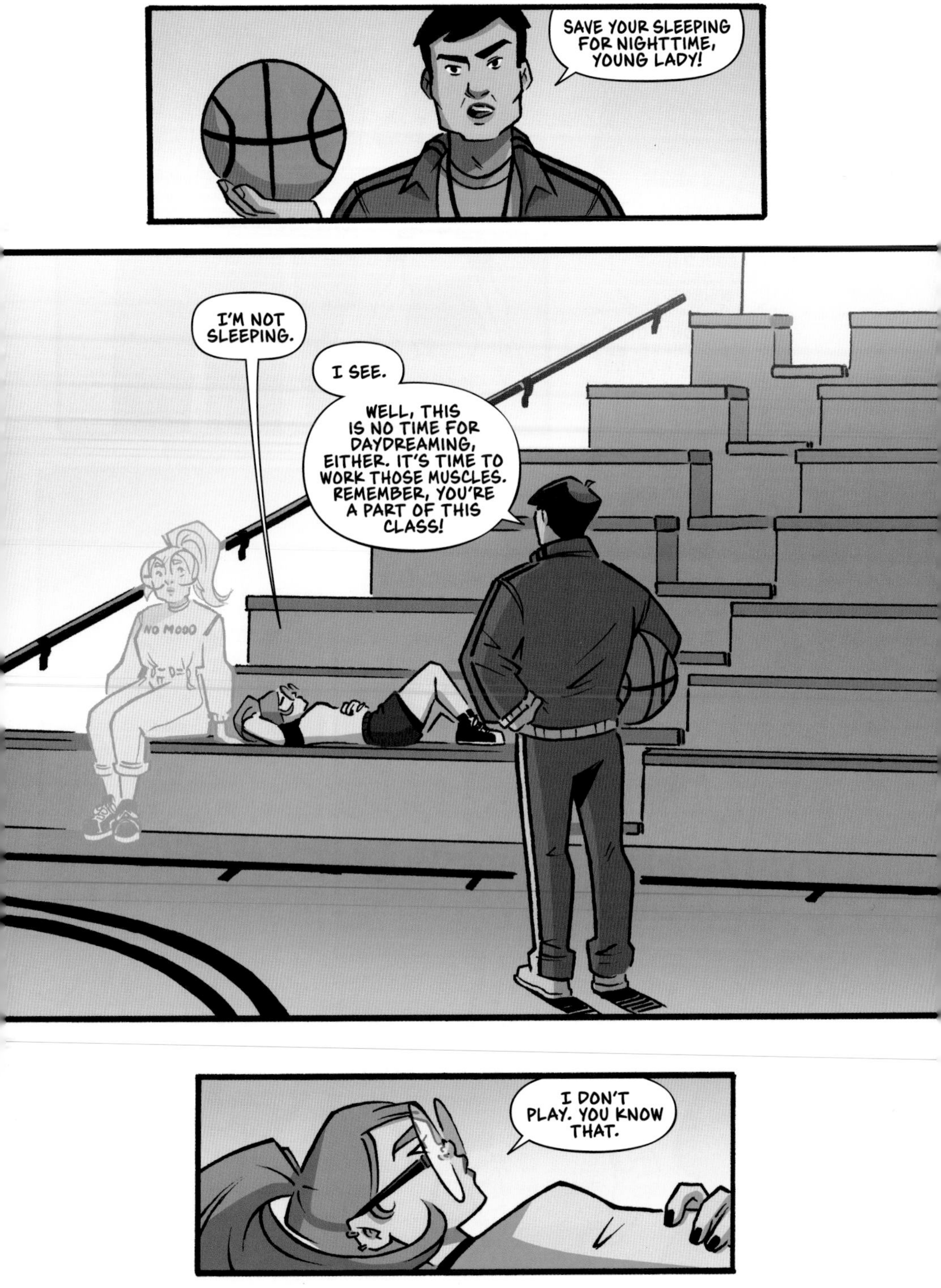
SAVE YOUR SLEEPING FOR NIGHTTIME, YOUNG LADY!
I'M NOT SLEEPING.
I SEE.
WELL, THIS IS NO TIME FOR DAYDREAMING, EITHER. IT'S TIME TO WORK THOSE MUSCLES. REMEMBER, YOU'RE A PART OF THIS CLASS!
NO MOOD
I DON'T PLAY. YOU KNOW THAT.

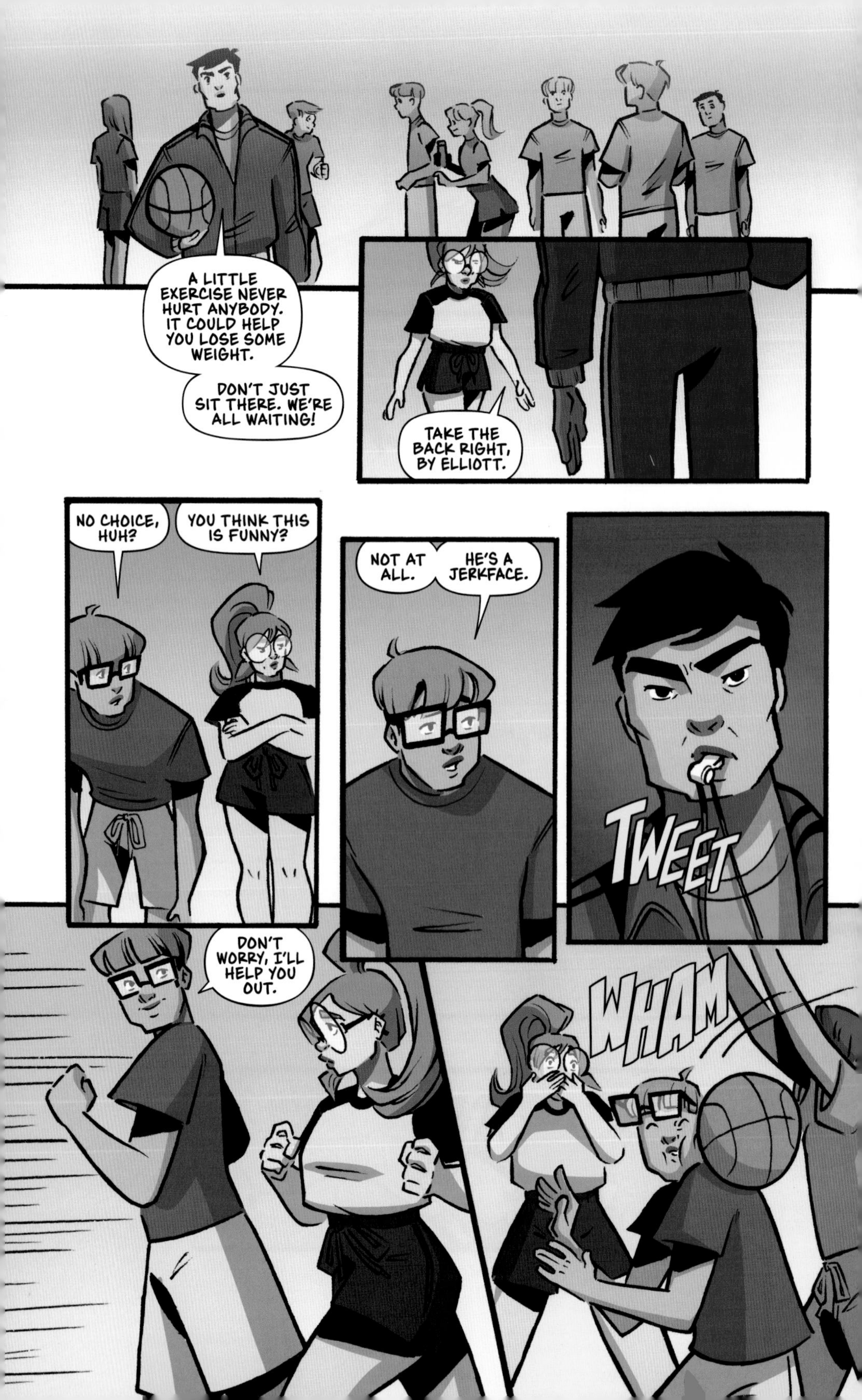

A LITTLE EXERCISE NEVER HURT ANYBODY. IT COULD HELP YOU LOSE SOME WEIGHT.
DON'T JUST SIT THERE. WE'RE ALL WAITING!
TAKE THE BACK RIGHT, BY ELLIOTT.
NO CHOICE, HUH?
YOU THINK THIS IS FUNNY?
NOT AT ALL.
HE'S A JERKFACE.
TWEET
DON'T WORRY, I'LL HELP YOU OUT.
WHAM

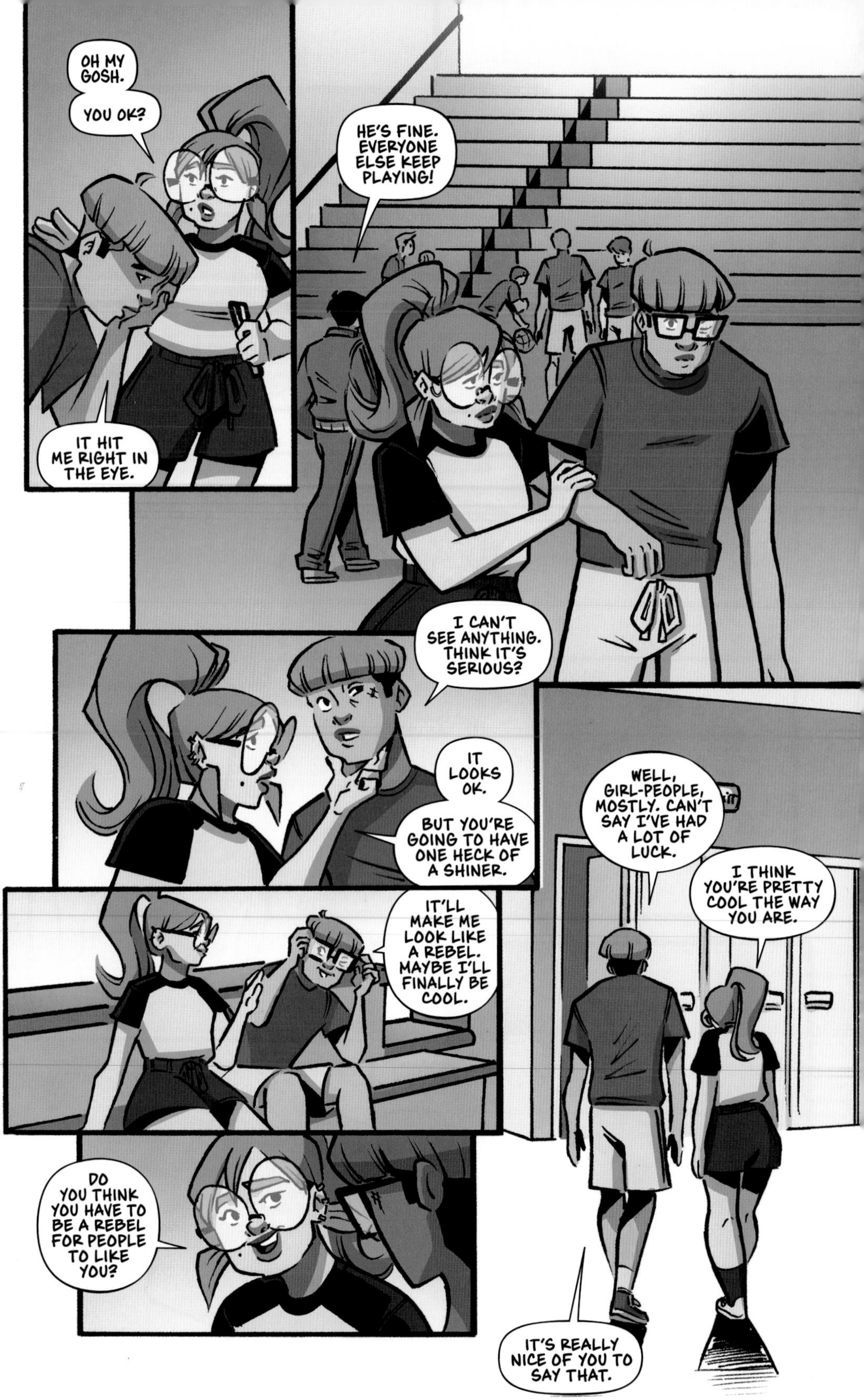
OH MY GOSH.
YOU OK?
IT HIT ME RIGHT IN THE EYE.
HE'S FINE. EVERYONE ELSE KEEP PLAYING!
I CAN'T SEE ANYTHING. THINK IT'S SERIOUS?
IT LOOKS OK.
BUT YOU'RE GOING TO HAVE ONE HECK OF A SHINER.
IT'LL MAKE ME LOOK LIKE A REBEL. MAYBE I'LL FINALLY BE COOL.
DO YOU THINK YOU HAVE TO BE A REBEL FOR PEOPLE TO LIKE YOU?
WELL, GIRL-PEOPLE, MOSTLY. CAN'T SAY I'VE HAD A LOT OF LUCK.
I THINK YOU'RE PRETTY COOL THE WAY YOU ARE.
IT'S REALLY NICE OF YOU TO SAY THAT.

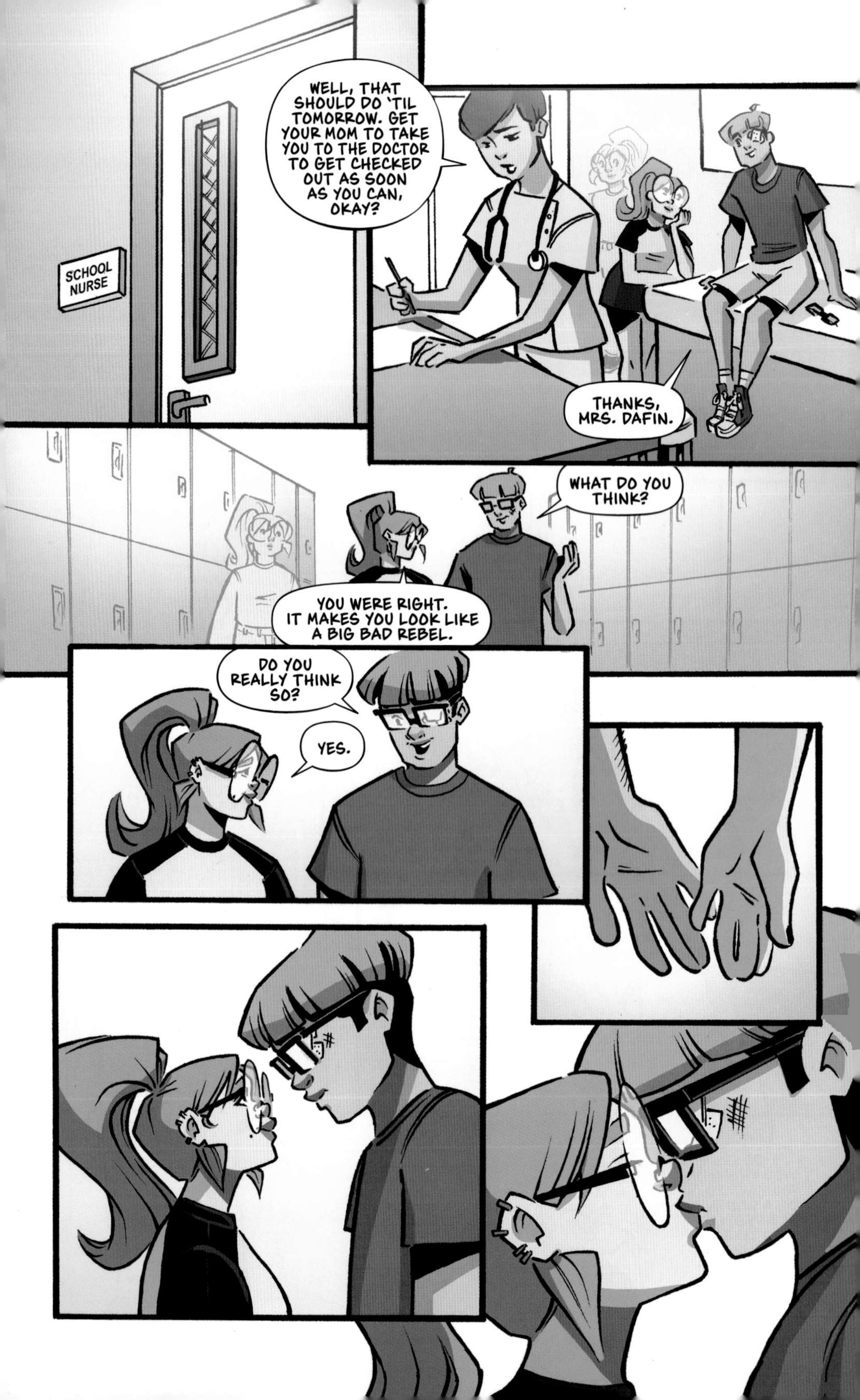
SCHOOL NURSE
WELL, THAT SHOULD DO 'TIL TOMORROW. GET YOUR MOM TO TAKE YOU TO THE DOCTOR TO GET CHECKED OUT AS SOON AS YOU CAN, OKAY?
THANKS, MRS. DAFIN.
WHAT DO YOU THINK?
YOU WERE RIGHT. IT MAKES YOU LOOK LIKE A BIG BAD REBEL.
DO YOU REALLY THINK SO?
YES.

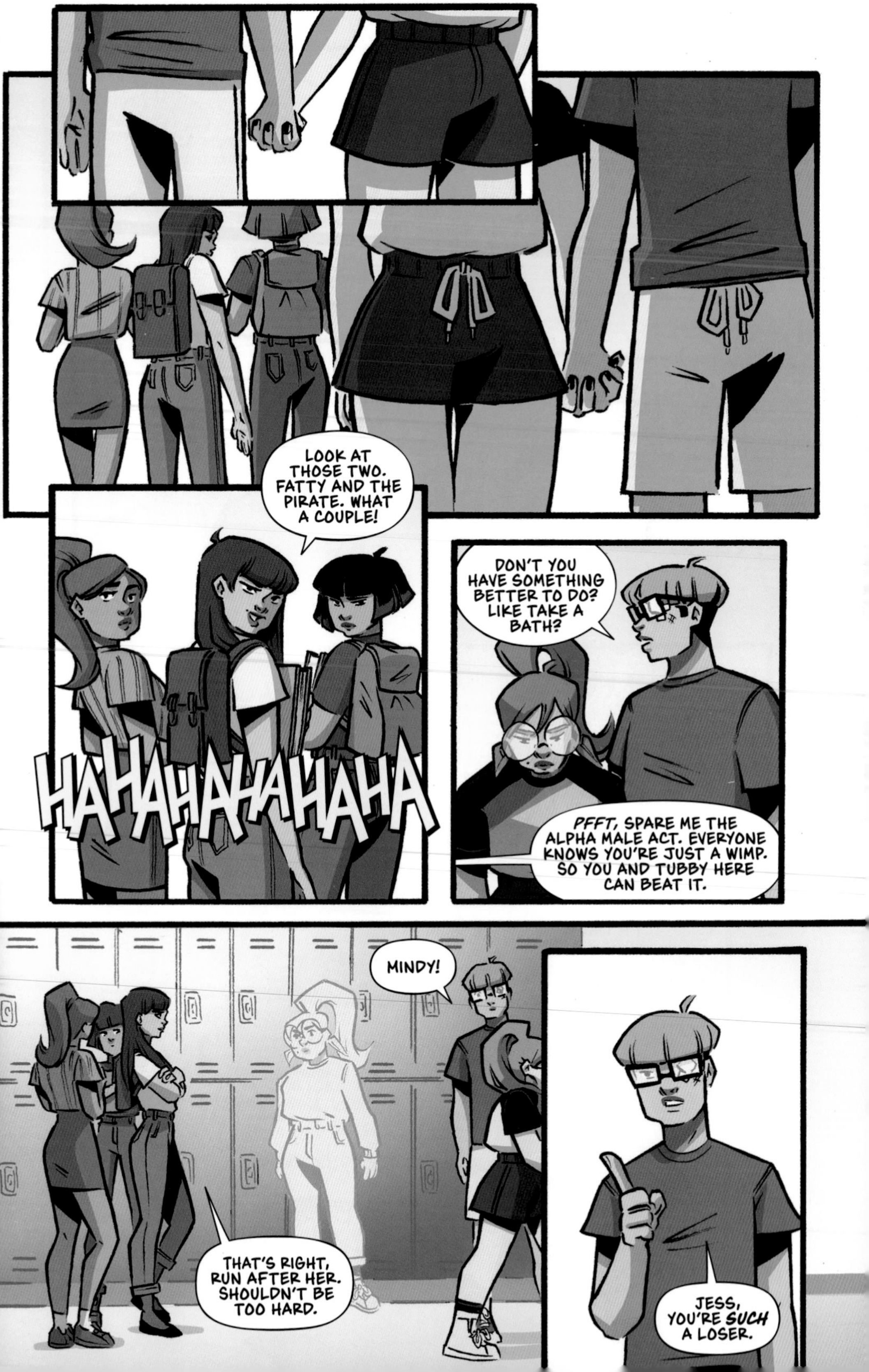
LOOK AT THOSE TWO. FATTY AND THE PIRATE. WHAT A COUPLE!
HAHAHAHAHAHAHA
DON'T YOU HAVE SOMETHING BETTER TO DO? LIKE TAKE A BATH?
PFFT, SPARE ME THE ALPHA MALE ACT. EVERYONE KNOWS YOU'RE JUST A WIMP. SO YOU AND TUBBY HERE CAN BEAT IT.
MINDY!
THAT'S RIGHT, RUN AFTER HER. SHOULDN'T BE TOO HARD.
JESS, YOU'RE SUCH A LOSER.

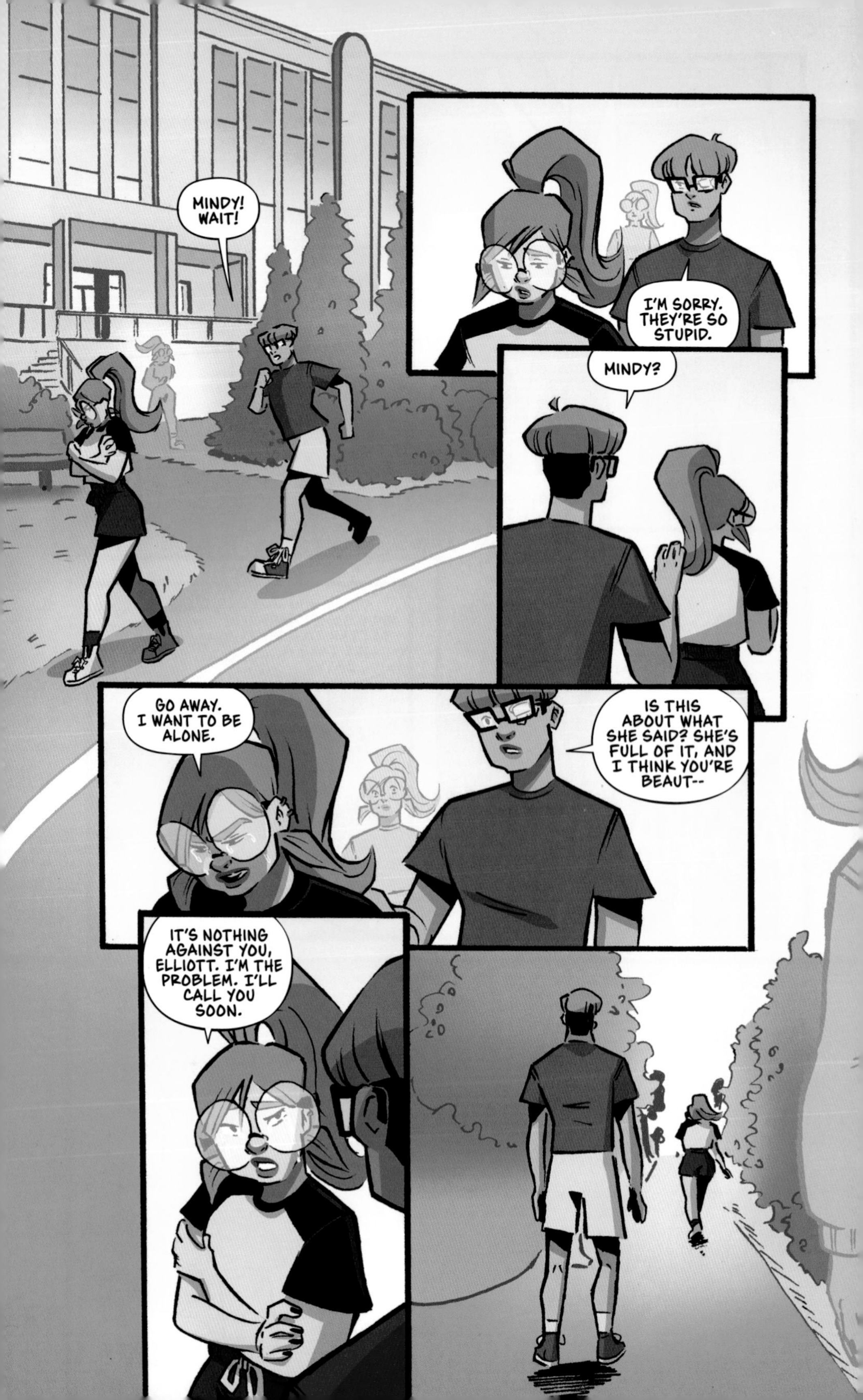
MINDY! WAIT!
I'M SORRY. THEY'RE SO STUPID.
MINDY?
GO AWAY. I WANT TO BE ALONE.
IS THIS ABOUT WHAT SHE SAID? SHE'S FULL OF IT, AND I THINK YOU'RE BEAUT--
IT'S NOTHING AGAINST YOU, ELLIOTT. I'M THE PROBLEM. I'LL CALL YOU SOON.

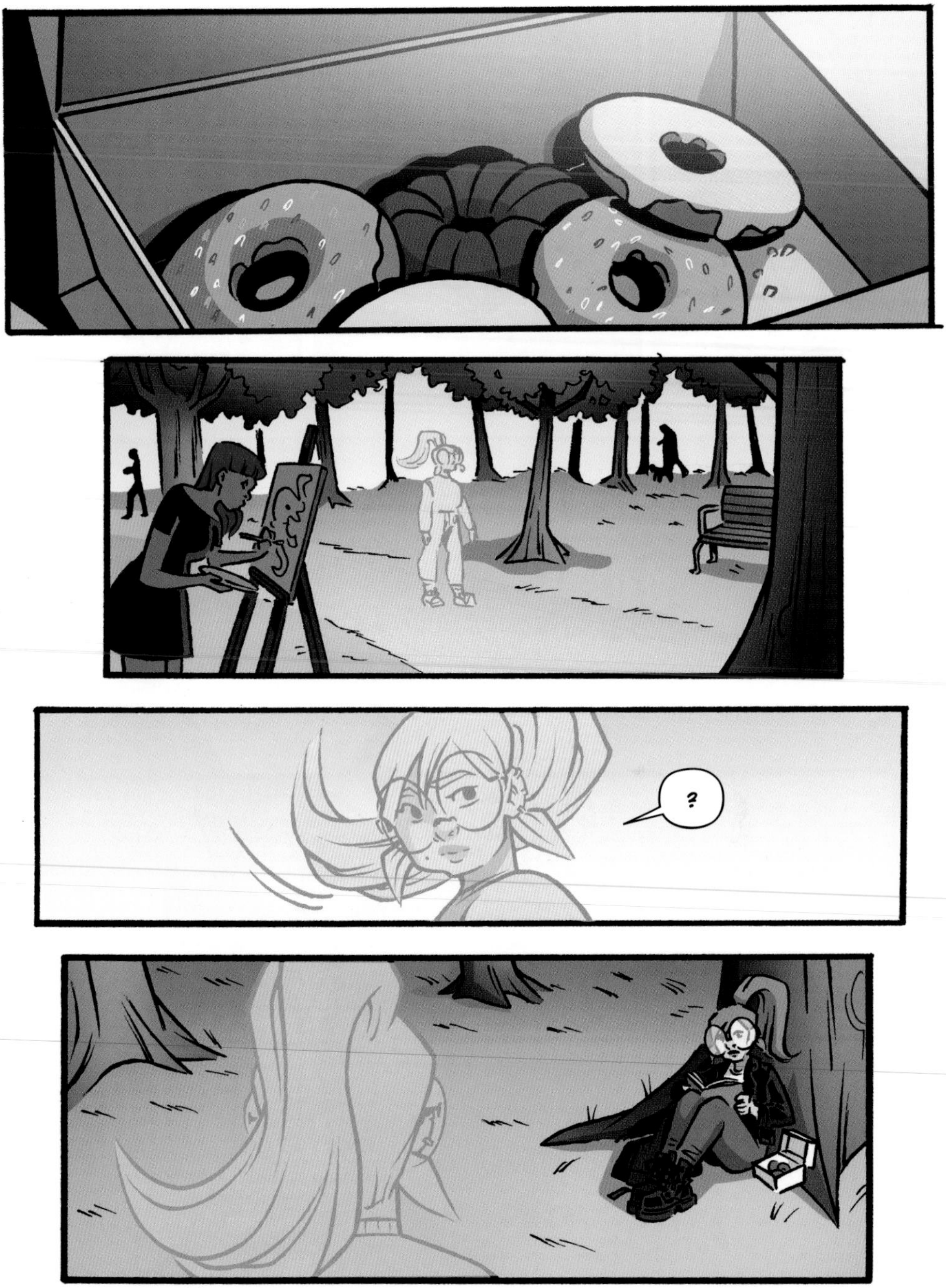
?

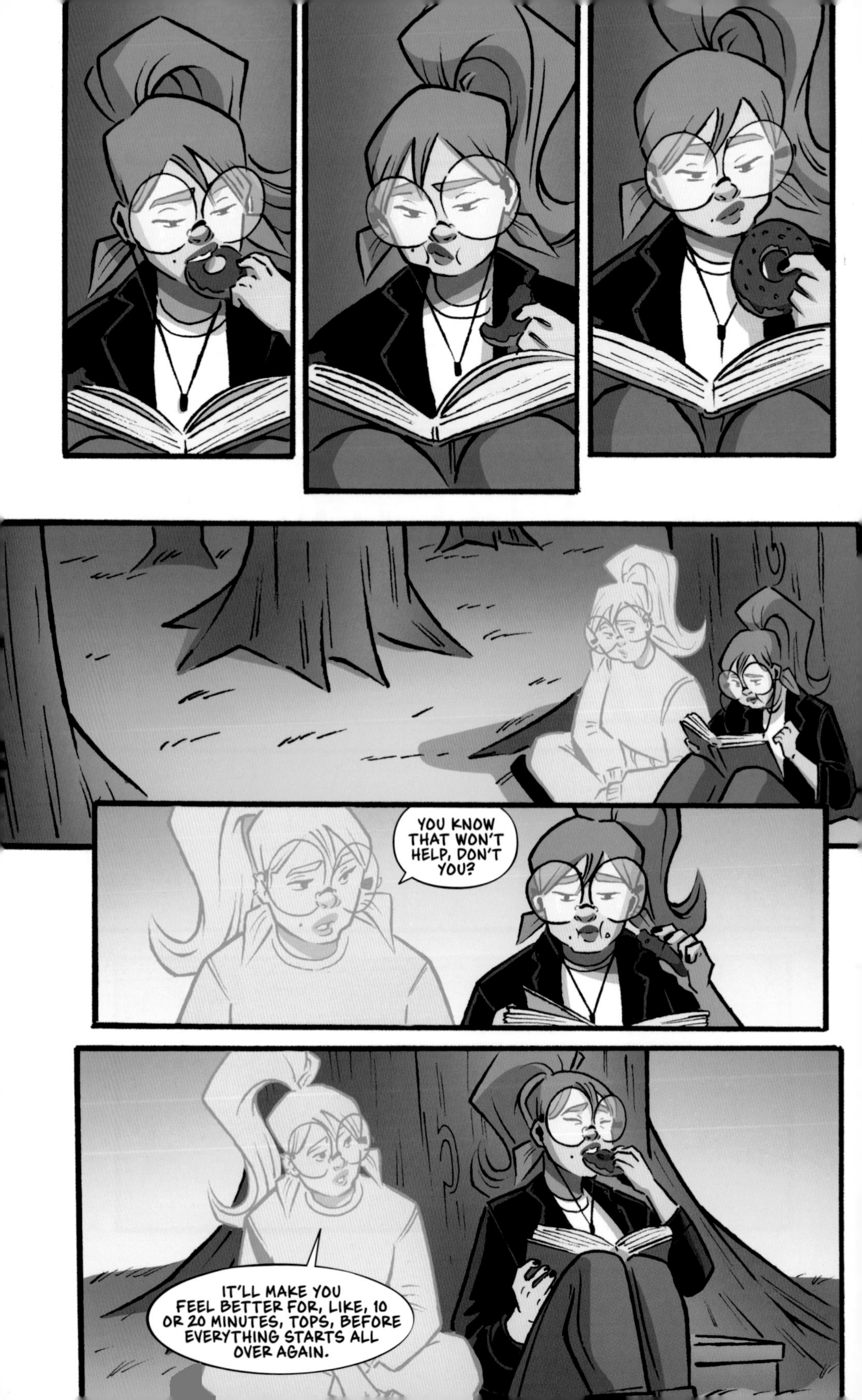
YOU KNOW THAT WON'T HELP, DON'T YOU?
IT'LL MAKE YOU FEEL BETTER FOR, LIKE, 10 OR 20 MINUTES, TOPS, BEFORE EVERYTHING STARTS ALL OVER AGAIN.

CAN YOU HEAR ME, MINDY?
SIGH
NO, OF COURSE YOU CAN'T.
WHAT'S THE POINT OF SEEING YOU IF I CAN'T TALK TO YOU?
SOMEONE EXPLAIN THAT.
IF I COULD JUST TALK TO YOU, I'D TELL YOU THIS DOESN'T MAKE ANYTHING BETTER. THAT IT'S JUST A DOWNWARD SPIRAL YOU CAN'T GET OUT OF. YOU JUST KEEP DOING THE SAME THINGS OVER AND OVER.
EATING WON'T FILL THAT HOLE, YOU KNOW? IT'LL JUST MAKE THE VOID INSIDE YOU BIGGER, AND YOUR NEED TO FILL IT STRONGER.

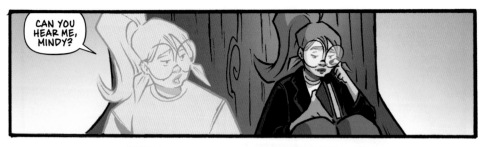

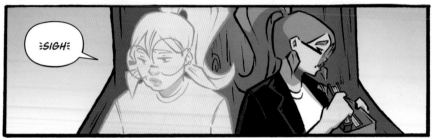

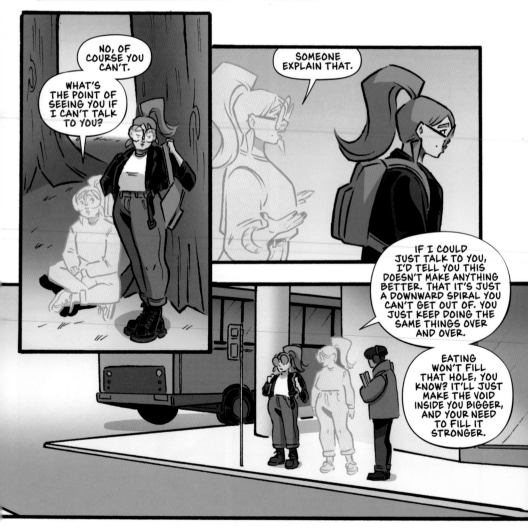

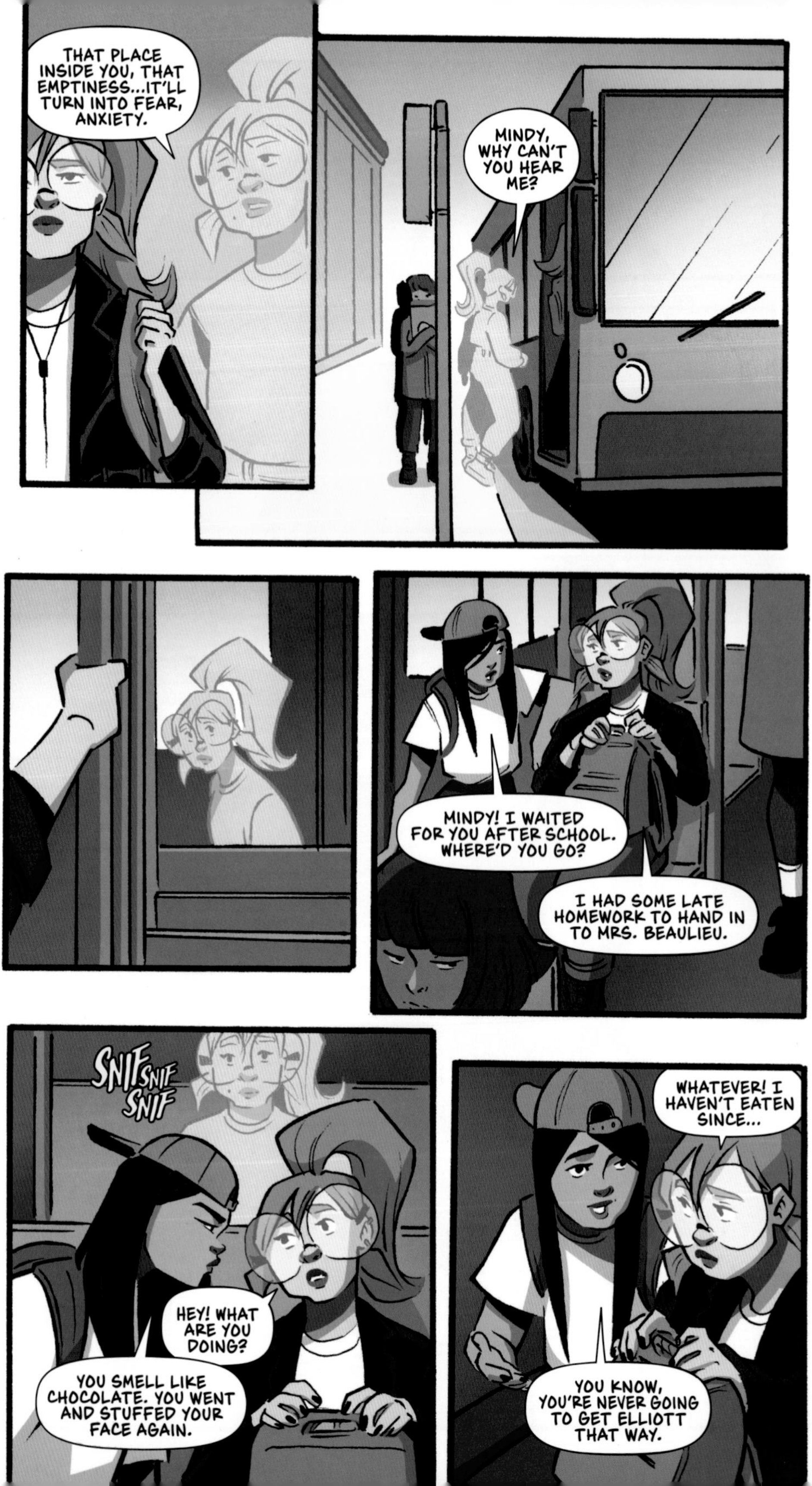
THAT PLACE INSIDE YOU, THAT EMPTINESS...IT'LL TURN INTO FEAR, ANXIETY.
MINDY, WHY CAN'T YOU HEAR ME?
MINDY! I WAITED FOR YOU AFTER SCHOOL. WHERE'D YOU GO?
I HAD SOME LATE HOMEWORK TO HAND IN TO MRS. BEAULIEU.
SNIF SNIF SNIF
HEY! WHAT ARE YOU DOING?
YOU SMELL LIKE CHOCOLATE. YOU WENT AND STUFFED YOUR FACE AGAIN.
WHATEVER! I HAVEN'T EATEN SINCE...
YOU KNOW, YOU'RE NEVER GOING TO GET ELLIOTT THAT WAY.

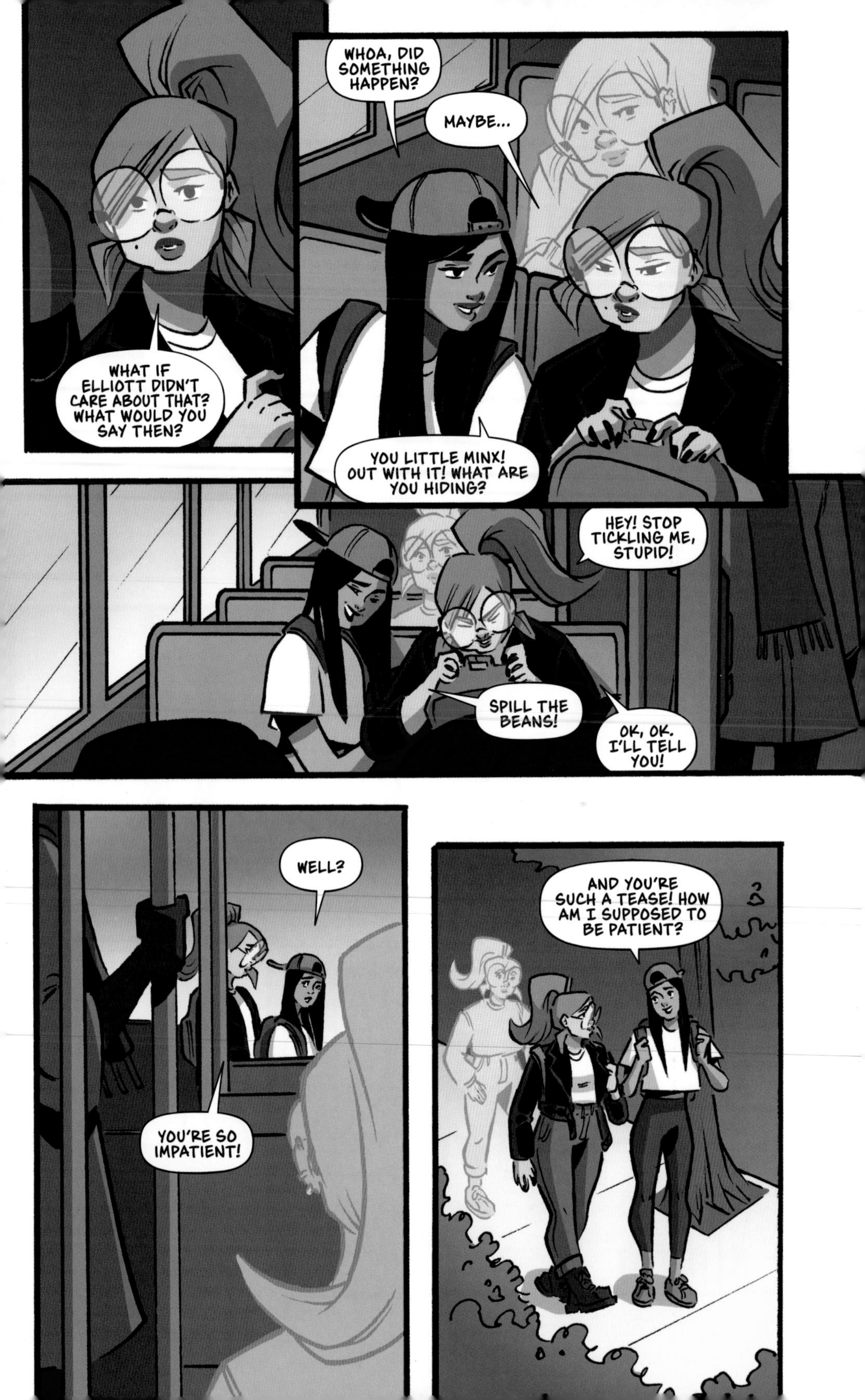
WHAT IF ELLIOTT DIDN'T CARE ABOUT THAT? WHAT WOULD YOU SAY THEN?
WHOA, DID SOMETHING HAPPEN?
MAYBE...
YOU LITTLE MINX! OUT WITH IT! WHAT ARE YOU HIDING?
HEY! STOP TICKLING ME, STUPID!
SPILL THE BEANS!
OK, OK. I'LL TELL YOU!
WELL?
YOU'RE SO IMPATIENT!
AND YOU'RE SUCH A TEASE! HOW AM I SUPPOSED TO BE PATIENT?

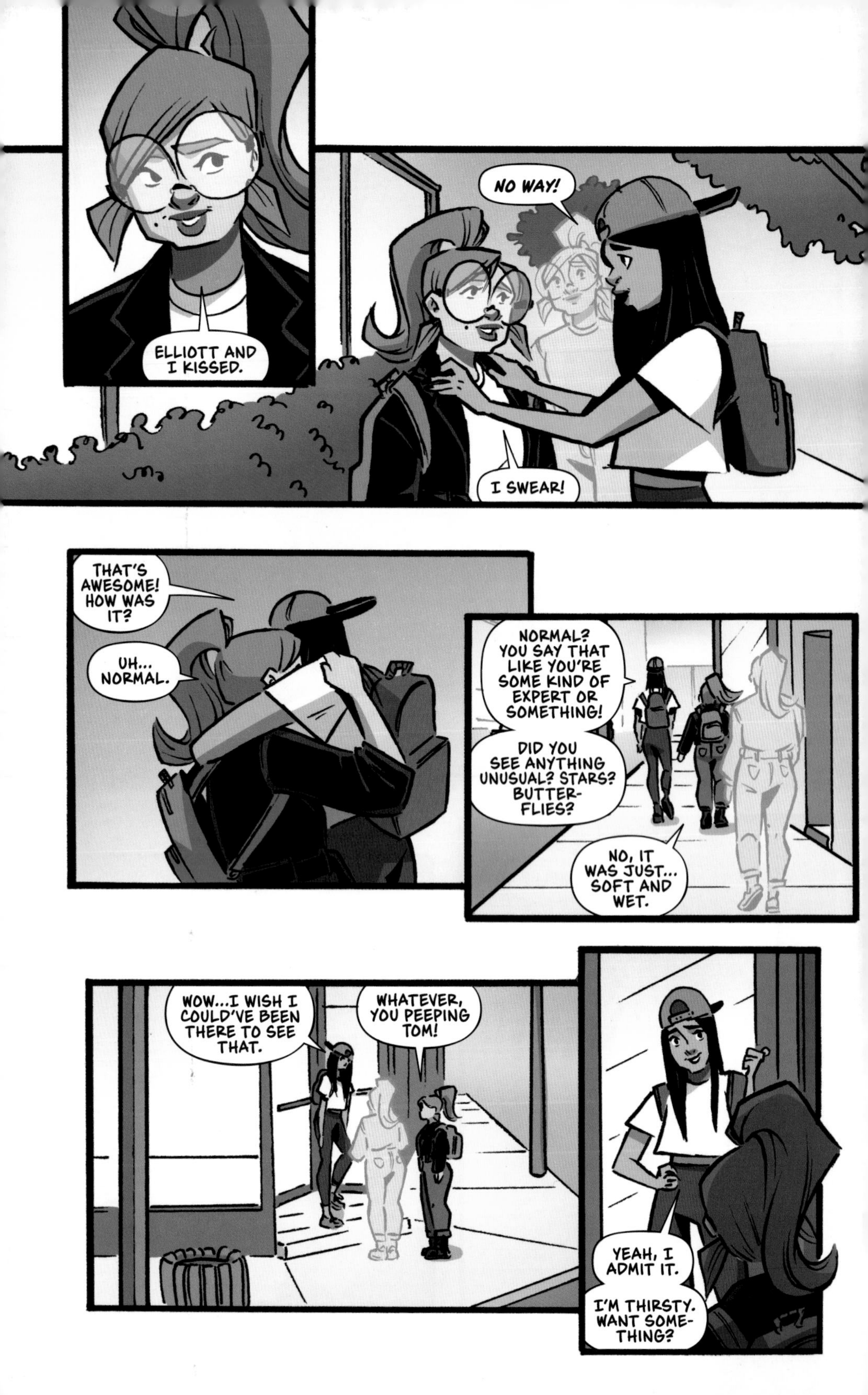
ELLIOTT AND I KISSED.
NO WAY!
I SWEAR!
THAT'S AWESOME! HOW WAS IT?
UH... NORMAL.
NORMAL? YOU SAY THAT LIKE YOU'RE SOME KIND OF EXPERT OR SOMETHING!
DID YOU SEE ANYTHING UNUSUAL? STARS? BUTTER-FLIES?
NO, IT WAS JUST... SOFT AND WET.
WOW...I WISH I COULD'VE BEEN THERE TO SEE THAT.
WHATEVER, YOU PEEPING TOM!
YEAH, I ADMIT IT.
I'M THIRSTY. WANT SOME-THING?

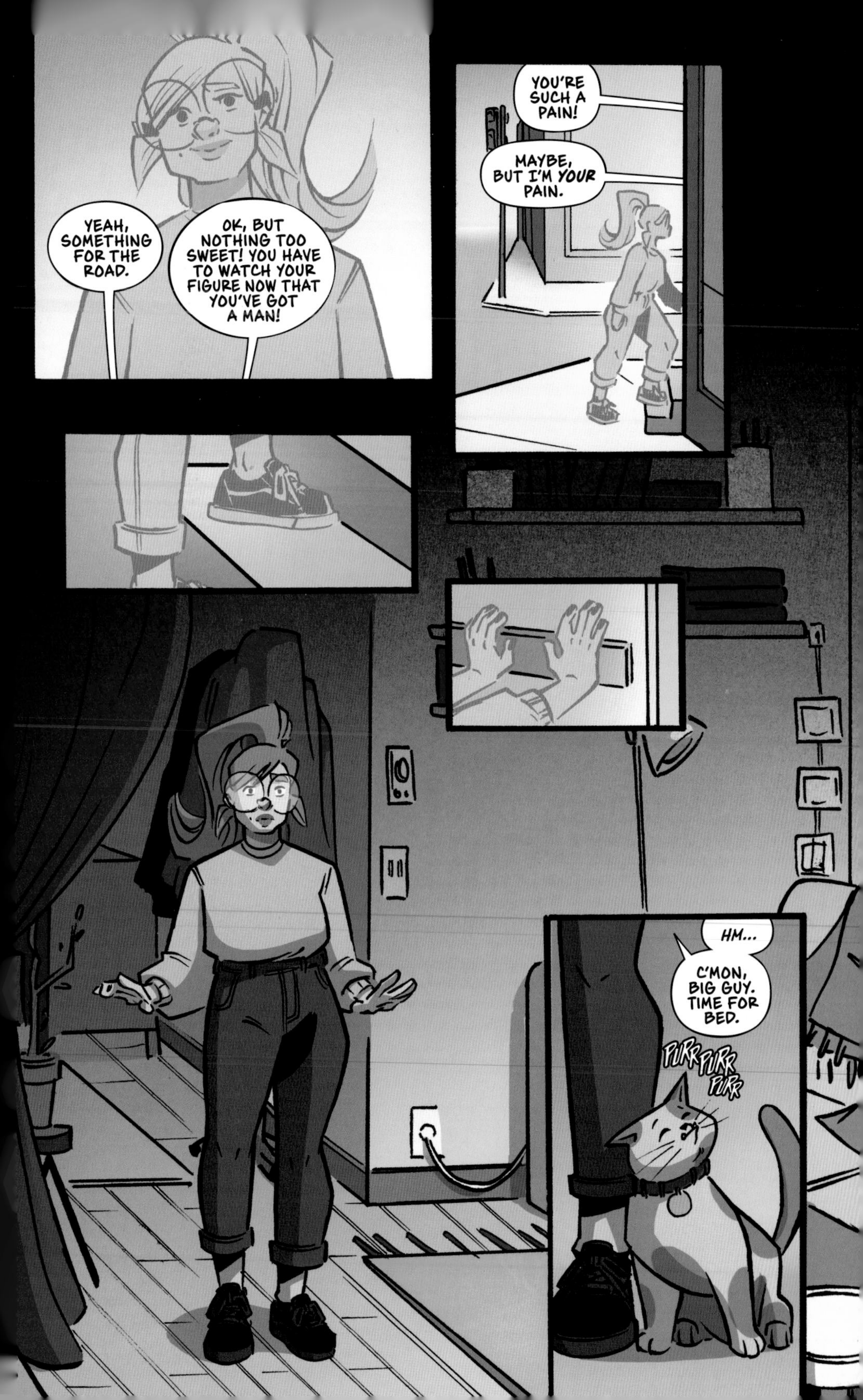
YEAH, SOMETHING FOR THE ROAD.
OK, BUT NOTHING TOO SWEET! YOU HAVE TO WATCH YOUR FIGURE NOW THAT YOU'VE GOT A MAN!
YOU'RE SUCH A PAIN!
MAYBE, BUT I'M YOUR PAIN.
HM...
C'MON, BIG GUY. TIME FOR BED.
PURR PURR PURR

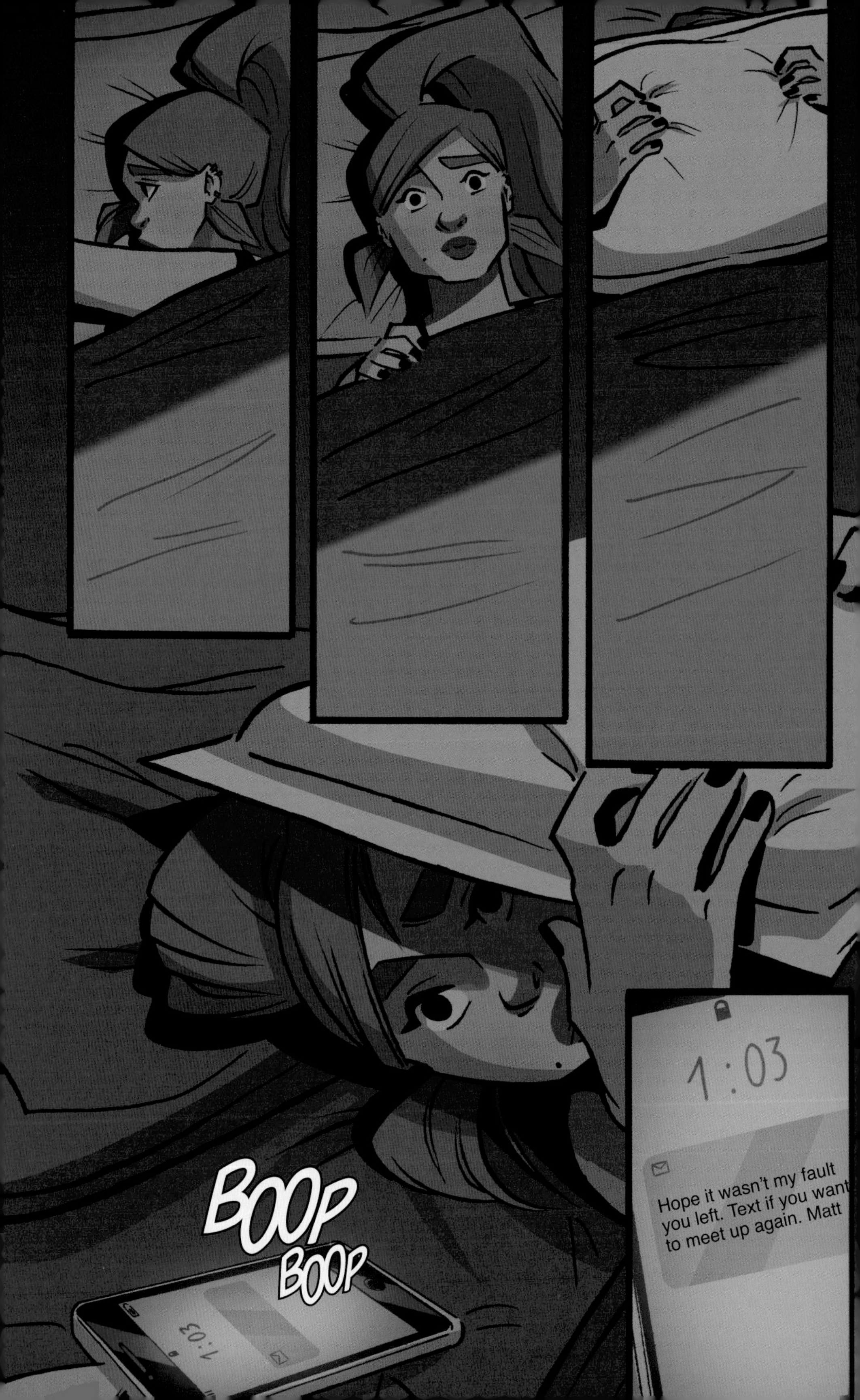
BOOP
BOOP
1:03
Hope it wasn't my fault you left. Text if you want to meet up again. Matt

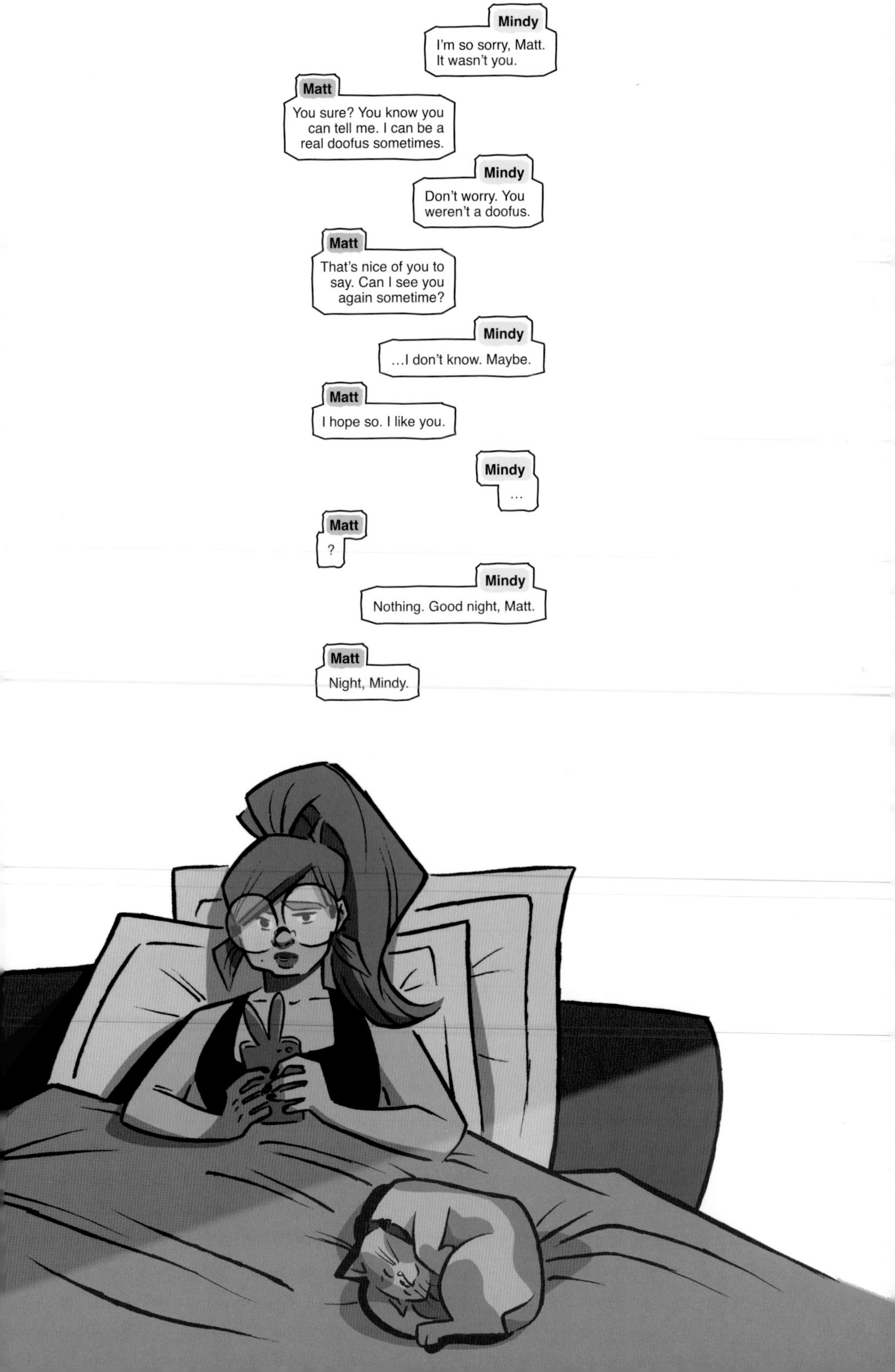
Mindy
I'm so sorry, Matt. It wasn't you.
Matt
You sure? You know you can tell me. I can be a real doofus sometimes.
Mindy
Don't worry. You weren't a doofus.
Matt
That's nice of you to say. Can I see you again sometime?
Mindy
...I don't know. Maybe.
Matt
I hope so. I like you.
Mindy
...
Matt
?
Mindy
Nothing. Good night, Matt.
Matt
Night, Mindy.

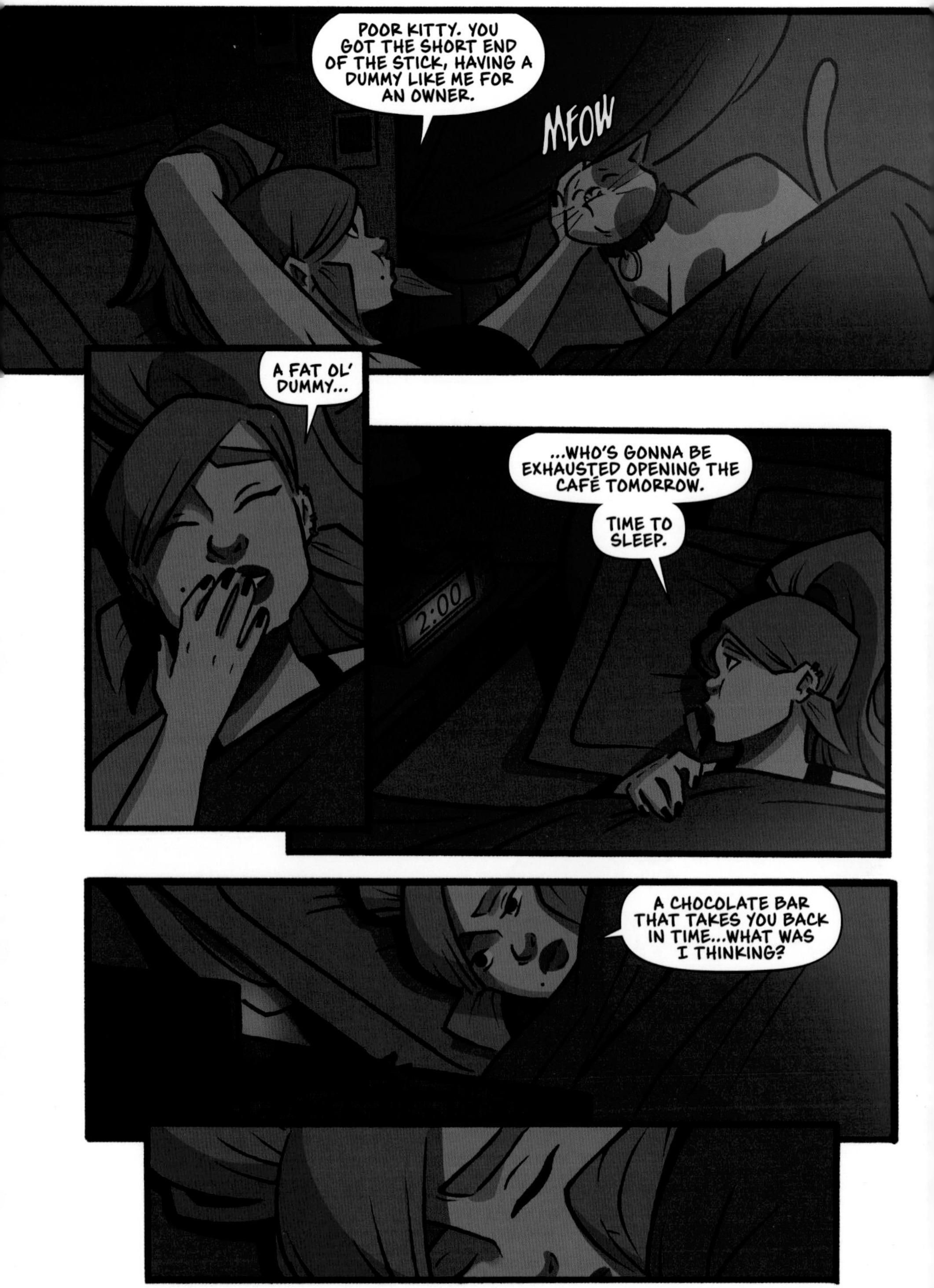
POOR KITTY. YOU GOT THE SHORT END OF THE STICK, HAVING A DUMMY LIKE ME FOR AN OWNER.
MEOW
A FAT OL' DUMMY...
...WHO'S GONNA BE EXHAUSTED OPENING THE CAFÉ TOMORROW.
TIME TO SLEEP.
2:00
A CHOCOLATE BAR THAT TAKES YOU BACK IN TIME...WHAT WAS I THINKING?

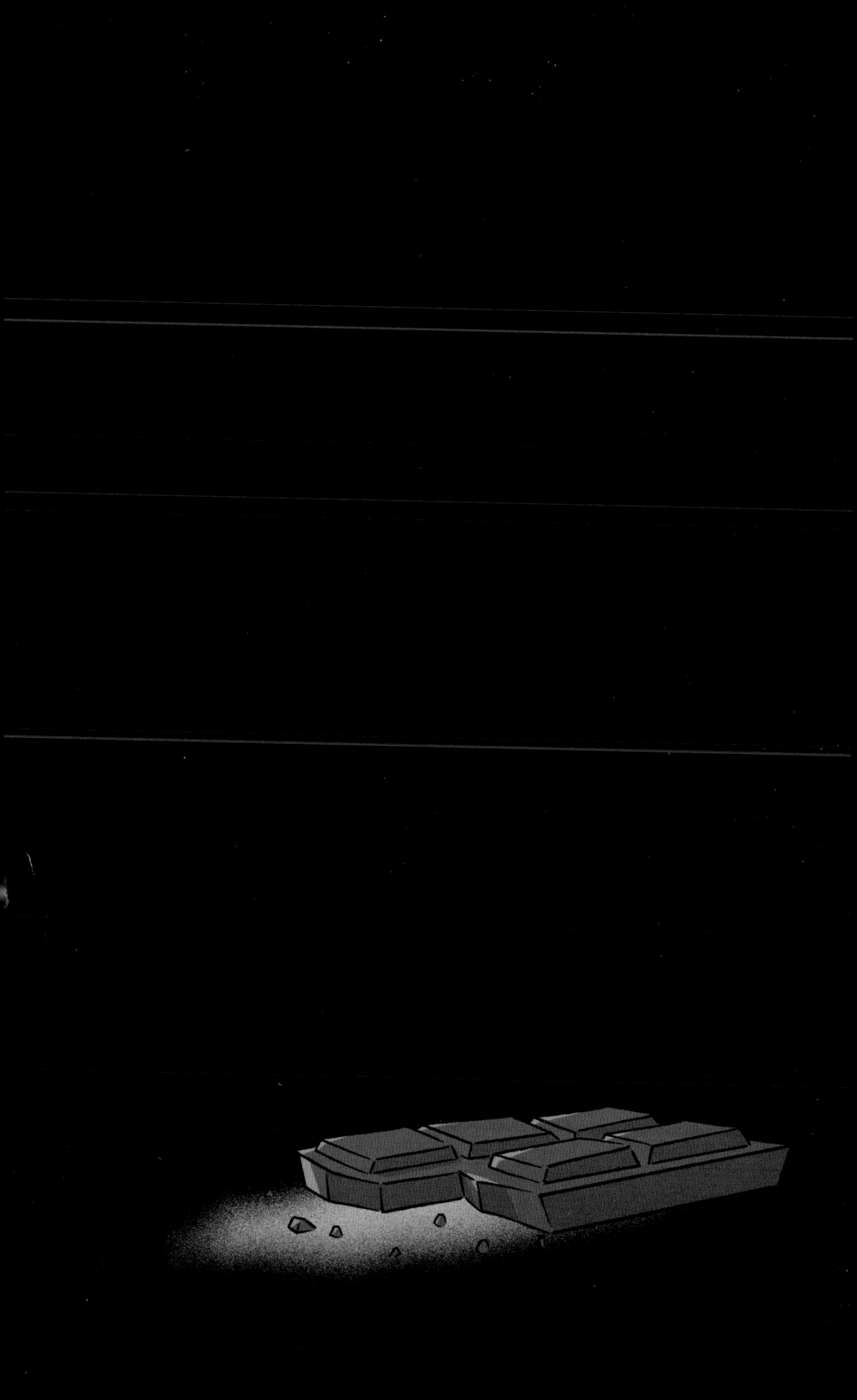

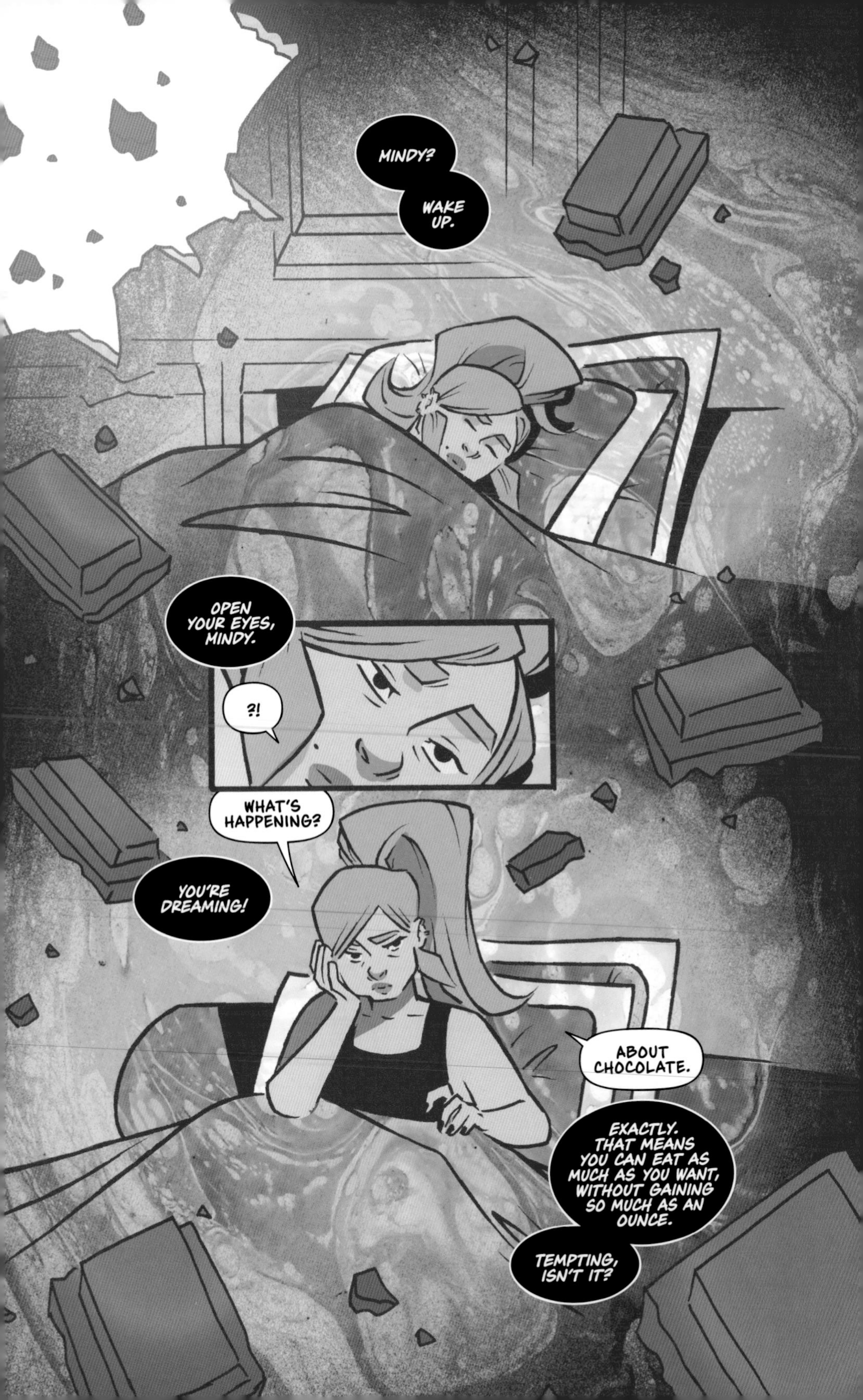
MINDY?
WAKE UP.
OPEN YOUR EYES, MINDY.
?!
WHAT'S HAPPENING?
YOU'RE DREAMING!
ABOUT CHOCOLATE.
EXACTLY. THAT MEANS YOU CAN EAT AS MUCH AS YOU WANT, WITHOUT GAINING SO MUCH AS AN OUNCE.
TEMPTING, ISN'T IT?

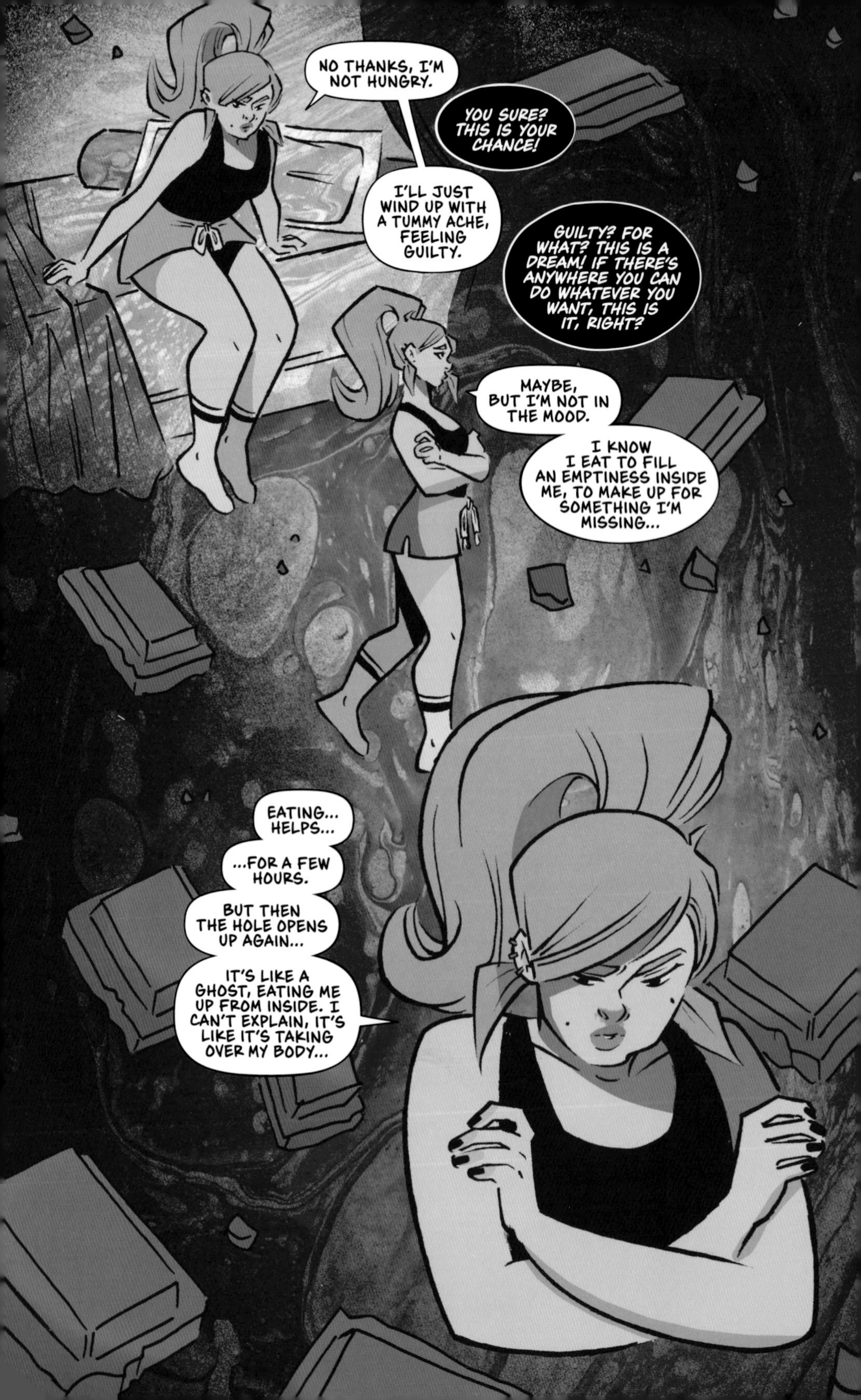
NO THANKS, I'M NOT HUNGRY.
YOU SURE? THIS IS YOUR CHANCE!
I'LL JUST WIND UP WITH A TUMMY ACHE, FEELING GUILTY.
GUILTY? FOR WHAT? THIS IS A DREAM! IF THERE'S ANYWHERE YOU CAN DO WHATEVER YOU WANT, THIS IS IT, RIGHT?
MAYBE, BUT I'M NOT IN THE MOOD.
I KNOW I EAT TO FILL AN EMPTINESS INSIDE ME, TO MAKE UP FOR SOMETHING I'M MISSING...
EATING... HELPS...
...FOR A FEW HOURS.
BUT THEN THE HOLE OPENS UP AGAIN...
IT'S LIKE A GHOST, EATING ME UP FROM INSIDE. I CAN'T EXPLAIN, IT'S LIKE IT'S TAKING OVER MY BODY...

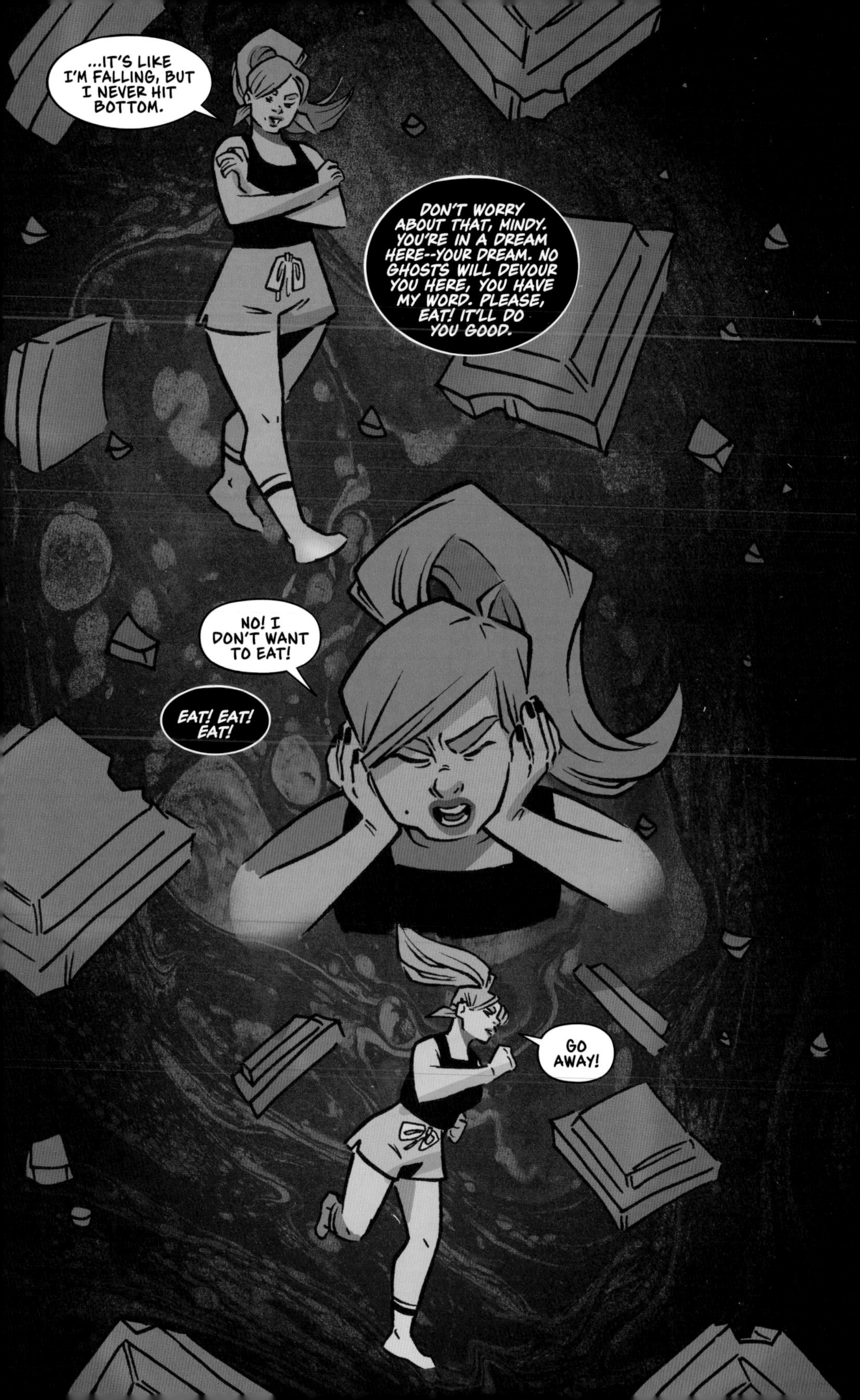
...IT'S LIKE I'M FALLING, BUT I NEVER HIT BOTTOM.
DON'T WORRY ABOUT THAT, MINDY. YOU'RE IN A DREAM HERE--YOUR DREAM. NO GHOSTS WILL DEVOUR YOU HERE, YOU HAVE MY WORD. PLEASE, EAT! IT'LL DO YOU GOOD.
NO! I DON'T WANT TO EAT!
EAT! EAT! EAT!
GO AWAY!

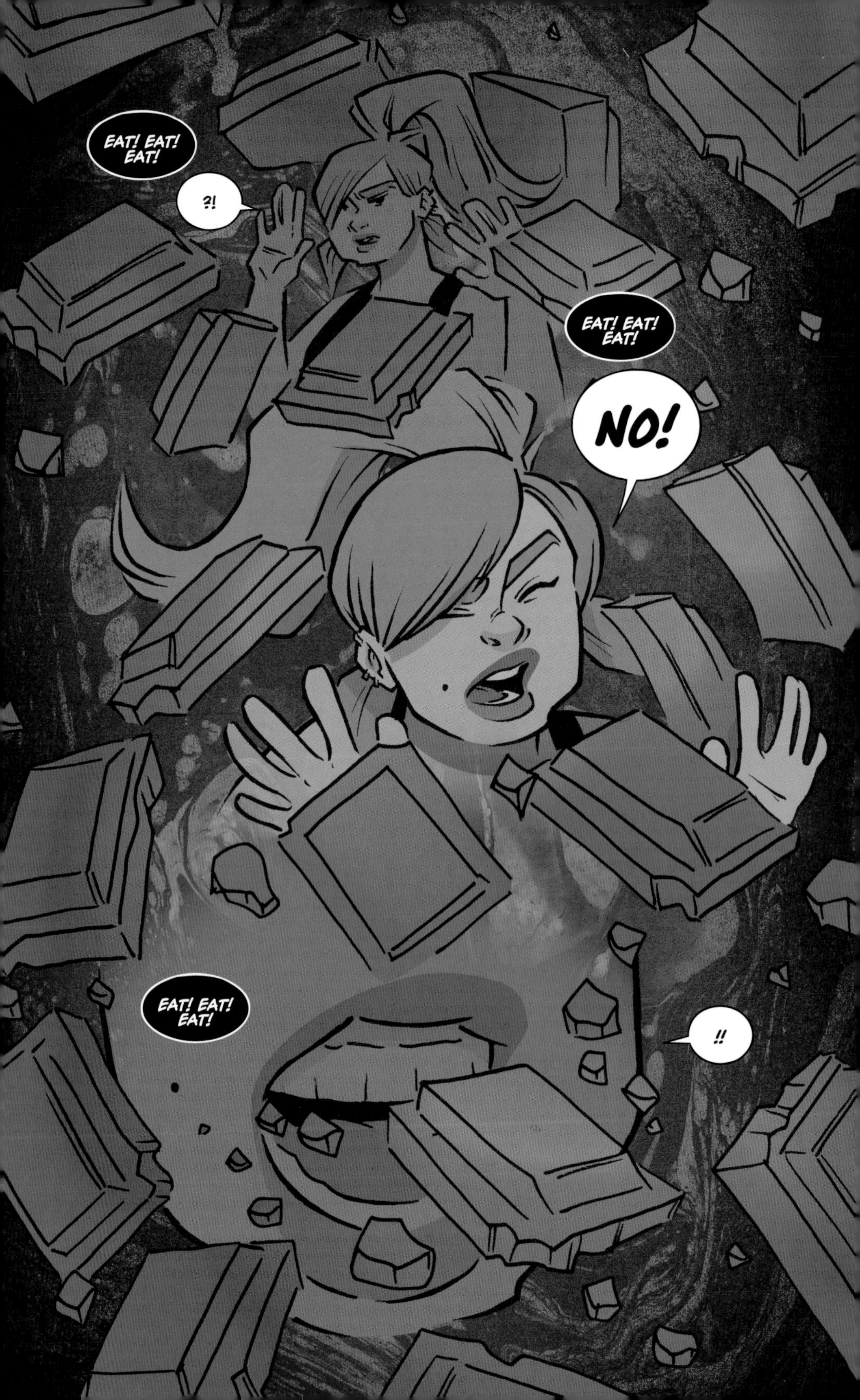
EAT! EAT! EAT!
?!
EAT! EAT! EAT!
NO!
EAT! EAT! EAT!
!!

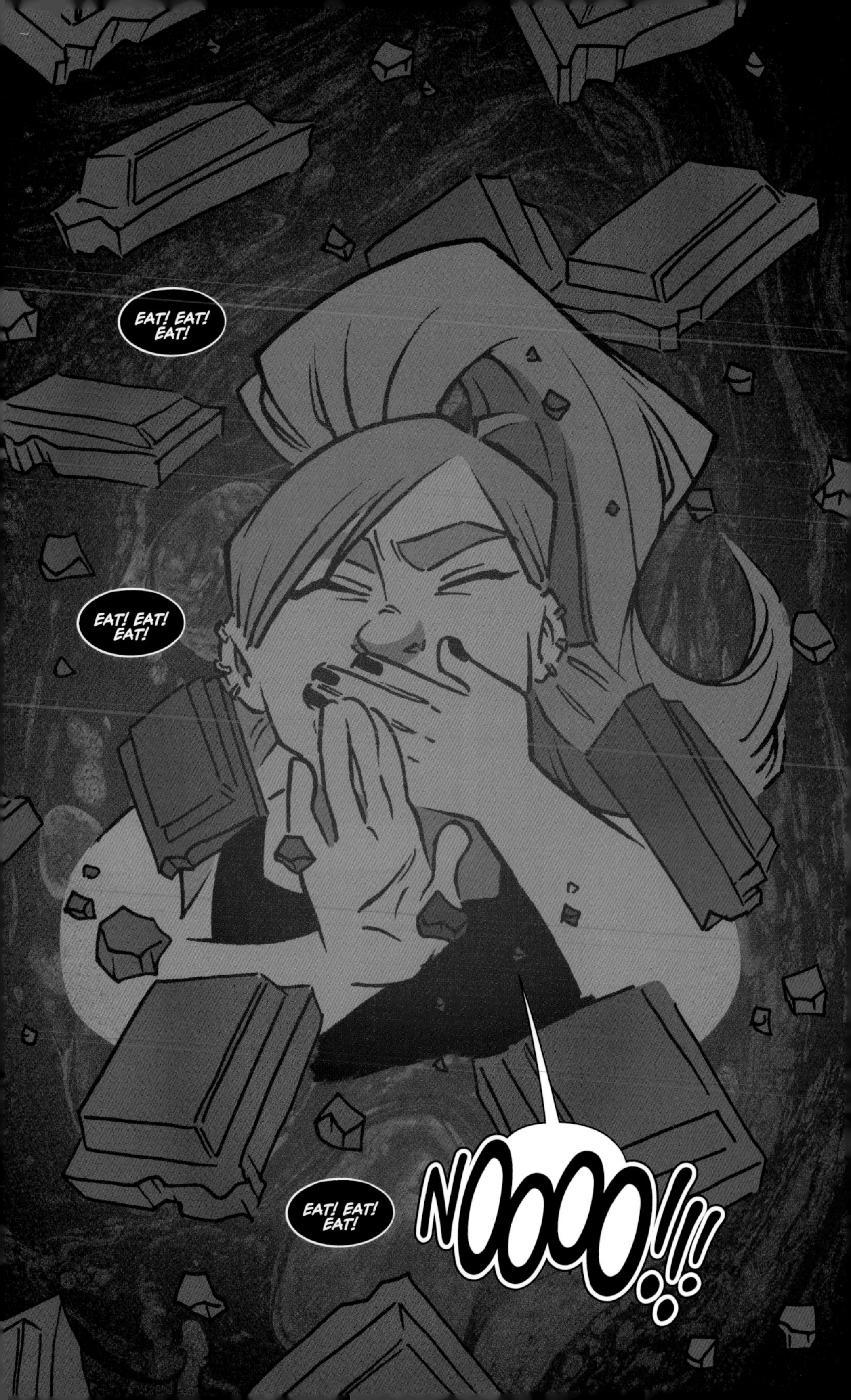
EAT! EAT! EAT!
EAT! EAT! EAT!
EAT! EAT! EAT!
NOOOO!!!

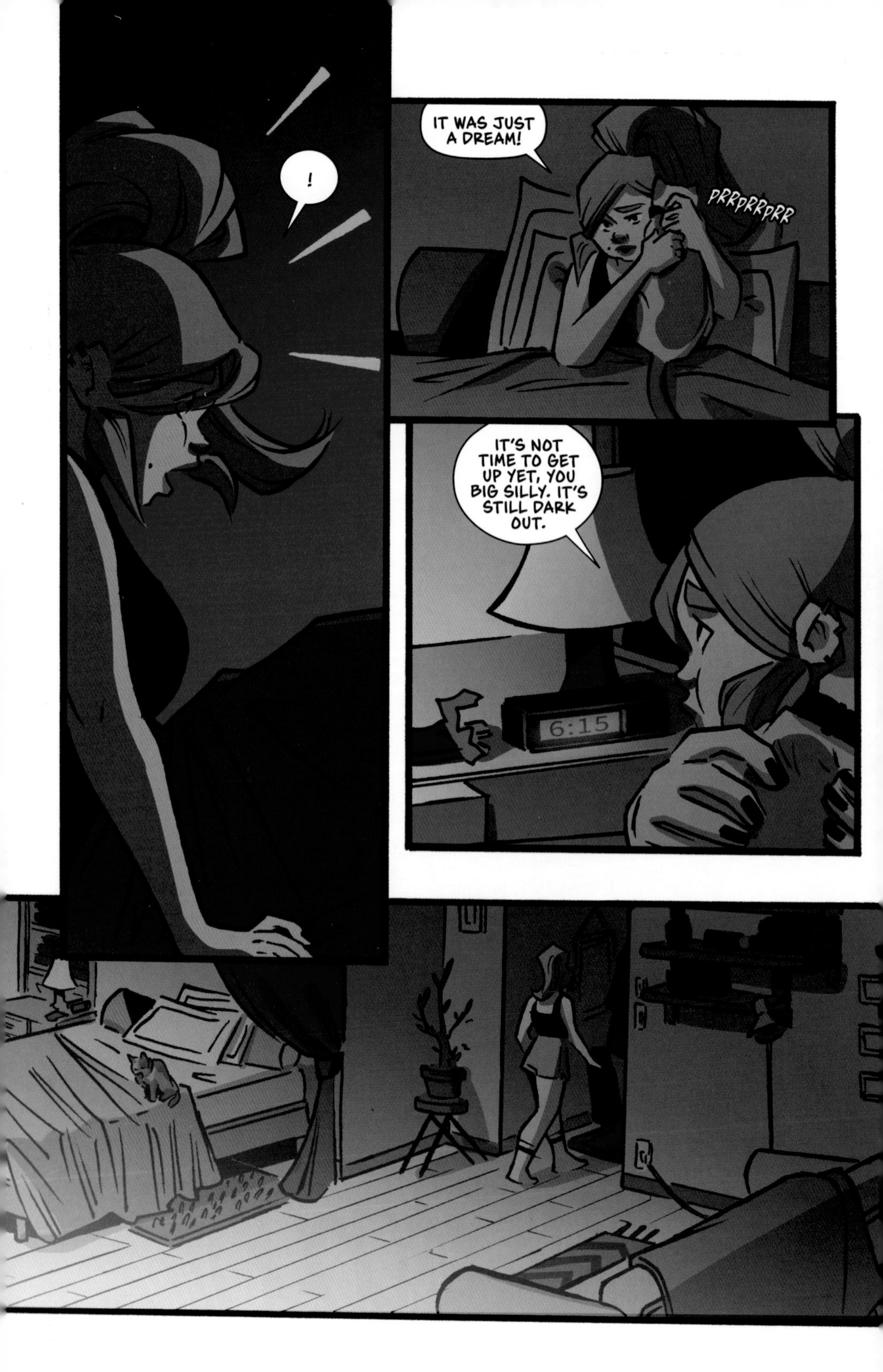
!
IT WAS JUST A DREAM!
PRRPRRPRR
IT'S NOT TIME TO GET UP YET, YOU BIG SILLY. IT'S STILL DARK OUT.
6:15

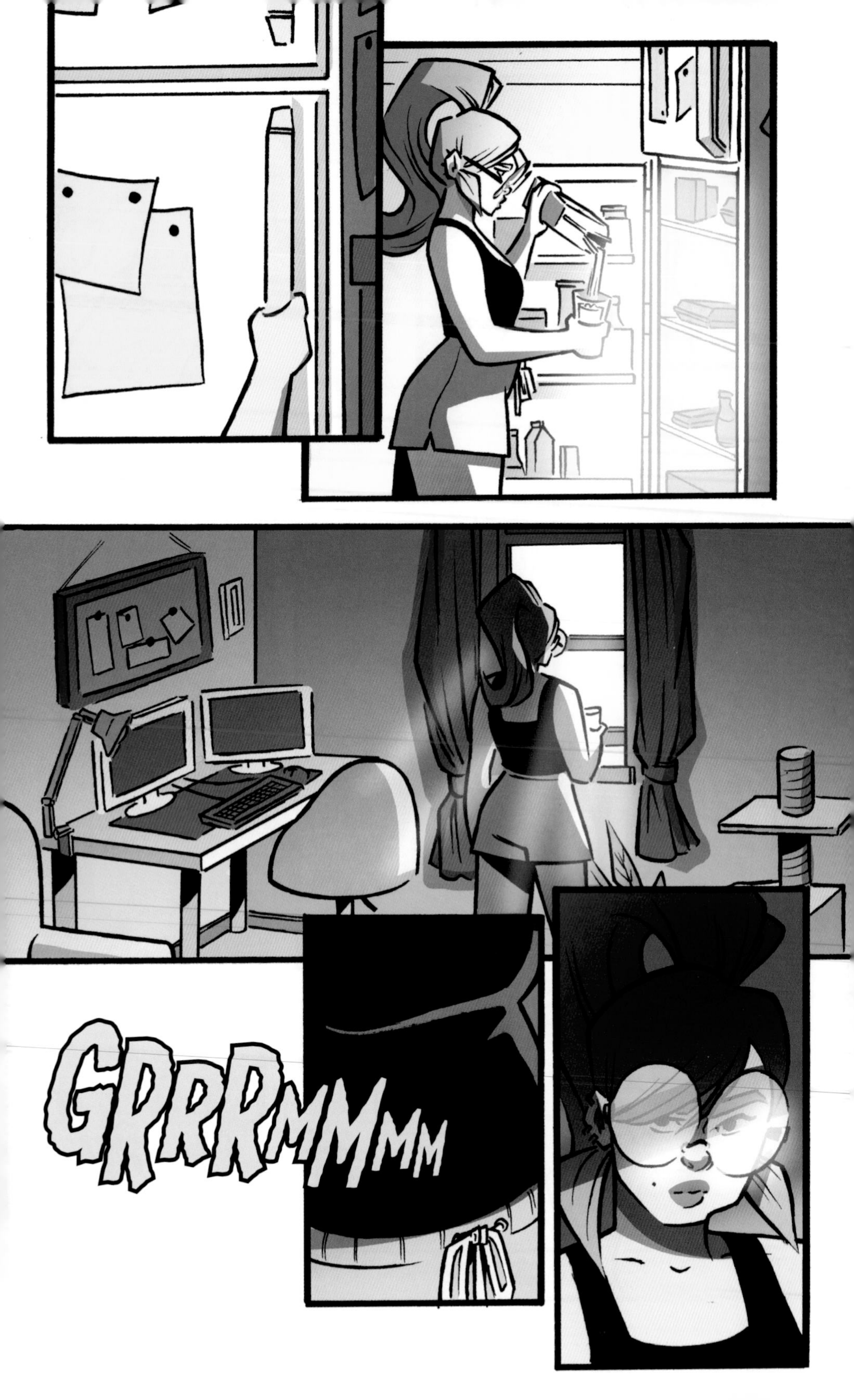
GRRRMMMMM

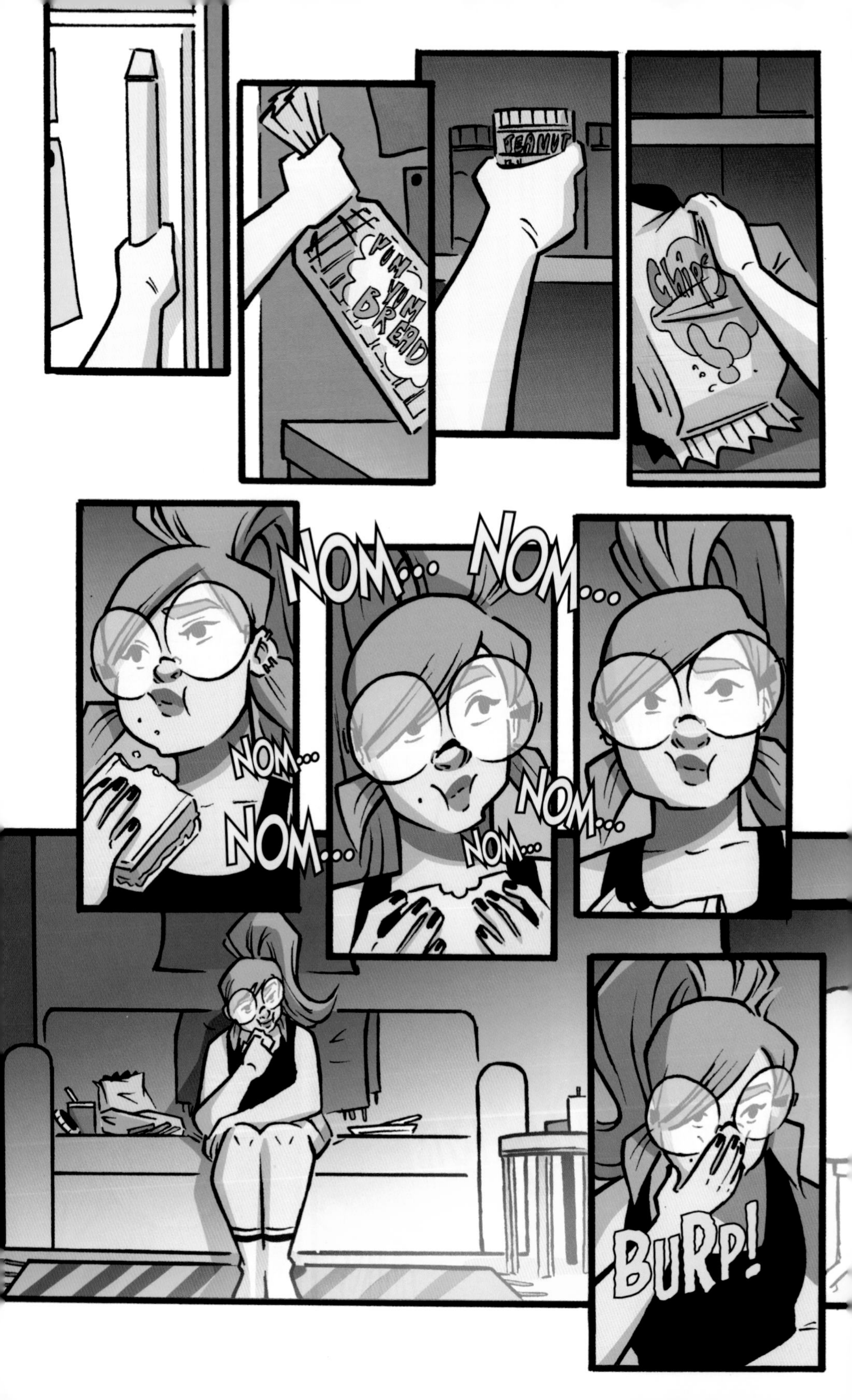
YUM YUM BREAD
PEANUT
Chips
NOM... NOM...
NOM...
NOM...
NOM...
NOM...
BURP!

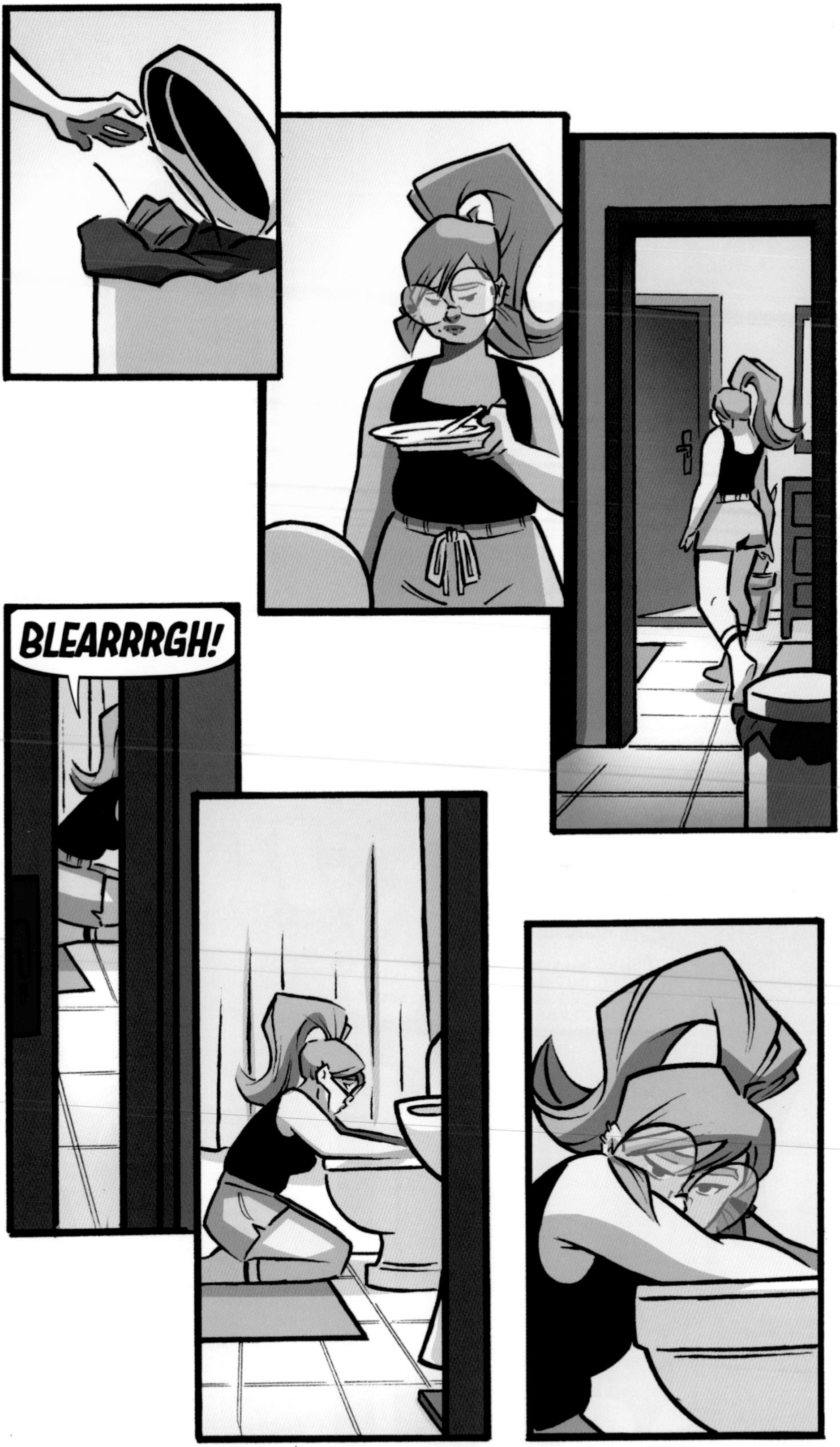
BLEARRRGH!

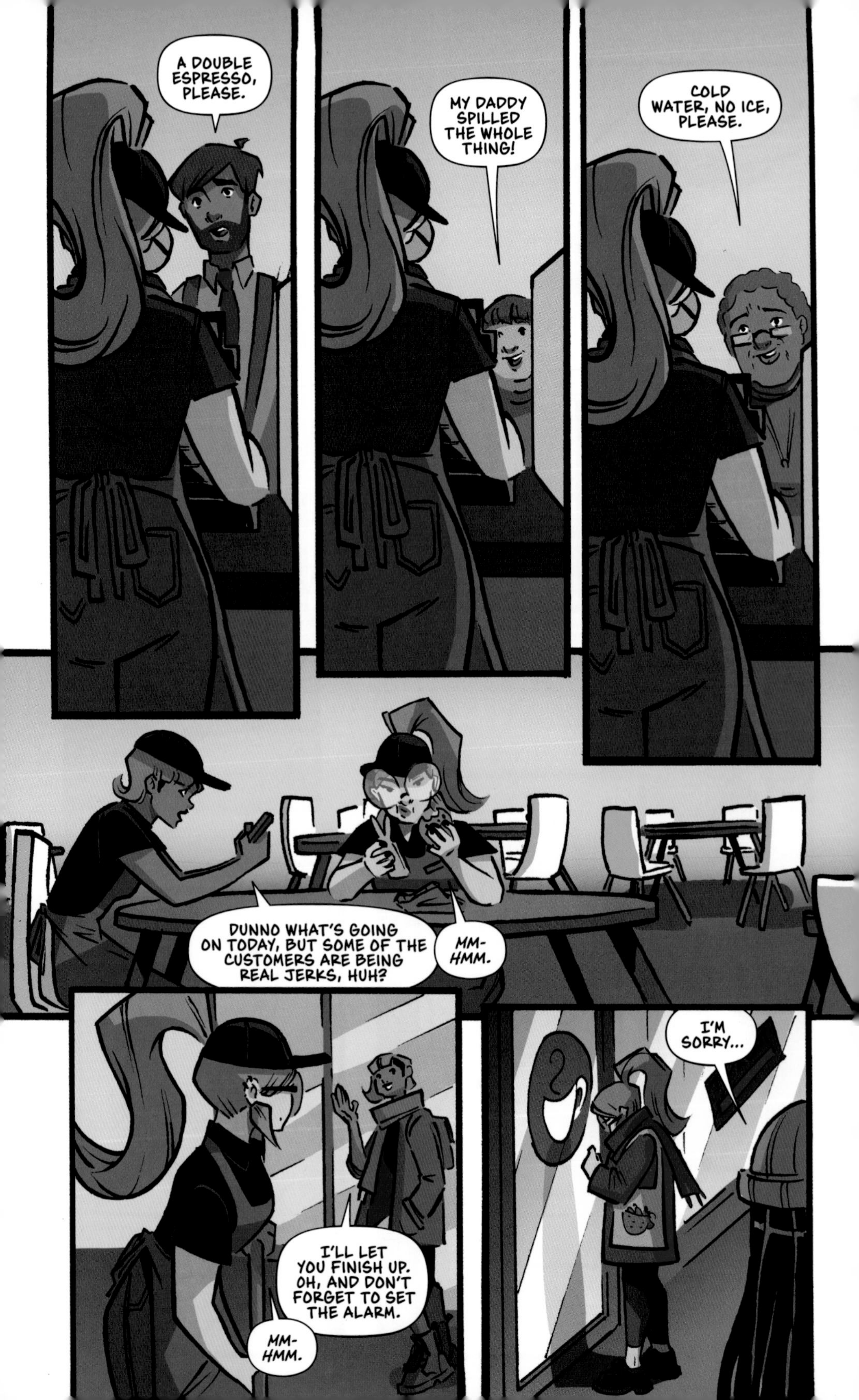
A DOUBLE ESPRESSO, PLEASE.
MY DADDY SPILLED THE WHOLE THING!
COLD WATER, NO ICE, PLEASE.
DUNNO WHAT'S GOING ON TODAY, BUT SOME OF THE CUSTOMERS ARE BEING REAL JERKS, HUH?
MM-HMM.
I'LL LET YOU FINISH UP. OH, AND DON'T FORGET TO SET THE ALARM.
MM-HMM.
I'M SORRY...

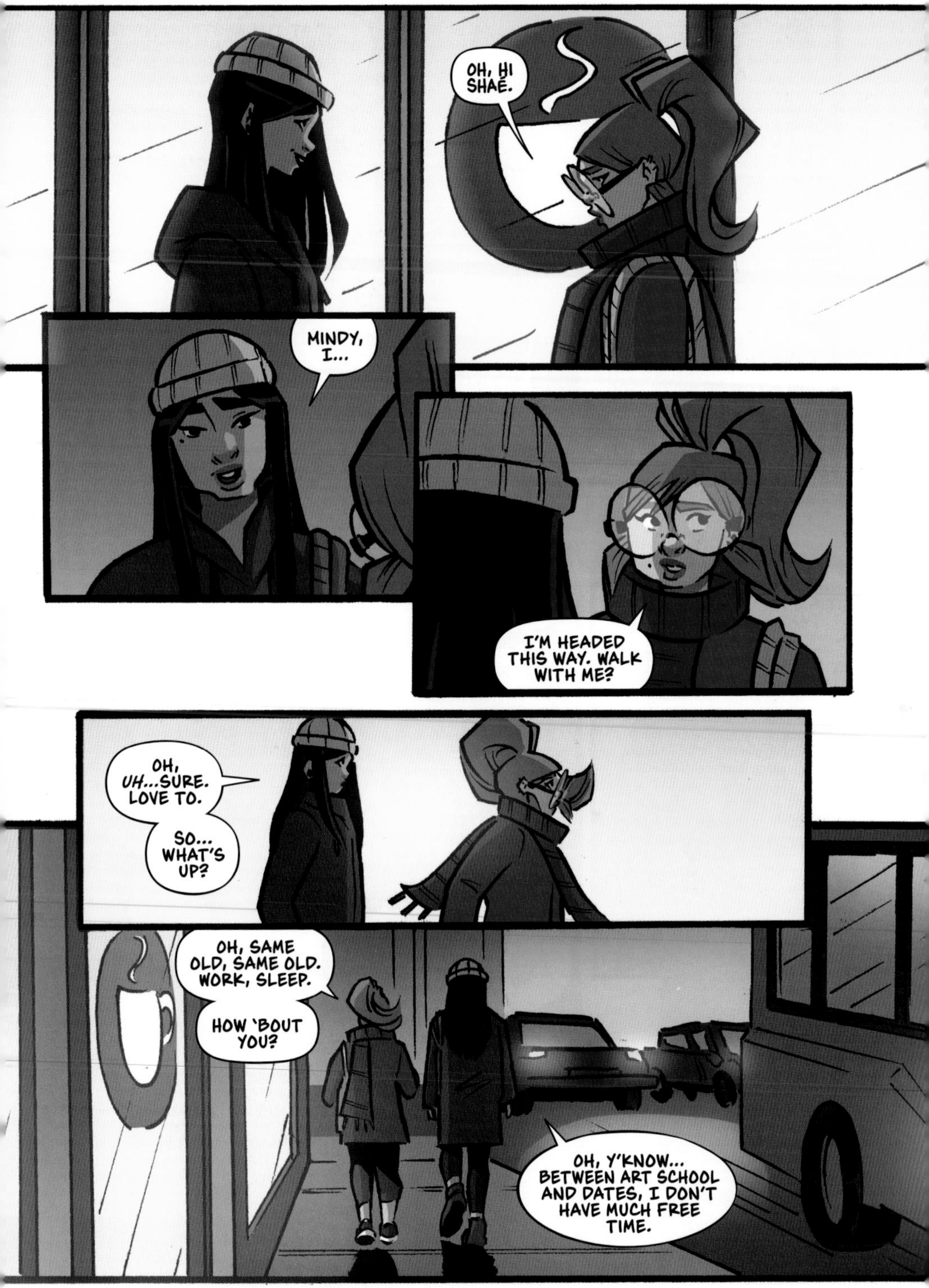

OH, HI SHAE.
MINDY, I...
I'M HEADED THIS WAY. WALK WITH ME?
OH, UH...SURE. LOVE TO.
SO... WHAT'S UP?
OH, SAME OLD, SAME OLD. WORK, SLEEP.
HOW 'BOUT YOU?
OH, Y'KNOW... BETWEEN ART SCHOOL AND DATES, I DON'T HAVE MUCH FREE TIME.

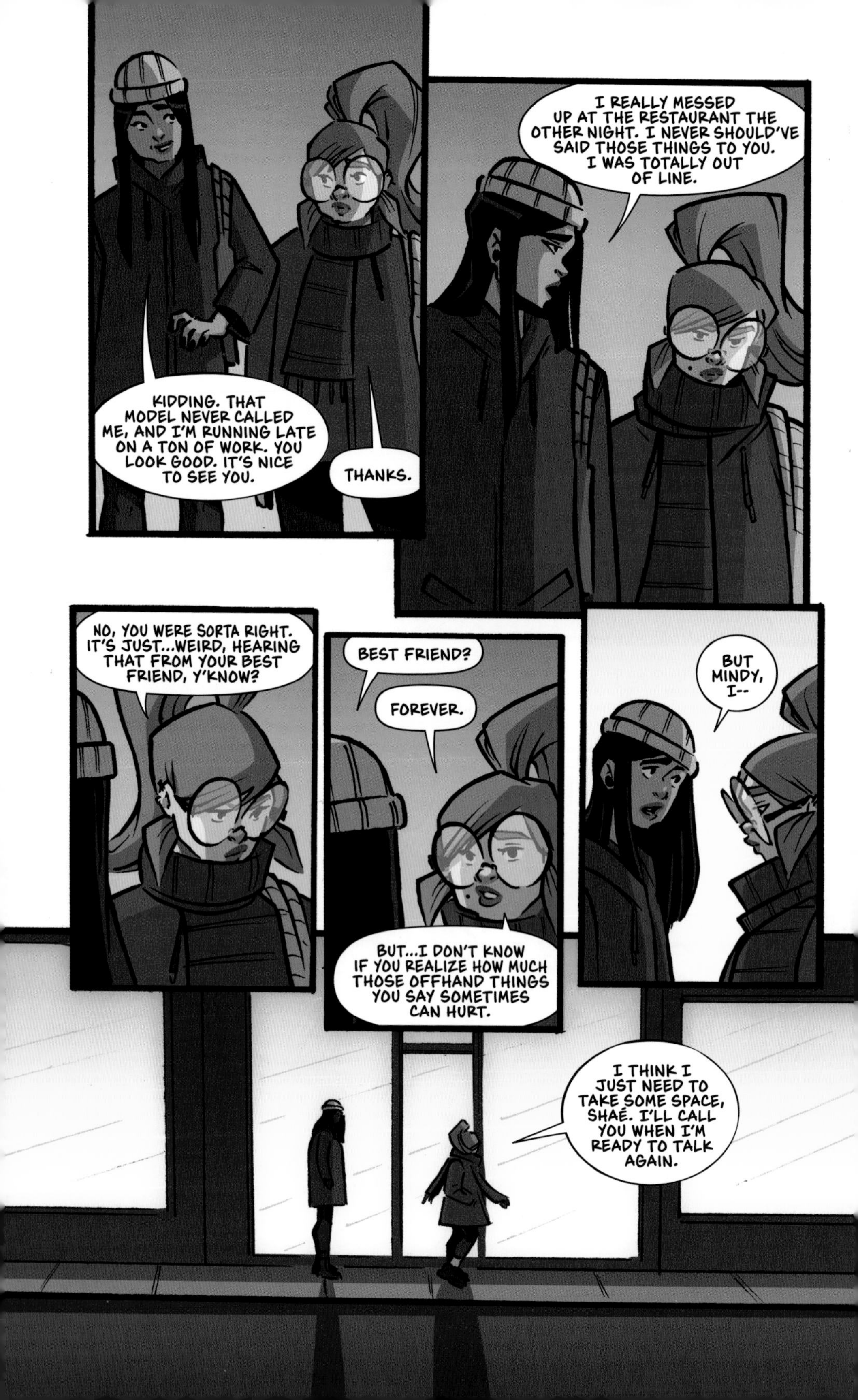
KIDDING. THAT MODEL NEVER CALLED ME, AND I'M RUNNING LATE ON A TON OF WORK. YOU LOOK GOOD. IT'S NICE TO SEE YOU.
THANKS.
I REALLY MESSED UP AT THE RESTAURANT THE OTHER NIGHT. I NEVER SHOULD'VE SAID THOSE THINGS TO YOU. I WAS TOTALLY OUT OF LINE.
NO, YOU WERE SORTA RIGHT. IT'S JUST...WEIRD, HEARING THAT FROM YOUR BEST FRIEND, Y'KNOW?
BEST FRIEND?
FOREVER.
BUT...I DON'T KNOW IF YOU REALIZE HOW MUCH THOSE OFFHAND THINGS YOU SAY SOMETIMES CAN HURT.
BUT MINDY, I--
I THINK I JUST NEED TO TAKE SOME SPACE, SHAÉ. I'LL CALL YOU WHEN I'M READY TO TALK AGAIN.

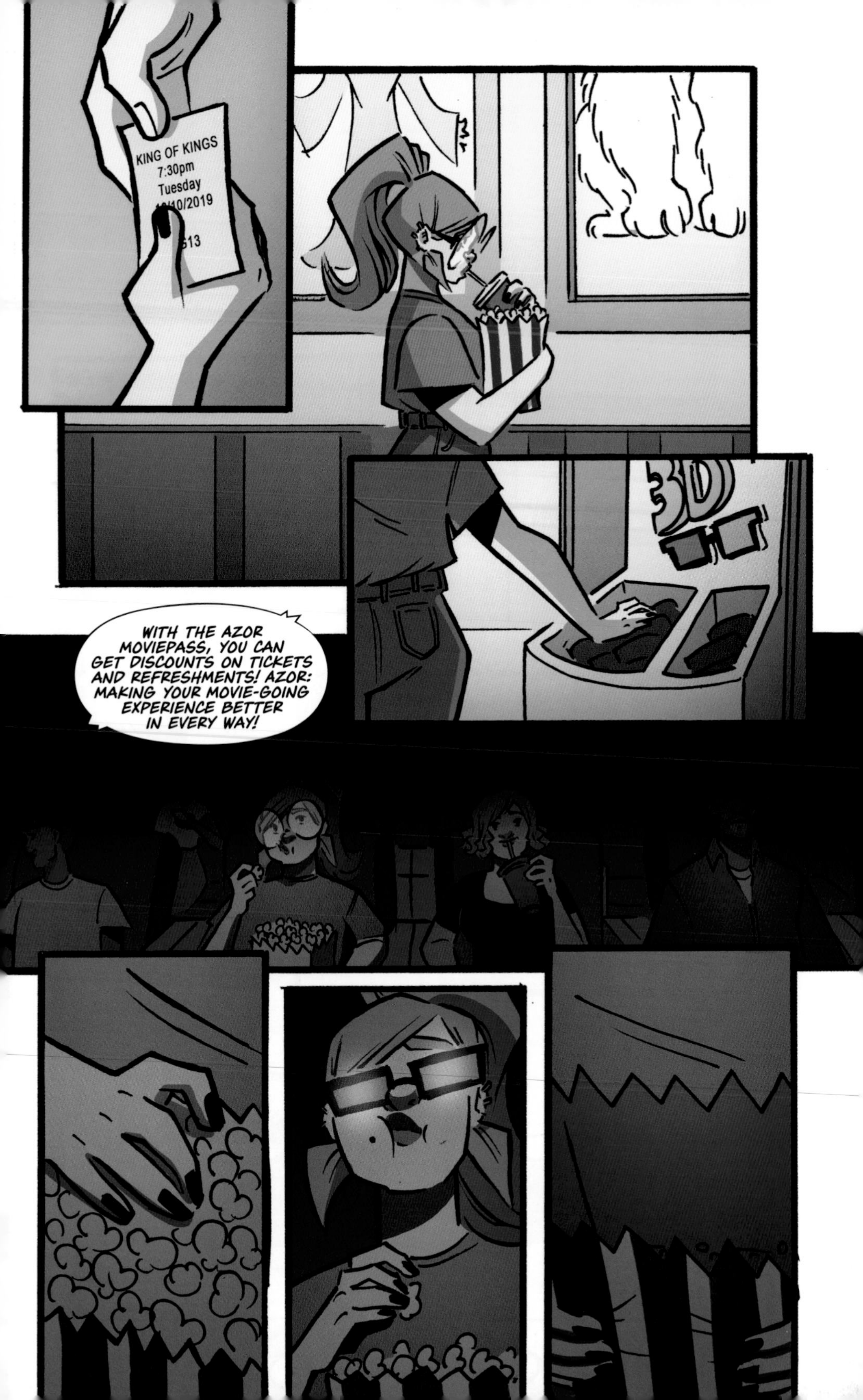
KING OF KINGS
7:30pm
Tuesday
3D
WITH THE AZOR MOVIEPASS, YOU CAN GET DISCOUNTS ON TICKETS AND REFRESHMENTS! AZOR: MAKING YOUR MOVIE-GOING EXPERIENCE BETTER IN EVERY WAY!

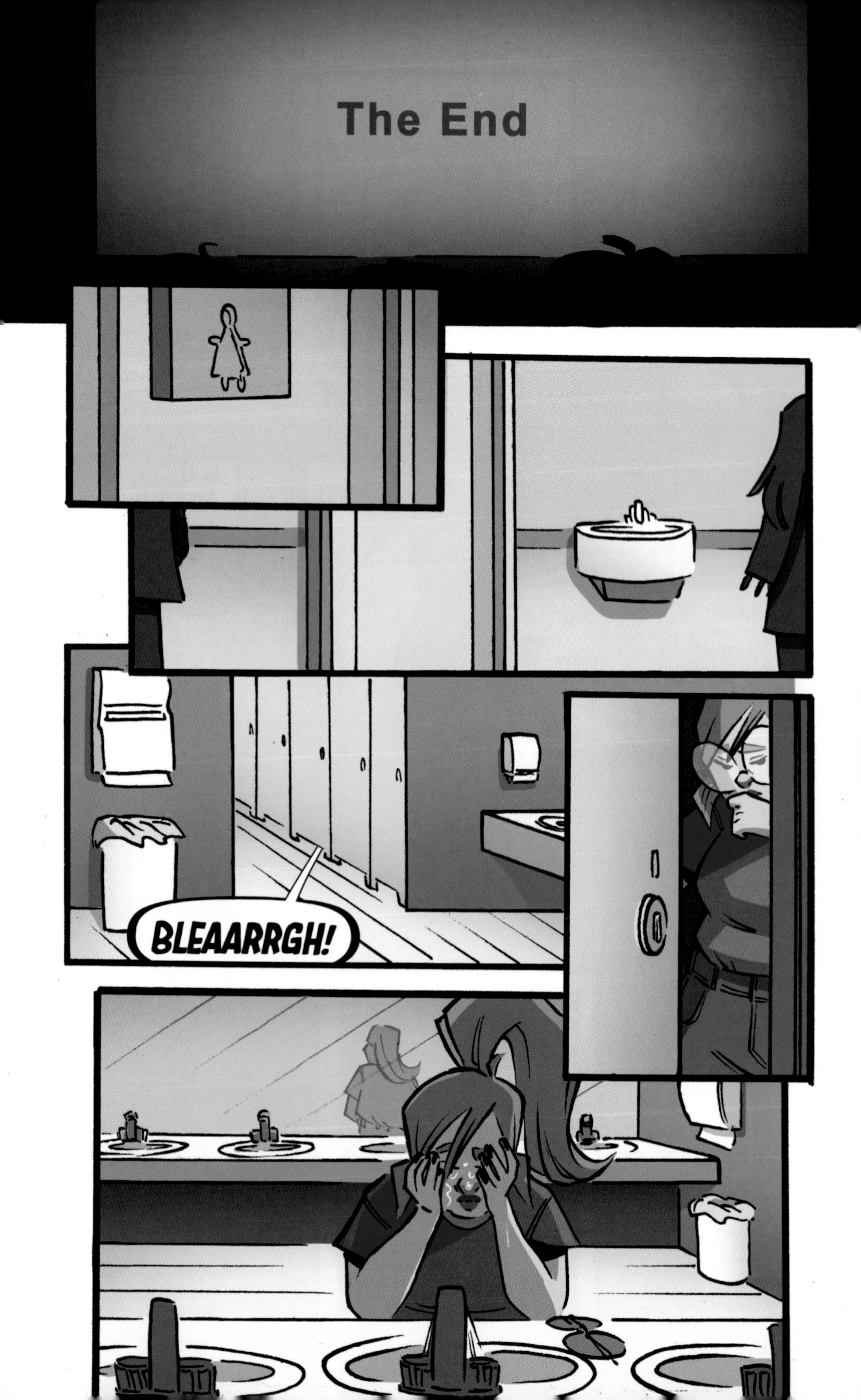
The End
BLEAARRGH!

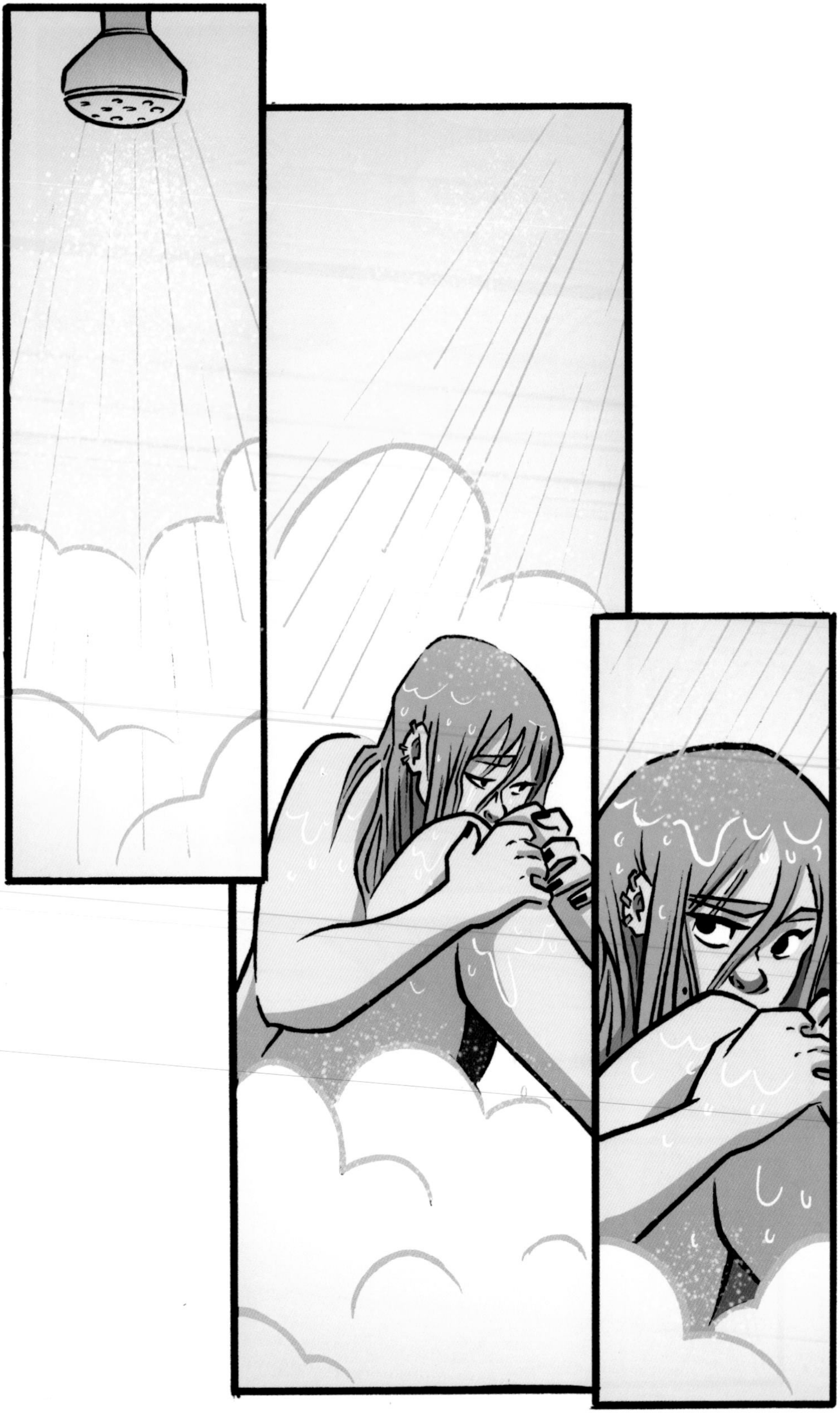

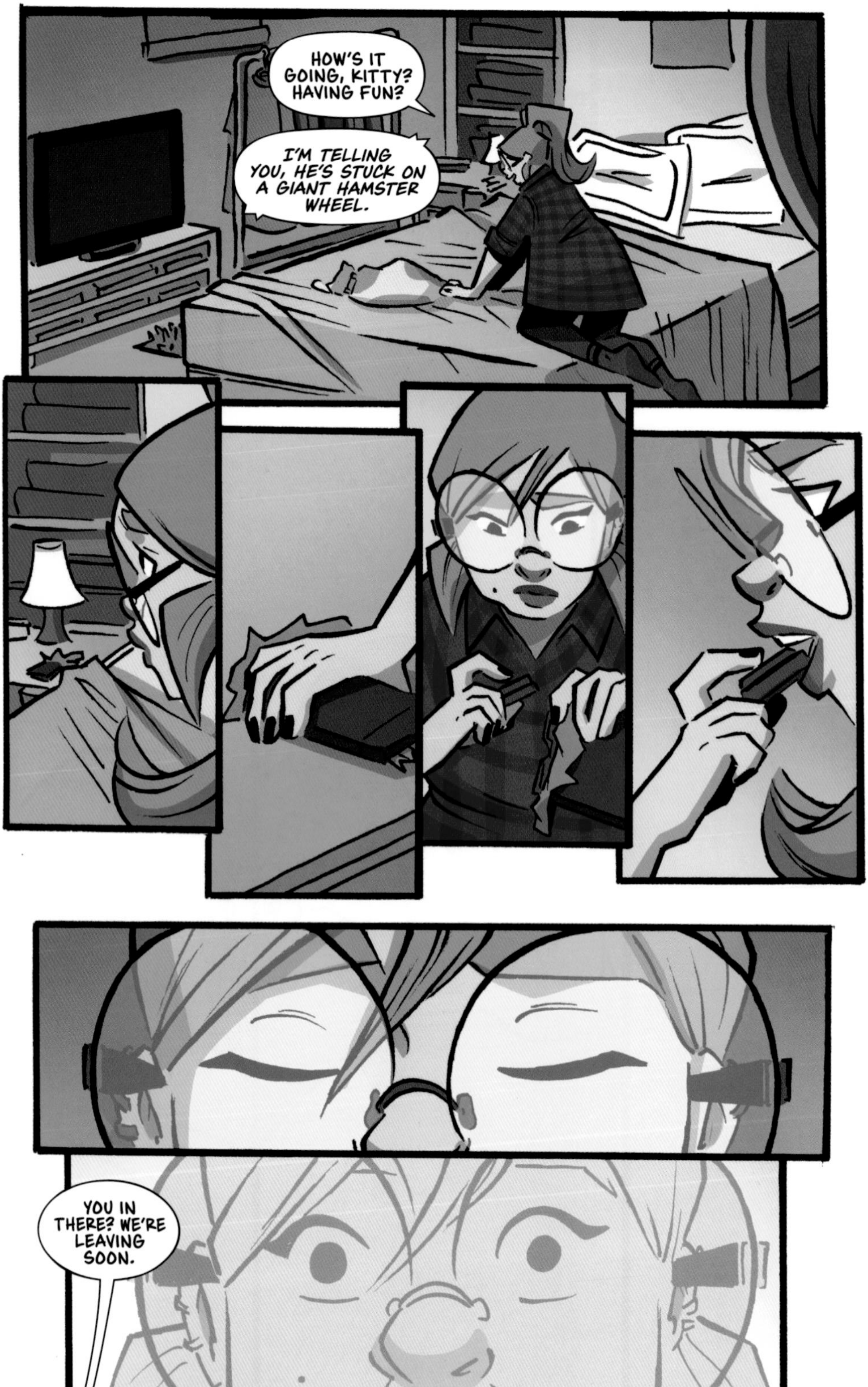
HOW'S IT GOING, KITTY? HAVING FUN?
I'M TELLING YOU, HE'S STUCK ON A GIANT HAMSTER WHEEL.
YOU IN THERE? WE'RE LEAVING SOON.

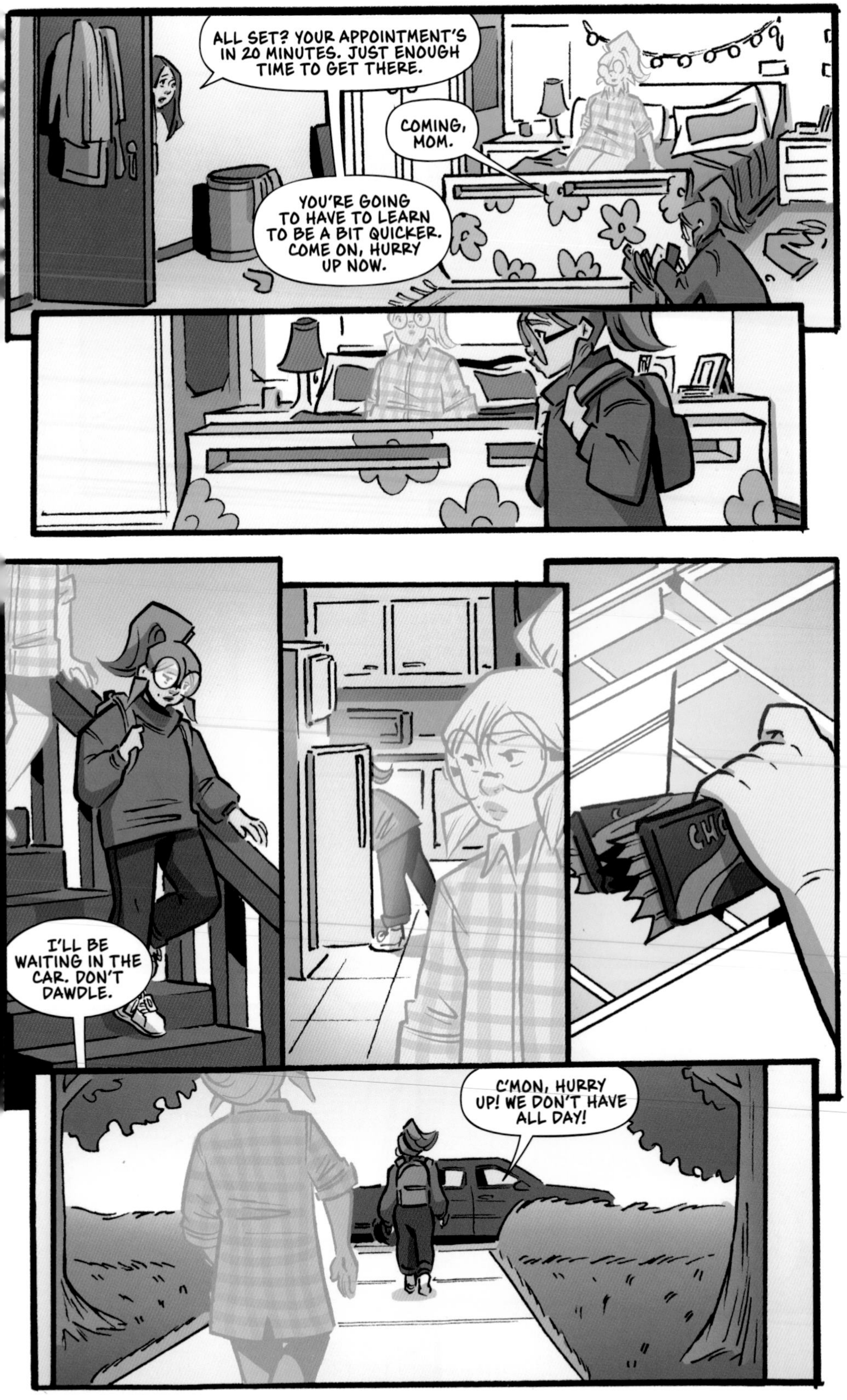
ALL SET? YOUR APPOINTMENT'S IN 20 MINUTES. JUST ENOUGH TIME TO GET THERE.
COMING, MOM.
YOU'RE GOING TO HAVE TO LEARN TO BE A BIT QUICKER. COME ON, HURRY UP NOW.
I'LL BE WAITING IN THE CAR. DON'T DAWDLE.
C'MON, HURRY UP! WE DON'T HAVE ALL DAY!

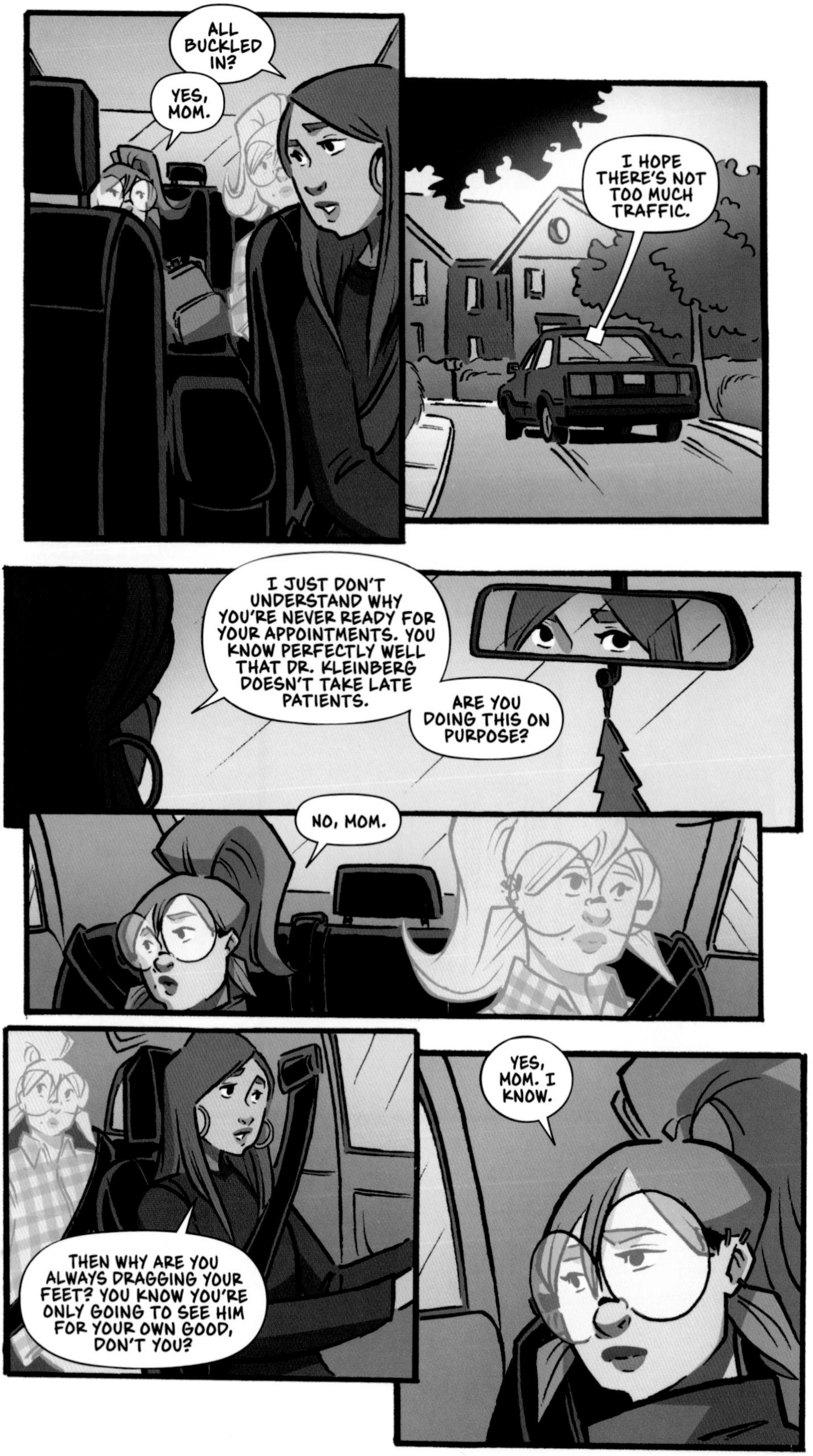
ALL BUCKLED IN?
YES, MOM.
I HOPE THERE'S NOT TOO MUCH TRAFFIC.
I JUST DON'T UNDERSTAND WHY YOU'RE NEVER READY FOR YOUR APPOINTMENTS. YOU KNOW PERFECTLY WELL THAT DR. KLEINBERG DOESN'T TAKE LATE PATIENTS.
ARE YOU DOING THIS ON PURPOSE?
NO, MOM.
THEN WHY ARE YOU ALWAYS DRAGGING YOUR FEET? YOU KNOW YOU'RE ONLY GOING TO SEE HIM FOR YOUR OWN GOOD, DON'T YOU?
YES, MOM. I KNOW.

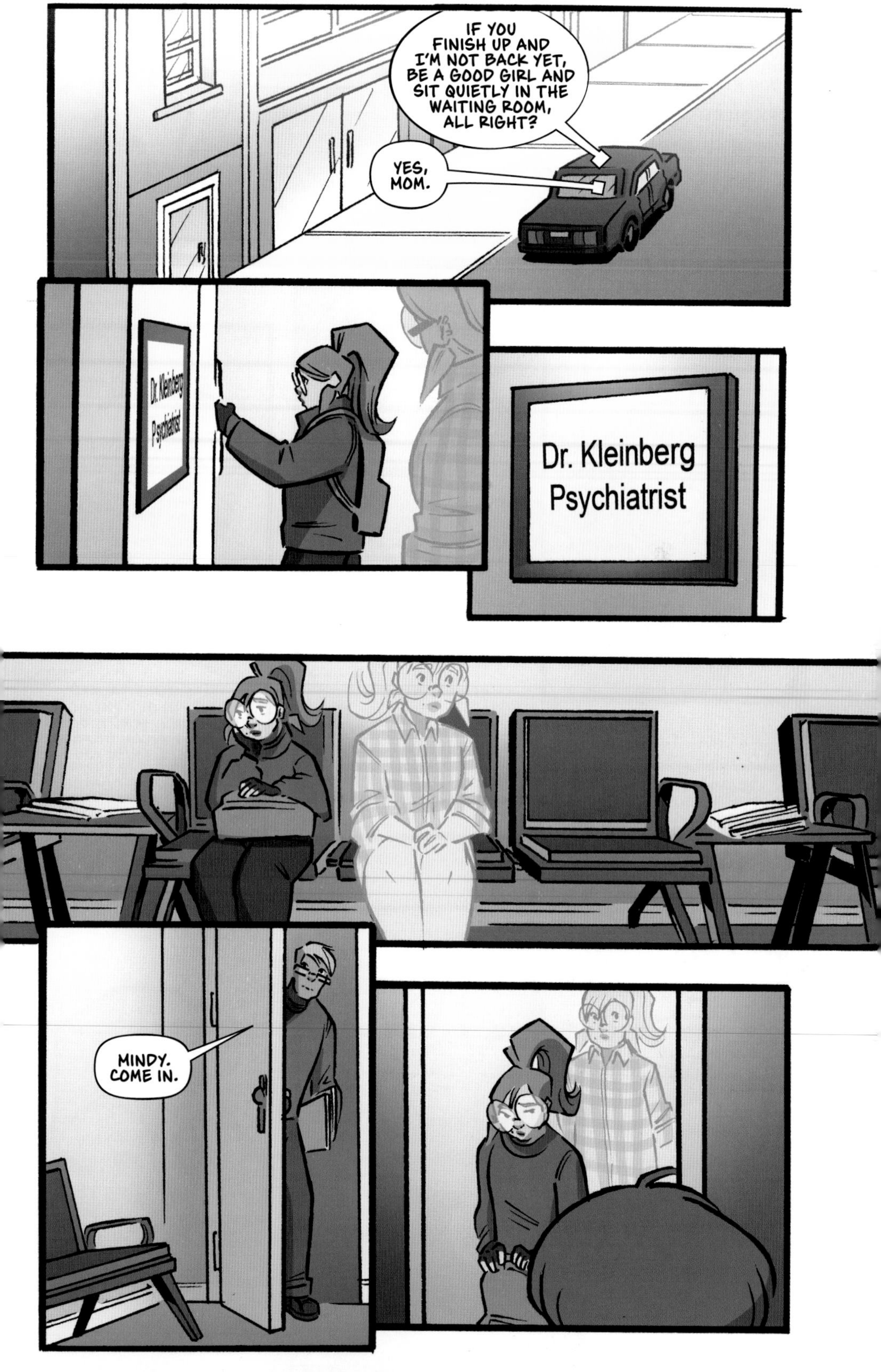
IF YOU FINISH UP AND I'M NOT BACK YET, BE A GOOD GIRL AND SIT QUIETLY IN THE WAITING ROOM, ALL RIGHT?
YES, MOM.
Dr. Kleinberg Psychiatrist
Dr. Kleinberg Psychiatrist
MINDY. COME IN.

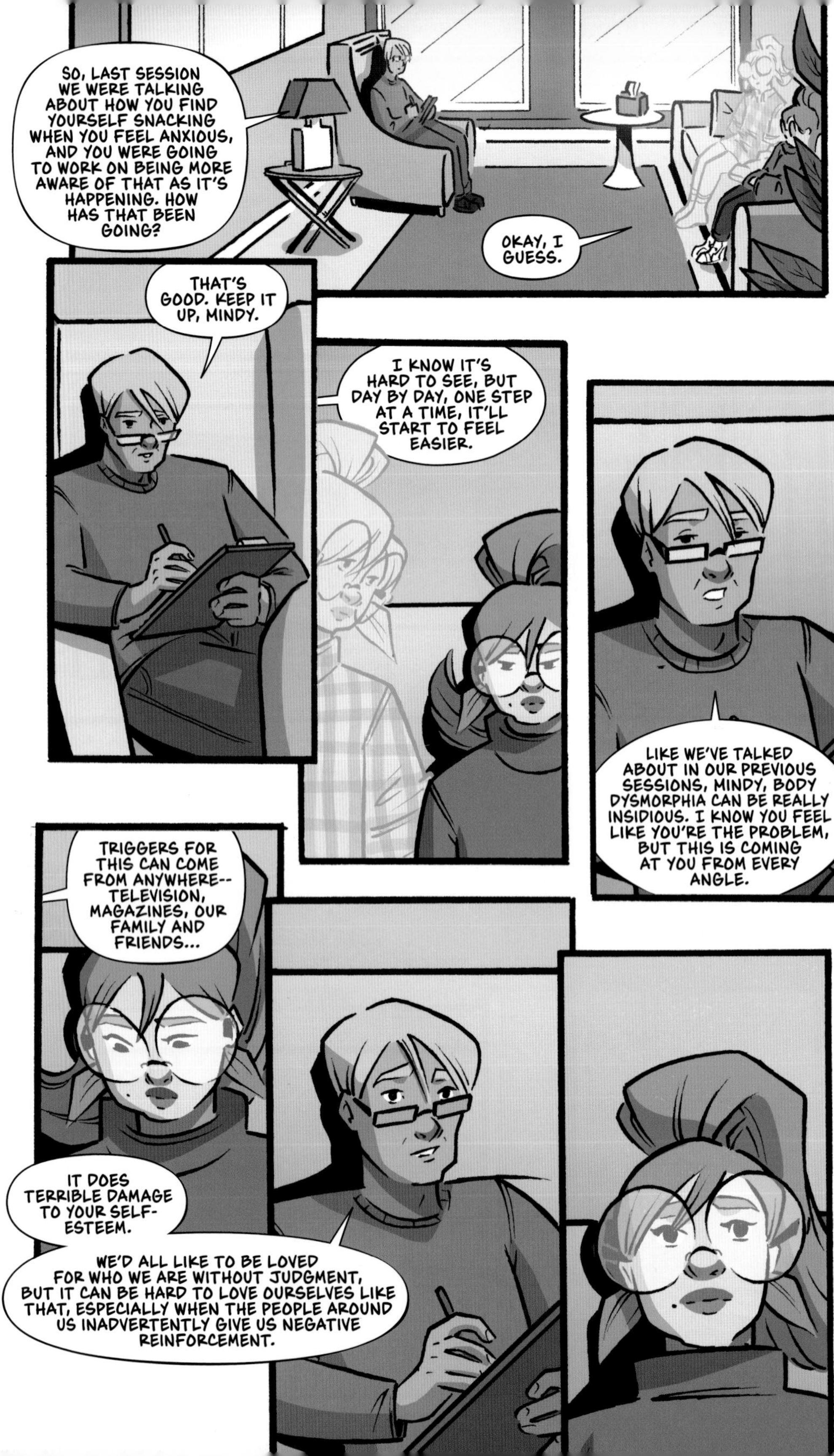
SO, LAST SESSION WE WERE TALKING ABOUT HOW YOU FIND YOURSELF SNACKING WHEN YOU FEEL ANXIOUS, AND YOU WERE GOING TO WORK ON BEING MORE AWARE OF THAT AS IT'S HAPPENING. HOW HAS THAT BEEN GOING?
OKAY, I GUESS.
THAT'S GOOD. KEEP IT UP, MINDY.
I KNOW IT'S HARD TO SEE, BUT DAY BY DAY, ONE STEP AT A TIME, IT'LL START TO FEEL EASIER.
LIKE WE'VE TALKED ABOUT IN OUR PREVIOUS SESSIONS, MINDY, BODY DYSMORPHIA CAN BE REALLY INSIDIOUS. I KNOW YOU FEEL LIKE YOU'RE THE PROBLEM, BUT THIS IS COMING AT YOU FROM EVERY ANGLE.
TRIGGERS FOR THIS CAN COME FROM ANYWHERE--TELEVISION, MAGAZINES, OUR FAMILY AND FRIENDS...
IT DOES TERRIBLE DAMAGE TO YOUR SELF-ESTEEM.
WE'D ALL LIKE TO BE LOVED FOR WHO WE ARE WITHOUT JUDGMENT, BUT IT CAN BE HARD TO LOVE OURSELVES LIKE THAT, ESPECIALLY WHEN THE PEOPLE AROUND US INADVERTENTLY GIVE US NEGATIVE REINFORCEMENT.

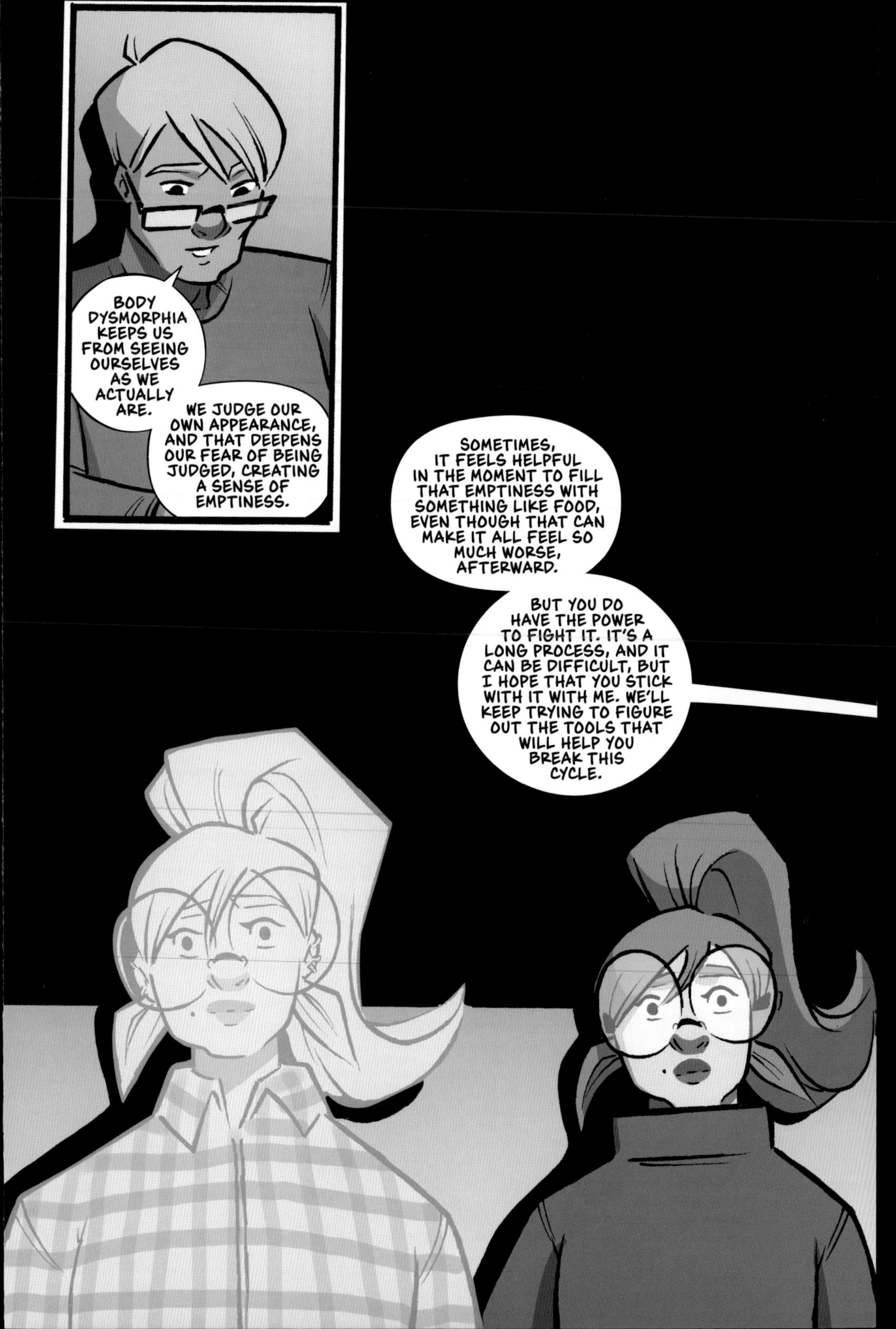
BODY DYSMORPHIA KEEPS US FROM SEEING OURSELVES AS WE ACTUALLY ARE.
WE JUDGE OUR OWN APPEARANCE, AND THAT DEEPENS OUR FEAR OF BEING JUDGED, CREATING A SENSE OF EMPTINESS.
SOMETIMES, IT FEELS HELPFUL IN THE MOMENT TO FILL THAT EMPTINESS WITH SOMETHING LIKE FOOD, EVEN THOUGH THAT CAN MAKE IT ALL FEEL SO MUCH WORSE, AFTERWARD.
BUT YOU DO HAVE THE POWER TO FIGHT IT. IT'S A LONG PROCESS, AND IT CAN BE DIFFICULT, BUT I HOPE THAT YOU STICK WITH IT WITH ME. WE'LL KEEP TRYING TO FIGURE OUT THE TOOLS THAT WILL HELP YOU BREAK THIS CYCLE.

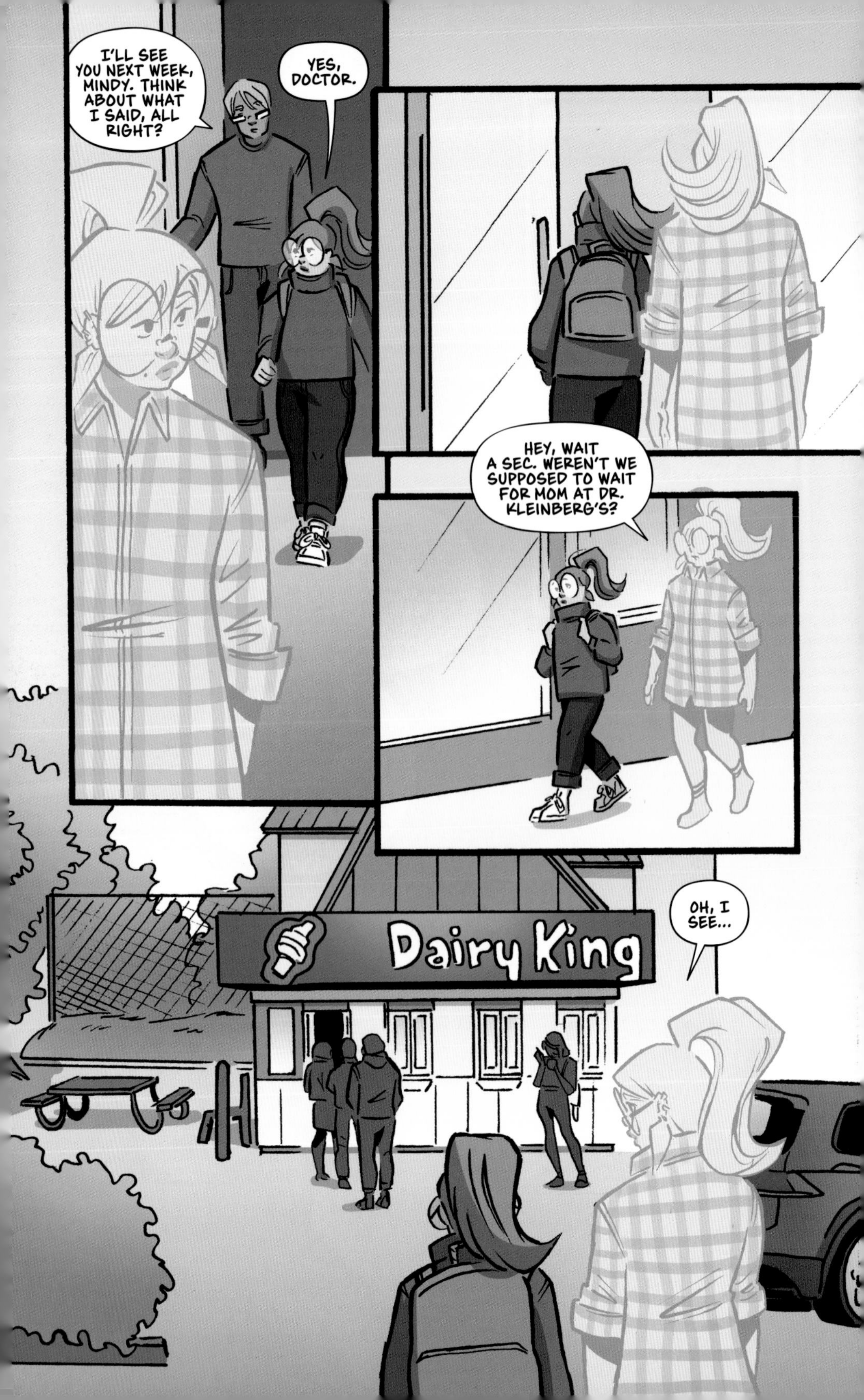
I'LL SEE YOU NEXT WEEK, MINDY. THINK ABOUT WHAT I SAID, ALL RIGHT?
YES, DOCTOR.
HEY, WAIT A SEC. WEREN'T WE SUPPOSED TO WAIT FOR MOM AT DR. KLEINBERG'S?
Dairy King
OH, I SEE...

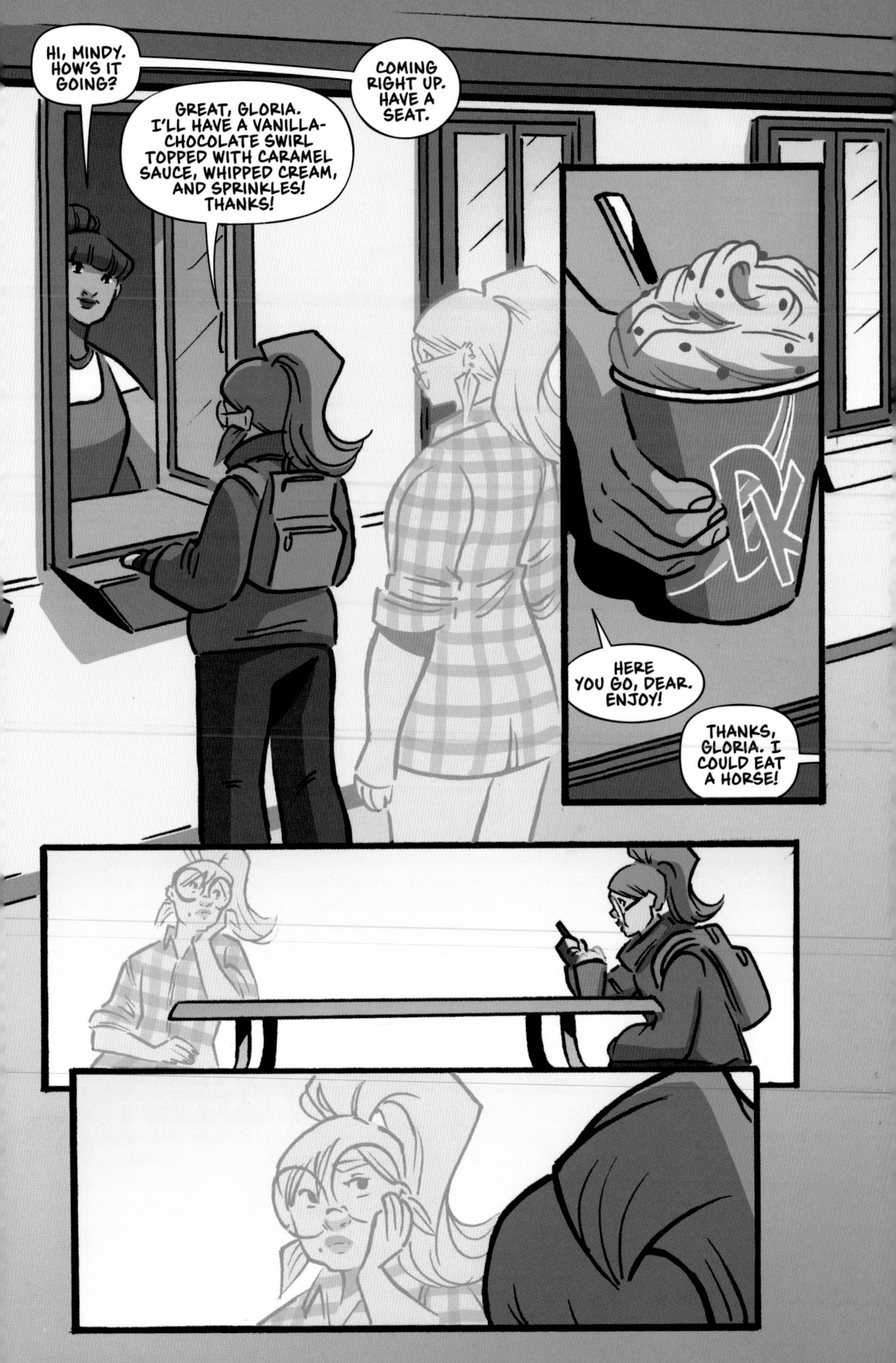
HI, MINDY. HOW'S IT GOING?
GREAT, GLORIA. I'LL HAVE A VANILLA-CHOCOLATE SWIRL TOPPED WITH CARAMEL SAUCE, WHIPPED CREAM, AND SPRINKLES! THANKS!
COMING RIGHT UP. HAVE A SEAT.
DK
HERE YOU GO, DEAR. ENJOY!
THANKS, GLORIA. I COULD EAT A HORSE!

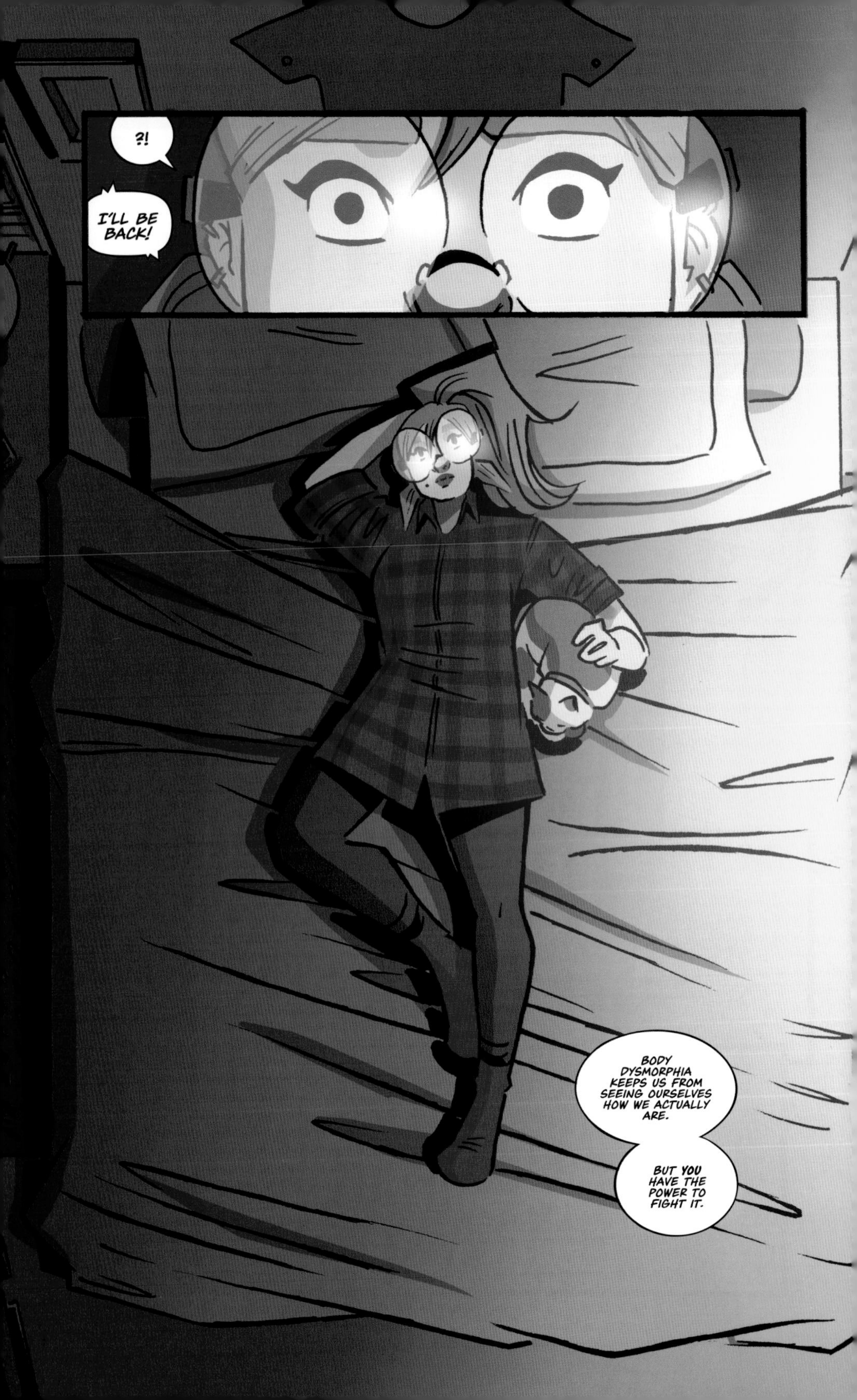
?!
I'LL BE BACK!
BODY DYSMORPHIA KEEPS US FROM SEEING OURSELVES HOW WE ACTUALLY ARE.
BUT YOU HAVE THE POWER TO FIGHT IT.

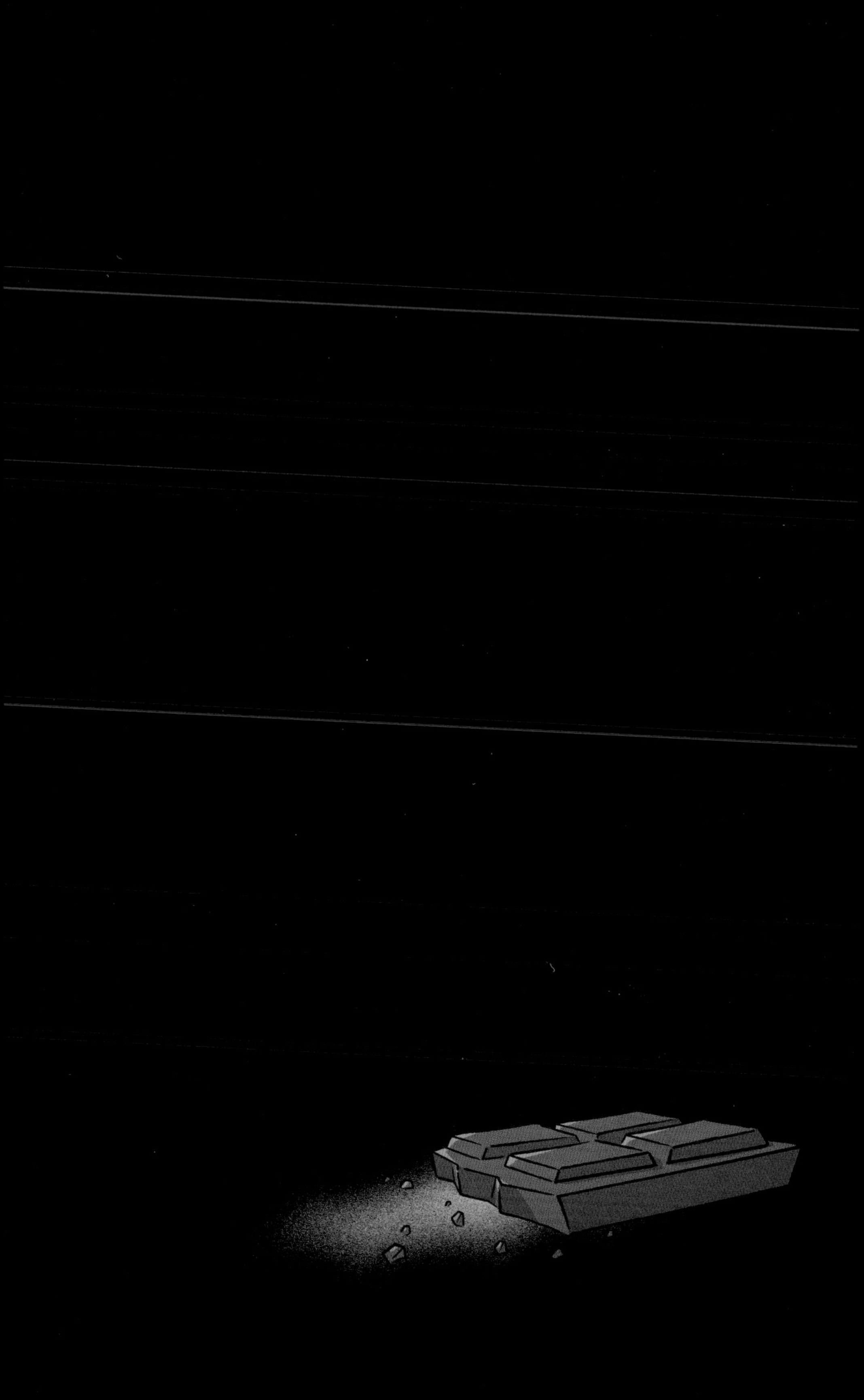

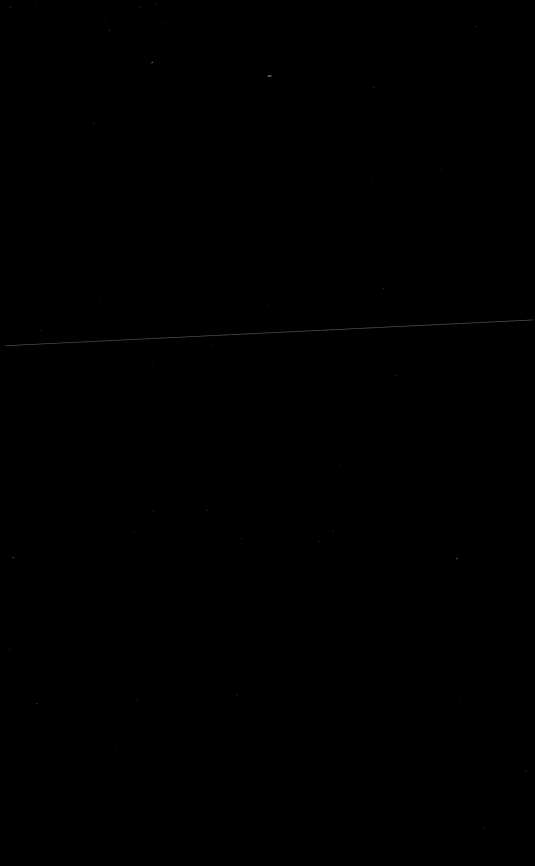

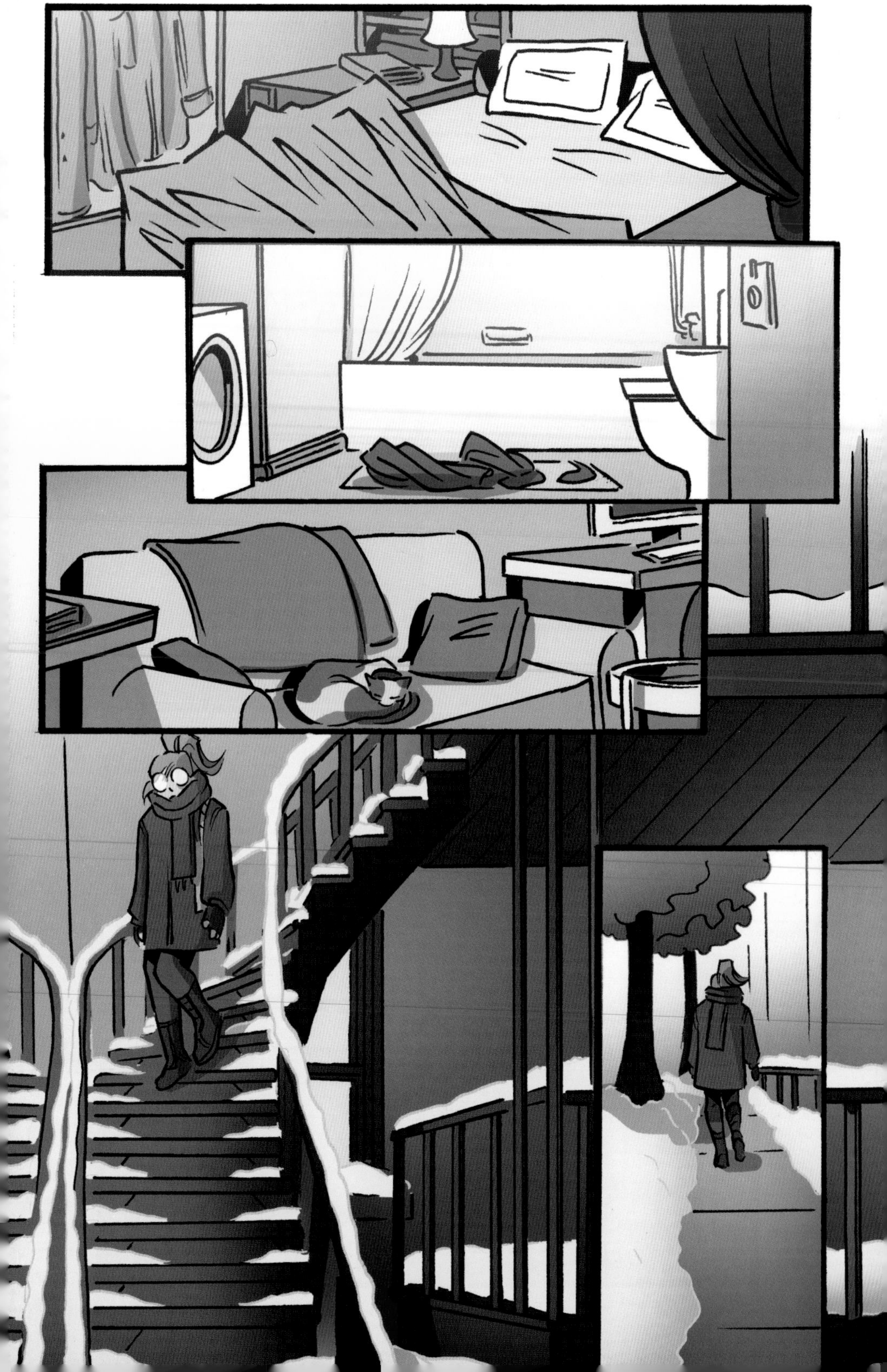

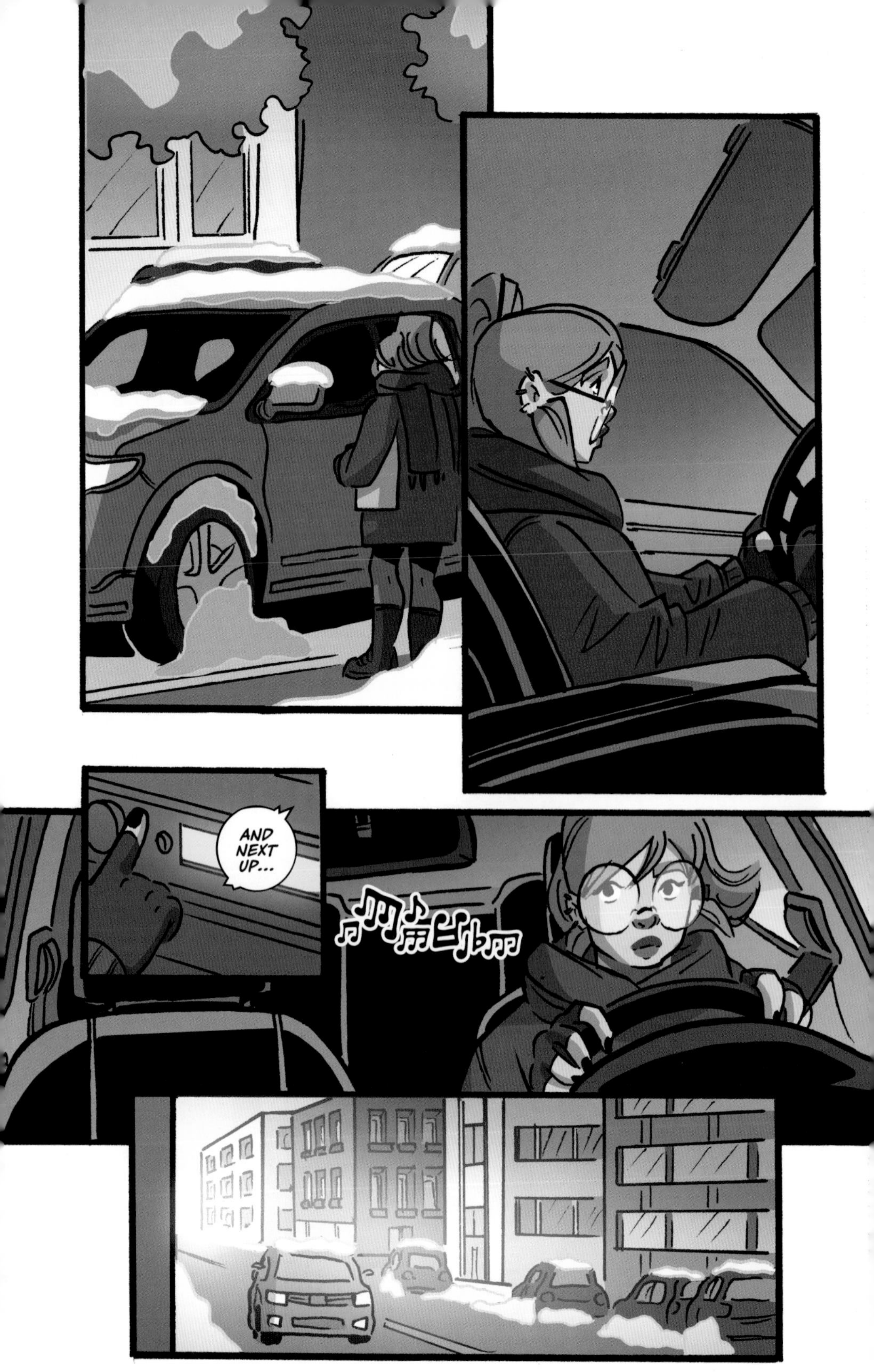
AND NEXT UP...

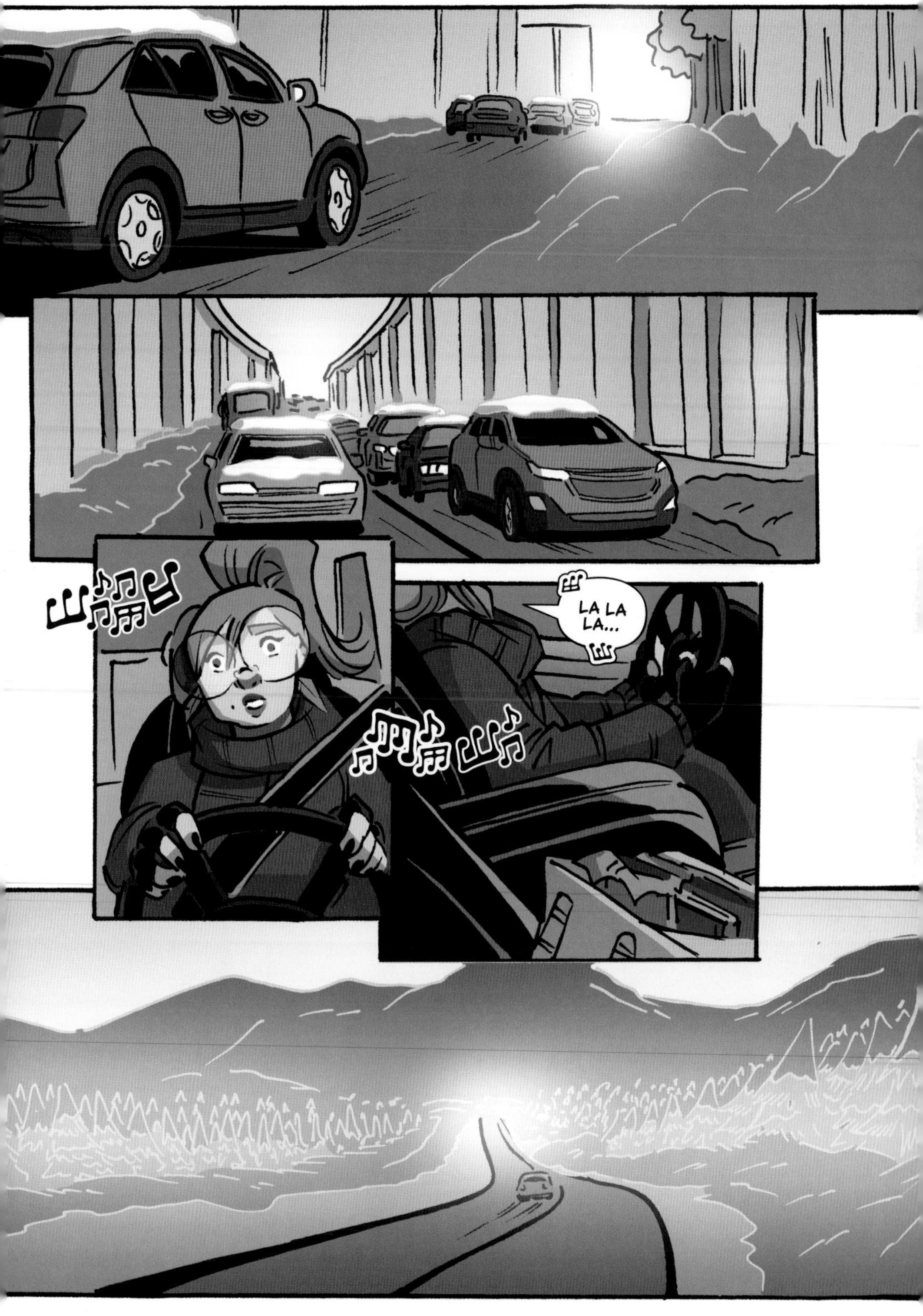
LA LA LA...

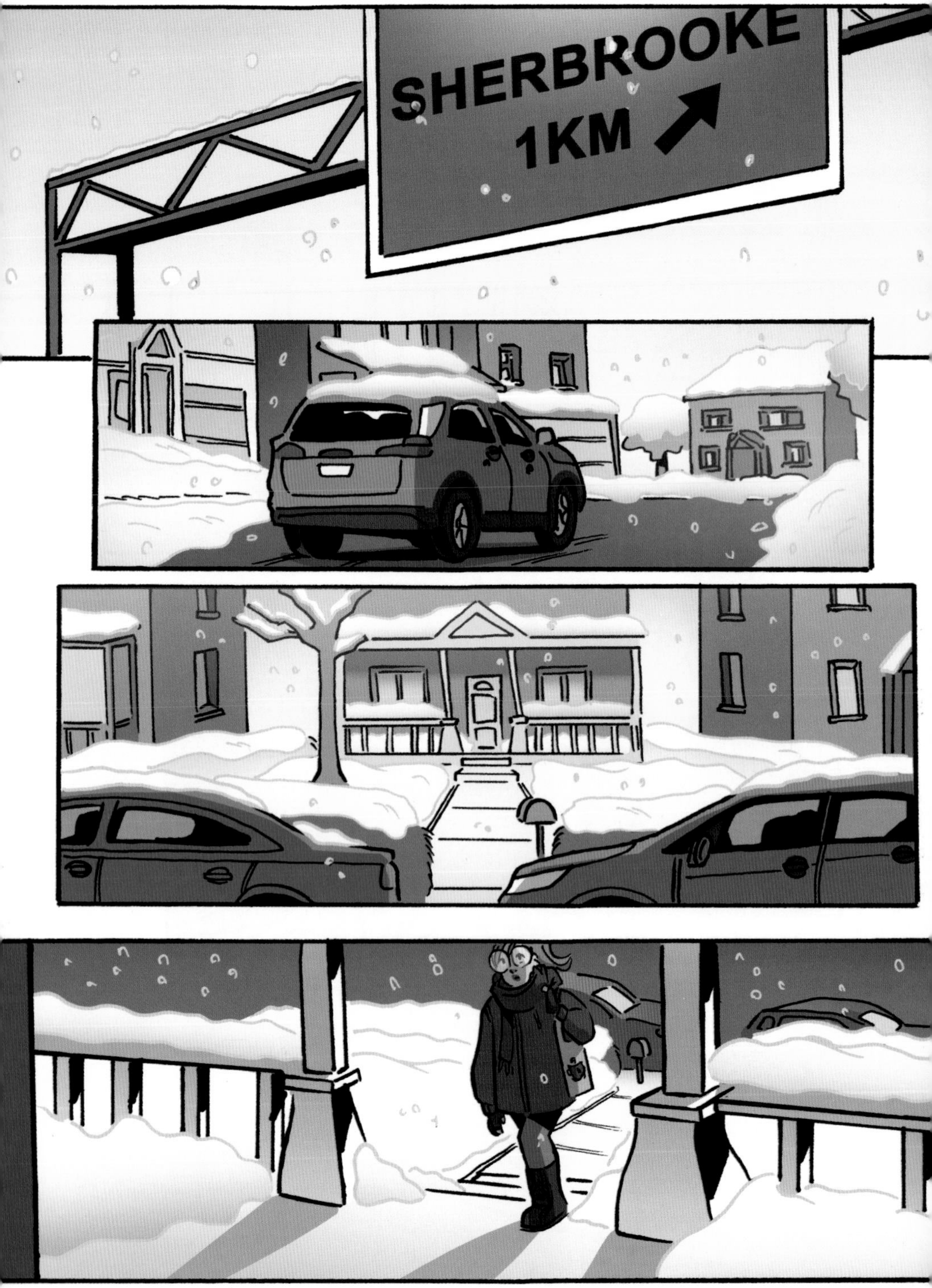
SHERBROOKE
1KM

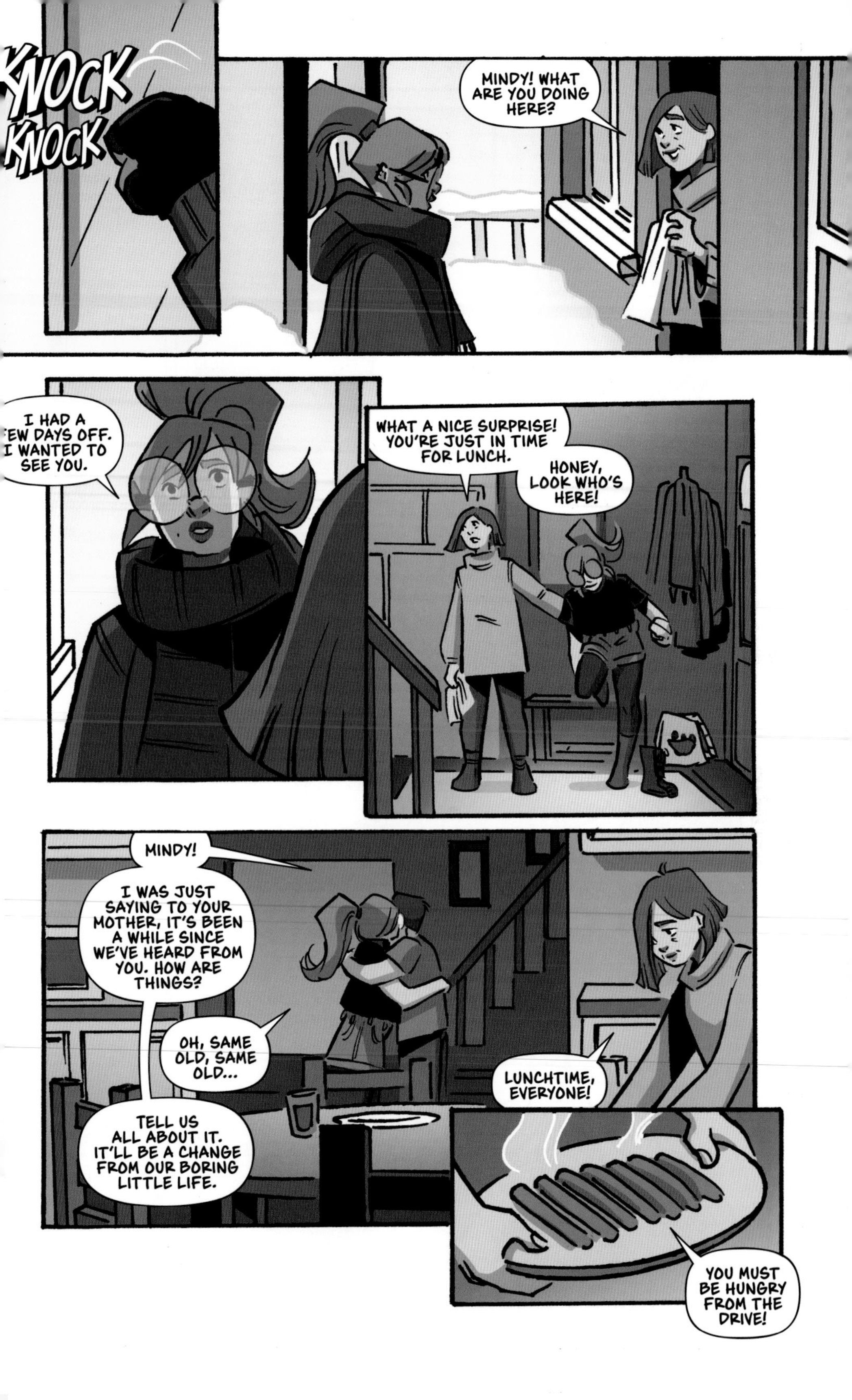
KNOCK KNOCK
MINDY! WHAT ARE YOU DOING HERE?
I HAD A FEW DAYS OFF. I WANTED TO SEE YOU.
WHAT A NICE SURPRISE! YOU'RE JUST IN TIME FOR LUNCH.
HONEY, LOOK WHO'S HERE!
MINDY!
I WAS JUST SAYING TO YOUR MOTHER, IT'S BEEN A WHILE SINCE WE'VE HEARD FROM YOU. HOW ARE THINGS?
OH, SAME OLD, SAME OLD...
TELL US ALL ABOUT IT. IT'LL BE A CHANGE FROM OUR BORING LITTLE LIFE.
LUNCHTIME, EVERYONE!
YOU MUST BE HUNGRY FROM THE DRIVE!

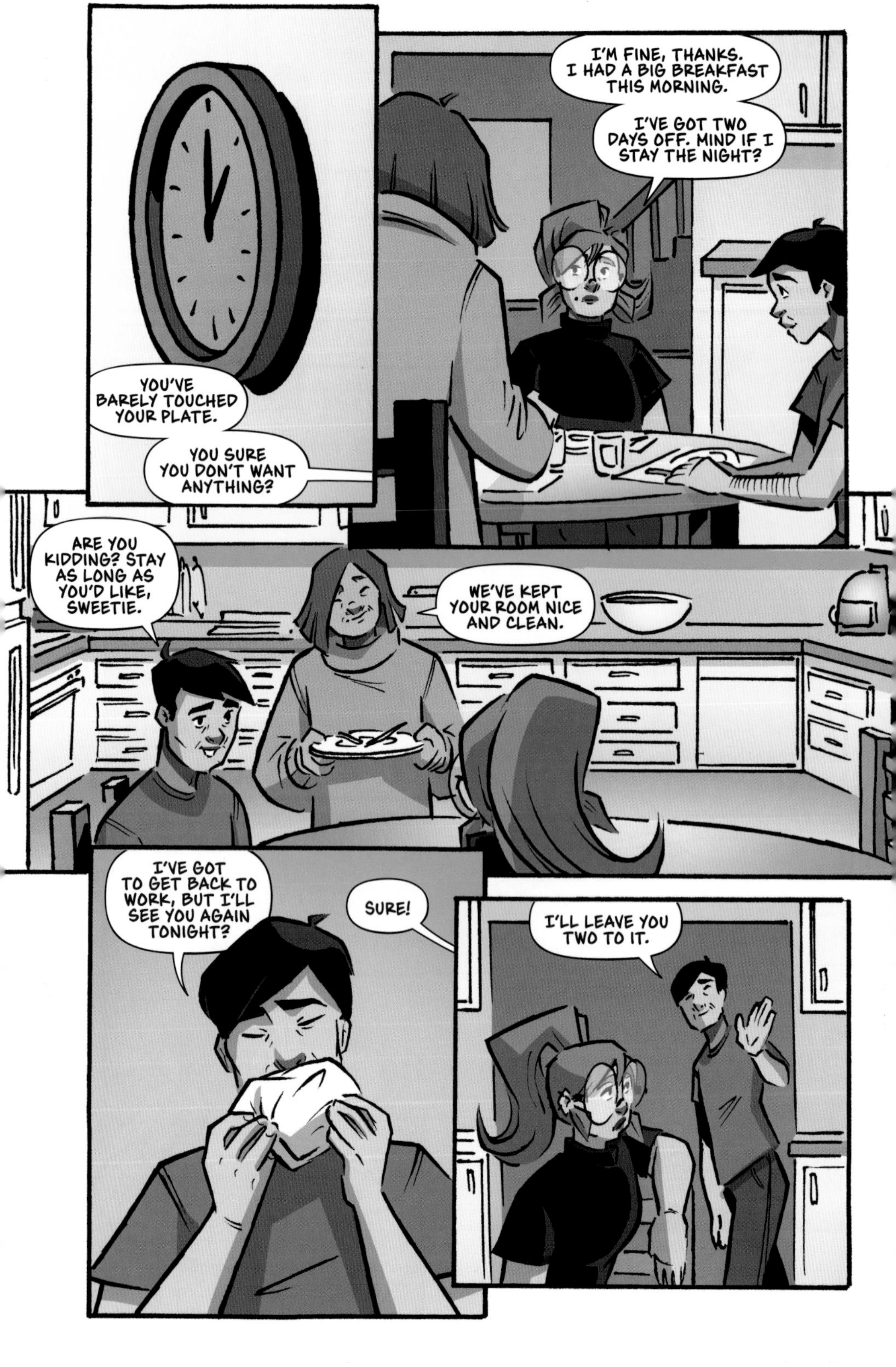
YOU'VE BARELY TOUCHED YOUR PLATE.
YOU SURE YOU DON'T WANT ANYTHING?
I'M FINE, THANKS. I HAD A BIG BREAKFAST THIS MORNING.
I'VE GOT TWO DAYS OFF. MIND IF I STAY THE NIGHT?
ARE YOU KIDDING? STAY AS LONG AS YOU'D LIKE, SWEETIE.
WE'VE KEPT YOUR ROOM NICE AND CLEAN.
I'VE GOT TO GET BACK TO WORK, BUT I'LL SEE YOU AGAIN TONIGHT?
SURE!
I'LL LEAVE YOU TWO TO IT.

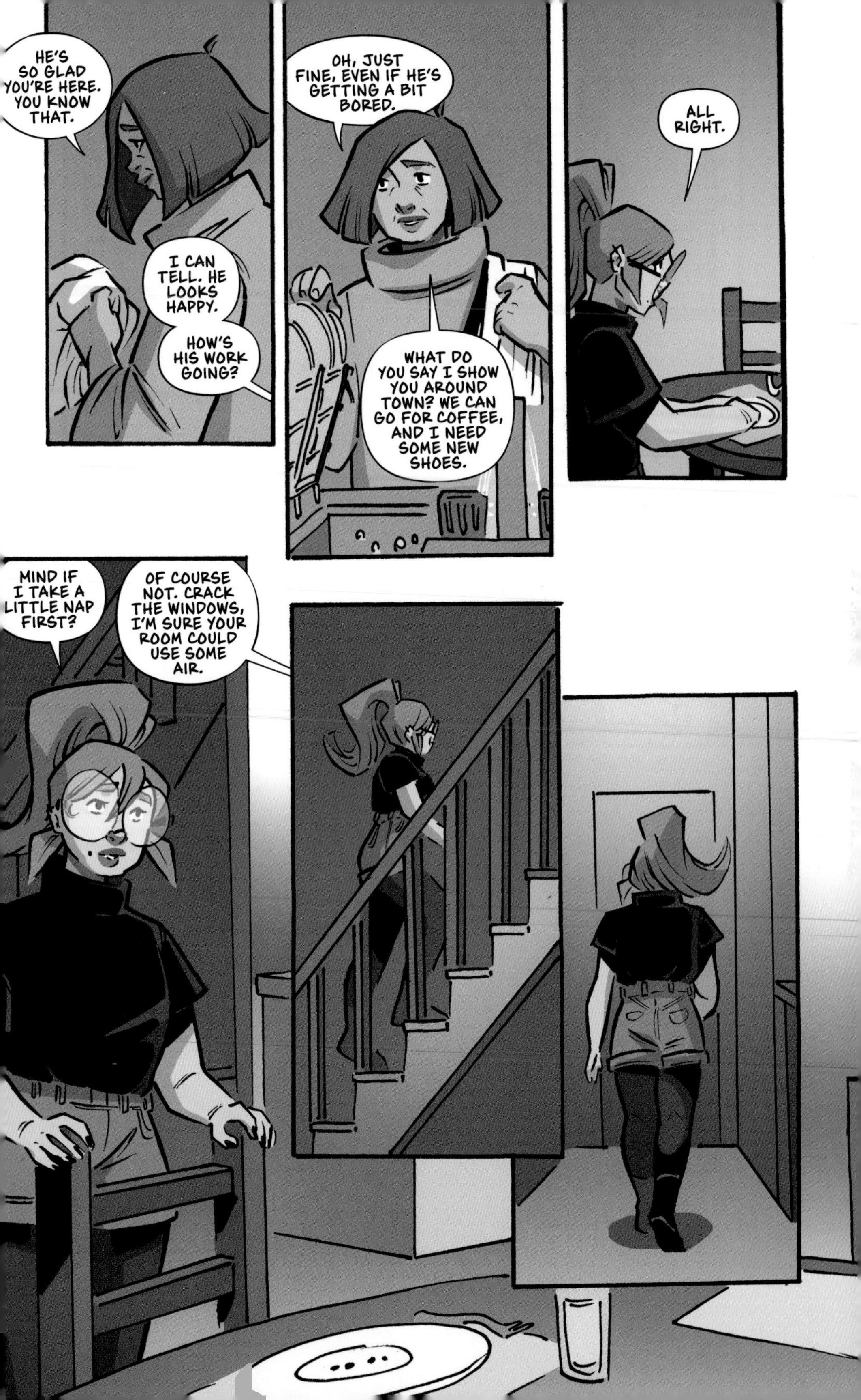
HE'S SO GLAD YOU'RE HERE. YOU KNOW THAT.
I CAN TELL. HE LOOKS HAPPY.
HOW'S HIS WORK GOING?
OH, JUST FINE, EVEN IF HE'S GETTING A BIT BORED.
WHAT DO YOU SAY I SHOW YOU AROUND TOWN? WE CAN GO FOR COFFEE, AND I NEED SOME NEW SHOES.
ALL RIGHT.
MIND IF I TAKE A LITTLE NAP FIRST?
OF COURSE NOT. CRACK THE WINDOWS, I'M SURE YOUR ROOM COULD USE SOME AIR.

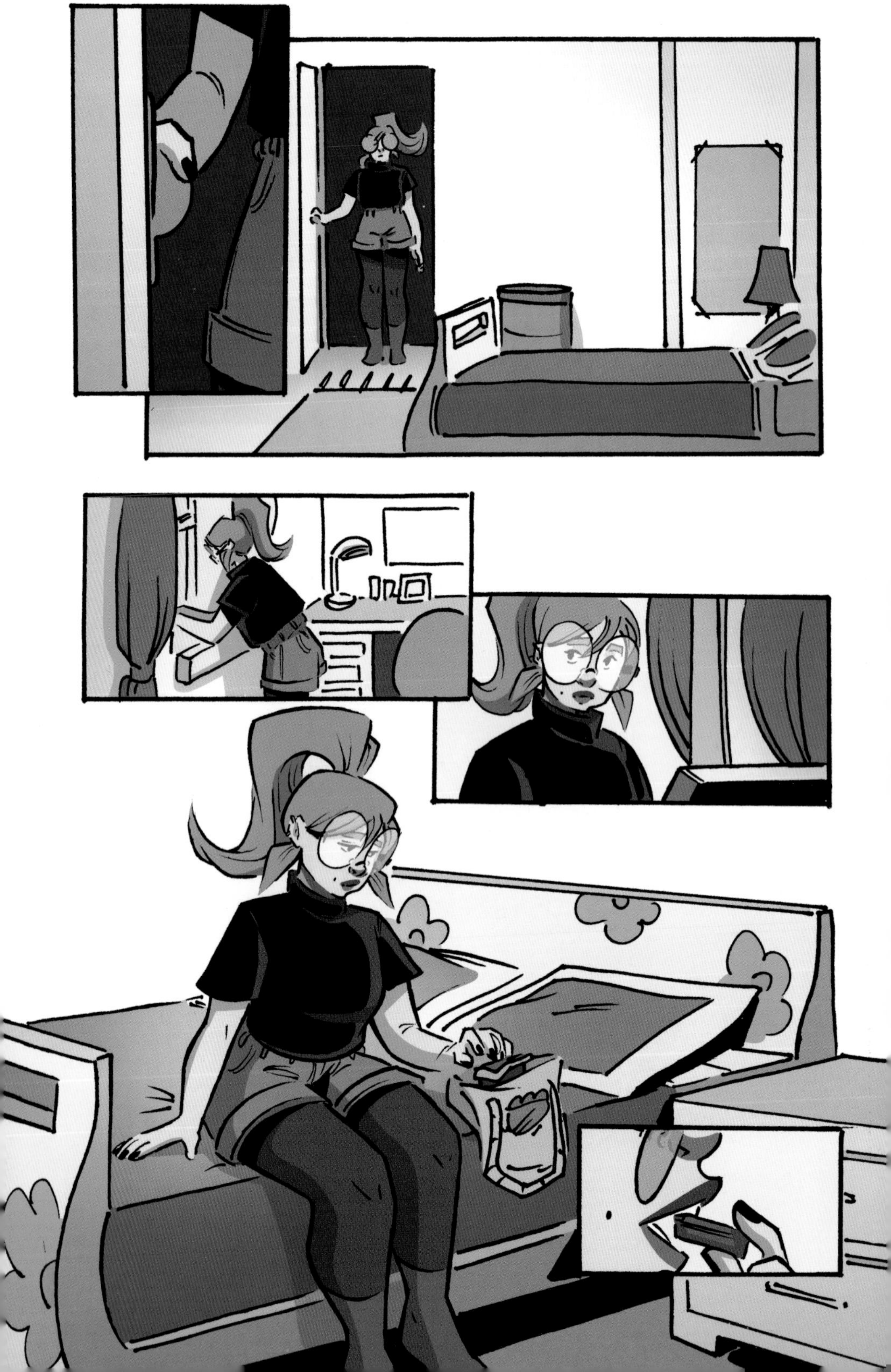

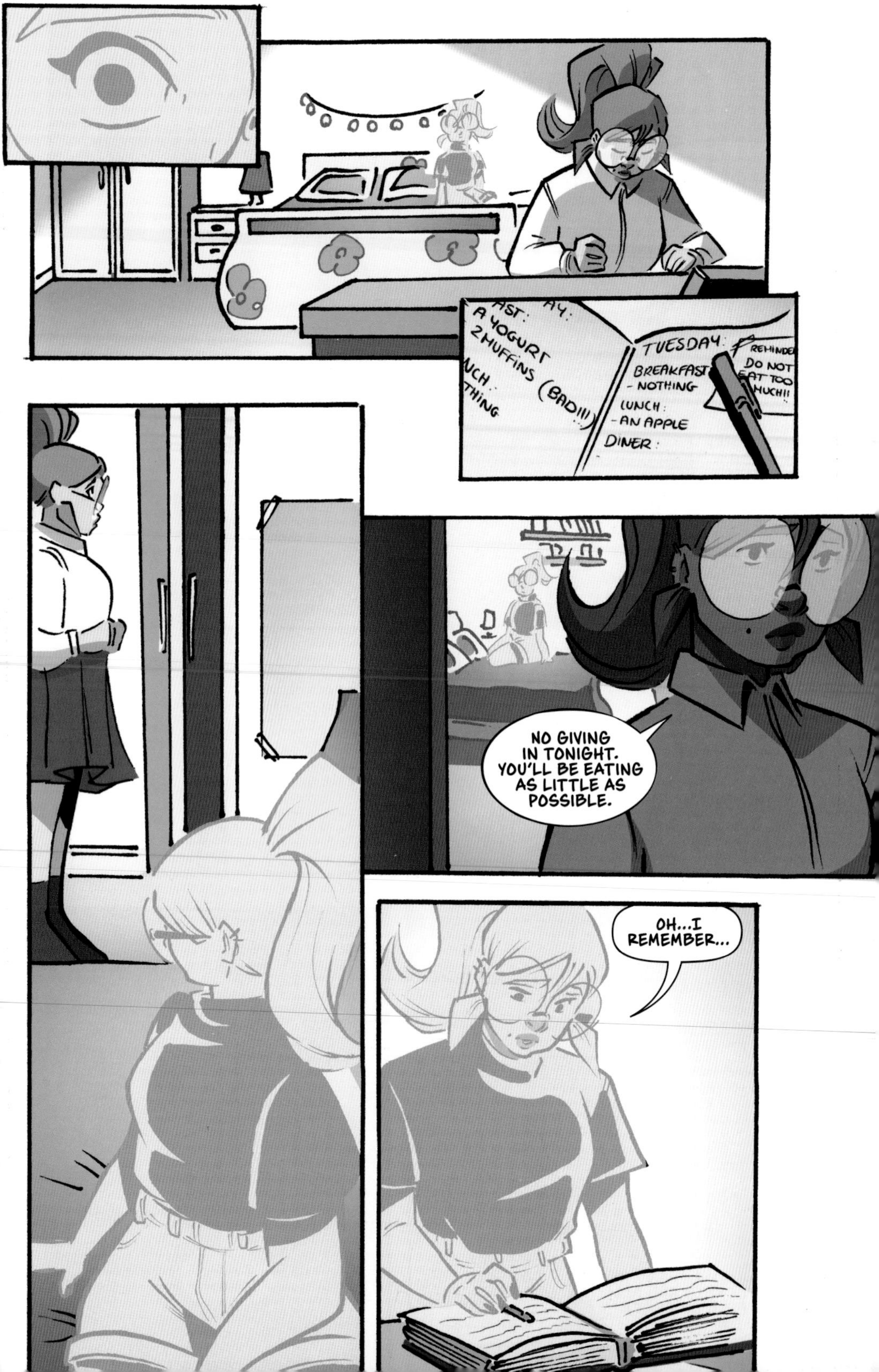
A YOGURT
2 MUFFINS (BAD!!!)
TUESDAY:
BREAKFAST:
- NOTHING
LUNCH:
- AN APPLE
DINER:
DO NOT
NO GIVING IN TONIGHT. YOU'LL BE EATING AS LITTLE AS POSSIBLE.
OH...I REMEMBER...

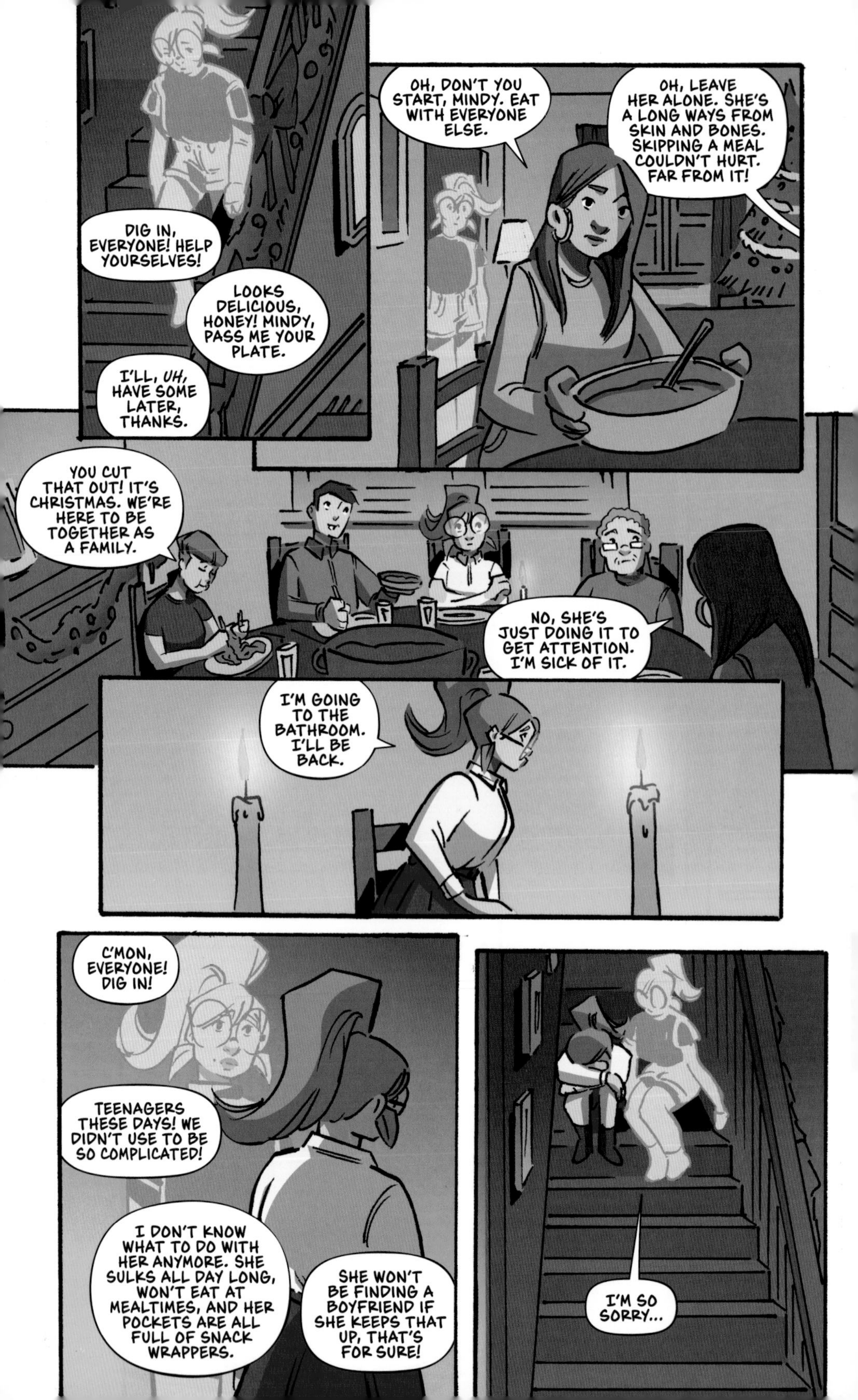
DIG IN, EVERYONE! HELP YOURSELVES!
LOOKS DELICIOUS, HONEY! MINDY, PASS ME YOUR PLATE.
I'LL, *UH*, HAVE SOME LATER, THANKS.
OH, DON'T YOU START, MINDY. EAT WITH EVERYONE ELSE.
OH, LEAVE HER ALONE. SHE'S A LONG WAYS FROM SKIN AND BONES. SKIPPING A MEAL COULDN'T HURT. FAR FROM IT!
YOU CUT THAT OUT! IT'S CHRISTMAS. WE'RE HERE TO BE TOGETHER AS A FAMILY.
NO, SHE'S JUST DOING IT TO GET ATTENTION. I'M SICK OF IT.
I'M GOING TO THE BATHROOM. I'LL BE BACK.
C'MON, EVERYONE! DIG IN!
TEENAGERS THESE DAYS! WE DIDN'T USE TO BE SO COMPLICATED!
I DON'T KNOW WHAT TO DO WITH HER ANYMORE. SHE SULKS ALL DAY LONG, WON'T EAT AT MEALTIMES, AND HER POCKETS ARE ALL FULL OF SNACK WRAPPERS.
SHE WON'T BE FINDING A BOYFRIEND IF SHE KEEPS THAT UP, THAT'S FOR SURE!
I'M SO SORRY...

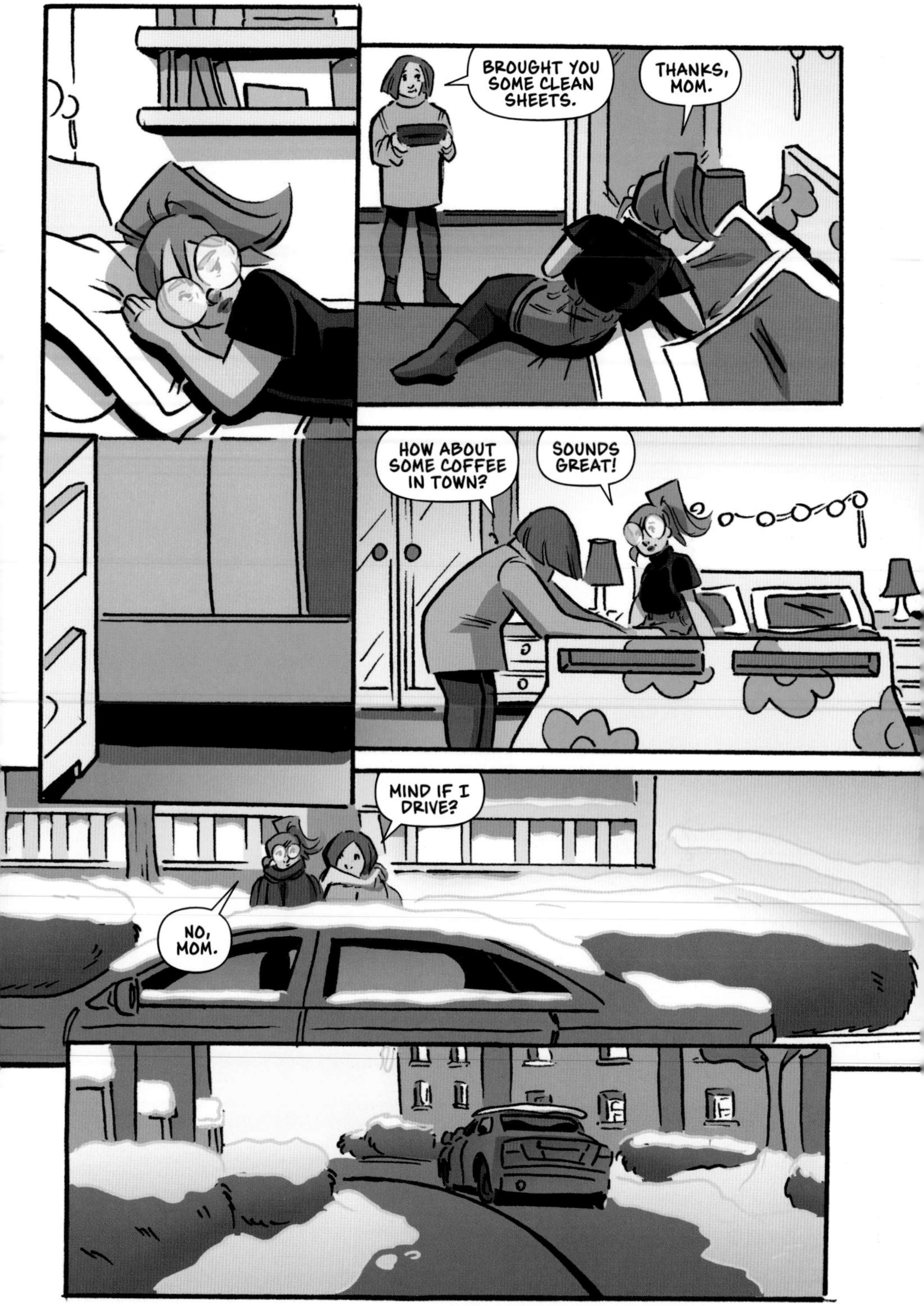
BROUGHT YOU SOME CLEAN SHEETS.
THANKS, MOM.
HOW ABOUT SOME COFFEE IN TOWN?
SOUNDS GREAT!
MIND IF I DRIVE?
NO, MOM.

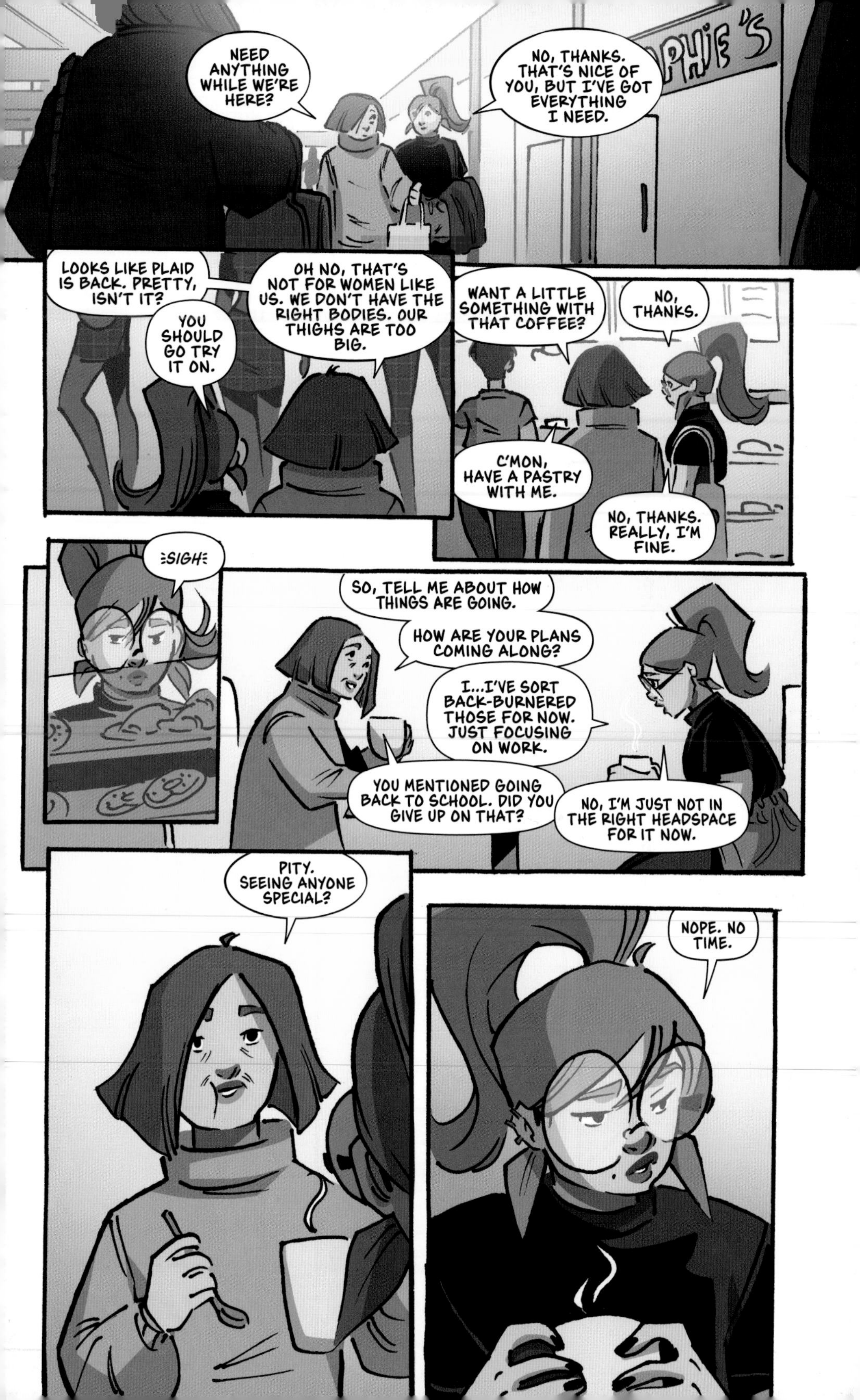
NEED ANYTHING WHILE WE'RE HERE?
NO, THANKS. THAT'S NICE OF YOU, BUT I'VE GOT EVERYTHING I NEED.
OPHIE'S
LOOKS LIKE PLAID IS BACK. PRETTY, ISN'T IT?
YOU SHOULD GO TRY IT ON.
OH NO, THAT'S NOT FOR WOMEN LIKE US. WE DON'T HAVE THE RIGHT BODIES. OUR THIGHS ARE TOO BIG.
WANT A LITTLE SOMETHING WITH THAT COFFEE?
NO, THANKS.
C'MON, HAVE A PASTRY WITH ME.
NO, THANKS. REALLY, I'M FINE.
SIGH
SO, TELL ME ABOUT HOW THINGS ARE GOING.
HOW ARE YOUR PLANS COMING ALONG?
I...I'VE SORT BACK-BURNERED THOSE FOR NOW. JUST FOCUSING ON WORK.
YOU MENTIONED GOING BACK TO SCHOOL. DID YOU GIVE UP ON THAT?
NO, I'M JUST NOT IN THE RIGHT HEADSPACE FOR IT NOW.
PITY. SEEING ANYONE SPECIAL?
NOPE. NO TIME.

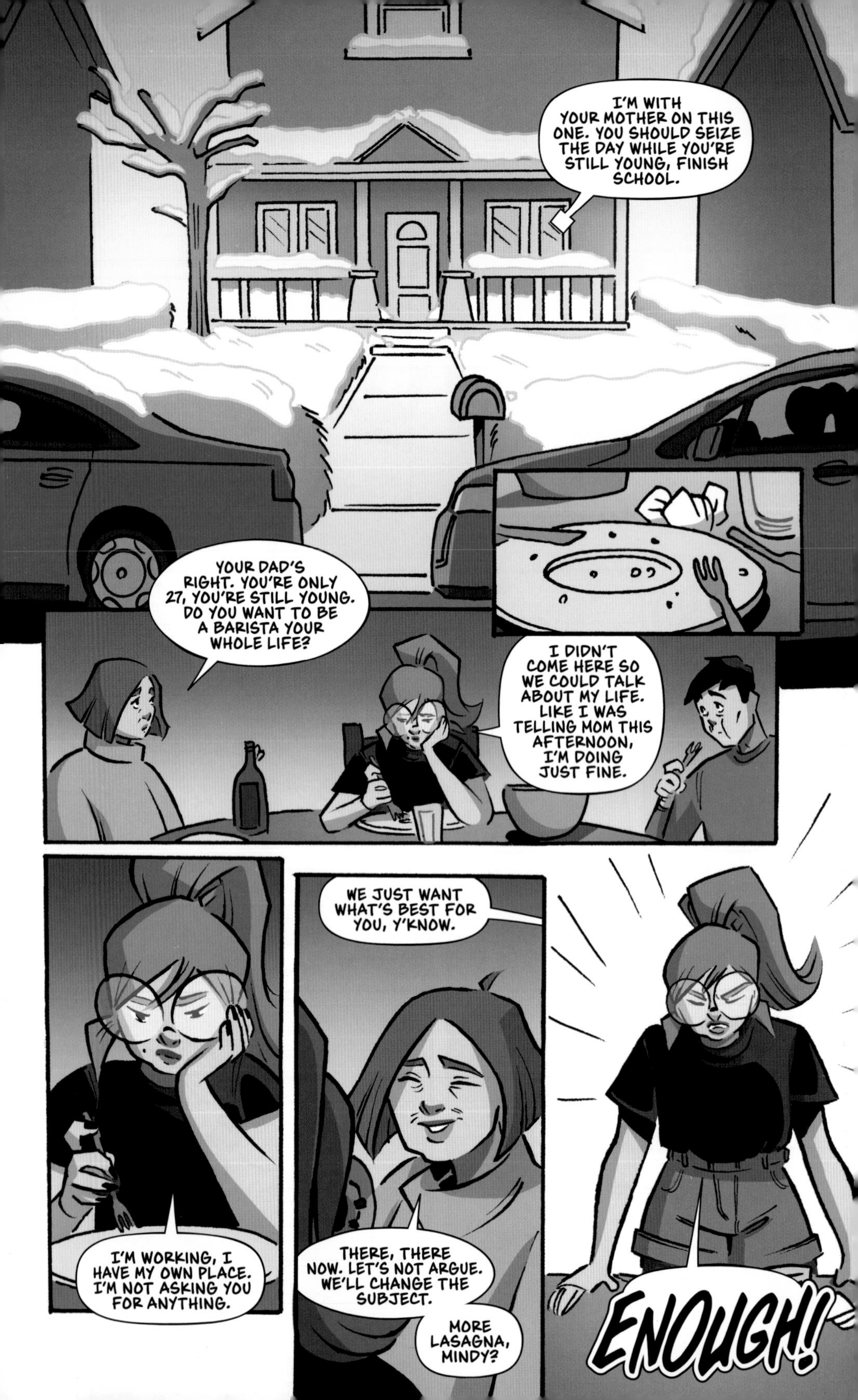
I'M WITH YOUR MOTHER ON THIS ONE. YOU SHOULD SEIZE THE DAY WHILE YOU'RE STILL YOUNG, FINISH SCHOOL.
YOUR DAD'S RIGHT. YOU'RE ONLY 27, YOU'RE STILL YOUNG. DO YOU WANT TO BE A BARISTA YOUR WHOLE LIFE?
I DIDN'T COME HERE SO WE COULD TALK ABOUT MY LIFE. LIKE I WAS TELLING MOM THIS AFTERNOON, I'M DOING JUST FINE.
I'M WORKING, I HAVE MY OWN PLACE. I'M NOT ASKING YOU FOR ANYTHING.
WE JUST WANT WHAT'S BEST FOR YOU, Y'KNOW.
THERE, THERE NOW. LET'S NOT ARGUE. WE'LL CHANGE THE SUBJECT.
MORE LASAGNA, MINDY?
ENOUGH!

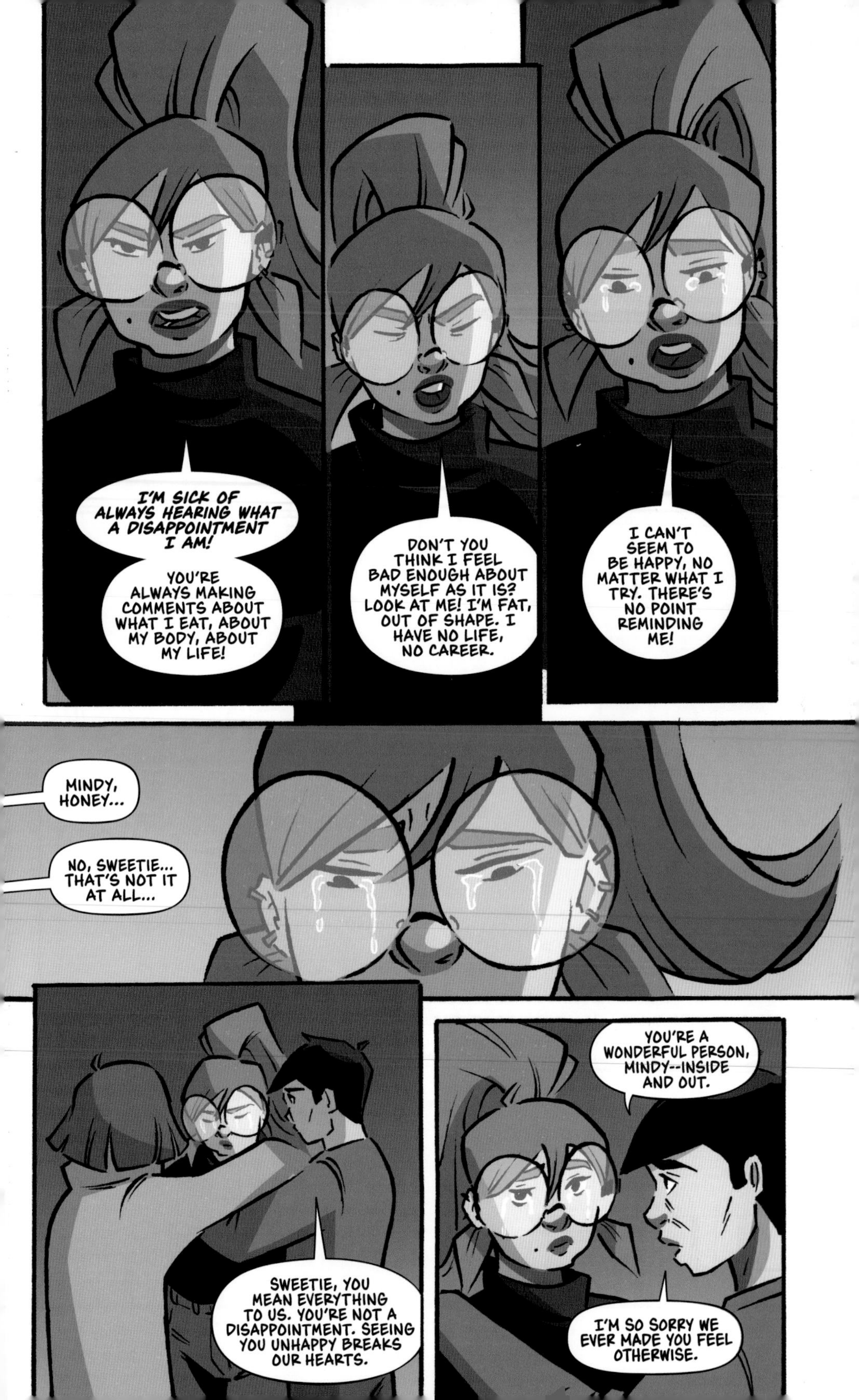

I'M SICK OF ALWAYS HEARING WHAT A DISAPPOINTMENT I AM!
YOU'RE ALWAYS MAKING COMMENTS ABOUT WHAT I EAT, ABOUT MY BODY, ABOUT MY LIFE!
DON'T YOU THINK I FEEL BAD ENOUGH ABOUT MYSELF AS IT IS? LOOK AT ME! I'M FAT, OUT OF SHAPE. I HAVE NO LIFE, NO CAREER.
I CAN'T SEEM TO BE HAPPY, NO MATTER WHAT I TRY. THERE'S NO POINT REMINDING ME!
MINDY, HONEY...
NO, SWEETIE... THAT'S NOT IT AT ALL...
SWEETIE, YOU MEAN EVERYTHING TO US. YOU'RE NOT A DISAPPOINTMENT. SEEING YOU UNHAPPY BREAKS OUR HEARTS.
YOU'RE A WONDERFUL PERSON, MINDY--INSIDE AND OUT.
I'M SO SORRY WE EVER MADE YOU FEEL OTHERWISE.

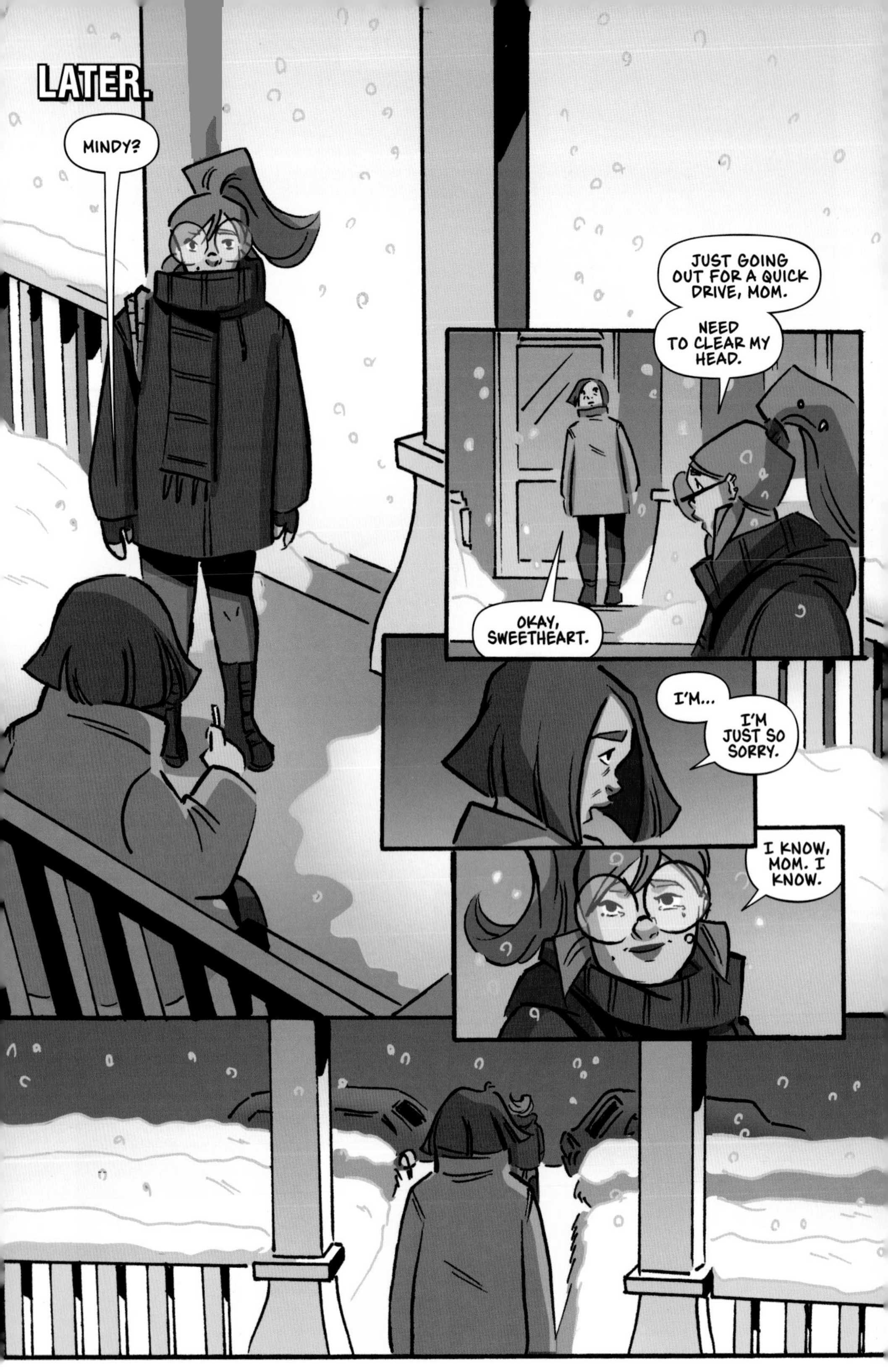
LATER.
MINDY?
JUST GOING OUT FOR A QUICK DRIVE, MOM.
NEED TO CLEAR MY HEAD.
OKAY, SWEETHEART.
I'M...
I'M JUST SO SORRY.
I KNOW, MOM. I KNOW.

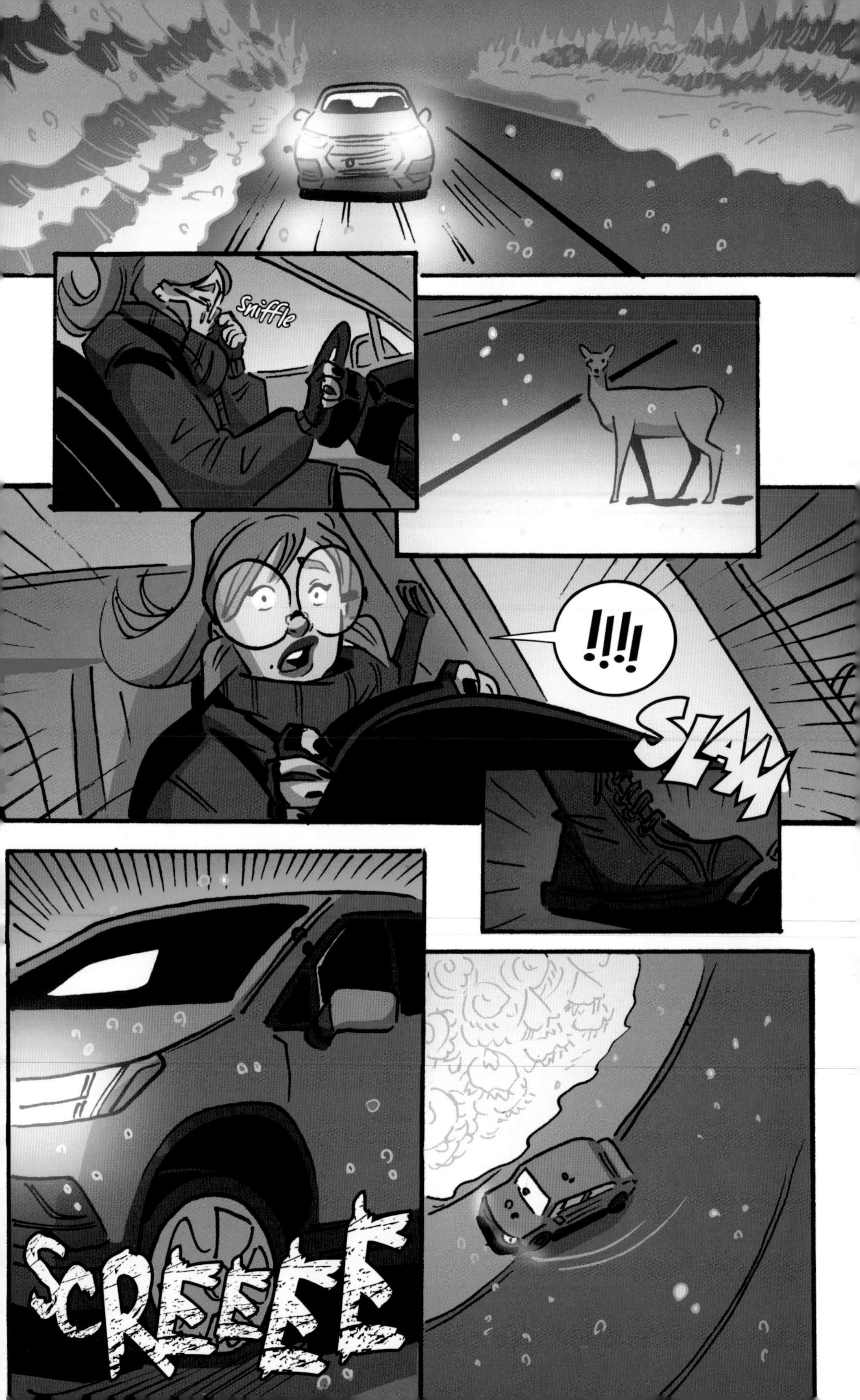
Sniffle
!!!!
SLAM
SCREEEE

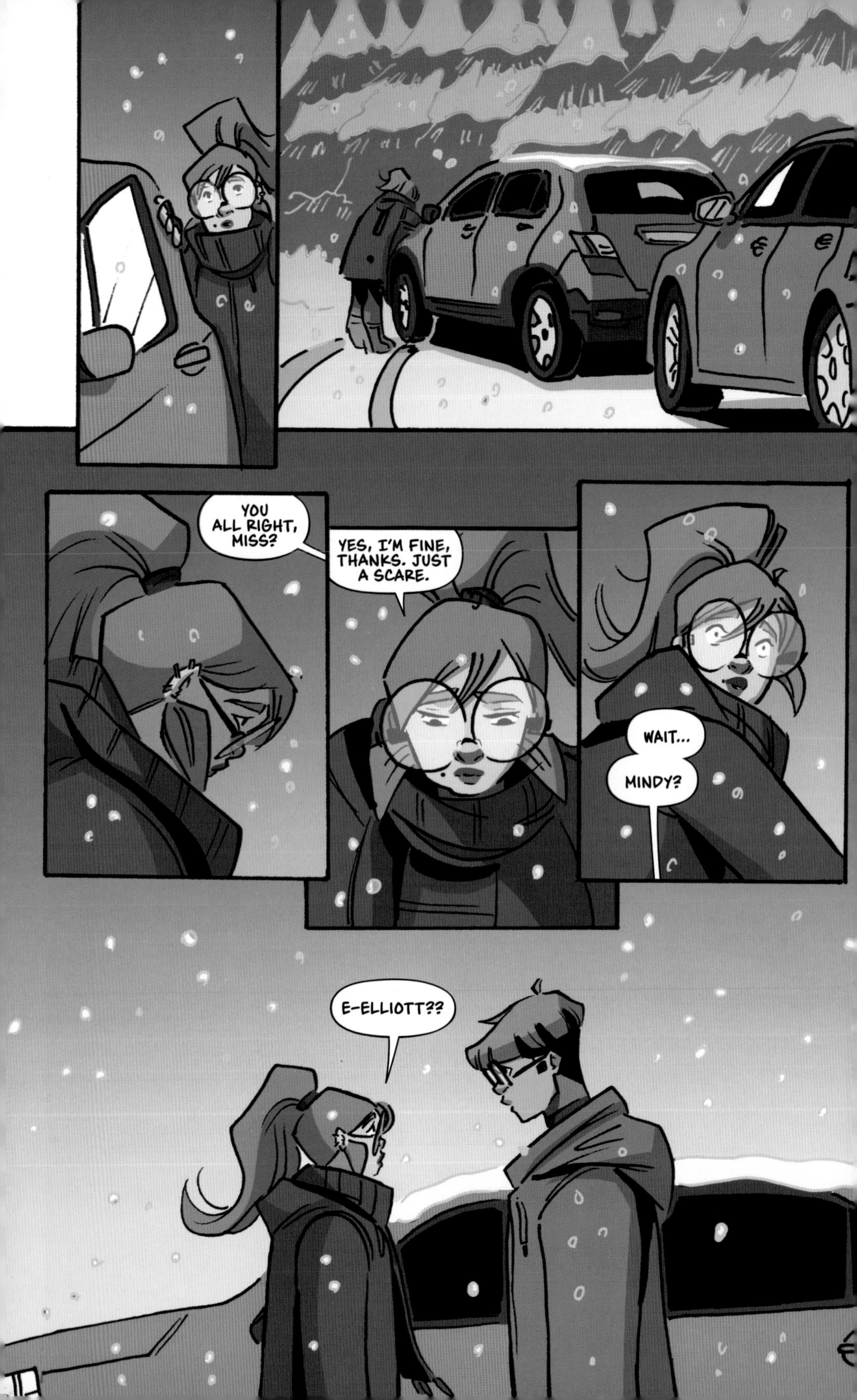
YOU ALL RIGHT, MISS?
YES, I'M FINE, THANKS. JUST A SCARE.
WAIT...
MINDY?
E-ELLIOTT??

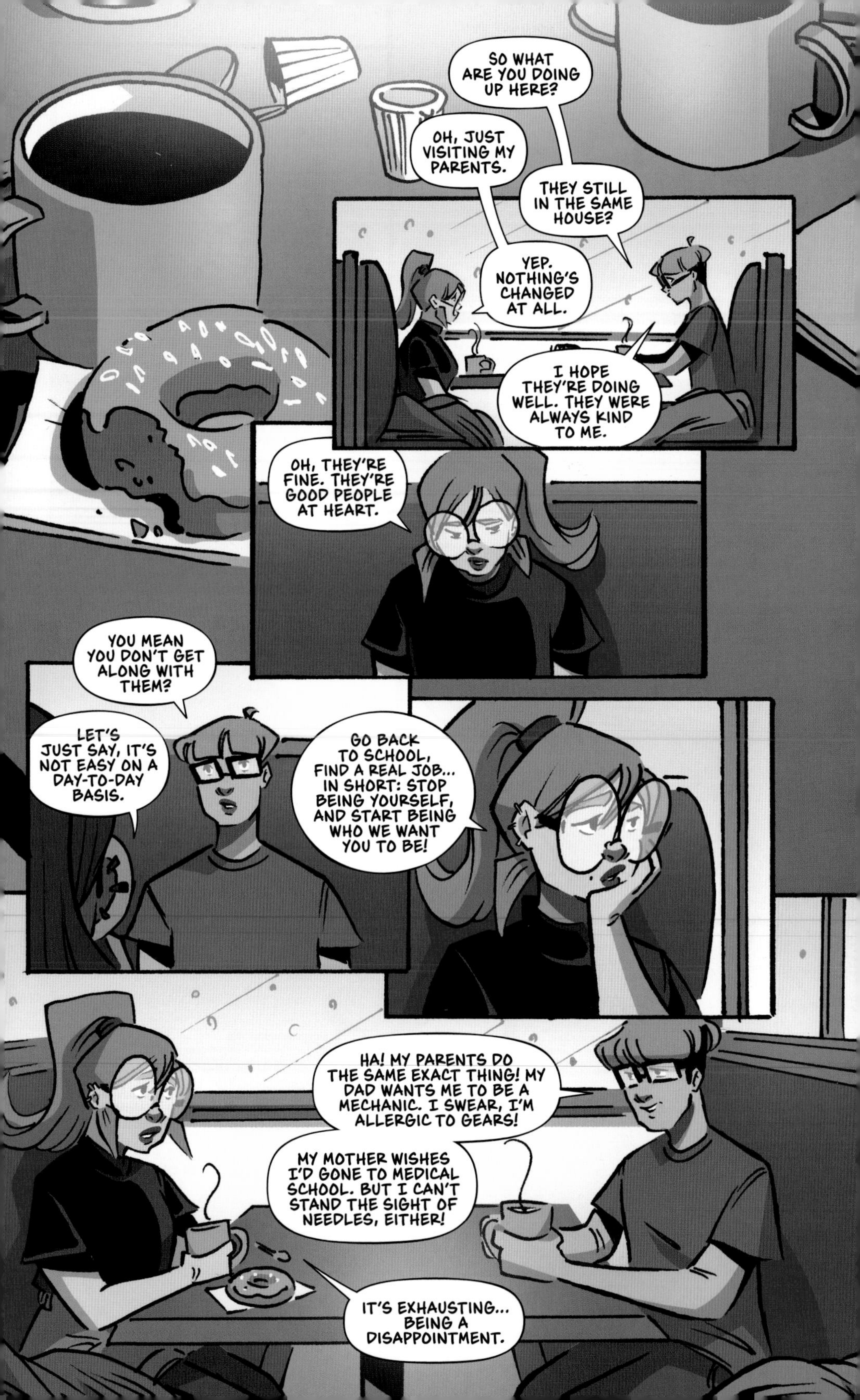
SO WHAT ARE YOU DOING UP HERE?
OH, JUST VISITING MY PARENTS.
THEY STILL IN THE SAME HOUSE?
YEP. NOTHING'S CHANGED AT ALL.
I HOPE THEY'RE DOING WELL. THEY WERE ALWAYS KIND TO ME.
OH, THEY'RE FINE. THEY'RE GOOD PEOPLE AT HEART.
YOU MEAN YOU DON'T GET ALONG WITH THEM?
LET'S JUST SAY, IT'S NOT EASY ON A DAY-TO-DAY BASIS.
GO BACK TO SCHOOL, FIND A REAL JOB... IN SHORT: STOP BEING YOURSELF, AND START BEING WHO WE WANT YOU TO BE!
HA! MY PARENTS DO THE SAME EXACT THING! MY DAD WANTS ME TO BE A MECHANIC. I SWEAR, I'M ALLERGIC TO GEARS!
MY MOTHER WISHES I'D GONE TO MEDICAL SCHOOL. BUT I CAN'T STAND THE SIGHT OF NEEDLES, EITHER!
IT'S EXHAUSTING... BEING A DISAPPOINTMENT.

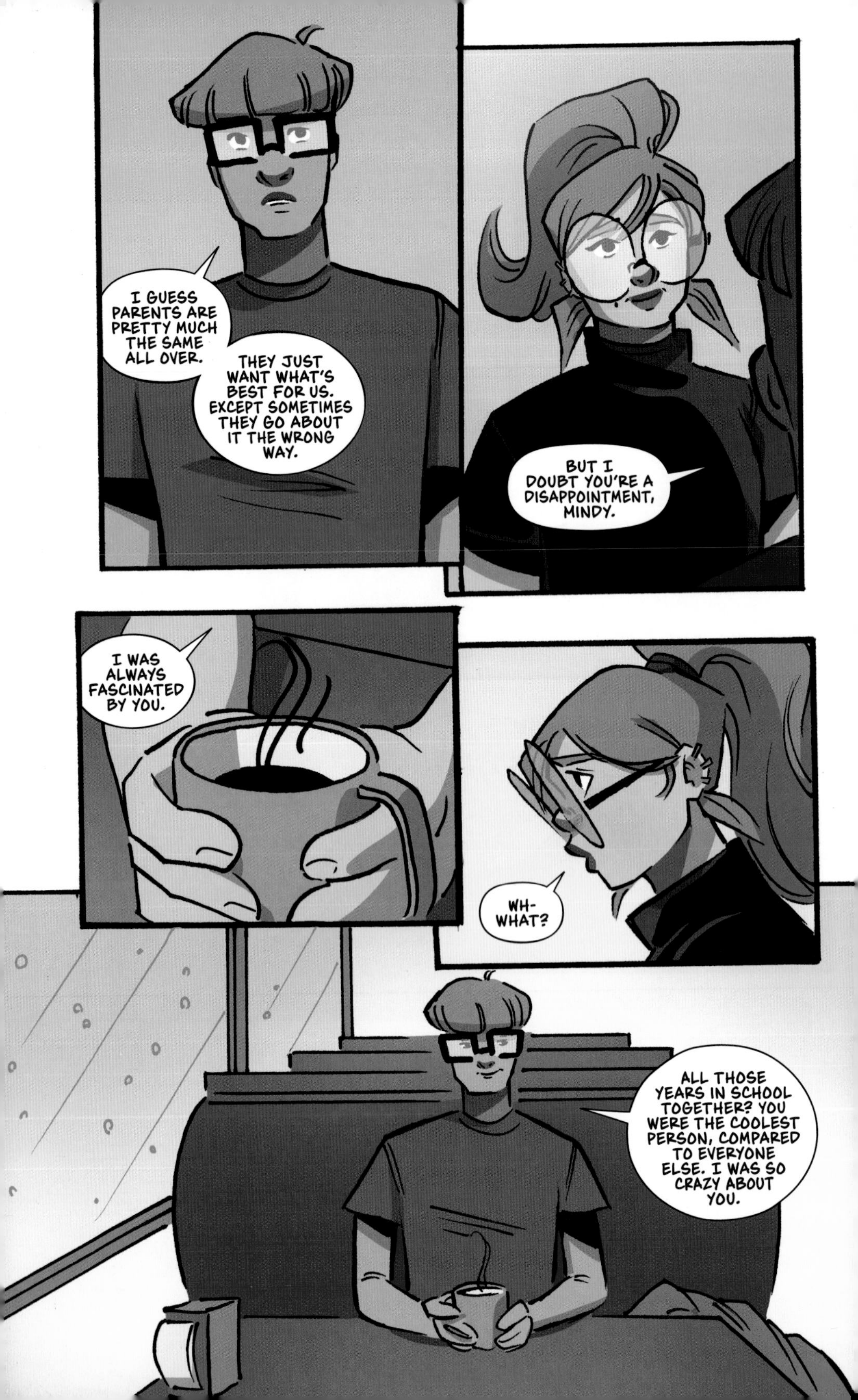
I GUESS PARENTS ARE PRETTY MUCH THE SAME ALL OVER.
THEY JUST WANT WHAT'S BEST FOR US. EXCEPT SOMETIMES THEY GO ABOUT IT THE WRONG WAY.
BUT I DOUBT YOU'RE A DISAPPOINTMENT, MINDY.
I WAS ALWAYS FASCINATED BY YOU.
WH- WHAT?
ALL THOSE YEARS IN SCHOOL TOGETHER? YOU WERE THE COOLEST PERSON, COMPARED TO EVERYONE ELSE. I WAS SO CRAZY ABOUT YOU.

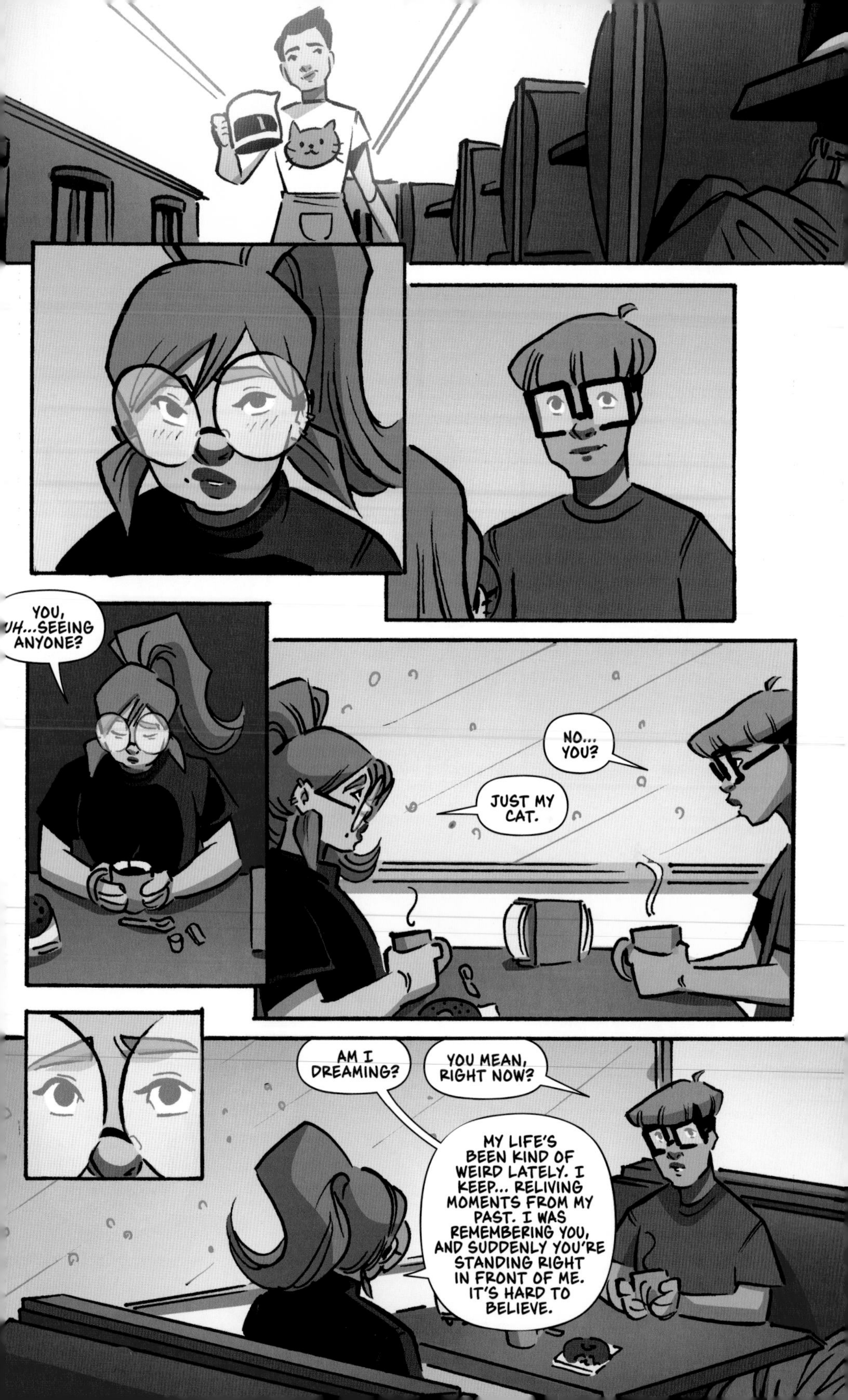
YOU, UH...SEEING ANYONE?
NO... YOU?
JUST MY CAT.
AM I DREAMING?
YOU MEAN, RIGHT NOW?
MY LIFE'S BEEN KIND OF WEIRD LATELY. I KEEP... RELIVING MOMENTS FROM MY PAST. I WAS REMEMBERING YOU, AND SUDDENLY YOU'RE STANDING RIGHT IN FRONT OF ME. IT'S HARD TO BELIEVE.

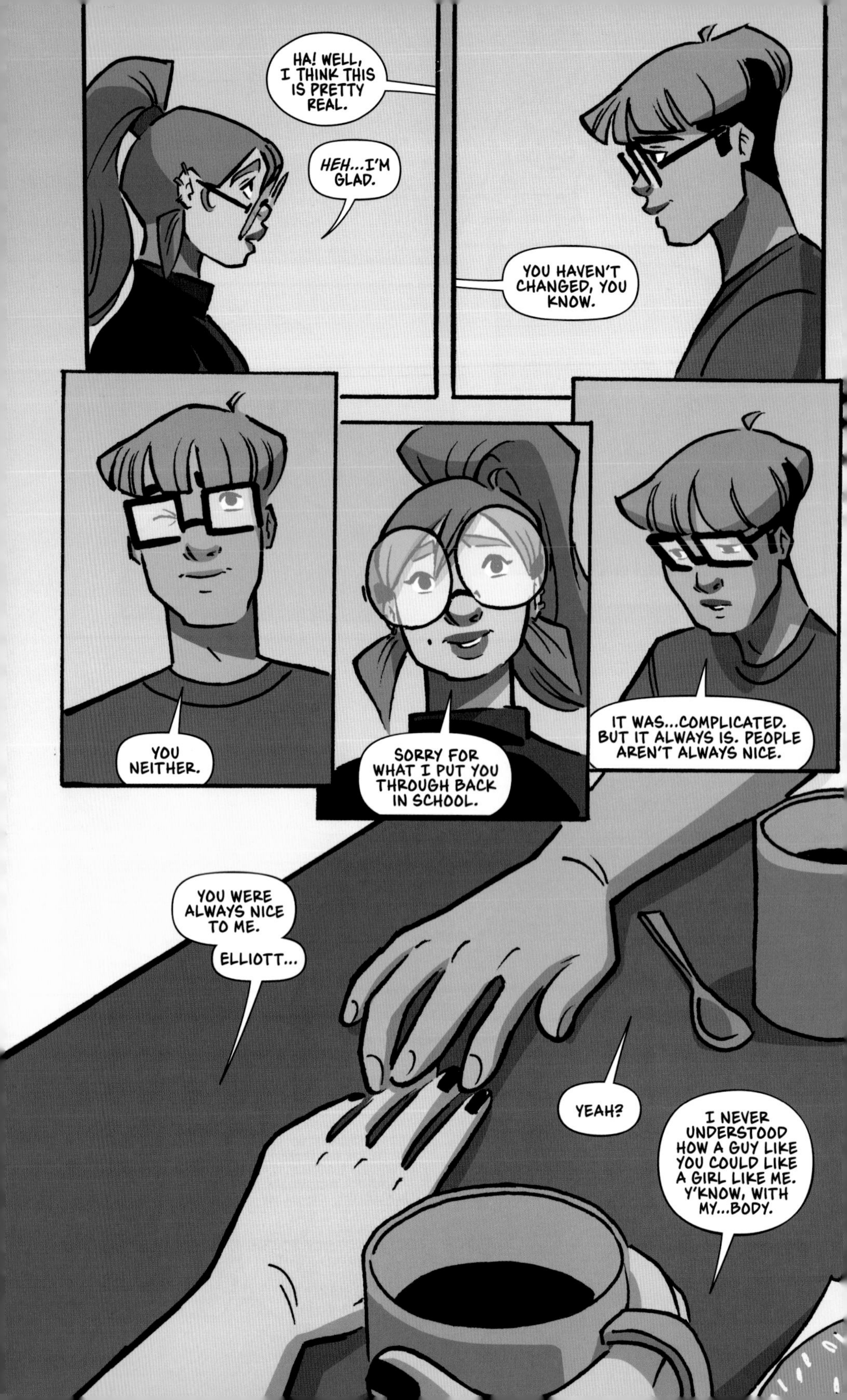
HA! WELL, I THINK THIS IS PRETTY REAL.
HEH...I'M GLAD.
YOU HAVEN'T CHANGED, YOU KNOW.
YOU NEITHER.
SORRY FOR WHAT I PUT YOU THROUGH BACK IN SCHOOL.
IT WAS...COMPLICATED. BUT IT ALWAYS IS. PEOPLE AREN'T ALWAYS NICE.
YOU WERE ALWAYS NICE TO ME.
ELLIOTT...
YEAH?
I NEVER UNDERSTOOD HOW A GUY LIKE YOU COULD LIKE A GIRL LIKE ME. Y'KNOW, WITH MY...BODY.

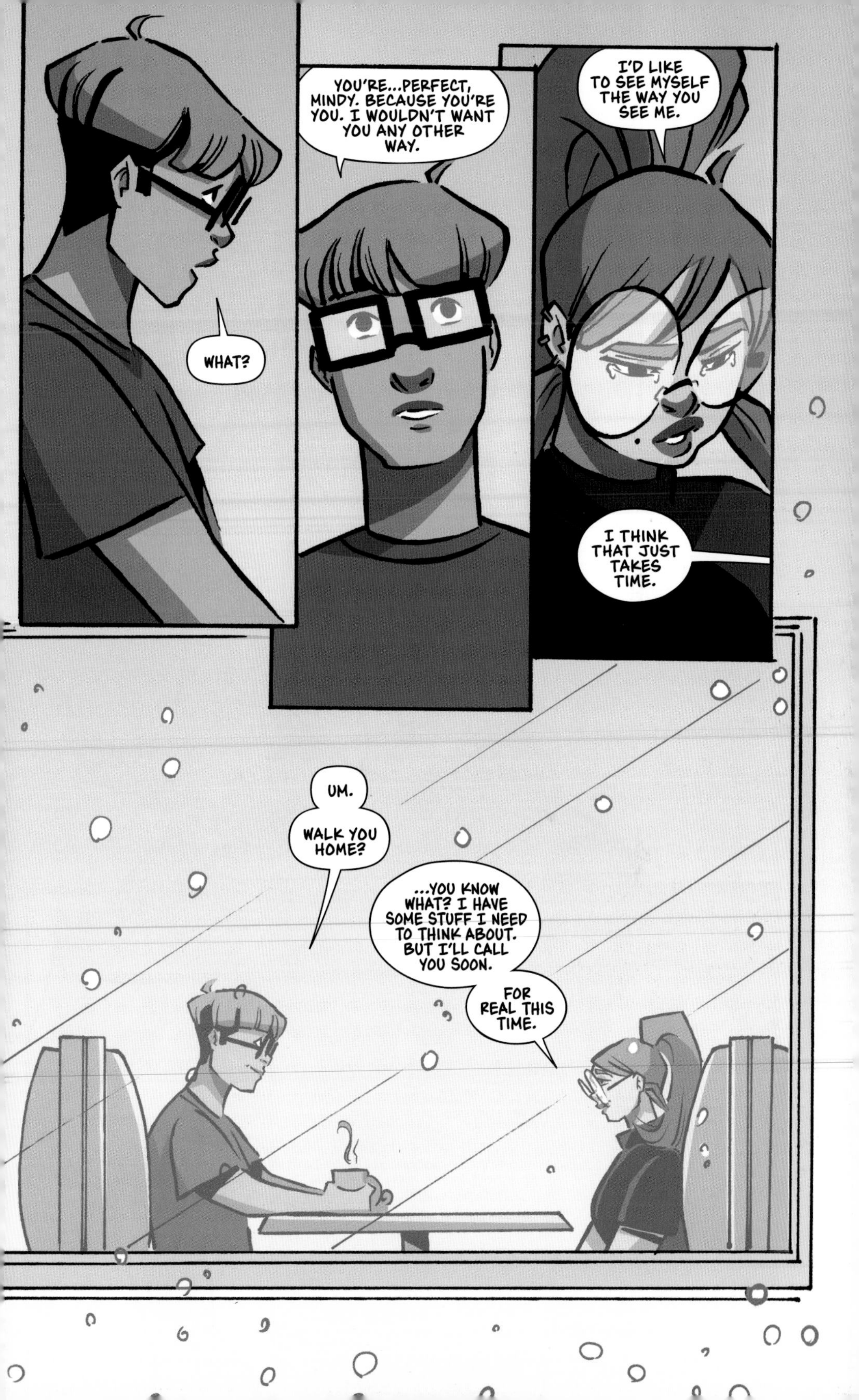
WHAT?
YOU'RE...PERFECT, MINDY. BECAUSE YOU'RE YOU. I WOULDN'T WANT YOU ANY OTHER WAY.
I'D LIKE TO SEE MYSELF THE WAY YOU SEE ME.
I THINK THAT JUST TAKES TIME.
UM.
WALK YOU HOME?
...YOU KNOW WHAT? I HAVE SOME STUFF I NEED TO THINK ABOUT. BUT I'LL CALL YOU SOON.
FOR REAL THIS TIME.

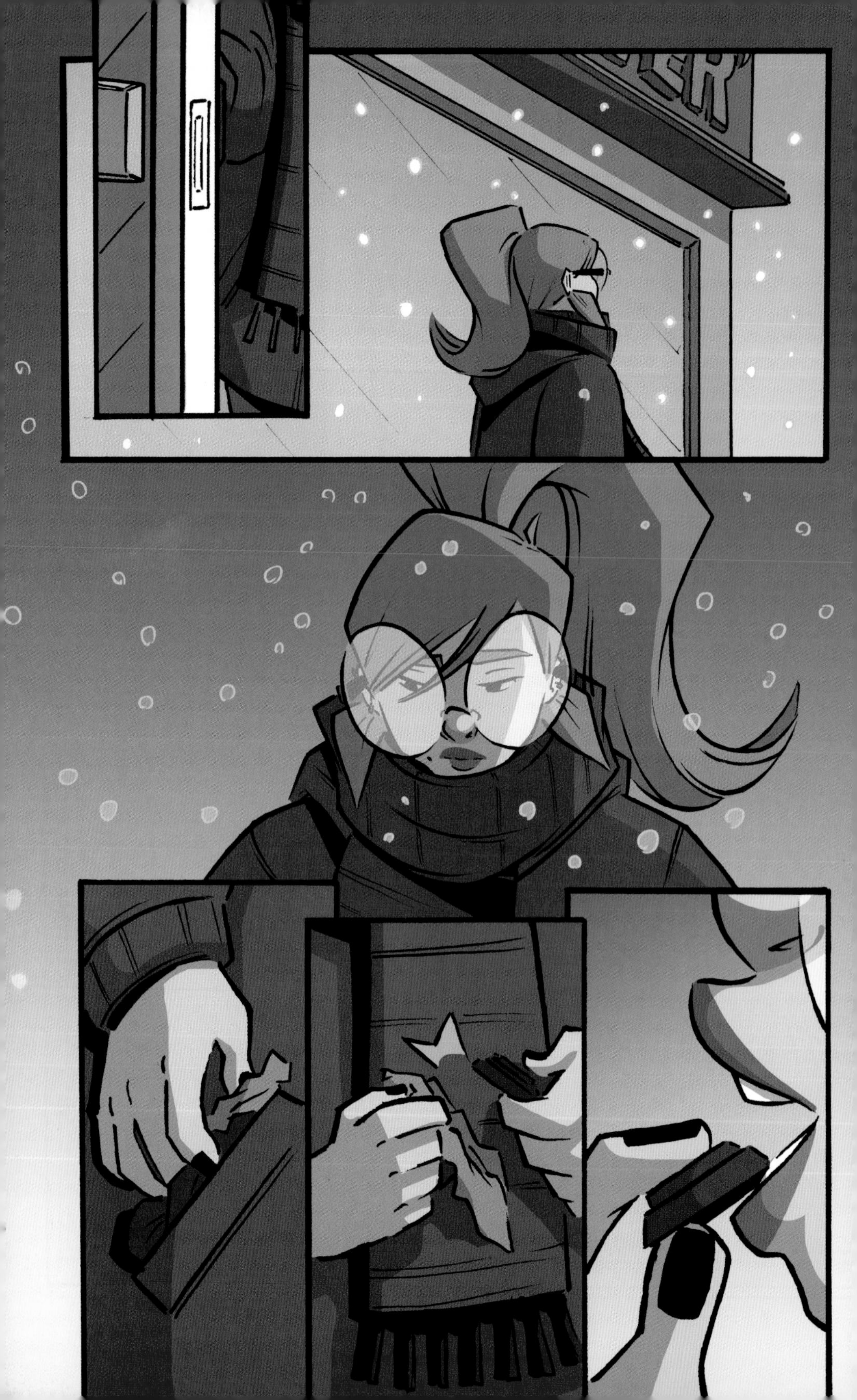

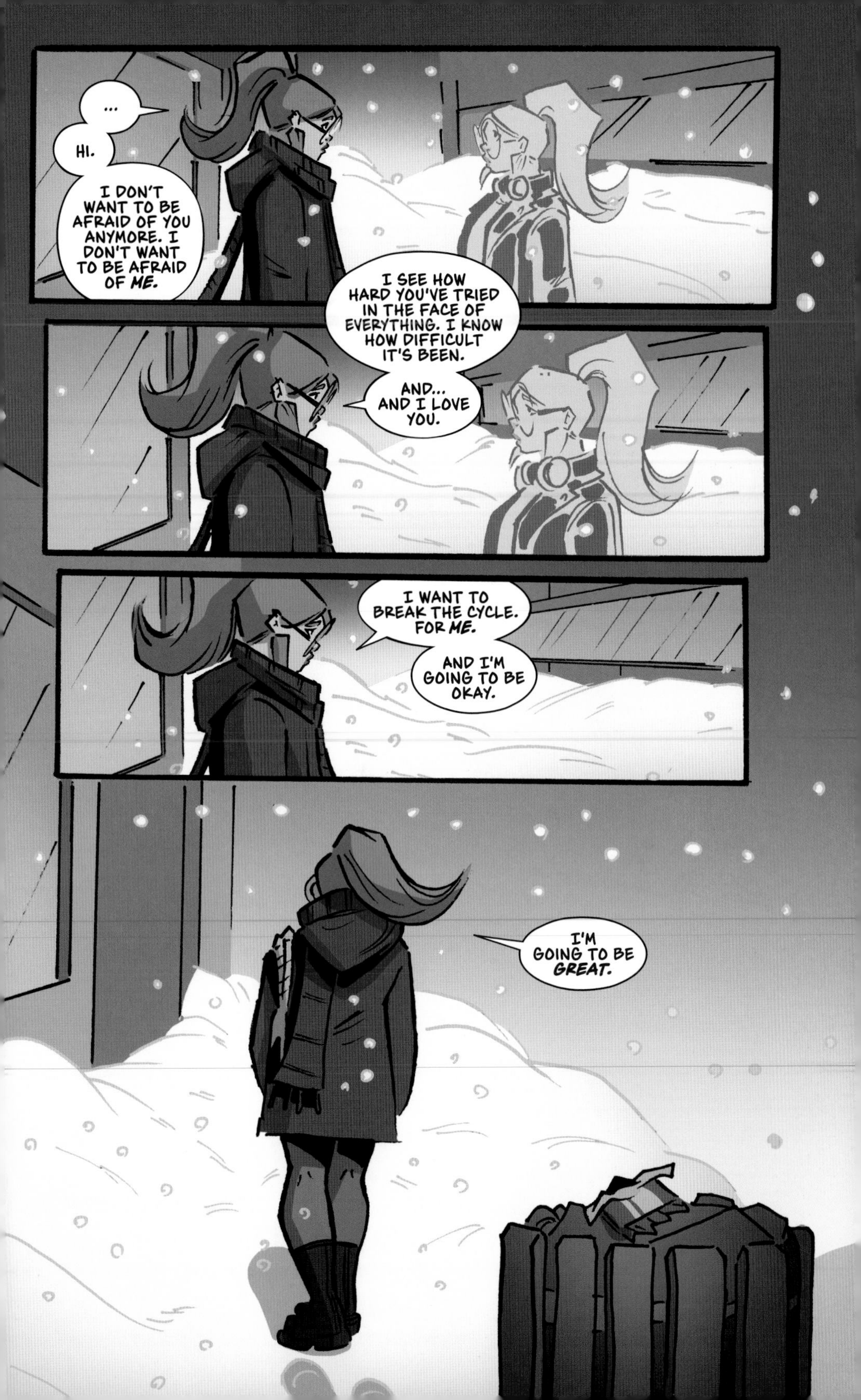
...
HI.
I DON'T WANT TO BE AFRAID OF YOU ANYMORE. I DON'T WANT TO BE AFRAID OF *ME.*
I SEE HOW HARD YOU'VE TRIED IN THE FACE OF EVERYTHING. I KNOW HOW DIFFICULT IT'S BEEN.
AND... AND I LOVE YOU.
I WANT TO BREAK THE CYCLE. FOR *ME.*
AND I'M GOING TO BE OKAY.
I'M GOING TO BE *GREAT.*

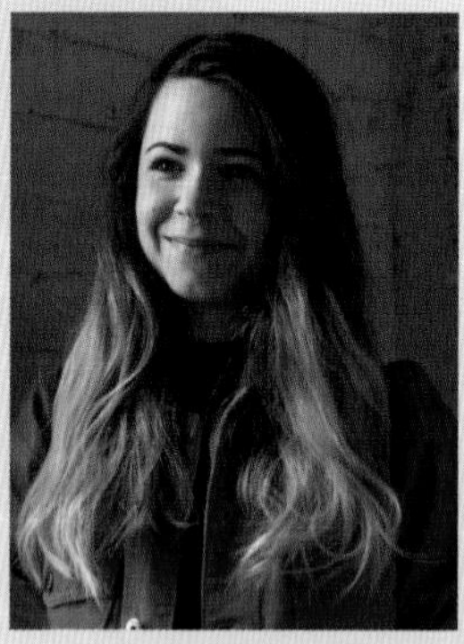

Photo by **Edwin Isford**

Sweeney Boo is a comic artist and illustrator. She grew up in the southwest of France, where she studied graphic design and listened to really loud rock music. She started working as a comic letterer and colorist for French publishers, and in 2015 she made the decision to move to Montreal, Canada. There, she started working at a mobile game company as a 2-D Artist, continuing to draw comics on weekends. Her comics debut was a cover and a short story for *Rat Queens* (Image Comics) in 2016. Later that year, she launched a Kickstarter campaign for *Eat, and Love Yourself*, a story about eating disorders, depression, body dysmorphia, and ultimately self-love: a subject really important to her. *Eat, and Love Yourself* was fully financed and was eventually picked up by BOOM! Studios for publication.

Sweeney lives a happy, full time freelance life: drawing all day, watching true crime shows, and eating lots of nice cheeses. She also has a feline assistant, Loki, who doesn't do much except sitting pretty while being a fluff and keeping her company.

If you, a friend, a family member, or anyone
you love is dealing with an eating disorder,
help and resources are available at
www.nationaleatingdisorders.org

For more resources, including a teaching
guide for **Eat & Love Yourself**, please go to
BOOM-STUDIOS.COM/eatandloveyourself

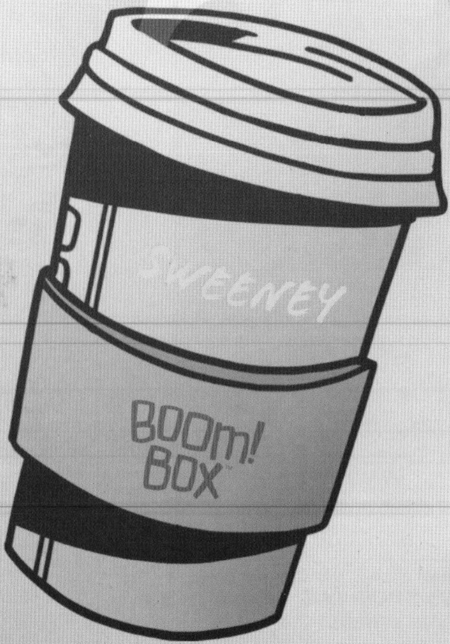
SWEENEY
BOOM! BOX

DISCOVER
ALL THE HITS

STEVENSON • ELLIS • WATTERS • ALLEN
LUMBERJANES
BEWARE THE KITTEN HOLY
NEW YORK TIMES BESTSELLING SERIES

Allison + Treiman + Cogar
GIANT DAYS
VOLUME ONE

From a writer of Disney's Moana
RIBON • FISH • PEER
SLAM!
VOLUME ONE

Hope Larson • Brittney Williams • Sarah Stern
GOLDIE VANCE
"Scoot over Nancy Drew..."
—Los Angeles Times
Volume One

THE BACKSTAGERS

TYSON HESSE'S
DIESEL
IGNITION

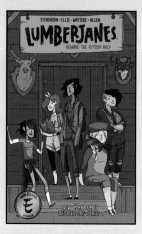

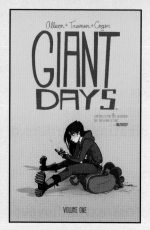

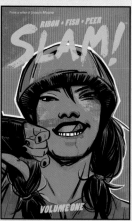

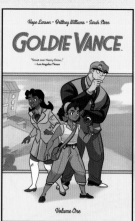

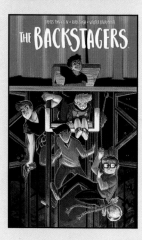

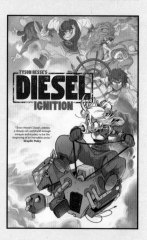

Lumberjanes
Noelle Stevenson, Shannon Watters, Grace Ellis, Brooklyn Allen, and Others
Volume 1: Beware the Kitten Holy
ISBN: 978-1-60886-687-8 | $14.99 US
Volume 2: Friendship to the Max
ISBN: 978-1-60886-737-0 | $14.99 US
Volume 3: A Terrible Plan
ISBN: 978-1-60886-803-2 | $14.99 US
Volume 4: Out of Time
ISBN: 978-1-60886-860-5 | $14.99 US
Volume 5: Band Together
ISBN: 978-1-60886-919-0 | $14.99 US

Giant Days
John Allison, Lissa Treiman, Max Sarin
Volume 1
ISBN: 978-1-60886-789-9 | $9.99 US
Volume 2
ISBN: 978-1-60886-804-9 | $14.99 US
Volume 3
ISBN: 978-1-60886-851-3 | $14.99 US

Jonesy
Sam Humphries, Caitlin Rose Boyle
Volume 1
ISBN: 978-1-60886-883-4 | $9.99 US
Volume 2
ISBN: 978-1-60886-999-2 | $14.99 US

Slam!
Pamela Ribon, Veronica Fish, Brittany Peer
Volume 1
ISBN: 978-1-68415-004-5 | $14.99 US

Goldie Vance
Hope Larson, Brittney Williams
Volume 1
ISBN: 978-1-60886-898-8 | $9.99 US
Volume 2
ISBN: 978-1-60886-974-9 | $14.99 US

The Backstagers
James Tynion IV, Rian Sygh
Volume 1
ISBN: 978-1-60886-993-0 | $14.99 US

Tyson Hesse's Diesel: Ignition
Tyson Hesse
ISBN: 978-1-60886-907-7 | $14.99 US

Coady & The Creepies
Liz Prince, Amanda Kirk, Hannah Fisher
ISBN: 978-1-68415-029-8 | $14.99 US

BOOM! BOX™

AVAILABLE AT YOUR LOCAL COMICS SHOP AND BOOKSTORE
WWW.**BOOM-STUDIOS**.COM